MAGGIE MAY AND MISS FANCYPANTS MYSTERIES

BOOKS 7 - 9

BOOKS BY ALEKSA BAXTER

MAGGIE MAY AND MISS FANCYPANTS MYSTERIES

A DEAD MAN AND DOGGIE DELIGHTS

A CRAZY CAT LADY AND CANINE CRUNCHIES

A BURIED BODY AND BARKERY BITES

A MISSING MOM AND MUTT MUNCHIES

A SABOTAGED CELEBRATION AND SALMON SNAPS

A POISONED PAST AND PUPPERMINTS

A FOULED-UP FOURTH

A SALACIOUS SCANDAL AND STEAK SIZZLERS

A PUZZLING POOCH AND PUMPKIN PUFFS

NOSY NEWFIE HOLIDAY SHORTS

HALLOWEEN AT THE BAKER VALLEY BARKERY & CAFE

A HOUSEBOUND HOLIDAY

TABLE OF CONTENTS

A HOUSEBOUND HOLIDAY

A NOSY NEWFIE HOLIDAY SHORT

ALEKSA BAXTER

CHAPTER 1

When I imagined my honeymoon—and I assure you I spent far more time imagining that than the actual wedding day—I never imagined that it would involve one over-active eight-year-old, his recuperating mother, and only phone calls with my gorgeous, sexy husband.

But that's what happened.

Because not long after Matt Barnes and I, Maggie May Carver, said "I do" the world decided to go into lockdown. At least we hadn't had any travel plans that were ruined. No resort in Fiji with a tropical bungalow that was standing empty, or lovely resort in some picturesque town in New Zealand or the Swiss Alps that was sending us a "we regret to inform you" notice.

Still.

No matter how I'd spun the potential possibilities for *la luna de miel* they had all involved my husband. Which meant that the reality really sucked.

But when there's a terrible infection spreading around the world and you're married to a cop and want to be able to take care of your elderly grandpa who suddenly finds himself housebound against his will, the choices are limited.

Since Matt was being exposed to every silly yahoo who thought being told to work from home meant hop into your car and go visit Colorado like you've always wanted to do, we'd made the painful yet practical decision to have him stay in the trailer with Jack, his brother, while Jack's new wife, Trish, and her son, Sam, moved in with me at what was supposed to be Matt's and my new home.

Jack had a job doing construction so he was still out and about and Trish simply wasn't up to taking care of Sam on her own just yet.

Neither was I for that matter. I think having a kid is a lot like being a lobster in a pot of slowly boiling water. Over time parents get used to all the pains and tribulations of parenthood—that's how a mom can heft a forty-pound kid onto her hip without batting an eye and make it through the teenage years without committing homicide, but one of us uninitiated fools tries to do the same? No. Not happening.

Which is how Trish could blithely ignore the sounds of her screaming under-stimulated, over-caffeinated child while Fancy—my now four-year-old Newfoundland—and I were not doing quite so well.

As Sam ran around the living room with a toy plane in his hand making vroom-vroom and shooting sounds while screaming about taking evasive maneuvers, I clutched my fifth Coke of the day to my chest and prayed for it all to end.

I'd always thought pandemics were some sort of fast-spreading wave of annihilation, not this slow-moving torture where nothing had really changed but at the same time everything had.

Fancy stared at me from the corner, her big amber eyes asking me what she'd done to deserve this. At least she'd stopped barking at him every time he moved. That had been the first three days. And it had not been fun chasing a hundred-and-forty-pound dog around the house trying to get her to stop.

Now she just sullenly slunk from room to room trying but failing to stay out of his way. It didn't help that we were in a two-story house and she wasn't one for stairs so she only had so many choices of where to hide.

She would've been outside where she'd been spending seventy percent of every day, but it was raining and thundering and I'd made her come in. Fancy would've happily stayed out there while tree limbs blew down and hail rained on her head, but the last thing I needed right then was an emergency visit to the vet.

I glanced towards the couch where Trish had her feet propped up on the dining room table. She flipped through her phone, never once looking up. How? How did she not notice the chaos around her?

"Sam," I said, trying not to snap the words out too forcefully, but probably failing. Even though Sam was downright adorable with his red hair and freckles, I was seriously at my limit.

"Yeah, Maggie?" He stopped, smiling at me from ear to ear.

"Will you do me a favor?"

"Sure. What?"

"I was going to go over to my grandpa's later and see how he's doing. Do you think you could draw him something for me? Like a plane? Or Lady?" (That was the miniature horse Jack insisted on throwing into my life every chance he got, including on my wedding day.)

Sam hesitated for a moment but he'd been raised with enough manners and was smart enough to know that my request wasn't really a request. He set down the plane. "Sure. Um…"

I took the plane and put it on top of the fridge. "You better get started on it now. I'd hate for it not to be done when I go over there."

"Okay."

As he slunk off towards the room he and Trish were sharing I tried to feel bad for banishing him to his room to do something quiet, but I couldn't.

Don't get me wrong, kids are cute. In small doses and at large distances.

At a loss for what to do next, I went to the kitchen and stared at the cupboards wondering what I should pick up at the store or order in.

I'd tried looking online for advice about what to store up on in event of an emergency but all the advice was for what to do if you had no running water or electricity and perhaps were living in a gym with a hundred other displaced people with nowhere to go. Under those circumstances it seemed canned goods and pasta and lots of water were the answer.

But what do you stock up on when the grocery stores are still open? And you still have power and running water?

Each time there was a story about an outbreak at a meat processing plant I ordered more meat, so we were good there. (For like the next century.)

What else, though?

I refused to buy into the craze for homemade bread that had spread through all my corporate friends.

A Housebound Holiday

Suddenly my Facebook feed was full of posts about sourdough starters and pictures of rye bread. (Who *ever* eats rye bread? Seriously.) I was surprised no one had bought raw wheat and a mortar and pestle yet, but give it enough time…

And I wasn't about to start my own garden. That seemed a step too far. If the world really came down to me surviving on only the vegetables I'd grown in the backyard and the sourdough starter I nurtured on a shelf each day, well, I was okay with just calling it quits at that point.

I'd miss Matt and Fancy, but no. I was just not going to go there.

But I still needed to stock up on *something*. Nice, made-by-someone else somethings. I just didn't know what.

Which is how I'd ended up with five spare jars of peanut butter, six extra boxes of peppermint tea, forty cans of soup, three dozen packets of tuna fish, thirteen cases of Coke (that I'd actually had before things went crazy but let's not dwell on that), and enough frozen meat to last for years.

Still, though, I felt like I was missing something. Maybe it was the non-food items I was missing.

But no. I had four mega-packs of toilet paper, two mega-packs of paper towels, three dozen boxes of Kleenex, six things of dishwasher detergent, two extra deodorants, one extra toothpaste, an extra shampoo, and an extra conditioner. Oh, and of course, three extra bags of Fancy's dog food and more treats than she could probably eat in a lifetime.

And yet…

Was it enough? What was going to happen next? What might be out when I wanted it?

And what was I going to want to eat that I didn't normally? Because my consumption of bacon and ice cream was through the roof.

(Not because of any "happy news" causing food cravings (although after two weeks with Sam around that would not have been happy news, thank you very much) but just because it turns out my comfort foods in times of uncertain crisis are fatty and sweet.)

I slumped into a kitchen chair and stared at the wall. I was stumped. I'd prepared as well as I could and now…

I sighed.

Now it was just a game of whack-a-mole trying to keep those I loved safe as they constantly came up with new and creative ways to endanger their health. Especially my grandpa who had somehow decided that this was all way overblown. He'd listened to me for the first week or so, but every time I turned around he was spouting some crazy half-baked idea that was bound to end poorly.

Just the day before I'd caught him trying to leave the house so he could run to the hardware store for a couple of screws to finish some project he hadn't worked on in a decade or more. I asked him if he really thought it was worth risking his life to construct a bird cage for a bird that didn't exist, and he'd just grumbled something under his breath about not being a child and being perfectly capable of making his own decisions.

I sighed again.

It was all a mess. The resort was on hold. I couldn't

see Matt or Jamie or Greta. The only bright light was that online barkery sales were thriving.

(The year before Jamie and I had started a dog barkery and human café together that had done okay, but then the land it was on was sold and the building was torn down to create a pet resort. Good news was that the person who tore it down, Mason Maxwell, married Jamie so when the resort was finally completed, we could reopen the barkery as well as a cattery and a coffee shop where Jamie could sell her delicious cinnamon buns. In the meantime, I'd left the online store up and running, and it generated enough sales to keep me from completely losing my mind.)

(And my income if Mason and Greta decided to pull the plug on the pet resort altogether. I mean, honestly, they could only pay me to sit on the sidelines for so long, right? And who knew how long it would be until we could launch a luxury pet resort given the current situation.)

There was one other bright spot. Or so I assumed.

I couldn't stumble across a dead body when I, and most everyone else, was pretty much trapped at home 24-7. (Something that had happened a disconcerting number of times since I'd moved to the Baker Valley of Colorado. I mean, seriously, how many people can die under bizarre circumstances in a series of small mountain towns? Answer: You'd be surprised.)

I glanced out the window. The storm was finally over.

"Come on, Fancy," I called. "Let's go for a walk." She scrambled to her feet and ran for the door, staring back at me like "what's taking you so long, get me out of here."

As I put on my shoes and grabbed my bag, I called out, "Hey, Trish, we're going for a walk. Be back soon."

She grunted, still not looking up from her phone. I debated asking Sam if he wanted to tag along—I knew he'd appreciate the chance to get outside—but I just couldn't do it. I needed to get away. I needed "me" time. Desperately.

Fancy cried at me, reminding me that she too needed to get away.

I hustled towards the door, leashed her up, and we dashed outside into the welcome of a mid-spring afternoon in the Colorado mountains, everything still green and fresh and alive.

CHAPTER 2

Because I had absolutely no desire to see anyone whatsoever, I led Fancy to the trail that ran up the mountain behind my house and my grandpa's house. The town of Creek is part of the Baker Valley, a string of small mountain towns off the highway surrounded by tall mountains. My grandpa's house sits at the end of town right at the base of one of those mountains, and my new home is right next door.

With the storm gone the sky was a bright, clear blue and everything smelled clean and vegetal.

(A weird word, I know, but how else do you describe that smell of living plants that can fill the air after a good storm? So different from New York where if it rained hard enough the storm drains overflowed and…Ugh. Anyway. That life was behind me now.)

It was about five hundred feet from the base of the trail to the top of the ridgeline of the nearest mountain and that's where Fancy and I headed.

After a year of being in Creek I managed the hike without gasping and needing to stop ten times along the way. (Altitude is no joke if you're not used to it.) From the top of the ridgeline we could see the entire town laid out before us. All forty-some houses, two gas stations, one church, one funeral home, and one pioneer museum which looked like they'd been around for a hundred years, and then the county seat, police station, and library which were all modern brick and shiny glass.

The town was definitely small and full of people who were a little too into each other's business, but it was home. The place I wanted to stay for the rest of my life. It had only taken me thirty-seven years and a few missed turns along the way to figure that out.

And I had Fancy to thank for starting me down that path. No way I could make her happy and live the life I'd been living in DC.

I pulled the elastic out of my blonde ponytail and twisted my hair up into a bun to get it off my neck. I liked having long hair, I just didn't like having it in the way, which sort of defeated the purpose of long hair. But I'd tried short hair. It wasn't a good look for me. At five-eight, one-sixty, longer hair was definitely more flattering.

(Which is not any sort of judgement on anyone else's weight or hairstyle choices, I might add. If you're happy as you are, be happy, whatever appearance or body shape works for you. But I digress. As always.)

Fancy, sick of waiting for me to ponder my life and fix my hair when there was a whole wet world to explore, tugged on her leash. As she led me through the knee-high grass, I was thankful that I always wore hiking boots while walking her because she was most definitely a cross-country sort of dog. Sure, I could keep her to a nice well-manicured trail, but what's the fun in that?

Of course, my lenience towards where she walked meant that in the spring I had to spend about twenty minutes after each walk checking her paws, legs, and belly for grass seeds. I always knew where one was by the way she'd slowly move her paw away from my grasp when I reached for it. But it still took some time and effort to find them all.

I think my record was fifty grass seeds in one walk. That one had required a set of tweezers to get them all out. But I figured as long as she enjoyed herself and I found them all, it was all good.

While Fancy stopped to sniff a very interesting tree, I glanced towards Luke's place with its backyard devoted to piles of junk. That's the one thing I don't think Matt had given enough thought to—us living next to Luke who had an annoying habit of walking around outside in skimpy little shorts and no shirt.

He was a good-looking man, no doubt about it, and always up for a little trouble-making—which women like my friend Jamie were sometimes drawn to—but I thought he was smarmy and that the world would be a better place without him.

And it was a nightmare having him live next door. Especially with Trish living with me. She was *definitely* drawn to that sort of man like a bee to honey. I'd caught them chatting in the front yard more than once. Her reunion with Jack and their subsequent marriage had been a bit of a whirlwind and now with them separated due to the lockdown I worried it might not stick. Not with a bad influence like Jack hanging around.

I didn't dwell on it too long, though, because as I was standing there on the ridge I saw my now eighty-three-year-old grandpa come out of his house and head for his truck.

"Where's he going?"

I grabbed my phone and dialed his cellphone. He hated the thing, but I'd managed to convince him that it didn't hurt to carry one. He glanced at the display and put the phone back in his pocket before getting in his truck.

I stamped my foot. "Why you…"

I stared, open-mouthed as he started up his truck and pulled out of the driveway. Maybe he was just going over to Lesley's house. Even though they were now married, they still kept separate houses. Since they were both staying home and away from danger they often went back and forth.

But no. He navigated his way to the highway, turned right, and drove straight out of town.

I cussed up a storm at that point.

What was he doing? Didn't he know how risky it was to be out and about? Didn't he understand that this thing could *kill* him?

I dialed Matt.

"Hey, Maggie. How's my girl?"

The sound of his voice alone made me smile. He was gorgeous, he was kind, and he was mine, all mine. Even if I hadn't seen him in person in two weeks.

"I miss you."

"I miss you, too. But I'm working right now. Is something wrong?"

He'd been extra busy the last couple of weeks dealing with people who had gone downright crazy thanks to the current situation. One woman who owned a vacation home in Bakerstown that she'd fled to for safety had actually called the police and demanded that they make her favorite coffee shop reopen.

A local man in Masonville had to have a truckload of fireworks confiscated because even though there was a fire ban in place he'd been setting fireworks off every single night for a week straight.

There were so many more like them…

Honestly, I didn't know how he did it. Matt was definitely a better person than I am.

"Sorry to bother you. But my grandpa just drove towards Masonville and I don't know where he's going. Will you track him down for me?"

"Maggie…"

"What?"

"He's a grown adult. He has the right to make his own decisions."

Fancy tugged on her leash. When I shook my head at her she sat down and started lecturing me in a very high-pitched, unending crying voice. For such a large dog she can be decidedly whiney at times. I grabbed a handful of treats to quiet her down as I answered Matt.

"I don't want him to get this, Matt."

"I don't either. And I'm sure he doesn't want to get it. But he knows the risks, and if he wants to take those risks…"

"Matt," I cut him off.

"Yes?"

"Just find him, please. And find out what he's up to."

There was a long enough silence on the other end of the line that I knew he was debating whether or not to argue further with me about it. But finally he just said,

"Okay. No promises. I am at work after all. But I'll see if I can't find him and make sure he's being safe. Maybe he just went fishing or something."

Fishing with a hundred other people, none wearing masks or keeping a good social distance.

"Thank you. Love you."

"Love you, too."

I hung up and looked down to find Fancy drooling all over herself, eyes fixed on the one remaining treat in my hand. "Here you go, silly girl."

She took the treat from my hand like the dainty lady she is and we continued on along the ridgeline, her sniffing at every little bush and me worrying about how to keep my grandpa safe. And how not to kill anyone before this all ended.

CHAPTER 3

The next day I decided to drop in on my grandpa and figure out what he'd been up to.

I'd learned by then not to drop in unexpectedly. I either called to get permission before I went over or I stood at the front door and knocked until my grandpa answered. No more just walking in and going looking for him, oh no siree. Only needed that experience once, thank you very much.

I didn't want him to tell me it was a bad time so I chose to walk over and knock, dragging Fancy and the drawing I'd had Sam do along with me.

Fancy, not schooled in the finer points of human behavior, didn't understand why we had to wait at the door we used to just walk through. She made her unhappiness at the delay known by crying at me.

"Fancy, I love you. But please stop."

Fortunately, my grandpa answered the door and she did. He'd just turned eighty-three the weekend before but he looked like he was in his sixties. Mostly because he was still a trim man whose hair had faded to a light brown instead of turning gray. He was wearing his customary summer wardrobe of jeans and a short-sleeved button-up plaid shirt.

"Maggie May."

"Grandpa."

I wanted to give him a hug, but since I didn't know where he'd been…

I let Fancy off her leash. She turned her crying act on him until he led her to the kitchen and gave her some sort of treat that she immediately took out the back door. I smiled to think that a year ago my grandpa would've said that the only good dog was one that lived outside and now here he was stocking up on Fancy's treats for when she came to visit.

"To what do I owe the pleasure, Maggie May? You'll see that I'm still here. Still alive and kicking. For all the good it does me." He plomped down on the goldenrod couch and reached for the front pocket of his shirt then grimaced when he didn't find the pack of cigarettes he'd kept there for most of his life. Life-long habits die hard.

"I tried to call you yesterday," I said as I sat down across from him on the other couch, moving over when a spring poked into my thigh. I stayed on the front-edge of the couch, not wanting to get too comfortable for my interrogation. "On your cellphone. Because I saw you were heading out while I was hiking."

"Huh. You know me and those new-fangled devices. Must've had it on mute. Or left it at home or something."

"Grandpa. You looked at who it was and put the phone back without answering."

He shrugged. "I was running late. Lesley and I were supposed to meet up for lunch."

"Where? Masonville? Because I watched you drive right out of town."

He crossed his arms. "If I needed a mother, Maggie May, I'd ask for one."

"Grandpa. It is not safe out there. I don't want to lose you."

"And I don't want to spend whatever time I have left cowering inside watching bad TV."

"It's just a year."

"A *year*?" He sat forward, staring at me.

"Yeah, a year. Probably. Maybe a little longer."

"I thought it was going to last for a month. If that."

"Not when we have such an uneven response and no good way to treat this thing."

"Maggie May. I love you. But I am not going to hide here in my house for the next year. It's not going to happen."

"But…"

"But nothing. I don't even know anyone who's sick."

"That can change any day. You know how many tourists flock to the valley in the summer. Matt's already having to deal with a bunch of fools trying to find somewhere they can go skiing with all the resorts shut down. Imagine what it's going to be like on Memorial Day. Or the Fourth. All it takes is one sick person and it's going to spread like wildfire. Unless you stay home. You can't get it if you're staying away from people."

He thought about it for a long moment. "So the issue is someone bringing it in from the outside?"

"Probably, yeah. I mean, there could be one or two people here who have it already. But most likely, yeah."

He pursed his lips. "What if there weren't any tourists coming in? What if it was just us? I read an article about that town, Gunnison, that never saw a case during the flu pandemic of 1918 because they locked down and didn't let anyone in."

I shrugged. "That's pretty much what New Zealand is doing. And Australia. But how are you going to do that here? We're not an island. People have second homes here, and we've already seen at least a couple bring it in with them that way. And I don't think you can just tell the rest of the state or the country to stay away. Pretty sure that's illegal under the constitution. You'd have to lock down all of America, and that's just not going to happen."

Warming up to my subject, I added, "Even here we couldn't pull something like that off. You know the big tourist companies aren't going to go along with that. They're losing money right now and have no local interests other than the tourist revenue. Why would they agree to a lockdown that cost them profits?"

"Hm." He looked far too thoughtful for my comfort. "But if we *could* keep people away…How long would we have to stay home for then?"

I sighed. "If you really could pull it off?" I thought about it for a moment. "Ideally everyone would stay where they are for at least two more weeks. Stock up on groceries, give up walking the dog or going fishing or *anything* else, just stay home and don't go anywhere. No construction. No take-out food. Nothing. I mean really lockdown, not this half-baked version we're doing now."

I scratched behind my ear, hating how dry my skin got these days. "If you did that, by the end of the two weeks anyone who had it would likely be showing symptoms. You could keep them and anyone they were locked down with isolated until they all tested negative, but let everyone else go back to their business. Of course, that doesn't cover those who have it and show no symptoms, so better to lock everyone down for two weeks and then test them all at the end of it, but that's not gonna happen."

He smiled. "Two weeks, huh? I can do two weeks."

"But that's assuming no one else was going to come into the valley after that. And assuming no one lies about their symptoms. And that people actually comply with the lockdown. But, yeah, theoretically, if all of that fell into place we could get back to normal in two weeks or so."

"So why don't we do that everywhere?"

I laughed. "Like we could coordinate that across so many states and countries? I mean, to wipe this thing out the world would have to pause for two weeks. New Zealand can pull something like that off because they're an island that's far away from everyone else. We're not. Getting Americans to all agree to do the same thing? That's like herding cats."

"But the valley's small enough, we should be able to do it here."

I shook my head. "You'd have to find a way to keep anyone else from coming in. And even people who'd been here at the time of the lockdown, if they left and wanted to come back they'd have to agree to isolate for another two weeks. No one is going to agree to do that, Grandpa. Would you?"

Even as we were having this conversation there was a small part of my mind telling me it was not a good idea to be discussing this hypothetical scenario with my grandpa.

See, my problem is, I'd probably sit down and help a murderer figure out the perfect way to kill someone as long as it was phrased as an intellectual challenge. Because when it's not real it just seems like some fun little theoretical exercise.

But to someone else? Well, my theoretical idea of how to do something might start to sound like a good plan. And my grandpa's past didn't exactly involve living by the law.

My grandpa scratched at his chin, clearly taking this seriously. "What about food? And supplies? How would you handle that?"

I swear, I'm my own worst enemy. Because instead of changing the subject, I answered. "Well, to be really safe I'd say you'd have to stop the deliveries at the border and then have some sort of contactless handoff. Or you'd have to test the drivers every time they arrived to make sure they weren't actively infective. But even that's not ideal unless you made them leave same-day. Best bet would be to stock up before you shut down and then limit deliveries from that point forward."

He sat back, thinking, which made me very nervous.

"Grandpa. You can't be taking this conversation seriously. It won't work. This is not Colorado of the early 1900s. You can't threaten people away with a shotgun or tell them they're not welcome in your town anymore."

"But if we could pull it off, we could go back to normal?"

"Theoretically, yeah. But that's like saying if I win the lottery I'll never have to work another day in my life. Problem is, how many people do you know win the lottery? And this is even harder to accomplish than that, because it's making a bunch of very different people with very different interests cooperate on something they may not want to cooperate on."

"Hm."

"Grandpa…"

"What?"

"Please don't do anything stupid."

Speaking of, I was about to ask him about where he'd gone the day before, but then Fancy started barking her head off in the backyard and I had to go deal with that instead. I loved her, but…

It had been a hard couple of weeks and I just needed a break. One little thing that would go my way.

CHAPTER 4

I called Matt when I got home. "Can you come by, please? I know you're working, but I really need to see you."

"Maggie, you know I can't risk exposing you because it'll expose your grandpa."

"You don't have to come inside. We don't have to touch. You can just stand outside the fence and I can see you, in person, for just a moment or two. Please. We'll stay six feet apart. I just…I need to see you Matt."

"Okay. I'll be right there."

"Thank you."

I paced the front yard until he finally pulled up out front. Our new house had a white picket fence in the front yard which meant that Fancy was waiting with me, too. She didn't know what she was waiting for, which is what made it all the more special when she saw Matt's vehicle stop out front and bounded to her feet and ran for the fence.

"Hey, gorgeous," he said to me as he came around the side of his SUV. He was as sexy as ever, especially in his uniform.

I went all melty inside at the sound of his voice. "Hey."

I wanted desperately to hug him and kiss him, but I couldn't. Fancy on the other hand…

She jumped onto the fence and started making pathetic, excited crying noises until he rubbed her ears and gave her a kiss on the nose and told her what a good girl she was.

I'd never been so jealous of my dog in my life.

"She misses you," I said as Fancy finally jumped down from the fence and ran to grab her newest toy—a pink fluffy bunny rabbit that I figured was a better toy for her than real rabbits.

"I miss her, too. And you."

We both stood there looking at each other, arms crossed, trying not to close that last little bit of distance.

"I wish this was over," I said.

Life has always balanced out for me. Something good happens and then something bad happens to offset it. Or vice versa.

But did life really have to follow my happily-ever-after wedding with a frickin' never-ending pandemic?

"Me too. But I'm afraid we have a long ways to go. Of course…" He glanced towards my grandpa's house. "If the reason we're staying apart is to protect your grandpa, then I think we're wasting our time."

"You found out where he's been going?"

"I saw his truck parked outside Russell's house yesterday along with about a dozen others."

"Did you talk to him?"

"I did. And he told me he doesn't know how many years he has left and he's not going to sit around at home alone on his couch watching the clock tick."

"Doesn't he realize he's going to have a heckuva lot fewer years if he isn't careful here?"

He shrugged. "You can lead a horse to water, Maggie."

"Yeah, yeah. I know. Can't make him do what he doesn't want to."

I debated telling Matt about the hypothetical conversation I'd had with my grandpa about locking the valley down somehow, but decided not to. It was probably nothing. Plus, what could he do about it? Talk to my grandpa again? Like that was going to work. No point in adding to his stress.

I glanced towards the house. "How's Jack? He giving you any trouble?"

"Nah. Barely see him. We're both working double-shifts right now. He's trying to save up for an extension to the trailer."

"An extension? What for?"

He grinned. "I think he and Trish are hoping to give Sam a baby sister or brother when this is over."

"Oh. I didn't know that. Good for them."

I tensed, waiting for Matt to say something about us having kids, but fortunately he didn't. Not that I didn't think he'd be a great father, it was just…Kids are complicated. And wanting them can sometimes destroy what's already there. So can having them. At least, from what I'd seen of my friends.

Oh, there were the happy, delighted, bonded-by-love couples, too. I just didn't have much faith that my personal story would go that direction. At least that was one upside to this whole mess, I had a very good excuse for not immediately trying to get pregnant now that we were married.

We stood there and stared at each other for a long, long moment until Matt's radio crackled with a call for assistance. Matt responded that he was on his way and then looked at me. "I better get going."

"Yeah."

I bit my lip, trying not to cry or run to him. He didn't move, just stared at me for another long moment.

"Love you," he finally said.

"Love you, too."

"This'll be over soon. And then we can start that amazing life we have planned."

"Yeah."

I knew it was a lie. So did he. But I felt better for it.

Fancy and I didn't take our eyes off him until he got into his SUV and drove away. Only then did we go back inside and have ice cream. Lots and lots of ice cream.

CHAPTER 5

The next day was Easter. We didn't want to endanger anyone's health, but Sam was young and there are only so many Easter egg hunts a kid gets in a lifetime, you know? So we'd dyed boiled eggs the night before and then Trish and I had hid them along with a dozen plastic eggs in the wild area to the side of my grandpa's house.

Jack and Matt came, but they sat on the other side of the clearing. Trish had to continuously remind Sam to keep his distance. It was heart-breaking.

I'd left Fancy locked up next door. It was her nap time and I didn't want to put her on the tether I'd have to use in the front yard of my grandpa's house since it didn't have a fence. For some reason she was fine on a leash, but put her on a tether and she forgot she was on it and would run to the end and get jerked backward.

While Trish helped Sam find the last few eggs my grandpa came over and stood next to me.

"Wouldn't it be nice if we could end all of this right now? Just open back up?"

"Of course it would, Grandpa. But unfortunately you can't intimidate a virus into doing what you want it to do. The only way to end this is to come up with a way to treat it or prevent it or to get people to stay away from each other long enough it stops transmitting. And, well, none of that's looking very promising right now."

He winked at me. "I have a plan."

"Grandpa." I turned to face him. "You think being stuck in your nice comfortable home with television and the ability to drive around when you want is bad, don't forget how much worse prison was. Not to mention those places are a nightmare right now. Do you really want to go back there?"

He just smiled. "Who's going to arrest me?"

"Matt. He wouldn't like it, but he'd do it."

"What's he going to charge me with?"

"I don't know yet. But I'm not liking the way your mind is going these days."

He took a long sip of his Coors and nodded towards where Sam had settled himself down on the grass to open each of the plastic eggs. Most had chocolate or other little candies, but the gold one had a twenty-dollar bill in it. I knew when he'd found it because his eyes went so wide they probably doubled in size and he ran around showing it to everyone.

Matt caught my eye and raised one eyebrow as Sam ran by, like, "Look isn't he cute. Don't you want one? I see you smiling over there." I just shook my head and laughed. Not the time, Matt. Not the time.

After the egg hunt we all settled into an appropriately distanced barbecue in the front yard with Matt and Jack at one table on the far side of the yard and Sam, Trish, my grandpa, and I at a table on the other side of the yard.

"How's Lesley?" I asked.

"Good. We've talked each night on the phone, but I didn't see her this week because she wanted to be able to spend the day with her grandkids. All of her kids and their families agreed to not go anywhere for the last week so they could safely be together."

"Good for them." I gave him a sidelong glance. "You know, I probably shouldn't be sitting so close to you given the fact that you've been sneaking off to hang out at Russell's house."

"Maggie May."

"Well it's true. You're being less safe than I am."

He didn't answer.

I tried to imagine what the next year of our lives was going to look like with us sniping at each other to see who was being safe enough and who was being too dangerous. And, really, how long could we expect a little kid like Sam to hang out at home?

This was a kid who'd ridden his bicycle through most of the valley to find me when his mom went missing. He wasn't the type to curl up in the corner with a good book. And there really are only so many fun TV shows or movies for kids.

After a while I had to image the fun of growing virtual radishes was going to wear off. (He was currently obsessed with some strange game that involved living on an island and growing radishes for animal creatures. He'd spent an hour trying to tell me about it and I still didn't get it. What happened to Pitfall? Or my personal childhood favorite, Happy Trails, which involved sliding little map squares around while your character tried to collect money bags and chase down the bad guy.)

(I know. Probably no one else on this planet played that game. But I had an old Intellivision game console that my dad gave me and I'd play it for hours until my thumbs developed blisters from the tiny little buttons on the controller. Now games were about, I don't know, building things? Growing things? Character development? It was weird. It confused me. I just liked games I could win. Puzzles I could solve. Where there was one answer.)

I looked around at our sad little family gathering. No Abe and Evan. No Greta. No Jamie and Mason. No friends of Sam's. Of course I wanted it over. I don't like feeling powerless.

But we'd make it through. All of us. Alive.

Because that much I could control. I couldn't change the fact that this thing existed. I couldn't change the fact that it had spread the way it had. I couldn't make some stranger stay home or wash their hands or keep their distance or make safe choices.

But I could do that for myself. And I could guilt the hell out of everyone around me until they did, too.

And if that failed…

Well, I wasn't above a little sabotage to protect those I loved. What's an alternator cable between friends, right?

CHAPTER 6

I tried to keep a better eye on my grandpa the next couple of days. He was supposed to be staying away from Lesley still since they'd both been potentially exposed at their respective parties, but he kept leaving the house anyway. The third day in a row he did it, I decided to use my spare key and sneak into his house to see what I could find out.

I know. I'm a horrible person. We have established this fact. It should not be new to you or anyone else.

And normally I would not break into anyone's home, let alone the home of someone I love and who should be able to trust me. But I knew he was up to something and I also knew that whatever it was was the type of thing that was going to land him in jail.

And since I loved my grandpa and didn't want to see that happen, I needed to know what was going on. So my options were follow him to wherever he was going, which was likely Russell's house, which would do me no good, or break into his house and see if he'd left any notes around anywhere.

It wasn't a proud moment. But it was a necessary one.

A Housebound Holiday

What I found printed out neatly on his kitchen table didn't make a lot of sense to me.

First, he'd printed out the rates page for the Homesteader's Haven, a luxury camping retreat on the edge of Bakerstown. The place had replica teepee and covered wagons that people could sleep in that were nicer than a four-star hotel room. It was like extreme glamping. The beds in each one were king-sized, there was cable TV, and A/C in the summer, which was, quite frankly, more than any of us locals had.

The only accommodation people had to make when they stayed there was that the restrooms and dining/cooking area were communal.

My grandpa had circled the rates and made a couple calculations in the margins for what it would cost for someone to stay for fourteen days straight. There were also some notes to the side that made it look like he'd called the place and asked what a long-term rate would be for staying there.

I flipped through the stack and saw that he'd done the same for a handful of other properties in the area, including the Creek Inn, which my friends Abe and Evan ran.

That gave me an idea and I called Abe to ask him about it, but he said he really didn't know what my grandpa was up to. Just that he'd wanted their long-term rate and some idea about their capacity.

"How are you guys doing?" I asked, knowing they had to be struggling with the shutdown of their business.

"We were lucky. We don't need to be open. We own the place outright, so we've just been enjoying some time off. Neither one of us want to take the risk of getting sick."

"And your staff?"

"Well, luckily, this is our slow time of the year, so we just kept the few year-round staff on payroll. Managed to get one of those loans so it won't even cost us anything for a couple months."

"Oh, that's good. How's Lucy Carrots holding up?" (That was their St. Bernard who was absolutely adorable.)

"She misses the guests. They spoiled her rotten. But I think she's enjoying having us around more. How's Fancy?"

"Did I mention that Trish and Sam are living with us right now?"

"Oh."

"Yes. Oh." I glanced out the window. "You know, I better get going. I'm standing in my grandpa's kitchen without his permission, and if he comes home and finds me it may not go over well."

"Maggie! You broke into your grandpa's house?"

"It's not really breaking in if you have a key is it?"

His silence told me what he thought of that one.

"Anyway. Better go. Glad you're doing well. Bye."

"Bye."

I glanced at the other papers in the stack, but they were just as confusing as the rest of them. Something about freezer trucks and their capacity and how they worked.

As I let myself back out the front door I knew my grandpa was up to something, but what it was exactly I still wasn't sure. Maybe making everyone who entered the valley quarantine for fourteen days? That certainly made a lot of sense, but I couldn't see it actually working.

Look at that family in Chicago who'd exposed a whole school because they wanted to go to a Daddy-daughter dance. I mean, seriously. People are…

Selfish. We'll go with selfish. Or perhaps, not self-aware? I don't know. Whatever they are, you can't rely on them to "do the right thing" on their own most of the time.

As I closed the front door and walked back to my house, I wondered what my grandpa was up to. It had to be more than just researching quarantine options.

CHAPTER 7

I grabbed Fancy and took her up to the big rock behind my grandpa's house. As she ate a doggie ice cream, I called Jamie to see how she was doing and to run everything by her. Maybe she could see something I couldn't.

"Maggie! How are you holding up?"

"You sound far too happy given the current circumstances. Can I offer you an eight-year-old child and his mother as house guests for the next year or so?"

She laughed. "Not going so well, huh?"

"I am not equipped for this. I should be hiding out somewhere with just me and Fancy. And *maybe* Matt. On a good day."

She laughed again.

"Seriously, why are you so happy? You're stuck at home, too."

"I know. But…"

I had a sudden suspicion I didn't want to hear what came next.

"But?"

"Well, we weren't going to tell anyone until we hit the three-month mark, but we're almost there, and…"

"You're pregnant?"

"I am! Isn't it great? Oh, I'm so excited. I've been looking at all these decoration ideas for the baby's room. I know you'd probably want to do something crazy like a zig-zag black and white border and red or something, but I think we're going to go with yellow and green pastel. And giraffes. Or elephants. Or maybe teddy bears. Or maybe all three. I don't know. There are so many choices. And with the lockdown happening, I've just thrown myself into it. I'm also doing a ton of research on baby foods. I see no reason I can't make my own."

I laughed. That was the one part of the conversation I could grab hold of. "From what I hear, you're going to be pretty darned tired those first few months. So maybe don't try to add making your own baby food on top of it."

"Yeah, you're probably right. But I'm still going to research it all and try different types anyway even if I don't make them for my own kid. Maybe I can start a baby food company up and have it running by the time the second one comes along. And then I can just grab a few jars out of the storage room when I need them. If not by the second, then certainly by the third."

"Exactly how many kids are you planning on having?"

I figured maybe you should have one and see how it goes before you start thinking you like it enough to add more into the mix.

"I don't know. At least three? Maybe more?"

I opened my mouth to mention to her that sometimes that wasn't possible. And that sometimes people change their mind after the first one or, most definitely, after the second one.

But then I closed it again.

This was a moment of joy in an otherwise bleak year and I was not going to ruin it with my realism. "I am so happy for you, Jamie."

"Thank you. I was so worried about getting pregnant, but here we are. And, I know the world is crazy right now and maybe if we'd waited a couple more months we would've put it off, but I'm so glad we didn't."

"I'll have to throw you a baby shower. Maybe a virtual one, given the circumstances."

"We'll have to Zoom once my belly gets big enough so you can see it."

"Absolutely." I wanted to cry. Because life was changing so fast. In good ways. But, scary ways. To hide it from Jamie, I changed the subject. "Speaking of…"

I told her about my grandpa and the strange conversation we'd had and what I'd found on his kitchen table and how worried I was that he was about to do something drastic.

After lecturing me about how I shouldn't have broken into his house, Jamie said, "I wonder what his plan is? I hope he can pull it off, whatever it is."

"Jamie!"

"I do. I want my best friend here for my pregnancy. And I want to be able to leave my house without worrying about catching this thing. Can you imagine?"

I shuddered, thinking of the few stories that had made the news about pregnant women whose kids had been born while they were in comas or who had kids that needed to be kept in the NICU that they couldn't see for more than an hour or two a day. I didn't want that for my best friend.

Heck. I didn't want that for my worst enemy.

"Yeah. I just…I don't want my grandpa to go to prison, Jamie."

"If he pulls this off, whatever it is, no one is going to put him in prison."

"Not even Officer Clark?" (Who had hated my grandpa forever and still probably thought he'd killed Jack Dunner despite all evidence to the contrary.)

"He has a newborn. You imagine he doesn't go to work every day scared about catching this? He's been staying at his cousin's to keep his wife and baby safe."

"Oh. I didn't know that."

"Yeah. So, no, I don't think even Officer Clark will arrest him. It's people outside the valley that are going to be the problem, not people in the valley. But if we don't let them in then they can't do anything about it, right? Pretty much everyone I know would be grateful for a way to get on with our lives already."

"But what about tourism? So many people depend on it to live. This may last a year or more. People have bills to pay."

"I'll put Mason on it."

"What do you mean?"

"His family has enough money. If they can't help people through this, then I'll divorce his sorry you-know-what. He can make loans if he really feels that's required, but I'd rather see him just help people out. That's what a community does, isn't it? We come together when we're needed? I mean, really. Debt is just so much paper. This is about lives."

"That may be what a community should do. But, well, look at the world. We don't do that for each other on a normal basis. Why would anyone start now?"

"Because it's the right thing to do. And this isn't the world. This is the Baker Valley. We can make it work here."

"Hm. If you think so…"

"I do. You should call Greta. And I'm going to go corner Mason before baby brain makes me forget."

"Do you already have baby brain?"

"I don't know. Probably not. I probably just have information overload from doomscrolling day in and day out. I'd rather focus on this instead. Make the world a better place, one valley at a time, right? Talk to you later. Bye."

"Bye."

As I stared down at my grandpa's house, I tried to figure out how I'd managed to *add* members to my grandpa's conspiracy rather than defuse the whole situation. But Jamie did have a good point. If we could all pull together and agree to get through this, we should be able to make it work.

And if Mason Maxwell put his family's money and clout behind whatever hare-brained scheme my grandpa was cooking up that made it far less likely he'd be arrested. And far more likely he could actually pull off the plan, whatever it turned out to be.

CHAPTER 8

So I called Greta. (Thanks to good marriage choices she had a few hundred million dollars to work with and she'd come from humble enough beginnings that she might actually be willing to do it, too.)

"Maggie, so good to hear from you," she said when she answered the phone, her German accent as present as ever.

"Greta. How are you holding up?"

"Well, it was sad to have to cancel my visit to see Jean-Philippe in Paris, but otherwise, I am good. I have taken up jewelry making."

"Really?"

"Oh yes. It is a very soothing hobby."

"What kind of jewelry?"

"All kinds. I have worked with nail polishes and necklace bases to create pretty swirled patterns. And I have worked with wire and beads and jewels. I will send you something. Or I will give you something next time I see you. If I ever get to see you again. We are not doing so well here, Maggie. This country…I love it, but…I do not understand."

"Oh trust me, neither do most of us. No matter what side of the divide we're on. Speaking of…If we turn the Baker Valley into an isolated enclave until all this passes, any chance you'd be willing to help the residents out so they don't all end up bankrupt at the end? Maybe make some loans that don't have to be paid back immediately to get them through?"

"An isolated enclave? Explain."

"I may have accidentally given my grandpa the idea that if he could somehow keep people from coming to the valley that he could go back to living his normal life in a couple weeks. I was going to try to stop him, but Jamie thinks it's a good idea and maybe she's right. Problem is, how do people make a living until then? Or, if not make a living, meet their obligations at least. I mean, honestly, a roof over your head and food on your table should be all we're worried about, but people have mortgage payments and credit card payments and car payments and, well, debt, you know? It doesn't go away."

"Ah, yes, I see. This is a challenge. Because the people are here, but the debt is not."

"Right. I wish we could just pause everything for a couple weeks—just all stay in place, no one owes anyone anything for that period of time and then it would be over. But that won't happen."

"Hm, yes. American priorities. How many people are we talking?"

"About fifteen thousand or so." (That was the population of the county at least. I'd looked it up on my phone before I called her.) "Some will have savings to get through with. Some will have businesses that can still run. Some won't have debt. But that's how many we'd have to help if we manage this."

(When had *I* joined the conspiracy? Sometime between sitting down on a rock above a small Colorado town and now it seemed.)

"And how long would we need to plan for?"

"Maybe a year?"

"Give me a moment." I heard the sound of her fingernails clicking on keys and the whir of an adding machine crunching numbers. Finally, she made a small harrumphing sound. "I think this would take two hundred million or so. It is not a small amount, but we can do this. Perhaps some loans for mortgages and other debt, but food we can just give. The question is, what is your grandpa's plan? Will it work?"

"Oh, and you won't be alone in doing this. Jamie is making Mason help, too."

"Good. Your grandpa's plan?"

"I don't know, to be honest."

"Hm. I will call him. We must make sure it is a good plan. I enjoy my jewelry-making but I would like to see you for coffee. And to have Hans and Fancy go to the park together. So we will do this. Even if your grandpa was not planning this, now I am. It will be good, Maggie. Goodbye."

She hung up on me and I wondered what exactly I'd started. Even if I had no further involvement in the matter, between the conversations I'd had with my grandpa, Jamie, and Greta, I had definitely been the one to spur things along from "wouldn't it be nice" to something that was actually going to happen.

I considered calling Matt to let him know about everything, but Fancy decided she'd had enough of hanging out on a rock and started pulling at her leash to please be walked.

CHAPTER 9

It was two in the morning a few days later when I heard a loud rumbling noise like the canyon outside of town was collapsing. Knowing what I knew about my grandpa's friendships with people who knew how to use explosives, I immediately jumped out of bed and threw on a sweatshirt and some shoes.

(The nice thing about sleeping in the type of pajamas that can be seen by your neighbors without causing a scandal is that you can be dressed and out the door in a minute or so if need be. A habit I'd acquired when Fancy was a puppy who needed to be walked immediately or else.)

It was only one block down to the highway and two blocks to the beginning of the canyon, so I didn't bother with my van, just walked briskly. I took Fancy with me since she wouldn't stop barking. She does *not* like to be woken from a deep sleep, thank you very much.

I couldn't see any signs of a rock slide, but what I did find were a series of large concrete construction barriers placed across the highway so that there was no access to the canyon, and my grandpa and Officer Clark looking smug and talking quietly as they leaned side-by-side against the barrier.

"Gentlemen," I said.

My grandpa stood up. "Maggie May. Figured you'd be out here as soon as you heard it."

"And what exactly did I hear, Grandpa?"

"Well, don't you just know that there are some horrible rockslides in Colorado? Shut the whole highway down sometimes. And it turns out we just had one ourselves. A big one. The type that will shut down the canyon for…gosh, I don't know. Months?"

"Did we?"

He nodded, a slight smile quirking his lips.

"And let me guess, the highway outside of Bakerstown had the same issue? Same night even? Such a strange coincidence."

"That it did. Or so Officer Clark here tells me. Tragic all those strangers won't be able to come here for Memorial Day or the Fourth."

"And if I was wrong about this thing? If it clears up faster than I think it will?"

"Well, wouldn't you know it? There might be some construction equipment that unexpectedly frees itself up and we can get things fixed much sooner. But for now, we're just gonna have to live here together and make it work. Good thing your friend Greta brought in a nice big helicopter for emergencies. And that Mason Maxwell arranged for all sorts of extra food to be stored on his property before all this happened. And, of course, I imagine the county council will put together some sort of financial assistance for all those who are impacted financially by this so no one suffers."

"What if someone doesn't like this?"

He shrugged. "Nice thing about those helicopters is they can fly someone right on out of here. But they won't be allowed to fly them back."

I shook my head in defeat. "You did good, Grandpa. But what about Evan and Abe? I assume they're stuck on the other side of that rock slide of yours?"

"Wouldn't you know it? They decided to stay at the Homesteader's Haven for a few nights so they were already in the valley when it happened. And it turns out Greta has a nice little furnished property she normally rents out that's just going to be sitting there vacant now that I'd bet they can stay in until this all passes."

"What if we're just locking the illness in with us, though?"

"Speaking of that, I heard the council is going to impose a lockdown starting at midnight tomorrow. One of those serious, European-type lockdowns where no one goes anywhere for two weeks. Someone needs food, they'll drop it off for them. Only exception are cops, fire, and doctors or nurses willing to stay at the hospital. Or so I hear."

"You thought of everything."

"Me? Oh no. You thought of everything, my dear. We just made it work." He winked at me as he walked over and put his arm around my shoulder. "Now. It's the middle of the night. How about we walk back home and let Officer Clark handle this 'til morning?"

EPILOGUE

Once people understood that they'd be taken care of through however long this mess lasted most were happy to have the valley walled off from the rest of the world for a while if it meant getting back to some sense of normalcy.

Greta flew the few remaining dissidents out of the valley and gave them a nice generous payment to settle in elsewhere until things cleared up. It helped that the council made it very clear that you either went along with the new plan or left.

I still figured it wasn't going to be quite as easy as it looked right now, because there would definitely be those who did not agree with what had been done, but I still had hope it would be better than the alternative.

And I was glad to know that I lived in a place where people were willing to make those sacrifices for one another. Mason and Greta could've bunkered down secure in their mansions and let the rest of the valley suffer, but they hadn't. And they weren't the only ones who'd agreed to help out. The county council had set up a donation fund and over 2,500 people had contributed in the first two weeks.

We were committed to helping one another through this. It felt good.

But what was even better was when Matt was finally able to come home two weeks later.

I was so excited I literally jumped on him as soon as he walked through the door even though I wasn't sure he was going to be able to catch me. I didn't care if we fell to the floor in a heap, at least we'd be doing it together.

After he finished kissing me hello he asked, "Where's Fancy?"

"At my grandpa's for the night. I know she's missed you and I know you've missed her, but I wanted twenty-four hours alone with my husband where all I have to think about is you and how wonderful it is that we can finally be together in this blessedly-silent home."

"All alone?"

I nodded.

"All alone."

"Then let's not waste a moment." He picked me up and carried me to our room.

(And the rest of that twenty-four hours? Well, that's none of your business now, is it?)

A FOULED-UP FOURTH

A MAGGIE MAY AND MISS FANCYPANTS MYSTERY

ALEKSA BAXTER

CHAPTER 1

July first and the good news was that the valley was still safe and walled off from a country that seemed increasingly bent on following the worst possible timeline. Bad news was that gave me more time to notice who my neighbors were.

Not my grandpa, he was great. Except for the small frown he gave Matt's and my front yard whenever we forgot to mow to his satisfaction. (A small frown that turned into pointed comments about how a man's home is a reflection on him and how much he values his neighbors.)

That I could handle. I'd spent a lifetime letting subtle critiques wash off without leaving a trace.

No, it was the other neighbor I was ready to murder: Lucas Dean.

I might have been able to forget his predilection for chasing any female he legally could get away with chasing. Or his inordinate fondness for hanging out in his yard in nothing but shorts so small they belonged in the 70's. And I could have maybe even forgotten his unfortunate habit of calling me Sunshine.

(I'm pretty sure half the time he didn't remember my name. I was tempted to wear a name tag around with M-A-G-G-I-E written on it in all capital letters until he got the point, but I resisted.)

What I couldn't forget, or forgive, was his apparent fondness for fireworks. And his complete obliviousness to how much those fireworks affected poor Fancy, my four-year-old Newfoundland.

I mean, picture it. There we were, sitting in our backyard in the shadow of a pine tree, hidden away behind a six-foot fence, me reading a book, Fancy snoring away, her foot just barely touching my leg, minding our own business, enjoying the day, relaxing in the almost but not quite uncomfortable heat, and suddenly…

BOOM.

A loud banging noise from next door and then a scatter of little explosions in the air.

Fancy, poor thing, jumped to her feet, furiously barking and looking for the culprit. How dare something disturb her sleep? How dare that loud noise go off and wake her? Where was it?

She ran around the yard, barking as loud as she could, demanding answers.

"Calm down, Fancy," I said quietly, as I slowly stood up.

(I don't believe in yelling at a barking dog, it never seems to solve the problem and just adds to the overall noise and stress of the whole thing.)

I managed to block her off and pointed towards the house. "Inside. Now."

She was headed there when another loud boom erupted from next door. She turned to charge towards the offending noise and I had to hop-skip my way into her path and get her turned back around and headed for the house again. "Inside. Go."

She went, bursting through the doggie door at the back of the house with enough force it was a miracle she didn't take the door with her.

I turned towards the six-foot wooden fence, ready to give Lucas Dean a piece of my mind, but before I could reach it, Fancy came charging around from the front of the house and resumed her barking.

(That was a rather unfortunate feature of our new home. It had doggie doors in the front *and* the back and unless I managed things properly Fancy would go in through one door but then immediately go right back out the other. She is too smart for my good, let me tell ya.)

By the time I wrangled Fancy back inside and blocked both doors so she'd stay there, things next door were once again quiet.

Who does that? Who sets off one or two loud explosions randomly during the middle of the day and then just goes on about their business as if it's nothing?

Is that fun? Can you even see fireworks in the middle of the day? I mean, really?

It seemed to me that the only reason someone would set off fireworks in the middle of the day is because they were a you-know-what who wanted to upset their neighbors.

I stewed about it all afternoon until Matt came home.

It was so nice to have my tall, dark, and handsome

husband walk through our door and give me a kiss, his blue eyes shining with love.

(In theory. Turns out that after a long shift in a cop car he could've maybe used a shower first thing. Still, a little man-stink was worth overlooking for the fact that I, Maggie May Carver, was now married to Matthew Barnes and that we could finally be together in the same house.)

"Hey, Maggie. How was your day?" he asked.

Since my days pretty much consisted of playing Sudoku on the computer and reading in the backyard, I normally didn't have much to tell him. But that day…

"You need to talk to Lucas Dean. Immediately."

"Why? Is it the shorts? Because I'm happy to talk to him about the shorts."

I laughed. "No. It's not about the shorts."

"Are you sure? I'd be happy to cite him for some sort of indecency violation so he'd cover up better."

"I'm sure you would. And if you want to mention it to him while you're over there, I'd be more than happy to be spared that sight on a regular basis. The only man I want to see in shorts that short is you. And even then…Not really my thing."

He narrowed his eyes at me. "You can't pretend he doesn't look good half-naked."

"Oh, he does. But I see a man's soul not his six-pack abs and that man is ug-ly."

Matt laughed. "So what do you want me to talk to him about?"

I stepped back and paced the room, my hands clenched into fists. "Fireworks. He set off two today. And three yesterday. And two the day before that. It has to stop."

"Maggie. It's the week before the Fourth of July. That's going to happen."

"It's a fire hazard." I flicked my blonde braid behind my shoulder and crossed my arms, glaring him down.

He raised an eyebrow at me.

"It is. And it upsets Fancy. Plus think about all the little kids and babies down for naps that were probably woken up by that. Or the veterans with PTSD. Or the…raccoons. And skunks. He keeps this up someday someone is going to get sprayed by a startled skunk."

Matt pressed his lips together. I knew he was trying not to laugh at me. "You're worried about the skunks, huh?"

"I'm serious about this, Matt. You talk to him or I will. And we both know that when I talk to people I make unfortunate death threats."

He squeezed my upper arms and smiled. "But you don't mean them."

I paused. "In this case I might."

"Maggie…I may be your husband, but I'm also still an officer of the law. Maybe don't joke about killing people in front of me?"

"Even if they deserve it?"

"*Especially* if they deserve it. Makes it much more likely they'll actually get killed and I'll have to investigate you."

I rolled my eyes. "Please. Like anyone would kill Luke. The universe is not that kind." I took Matt's hands in mine and gave him my best doe-eyed look. "So you'll talk to him for me?"

"Can it wait until after dinner?"

I nodded and wrinkled my nose. "Actually, dinner and a shower." I sniffed again. "Shower first."

I gave him a quick kiss on the cheek to take the sting out of my words and then headed into the kitchen to check on the pub-style cod I had baking away in the oven.

(My latest round of panic-buying of meat I'd decided to diversify a bit and was now stuck with various weird fish dishes that weren't bad, but weren't as emotionally satisfying as a good red-blooded steak. Life, I tell ya. If it isn't one thing it's another.)

CHAPTER 2

The next day Luke was outside mowing his yard when Fancy and I stepped out our front door.

Unfortunately, our front yard did not have a six-foot fence so I had to actually see him. (It had a cute little white picket fence instead, which was theoretically what you want in the perfect home, except, well, neighbors.)

I paused for a moment to smile at him because he was actually wearing a tank top with his too-short shorts.

He stopped the mower and sauntered over, pulling his baseball cap down a little lower. He *was* a good-looking man. On the surface. If you go for that "let's sneak off behind the bleachers for some fun" look.

He leaned forward, pressing his hands into the gaps between the white slats on the fence as I kept Fancy from going over to say hi. "Didn't figure you for a snitch, Sunshine," he said.

"I hate that word, you know. Snitch. It's the type of word people who do bad things use to make other people feel guilty about telling on them."

He winked. "I think that would be the point, don't you? Why'd you call the cops on me, Maggie?"

"I didn't call the cops on you." I fought the urge to cross my arms defensively. I hadn't called the cops. I'd waited until Matt got home.

"No? Then why was Matt on my doorstep first thing this morning, dressed in his full uniform with his hand on his gun, wanting to talk to me for just a moment?"

I tried not to laugh at the image. "Seems he doesn't like you peacocking around." I nodded at the tank top. "Nice to see you wearing some real clothes for once."

He leaned forward. "Like I told him. It's not my fault his wife can't take her eyes off me." He dropped his voice lower and purred, "You know, you ever get lonely over there, I'm right next door. I'm sure I could satisfy your needs..."

I said something back that I won't repeat here. I'm sure you can figure it out.

He just laughed and took a half-step back. "Always such a pleasure to talk to you, Maggie. By the way, you should know I've still got a *whole* lot of fireworks that need setting off and I plan to do so."

"I thought Matt talked to you about that."

"He did. Told me I couldn't set them off except for the weekend. So Friday night? Get ready to rumble."

Before I could say anything else about it, he turned and strolled away, adding an extra little swagger to his step just for my benefit. I huffed and stormed over to my grandpa's where I'd been headed before Luke accosted me, poor Fancy trailing along at my side trying to figure out what was wrong.

After I politely waited for my grandpa to open the door and let me inside, I stomped into the kitchen and grabbed a Coke. "I hate that man. I hate him with a passion. I wish he'd die."

Fancy fled for the backyard as my grandpa leaned against the doorway into the kitchen, looking as calm and composed as ever in his blue jeans and short-sleeved checkered button-up shirt. He was eighty-three, but you'd never know it from looking at him. He could easily pass for a man in his sixties since his hair was a faded brown instead of gray and he'd kept trim.

"Who is it you want to die today?" he asked, nonplussed.

"Who do you think? Lucas Dean. Haven't you heard the fireworks he keeps setting off?" I barely stopped myself from slamming the fridge closed, knowing that my grandpa would have my head if I did.

"You're upset about fireworks?" He raised one eyebrow.

"Do you realize how much they upset Fancy? It's horrible. It's *torture*. And anyone who tortures my dog deserves to die." I threw myself onto one of the kitchen table chairs.

"Maggie May."

"What?" I snapped, taking a long, long sip of soda. "You know hurting animals is the first step to becoming a serial killer."

He shook his head and grabbed himself a Coke, but much more calmly. "Fireworks are as American as apple pie and the flag," he said, joining me at the table.

"Oh please. I hate the Fourth of July. All it is is a holiday where people get drunk and show how American they are by setting off loud explosives that traumatize small animals and half their neighbors. It's absurd. Whatever its original purpose, it doesn't serve it anymore. Not that any of them do, really. Name me one holiday that isn't about getting drunk or getting gifts."

He raised an eyebrow at me, but didn't comment further.

I looked closer. "You're not planning on setting off fireworks, too, are you?"

"Here? No. Maybe down at the park. But that's far enough away you shouldn't be too upset by them."

I nodded, still wanting to punch something. (Not that I've ever punched anything in my life. That would hurt. It's just the thought of punching something that gives me a deep feeling of satisfaction sometimes. Call it positive visualization. Almost as good as the real thing and far less likely to land me in jail.)

"So." I took a deep breath, calming myself and deciding it was time to change the subject. "Lesley coming over for lunch?"

He nodded. "Would you like to join us?"

"If you don't mind. All I'm going to do if I stay home is storm around the house thinking of creative ways to kill Lucas Dean. And my cop husband has informed me that's not something I should do. Especially if I then talk about it out loud."

My grandpa smiled. "He does have a point."

"Yeah, whatever. How's the baseball season going?"

It wasn't the most eloquent way to change the subject, but I knew my grandpa and he loved coaching the local baseball team. We weren't a big town—Creek had about forty houses total—but every year we somehow managed to gather together enough kids to form a local baseball team that my grandpa coached. It was the highlight of his year working with those kids and I was so glad he was going to be able to coach them this year in safety.

"We have some great players this year…" he said as he sat down at the kitchen table.

We spent the next twenty minutes talking about batting averages and which kids had the heart to persevere even if they weren't there yet.

It was good. Good to spend time with my grandpa talking about something that mattered to him and just relaxing and enjoying the day.

I'd almost forgotten about Lucas Dean, but then…BOOM. Another firework went off. I cussed up a storm as I headed out the front door to tell him exactly what I thought of him, leaving my poor grandpa to calm down Fancy.

CHAPTER 3

Luke was standing in his front yard, grinning like an idiot, as I rushed towards him.

"It wasn't me," he said, holding his hands up in the air.

I jabbed my finger at him. "Then who was it? Because it sounded like it came from here."

"You gonna call the cops on me, Maggie. Take that husband of yours away from writing speeding tickets to give me another lecture about the rights of *dogs*?"

"I hate you. You know that?"

"Now, now, Maggie. Don't get so worked up. You're such a buzzkill."

I barely stopped myself from stomping my foot. "Another one of those words that people love to throw around when they're being jerks and don't want someone to stop their fun."

A man I didn't recognize came banging out of Luke's house. He was about the same age as us—late 30's—but hadn't kept himself in very good shape. His white t-shirt was stained in a few spots and untucked where it hung over his belly which in turn hung over his loose-fitting jeans. He had a nasty glint in his eye.

"Who's this?" he asked, eyeing me up and down in a way that made my blood boil.

I opened my mouth to tell him none of his business, but Luke beat me to it. "My neighbor. The one I told you wasn't going to appreciate you setting off that firework."

The guy scratched the sparse patch of stubble on his chin. "Huh. She gonna be around when you have your party on Friday?"

"Probably. She's always around killing my fun." Luke winked at me.

"Too bad." He turned back towards the house. "Come help me with the keg when you're done flirtin'. I'd like to tap it and see if it's any good since we're confined to this local brew stuff what with the valley being shut down and all."

I grimaced in disgust at the thought that I was *flirting* with Luke. This was not some rom-com enemies-to-lovers story. I was married, for one. And Luke was an ass, for two. (Yes, I did just use that word.) Plus, any man who'd do something to upset my dog was an absolute no. That is not redeemable in my opinion.

"Better get going," Luke said. "See you around, Sunshine." He turned and swaggered back inside.

That left me standing in the middle of the street fuming at his front door with nowhere to direct my anger. Fortunately for me, Lesley pulled into my grandpa's driveway just then and I immediately calmed down. She's so mellow and put together it's almost impossible to stay angry when she's around.

She stepped out of her perfectly maintained Lincoln and waved my way. "Hi, Maggie."

I walked over to her. "Hi, Lesley. How are you?"

Even on a random afternoon when all she was doing was going over to see my grandpa (who was her husband, but they still weren't living together), she looked perfectly put together, her pure-white hair styled into a subtle chignon, her jewelry that perfect balance of noticeable but not gauche. She was even wearing makeup and short high heels to go with her tailored slacks.

I adored her. She was great for my grandpa. But I was glad that the world didn't expect that level of put-togetherness from me, because I would've never managed to pull it off. It didn't matter how much time and care I put into getting dolled up, there was always something wrong with my outfit. A run in my hose. A chipped nail. A loose string on my hem. I'd never managed perfection a single day in my life.

Which was fine with me. Because perfection was simply not something I strove for. Too much effort for too little gain. I was pretty sure when I went to my grave no one was going to stand around and talk about how unfortunate it was that my shirts were sometimes wrinkled.

(And if they did, well, that was on them not me.)

"Are you joining us for lunch?" she asked.

"If that's okay with you." I silently pleaded with my eyes that she'd say yes.

"Of course, dear. Will you grab the casserole from the backseat?"

"Absolutely."

As we walked inside I sniffed at the edge of the aluminum foil to see what she'd made. Whatever it was, it smelled remarkably delicious. All fatty cheese and meat and bread of some sort. My stomach grumbled in anticipation.

My grandpa held the door open for us. "I gave that mutt of yours an ice cream to calm her down," he grumbled at me after giving Lesley a kiss on the cheek.

"She's not a mutt, Grandpa. And don't act like you don't love her just as much as I do." I handed him the casserole. "I'll go check on her, make sure she's okay. By the way, this time it wasn't Luke, it was some guy who's helping him set up for a big party on Friday night."

"What happened?" Lesley asked as I went in search of Fancy.

I heard my grandpa start to fill her in as I stepped outside. Fancy looked up at me, but didn't stop licking at her ice cream for a single moment. Once she got started on those things she was relentless. Other dogs I knew just took the entire container in their mouths and crunched it to pieces, paper wrapper and all. But Fancy would sit there for five minutes straight licking at the ice cream over and over again until it was all gone, leaving the container behind in almost pristine condition.

It was like that old Tootsie Pop commercial where they asked how many licks does it take to get to the center of the Tootsie Pop. Fancy would know the answer. Most dogs would just bite the thing before the end like the owl, but not Fancy

What can I say? My dog is as weird as I am.

I patted her head. "You okay, girl?"

She just kept licking.

"I'll take that as a yes."

I glanced in the direction of Luke's house. Clearly I was going to have to do something on Friday, because I could not have fireworks going off right next door for hours without it completely traumatizing Fancy. I growled in annoyance. Why couldn't he just go to the rodeo to see fireworks like everyone else?

CHAPTER 4

Fortunately, Jamie, my best friend, and Mason, her somewhat-acceptable-when-he-wasn't-being-too-obnoxiously-rich husband, invited me over for a little pre-Fourth barbecue on Friday night. Which meant that I was able to take Fancy and get away from the house before Luke's party got into full swing.

It had started around two with a bunch of uncouth men hanging out in his front yard getting drunk, but at least they'd held off on the fireworks until after I left.

Jamie, being the agreeable, wonderful person she is had told me I could come by at any time I wanted, but I didn't head over there until four.

She and Mason lived on a large plot of land outside town in a very colossal mountain-man-chic sort of home that involved lots of wood and natural stone. (It was his before they got married. If Jamie'd had a say there would have been more…*grace* to the place. More subtlety. But it was what it was. I had no doubt that given a few years she'd tone down what could be toned down.)

She was standing on the porch when I pulled up, glowing with happiness. And I do mean glowing. You know how they say some people get that pregnancy glow? Well, that was Jamie. About five months in she had the cutest baby bump in the world and was all health and joy from head to toe. Honestly, I don't think she'd stopped smiling since she found out she was pregnant.

She had her long brown hair braided back from her face and was wearing a bright yellow sundress that made her the poster child for being happily pregnant. I could just see the words shining in the air over her head. "Pregnancy is great! You should be pregnant, too! Everyone should be!"

It wasn't fooling me though. *I* knew that pregnancy was not all cute little feet pushing against bellies and good hormone surges. I'd *heard* things. Maybe she just wasn't at that stage yet. Although, Jamie being Jamie, she'd probably just laugh and smile right on through to the end, swollen ankles, acid reflux, hemorrhoids, and all.

Although, if we're being honest here, it was the thought of not being allowed unlimited quantities of Coke that scared me the most when it came to being pregnant. Going through one of the most life-changing events you can experience without caffeine as a crutch?

Haha. No.

As soon as I let Fancy off her leash she went tearing around the side of the house to find Lulu. No longer a puppy, Lulu—Jamie's golden retriever—could now give Fancy a run for her money. Of course, she was still only about half Fancy's size. Fancy was a hundred-and-forty pounds, Lulu was probably seventy. But what Lulu had that Fancy didn't was stamina.

Within five minutes, Fancy was ready to sprawl in the shade somewhere and take a nap while Lulu was still puppy pouncing around her and yapping to keep going. Jamie had never been the best at disciplining Lulu, but fortunately Mason had no problem being firm with her, so we left him on guard duty as Jamie excitedly led me through the house to the baby's room.

"I can't wait to show you what we're going to do," she exclaimed as we climbed up to the second floor and made our way down the long hallway towards the master bedroom. She stopped at the room next door to the master and opened it.

And…

Well, it was a room. Plain white walls. Boring light gray carpet. At least it didn't have the wood and stone theme that dominated most of the house. There was one small side table by the door but nothing else.

Jamie stepped into the center of the room. "So this is the room we're going to use for the nursery. I finally got all of Mason's stuff cleared out so we can start painting and putting down the new carpet. Here."

She grabbed a binder off the table and shoved it into my hands. (Jamie loves binders. I was surprised there was only one so far.) She opened it up for me. "The first tab is the furniture we're going to order. What do you think?"

It was…fine. Nice white wood furniture. Nothing too exciting except the price tag. There was a rocking chair and a crib and a dresser and it all looked okay enough to me, but what did I know? I couldn't see from the picture what made the furniture better than a dresser you could get at Target. I'm sure it was much nicer. Probably last a hundred years or something. Too bad it was only needed for probably six months.

Fortunately, Jamie didn't really want my opinion, because she kept right on talking. "And the next tab is the paint colors we're going to use. It's so important these days to be gender-neutral, you know. So no trucks if it's a boy and no curly-haired dolls if it's a girl. Just puzzle toys and stuffed bears and things like that. We don't want to program our kids with unhealthy ideas."

"But what if your kid really loves trucks? Or curly-haired dolls? Are you just going to deny them?"

She blinked at me, like the thought had never occurred to her. "We're not going to allow them screen time."

"Still. I'm not even saying if you have a boy that he'll be the one who likes trucks. You could have a girl who likes trucks. Or action figures. Or building things. Or a boy who likes curly-haired dolls. You never know. But I'm pretty sure whatever gender your child is they're going to like some sort of gendered toy at some point."

She frowned, and I laughed and patted her on the shoulder. "Don't worry too much about it, Jamie. As it turns out, most kids grow up just fine no matter what their parents subject them to. So. Gender-neutral paint colors. And," I flipped to the next tab, "giraffes and teddy bears."

She nodded, but her brow was all wrinkly and she was pressing her lips together a little too tightly. As I watched in horror, her eyes filled with tears.

"What is it? What's wrong? Did I say something to upset you? Jamie!"

She shook her head. "It's nothing. I just…" She waved her hands around. "I want it to be perfect. I want to give this baby the best life they can possibly have. And there are so many decisions and so many ways it can go wrong and…Maggie, what do I do?"

I laughed and gave her a quick hug. "It'll be okay, Jamie. I think kids are pretty resilient, all things considered. And I've never seen you mess anything up in your entire life." I pushed back and looked her in the eye. "But even if you do mess this up a little bit, it's okay. You have Mason and you have me and you have all your other friends and you aren't alone in this. People have kids every day. Some of them probably barely crack a book about it before they're suddenly holding a screaming infant in their arms. They make it through. So you will, too. It's biology."

"But there are so many theories out there and so much you need to do. And you have to feed them the right foods. And…"

"Jamie. Look at me. My mom put Karo syrup in water and fed it to me when I was a baby because I was so damned hungry all the time. But you know what? I turned out fine. Maybe with a certain soda addiction I wouldn't have had otherwise, but seriously. If our parents could do things like that—because you know your mother did crazy stuff like that, too—and we could turn out just fine, you'll be fine, too. Plus, honestly, a little bit of dirt and bad food and scraped knees is good for a kid. You can't coddle them too much if you actually want them to move on and be independent someday."

"Your mom gave you Karo syrup?"

I nodded. "*And* she let me run around pretty much buck naked until I was maybe three or four. I mean, not always, but there are definitely pictures enough to show it."

(My favorite one was of me sitting on the sink with a toothbrush in my mouth, tanned from head to toe so I'd obviously been spending a large amount of time outside sans clothes. And, come to think of it, I was quite possibly even older than four in that photo. If I and the world could survive that, Jamie's kid was going to be just fine.)

Jamie bit her lip.

"It's going to be fine, Jamie. I know it will. You think maybe this was a bit of pregnancy hormones? I mean, I'm never a fan of when men suggest hormones as a cause for things, but I hear it's pretty real when it comes to pregnancy."

She chuckled. "Yeah, probably. Mason doesn't know what to do with me these days because half the time I'm happy and excited and half the time I'm scared and crying. Or angry. I *yelled* at him yesterday. I never yell. But he left a pan on the stove after he made breakfast. And it was filthy. Who does that?"

"Have you ever been to my home?"

She shuddered. "Yes."

I laughed and put an arm around her shoulders as I led her back down the hallway. "Try to give him a break, this is all new to him, too, you know."

She nodded. "I know. You're right. But it was filthy, Maggie. Just thinking about it now…Ugh."

As we walked down the stairs back to the main level Fancy scrambled to her feet from where she'd been lying at the base of the stairs.

"You silly goof," I told her, bending down to rub her ears and kiss her nose.

"Why didn't she just come up?" Jamie asked.

"Yeah, no. Fancy and stairs do not go together. That's one of the reasons I don't think we'll stay where we are long-term. Half of the square footage is up a flight of stairs Fancy won't use."

Mason came in from the back porch with a plateful of grilled hamburger patties that smelled delicious. "You'd actually choose your house to accommodate your dog?" he asked.

"Yes. Of course. Wouldn't you?"

He chuckled. "No."

"You and my grandpa. But for me Fancy's comfort is probably number two on the list of what I need in a home. My own comfort being number one."

"And Matt's comfort?" he asked.

"Matt's comfort is my comfort." I batted my eyes at him and made my way to the fridge to grab a Coke. Just the thought of being deprived of my beloved addiction made me need one.

As I watched Jamie and Mason set out all the fixings for cheeseburgers and banter back and forth, I couldn't help but smile. I was so happy for them and so glad to be able to just hang out with them and enjoy a good meal together.

We were all blessed. Truly.

CHAPTER 5

I stayed at their house until the sun went down and then gave it another hour just to be safe. I figured Luke couldn't possibly have more than an hour's worth of fireworks to set off.

I was wrong.

As I drove up the street towards my house I could see the haze from all the fireworks that had already been set off. Another one screamed its way into the sky as I reached my driveway, a group of men and women with beers gathered on the front lawn cheering as it exploded in a shower of bright lights.

"Welp. I guess we're going for a drive, Fancy," I said, continuing on past my house and turning back towards the highway.

The good thing about living in a fairly rural area is that I could easily find a stretch of road far enough from any homes that we could avoid more fireworks.

I drove along the highway towards Masonville with the windows down. It was a gorgeous night, the sky clear of clouds and a deep dark blue, the stars shining bright above us, the breeze that blew through my hair pleasantly cool but not cold.

I didn't even bother trying to go the speed limit. (For once.) I wasn't trying to get anywhere. I was just killing time. So I drove along slowly, enjoying the feel of the breeze and the sound of Lizz Wright crooning about how she idolized someone.

There's a peace to being away from everyone, driving down a two-lane road through the countryside when it's already dark out, your headlights and the stars the only light, the air carrying the scent of fresh, healthy vegetation and maybe a hint of rain.

By the time I turned around outside Masonville and headed back towards Creek I was actually feeling calm and happy. Let Luke and his friends celebrate the holiday with too much booze and bad decisions. I had what I wanted: Fancy snoring away in the back of the van, a gorgeous night, and a gorgeous husband who'd be home sometime around three or four in the morning.

Of course, that peace evaporated as soon as I returned home and saw that Luke was *still* not done. Rather than drive around even more and risk some stupid drunk driver taking us out, I decided I'd just barricade Fancy and myself as far from the noise as we could get and hope it would be over soon.

I pulled into the driveway and made my way around to Fancy's door. I figured Luke would have the courtesy to maybe refrain from setting off the next firework until we were inside. But no. Of course he didn't.

(I should've known. Assholes gonna asshole. But I always have this small hope that my fellow humans are actually going to prove to be decent even though I should know better by now.)

As I let Fancy out of the van, a Roman candle went off ten feet away shooting loud streaking light and sparks in every direction. Poor Fancy lost it and started barking her head off, lunging towards the noise and light.

Luke just laughed.

I shouted four words at him. I'm sure you can guess which ones.

Because, seriously? Who does that? I know you're not supposed to cuss at a neighbor, but why can't neighbors return the same respect? I mean, really? You set one of those things off when there's a dog right there?

Yeah. Bleep you, Lucas Dean.

I herded Fancy inside as Luke continued to laugh at us. But I stopped in the door and turned and looked at him with every ounce of hate I felt. Seriously, some people can die as far as I'm concerned and the world would be a better place for it.

(Yeah, I know, how awful of me. What can I say? I'm pretty sure I must be one of those people who'd actually kill the enemy during war, not just shoot around them like most soldiers who haven't been trained supposedly do.)

Fancy and I spent the next half hour huddled on the floor of the walk-in closet in the bedroom with all the bedroom windows blocked with heavy blankets to muffle the sound as much as possible.

Even with all of my effort, Fancy still occasionally barked. I swear, a few of the ones they set off actually shook the house. But eventually they tapered off to just the occasional small pop of sound here or there and we were able to fall asleep on the floor, side-by-side.

When Matt finally came home from work at three or

four or whatever time it was, Fancy immediately jumped to her feet and cried until I woke up and let her out.

"There you are," Matt laughed as we emerged from the closet. "You okay?"

"I'd be better if Lucas Dean were dead," I said as I walked Fancy to the kitchen and opened the back door for her, figuring it was safe enough to let her outside now. If someone still had fireworks to set off I'd send Matt after them.

"Maggie, what did I say about making death threats against people?"

"Not a good idea. Blah, blah, blah. Yeah, yeah, yeah." I leaned into his chest, still half asleep.

Matt pulled back and kissed the tip of my nose. "It's not, you know."

I snuggled back against him and sighed in contentment. "I know. But you can't expect me to control my thoughts when I'm this tired, can you?"

"Fair enough. Come on. Let's get you into a real bed. The floor doesn't look all that comfortable."

"It's not. Trust me." (The carpet in that closet was *old*. And thin. And my hip and shoulder hurt from lying on what was essentially bare ground.)

We shuffled down the hall, linked together in that casual way couples have, and I couldn't help but smile. I'd never actually pictured myself in a moment like that, but now that I was in it, I couldn't imagine a better place to be.

CHAPTER 6

Fancy woke me the next morning at 5:37 AM on the dot with a small little cry that said it was time to rejoin the world of the living. Rain, shine, summer, winter, it doesn't matter to Fancy. Too early for sanity is the time to be awake.

Since it was getting towards the middle of summer, I leashed her up and took her for her walk first thing before it could get warm. I muttered a few extra curses at Luke as we walked by his house and I saw all the burned-out, discarded firework wrappers spread all over the street. Not only had he set off fireworks for hours, he was a litter bug, too.

Figured.

But I couldn't hold on to my grumpiness for too long. It was a gorgeous, gorgeous morning with enough clouds in the sky over the mountains to paint them in sherbet pinks and oranges. And no one else was up, so there was this expectant stillness to the day. Like anything was possible.

Fancy and I made our way down to the baseball park and sprawled in the grass in center field. She was in her happy place because she liked to be outside in really nice grass. I was, too, because I loved the view of Creek in the early morning with its little homes and the mountains surrounding me on all sides and the blue, blue sky above.

It was glorious. Amazing. Perfect.

Which is why you know it didn't last. Not even long enough for me to walk back home.

A truck screeched to a halt at the edge of the ball field. "That's not good," I muttered as I narrowed my eyes trying to figure out who it was. "Oh, yeah. Definitely not good."

It was Trish, my sister-in-law? (I was still getting used to all the family relationships I'd married into.) She was red-haired, long-legged, and always in some sort of trouble or other.

She had the worst taste in men I'd ever seen. And I say that even though she'd finally settled down and married Matt's brother, Jack. When she stayed with me during the early parts of the lockdown she'd spent far more time than I thought was advisable talking to Luke through the front fence. And Jack, as good as he was with Trish's son, Sam, was about one step away from turning back to his criminal roots on any given day.

So Trish seeing me at the ball field and deciding to come talk to me at six in the morning was a very, very bad sign.

"Hey, Trish," I called as she made her way towards me in her slim-fitted jeans and tank top.

Fancy wagged her tail once, but didn't make a move to get up. (She loves pretty much any man, but women she's mostly indifferent to.)

"Hey, Maggie," Trish said when she finally came

close enough to not have to shout. She tried to smile, but it was forced.

This was definitely not good. I wanted to close my eyes and lie back in the grass and pretend she wasn't standing there, but that's not what family does, is it? Or polite people, but I'm not one of those.

"What's up?" I asked.

"Um…" She twirled a lock of hair around her finger and chewed on her lip like she was still a teenager.

"Sit. Seriously. You're looming over me up there." Maybe sitting would calm her down enough for her to tell me what was going on.

She glanced at the grass like it would permanently ruin her jeans, but finally sat down across from me. I realized as I looked at her that even that early in the morning she was wearing mascara and lipstick and had clearly taken the time to style her hair not just throw it back like I always do.

"What is it, Trish? Is it Jack? Is it Sam? What are you doing out so early?"

"No, it's not Jack or Sam." She fiddled with her perfectly-manicured nails, not willing to look at me.

"Well then?" I asked, losing patience.

She bit her thumb for a moment before answering. "I was just at Luke's."

"Luke's? Lucas Dean's? My neighbor's?"

She nodded.

I tried not to roll my eyes. "I didn't see you when I left the house. So you either weren't there that long or you'd parked your truck out of view somewhere. Which is it?"

"I…I wasn't there very long."

"So….? What happened? Why are we having this

conversation?" I knew she was family now, but c'mon already. Tell me what the problem was.

She fiddled with her nails some more, not looking at me.

"Trish," I snapped, wanting to shake her until she just said whatever it was she wanted to tell me.

"He's dead. Luke's…dead." She curled in on herself like a pretzel, twisting her legs up and wrapping her arms around them.

I sighed in disgust. "Of course he is."

Because that would be my luck, wouldn't it? Most people go through their life and they never know anyone who gets killed or dies unexpectedly. But me? Since moving to the Baker Valley? Well, let's just say the body count was not encouraging. And it would have to be Luke who was dead, the man I'd not so subtly threatened with significant bodily harm and who lived right next door.

My life. I tell ya.

Trish stared at me. "You knew already?"

"No. I did not know already. Just…Ignore me. Sometimes I say what I'm thinking and I really shouldn't." I pinched the bridge of my nose. "So Luke's dead."

She nodded.

"Was it natural causes? Did he slip and fall while drunk?"

One could always hope. Although since Trish was talking to me about it in the middle of a ballpark, it wasn't likely.

"Not unless he slipped and fell on a knife. In his back."

I rubbed at my face, trying to think. It was too early for this. Just because I could get up at unholy hours, didn't mean my mind was awake yet. "Did you touch anything while you were there?" I asked.

She nodded.

"*What* did you touch?"

"Um…" Trish looked up at the sky, trying to remember and ticking each item off on her fingers as she named them. "The rock where he keeps his spare key. The key. The front door. The table by the front door. The door knob—both sides. The kitchen table. A beer bottle. Um…"

"Stop. That's enough." I sighed. "Did you touch the body? Step in the blood? Move it around any?"

"The blood? Did I move the blood?" she asked, confused.

"The body. Did you move the body?"

"Um…I don't think so. He wasn't wearing a shirt and he was facedown so I could see the wound without moving him. And it was pretty clear he was dead, so I didn't feel for a pulse or anything." She glanced at the bottom of her sandals. "No blood."

"Right. So as far as the cops or anyone else knows, you could've left those prints there some other time."

She nodded.

"Why didn't you just call the cops when you found him?" (Instead of ruining my delightful morning in the park, I wanted to add.)

"Because it looks bad. I mean…I'm married to Jack and…"

"Yeah. It does." I gave her a look. That look you give a woman who makes terrible choices in men who's just told you she was trying to visit some guy who wasn't her husband at six in the morning.

She shrunk away from me. "Jack's a good guy. I love him. I do. And he's great with Sam. But with everything that's been going on he's been working really hard. He isn't there much. And Luke…"

"Was."

She nodded.

I wanted to say more, but her marriage issues were not my immediate problem. Not yet at least.

"What made you go by the house? Was this pre-arranged?" I asked, trying to figure out if I was sitting across from a murderer or not.

"No. It wasn't like that. We normally text back and forth in the middle of the night. Neither one of us sleeps too well." She started pulling up the grass and stacking it in a small pile, reminding me of that time when I was six and my neighbor hired me to pull grass for him so he could make little bags of Colorado Weed that he sealed with a roach clip and sold to tourists. Only many years later did I finally understand why my mom was so horrified when she found out about it.

Unaware of my wandering thoughts, she continued, "But I texted him at two and he didn't answer. And then I kept texting him every half hour or so until six and he still didn't answer. So I figured I better go check on him."

"Why? For all you know he could've been with some floozy from the party."

"I know. But when I left the party he said to text him later. And there was really no one there that looked like his type."

I laughed. "Luke's type is anyone breathing between

the ages of seventeen and seventy."

"He's not like that, Maggie. It's just an act."

I tried not to choke on that one.

"So what do we do?" she asked.

"Could just stay out of it," I suggested with a hopeful smile.

I wasn't a huge fan of calling the cops when I found dead bodies. It seldom worked out well. Then again, *not* calling the cops hadn't worked out so well for me either. Really, when you find a dead body it's kind of a lose-lose situation whatever you do.

She looked at me in shock. "He's dead. We have to tell someone."

I narrowed my eyes. Did we? Did we really? I mean, someone else was bound to drop by at some point, weren't they? And not like Trish had any interesting information about the murder.

Then again…I was pretty sure this fell under the heading of things you're supposed to tell your spouse about, especially when your spouse is a cop. Matt and I had agreed that everyone has little secrets they keep and that we didn't really need full unfettered access to one another's emails and social media accounts and all that, but we'd also agreed not to keep any big secrets from each other either.

I figured the fact that Matt's brother's wife had found a dead body probably fell under the big secret category. Especially since I had also threatened to kill the victim on more than one occasion, including just a few hours before Trish found him dead.

Darn it.

I sighed. This married thing, it made life a lot more

complicated.

"Okay. Here's what we'll do. We'll tell Matt. See what he thinks about it and go from there. Just stay somewhere he can reach you."

She squeezed my arm. "Thanks, Maggie. I knew you'd know what to do."

I resisted the urge to snort at her comment. I had no clue what to do. But hopefully Matt would.

As Fancy and I trudged back home, I grumbled about how it was far too early in the morning to be dealing with murder. Far too early. Murders should only be committed or discovered after ten in the morning at the earliest. And ideally after noon. And before six. Why ruin a good evening?

But no. People had to be all inconvenient when they were murdered, didn't they?

CHAPTER 7

Matt, of course, was still in bed when I returned home. I couldn't blame him, he'd worked a late shift and was going to have to work another one that night.

I sat on the bed and looked at him for a long moment, sprawled on his belly, his mouth slightly open as he almost but not quite snored. I loved every line of him even if he wasn't as perfectly handsome this up-close as he'd been the day I met him. Reality does that, you know. Takes away all the shine. But good thing is it replaces it with something much deeper and more lasting.

I debated not waking him and just telling him about Luke when he finally did get up which would probably be in about four hours or so. That was fair, wasn't it? He wouldn't feel betrayed by that would he? I'd still be telling him about what Trish had found at the first opportunity I had. I'd just also be giving someone else a chance to discover the body first.

Unfortunately, he's a light sleeper. All that military training, I suspect. He opened one eye and looked at me. "Hey. How was your walk? Come back for a cuddle?"

He rolled over and lifted his arm up, inviting me to burrow in against his chest.

"I wish. Unfortunately..."

He yawned and flipped over onto his back, tucking one hand behind his head. "Unfortunately?"

I stared at the ceiling so I wouldn't have to see his expression as I asked, "Remember how I'm not supposed to wish people dead because they might end up dead and then it would be all awkward?"

"Yes." He was fully awake now.

"Well..."

"Lucas Dean is dead?"

I nodded.

He sat up. "And how do you know this?"

"That's the even more awkward part." I rubbed at the back of my neck as I filled him in on Trish's little visit and our conversation at the ball field.

By the time I was done he was already half-dressed and looking for his phone. "Any reason for Trish to lie about this?" he asked. "Do you think she could've done it?"

"No. And no reason to lie that I can think of. She doesn't strike me as the diabolically-clever, plant-an-alibi sort."

He sat back down on the bed. "It's going to kill Jack to find out about those text messages. And the fact that she came here looking for Luke."

"Does he have to know?" I asked, wincing as I said the words because I already knew the answer.

Matt gave me a long, long look.

I hunched my shoulders. "What? It's a fair question. He loves Sam so much and Luke's dead so not like anything is going to happen there with Trish, so why force him into making a choice maybe he doesn't want to have to make?"

"He needs to know, Maggie. Luke isn't the only one willing to pursue a woman he shouldn't."

"True. Up until a little bit ago, Jack was in that camp, too, you know."

He rubbed his fingers through his hair, ruffling it in five different directions. "Some people manage to work through these things. It doesn't have to be the end."

It was my turn to give him a long, long look. "It would be for me. Just sayin'."

"Oh me, too. Just so *you* know."

"Alright then. As long as we're agreed on that." I smiled at him.

He smiled back. "We are."

We sat there for another long, awkward moment until he finally stood. "Well, better go see what I can see."

I followed him to the kitchen. "You know, Luke did leave a lot of firework debris in the yard. Maybe you could knock on his door to tell him to pick it up?"

"And then go inside when he doesn't answer even though I'd normally just assume he was too hungover and swing back by later?"

I shrugged. "Could be something is visible from one of the windows."

He shook his head. "Or I could just tell dispatch I was tipped to the fact that there was a dead body in his house and do it the right way." He tweaked my nose. "You're a bad influence on me, Maggie."

"Clearly not bad enough." I nodded towards the phone in his hand. "I was just trying to keep Trish out of it."

"I know. But if she was sending him text messages all night, there's no way to keep her out. She'll be interviewed no matter what. Might as well be sooner rather than later."

"Good point."

I went to feed Fancy her breakfast while Matt called it in.

CHAPTER 8

By ten that morning there were three cop cars pulled up outside Lucas Dean's house. My grandpa came to join me in my yard as I stood and watched Matt talk to Sue, the coroner, while two other officers brought a body bag out.

"What happened?" my grandpa asked.

"What do you think?"

"Really? Someone killed Luke?"

I nodded. "Certainly no lack of suspects is there? I mean pretty much every father of a teenaged daughter and every husband in the county has to be at least considered for a moment."

"And every neighbor who threatened to kill him for setting off fireworks, especially after last night's display." He gave me a pointed look.

I glanced sideways at him. "That's not funny, Grandpa."

"No. But it's true. I told you it wasn't a good idea to walk around threatening to kill the man."

"Yeah, yeah. You and Matt."

"Who found him?" he asked.

I scrunched up my face, trying to decide what to say. It was going to get out anyway, wasn't it? Can't keep a secret like that in a small town. Still. It felt a little gossipy to be the one passing it on.

"Trish. She told me. I told Matt. He called it in."

My grandpa raised an eyebrow but didn't say any more about it.

"Don't tell anyone, though," I added. "I mean, it'll probably get out, but, you know."

"Alright. As long as you promise not to get involved in investigating the murder."

I laughed. "Please. Like I would. Whoever killed Lucas Dean did the world a favor."

"Maggie May." He used that tone of voice that said I'd done something wrong like forget to clean up the bathroom or wash the dishes.

"What? I am a firm believer that there are certain people who make the world a worse place than it needs to be. And that if those people were not around that the world would be, on balance, a nicer, kinder place to live. Lucas Dean was one of those people."

He shook his head in disappointment. "If you went around killing every philandering loud-mouth who liked fireworks you'd be taking out a large part of the population. Maybe save your divine wrath for actively evil people like Ted Little."

I shuddered at the name. "That man, too. Ugh. Thanks for the reminder, Grandpa."

He turned to look at me, searching my face. "But you can see the difference between the two, can't you, Maggie May?"

I looked back at him, holding his gaze. "Look,

Grandpa, here's the deal. While I fully believe that there are people who make the world a worse place by being in it I'd never actually advocate for taking those people out. Even Ted Little. Because I'd have no control over who got to wield that sort of power. And, as you point out, my list of people who make the world worse could be very different from someone else's. That's how we get frickin' holy wars, right? You don't believe in the right divine power, so you must die? I get it. I do. But there's a little fantasy world in my head where I get to point to bad drivers and mean people and, poof, vanish them to some other alternate reality where they no longer make my life unpleasant. And in that little fantasy world, Lucas Dean would make my list of people who go poof."

I crossed my arms and turned back to see them closing the door to the coroner's van. I added, "He laughed when Fancy freaked out over the fireworks, Grandpa. Laughed. Not a single sign of remorse. And don't even get me started on how he treated Jamie all those years. Or Katie. Or any number of other women."

"Hm." My grandpa grunted as he stared forward, arms crossed.

"What?" I demanded, exhausted and annoyed.

"Nothing. Just keep in mind that people who think the way you do about setting certain people aside and aren't so hesitant to use their powers are how otherwise decent people end up spending years of their life in jail. Unless you think a man deserves to be in jail for life because he stole one little thing? Or sold a little pot?" He looked at me sideways, one eyebrow raised.

I sighed and rolled my eyes. "Alright, Jean Valjean, you've made your point. I'll now go sing Kumbaya and love and accept everyone, no matter how horrible they make my life."

"Maggie May," he snapped.

"Sorry," I snapped right back.

I was kind of sorry. I mean, he had a point. But…

I know. He had a point.

I mean, he was living proof that bad decisions when you're younger don't have to define who you become. And if he hadn't eventually been given a second chance think of all the kids he'd coached whose lives would've been less because of his absence. Kids like Matt.

And what about me. Until Matt, after I lost my parents my grandparents were all I had in this world. My grandpa was my anchor. If no one had given him that second chance—or third chance as it turns out—where would I be?

So, yeah, fine. Forgiveness. Blah, blah, blah. It's wonderful, it's great. We should all do it.

But I still wasn't going to shed a single tear for Lucas Dean. Or be sad about the fact that he was gone.

Jamie was, though, which is why I excused myself and drove on over there before the gossip mill could reach her. She was blissfully happy with Mason and so much better off with him than she'd ever been with Luke, but fact was that Luke had been "that guy" for most of her teen years and well into her twenties and thirties and you don't just forget that because you find something better.

CHAPTER 9

That night I fixed myself a big, old celebratory dinner of petite filet mignon wrapped in bacon, baked potato, and grilled asparagus. It was heavenly. And Matt wasn't there to make me feel bad about it. I luxuriated in a peaceful evening devoid of fireworks next door and filled with the delicious taste of high-quality red meat. I even had a glass of red wine to go with it.

(I know. I'm horrible. But we long ago established that fact.)

Luke being gone was like removing that little pebble that's been stuck in the toe of your boot all day rubbing your foot raw. It was such a relief. I just knew things were going to get better.

Except they didn't.

Because the unimaginative police could only see two suspects: Trish, because she'd found the body in the middle of the night, which, fair enough. And me. Seriously, just because I'd walked around telling people I wanted him dead did not mean I killed him. Didn't they realize I was smarter than that?

(If I was actually going to kill someone I certainly

wouldn't tell everyone about it right before I did it. Come on now.)

And really, the people I had told about that should've kept their mouths shut. But one of the things I loved about Matt was that he was the guy who wouldn't shy away from doing the right thing even when it was a challenge. So the next afternoon I found myself once again in the Creek jail interview room sitting across from Officer Clark and my husband.

That room was not designed to make a person want a return visit. It was poorly lit, cramped, and smelled slightly of disinfectant and stale body odor. There might've also been the scent of various bodily fluids, but I stared straight ahead and tried really hard not to think about it.

"Maggie," Matt said, "where's your lawyer?"

"Do I need one? I mean, really? We both know I did not do this."

He crossed his arms and stared me down, his eyes begging me to take this seriously. Surprisingly enough, Officer Clark didn't step in and try to get me talking but instead waited for Matt and me to finish our silent conversation.

Finally, I rolled my eyes. "Fine. Give me a minute." I pulled my phone out of my purse and dialed Mason Maxwell's number.

"Ms. Carver. How can I help you?"

I glared at Matt because I couldn't glare through the phone at Mason. "You're married to my best friend, Mason, you can call me Maggie."

"Then this is a personal call?" he asked.

"No," I growled, thinking it was a very good thing he

wasn't there in the room with me the way he was being so obnoxious.

"Let me guess. The police want to talk to you about Lucas Dean's murder and you want me present while they question you."

"Pretty much."

"When?"

"We're sitting in the interrogation room right now if you wouldn't mind dropping by."

I could hear him sigh through the phone and pictured him pinching the bridge of his nose, reminding himself how much he loved his wife. "Tell me you have a better alibi for this murder than you did for the last one."

"I can promise you no one saw me running away from the crime scene this time around. Beyond that…Well, maybe not so much." (Matt had been at work when Luke was killed after all.)

"Is that because you weren't there? Or because you *walked* away?" he asked, all snide and annoying.

"Mason Maxwell," I snapped, fed up with his stupid questions. I was not in the mood to be poked at by an uptight jerk whose only redeeming quality was that he'd somehow convinced my best friend to marry him and bear his spawn.

(Yes, I know. I was being unfair. He's actually a decent enough guy once you get to know him, but did he have to be so *lawyerly*?)

"It is a fair question, Ms. Carver," he replied, completely calm.

I took a deep breath before answering. "I wasn't there. Now, can you please get down here so we can clear this matter up? I had to leave Fancy with my grandpa and she's going to have a sick tummy by the time I get out of here because he feeds her a treat every time she bats her eyes at him."

There was a slight pause. "You realize I do have other clients."

"I do. But I also know that you probably have orders from Jamie to drop everything and come help me out as soon as I call. Am I right?"

He sighed. "You are. I'll be there in ten minutes."

I hung up and smiled at Matt and Officer Clark. "My attorney will be here in ten. Any chance I can run home and grab a Coke while we're waiting?"

"No," Officer Clark answered. "You're a suspect here for questioning in a murder. You can't just leave."

Before I could open my mouth to respond, Matt put a hand on his shoulder. "It's alright. I'll escort her home, Ben. She won't be out of my sight for a moment."

As Matt and I stepped outside into the almost too-hot late afternoon heat, I shook my head. "That man needs therapy, Matt."

"Who?"

"Officer Clark. Honestly, what is wrong with him? He wasn't going to let me go home to grab a Coke? Some people take their jobs way too seriously."

"That's because there are protocols, Maggie. And those protocols do not involve letting a suspect leave the premises to obtain a personal beverage and bring it back into the interview room."

"Not like I'm grabbing myself a beer."

"Maggie." He grabbed my upper arms and leaned down so we were eye-to-eye. "You need to take this seriously. You are a suspect in a murder of a man you were known not to like. You have no alibi for the time of the murder. I know you think it's something you can just laugh off because you obviously didn't do it, but the more you do that the more seriously we have to treat it. Don't make me arrest my own wife. Especially if it's just because she wants to be difficult."

I ran my tongue along the bottom of my top teeth as I stared back at him. Finally, I sighed. "Fine. I will be the model interview witness so we can get this behind us."

"Thank you," Matt said in that tone of voice that implied he should've never had to ask me to behave in the first place.

CHAPTER 10

We walked the rest of the way home and back in silence, but I was a model witness for the entire hour and thirty minutes of questioning.

How they came up with that many questions when I hadn't done anything, I don't know. But they walked me through my entire history with Lucas Dean from diapers to death. Every little interaction we'd ever had was covered with a nitpicking level of detail that had me wanting to scream and crack sarcastic jokes.

But I'd promised Matt, so I was succinct and sincere and articulate and straight-forward and everything a good little witness should be.

It's fascinating really, how much of police interrogation can be driven by the perceptions of the people in the room. Did they trust me? Did I trust them? Did they really think I'd done it or were they just checking boxes? Did I have something to hide or did I feel I could be completely honest with them?

All of that goes into an interview. Into the way the questions are asked, the answers are given (or not given), and the direction the conversation takes.

Fortunately for me I trusted Matt and so did Officer Clark, so it was more formality than genuine attempt to break a suspect.

As Matt walked me towards the exit past the four desks, two facing each other on each side of the room, I saw that Jack and Trish were sitting in two of the three small plastic chairs against the front wall in the "waiting area" past the reception desk. They sat like strangers, not looking at each other, arms crossed, bodies tensed.

Matt glanced towards his brother, but turned his attention on Trish. "Come on, Trish, it's your turn."

She too glanced towards Jack as she stood and followed Matt, but Jack never once took his attention from the spot on the floor in front of his feet that he was glaring at. I waved Mason off with a quick thank-you and sprawled in the seat next to Jack.

"Well, that was fun. I'd rank it right up there next to a root canal except I've never had one." I nudged him in the ribs. "Hey, at least it's not you in there this time."

He turned towards me at last, but the usual mischievous spark that I always associated with him was missing. He was just some good-looking dark-haired guy who'd found out his wife was cheating on him. (Maybe not physically, but she certainly hadn't been honoring their relationship.)

I bit my lower lip. "Look, Jack, it's not my place, yeah? I know that. But there's this thing that happens when you're usually the person on the outside of relationships looking in like I was for most of my life. You start to see certain patterns. Certain paths relationships go down on a regular basis. And for you guys…"

He continued to stare at me, neither encouraging nor

denying me.

"Well, there's this Jim Croce song. And it's not a popular one but it was on his 40th anniversary collection or whatever. And it talks about this guy who's working non-stop to build this woman he loves a castle or something. I don't know. I'm not good at describing this. But the song is about how he's off trying to give her everything in the world he thinks she deserves and all she actually wants is him to be there with her. She's lonely and feels trapped all alone at home. So I don't know. Maybe think about it. I know you want to have the money to expand the trailer so you guys can have everything you want in life, but maybe all she really wants is you."

He sat back in his chair. "Or maybe I'm just not the man who can give her everything she wants. Not without a lottery win." He scuffed his foot on the ground.

We both spared a silent moment for the story that had been on the news a couple nights before about someone in the county buying a winning lottery ticket worth over a million bucks. Whoever it was, they hadn't come forward yet. Must be nice to have that kind of windfall.

But that's not life. I long ago learned that if I was going to get anything in life it was going to be through hard work and hard choices.

So I elbowed him in the ribs. Hard.

"Ow," he grunted. "What'd you do that for?

"So you'd quit being a self-pitying idiot. You are great with Sam and a helluva lot better catch than Trish deserves. All I'm saying is maybe dial back the working all hours of the day for a bit. Don't give the Lucas Deans of the world a chance to snake their way in there."

"Do you think she did it?" he asked.

"No. Do you?"

He shook his head. "Did you ever see them together while she was living with you?"

"Not in the way you're thinking. They'd stand six feet apart at the fence edge and talk a lot, but I never saw them cross that line. I know that can still feel like a betrayal, but…People come through these things. Sometimes stronger than ever."

He leaned his head back against the wall. "I don't know who I am these days, Maggie. I used to know. I was the fast-talking con man who could get anything he wanted if you gave him enough room to operate. But now…Now I'm just some guy who works construction and comes home to sit on the couch and watch TV and drink a beer. I have a wife and kid now. I never…I don't know."

I didn't know what to tell him. The "your old life would land you in jail eventually" argument didn't seem all that convincing in the moment.

"Maybe you need to find a sales job," I suggested.

"A sales job?" He gave me a skeptical look.

"Yeah. Cars, real estate, tractors."

"Tractors?"

"I was just trying to think of big ticket items you could sell here in the valley. Once things open back up that is. I mean, you could take all that fast-talking charm that used to get you into so much trouble and apply it to making sales instead. Ethically, please. No selling lemons to some poor old lady looking for a reliable car to drive around in during the winter. But…Something that lets you shine for who you are. Construction isn't going to do that. Put those amazing people skills you have to use somehow."

"I'm an ex-con, Maggie."

"So? I've known ex-cons who were car salesmen. And brokers. You could sell investments to people. Ethically."

He grinned and I saw a little spark of the old Jack. "Ethically."

"Yes, please. I like having you around."

He leaned his head back against the wall. "I'll think about it."

"Alright. Good." I nudged him in the shoulder. "I'll see you later. Hope you're not here too long, but they're being annoyingly thorough in there."

As I made my way back home I wondered who had killed Lucas Dean. And why. I had no interest in actually investigating the murder, I was glad he was gone. But I was curious.

CHAPTER 11

After that things settled down for a few days. The cops were convinced enough that it wasn't me or Trish who'd killed Luke, but they didn't really have a good lead on who else it might've been. Turns out Luke hadn't really been seeing anyone. Or if he had there was no sign of it on his phone or email.

Basically it was all at a dead end and well on its way to being a cold case.

Until they found the second body. And then suddenly we had a real killer in our midst.

I found out about it when Matt came home that day from work. He barely gave me a kiss before walking around the house, checking all the windows to make sure they were locked.

(Of course they were. I'm a paranoid freak, so not only were they locked, they were closed with heavy curtains keeping anyone from looking inside. I'm not sure I've ever had a stalker, but if I have they didn't get to see much. My mom was always big on wide-open windows that you could see out of. Made me shudder. Because any window you can see out of, someone else can see in. If it weren't for Fancy I'd also lock the front and back door at all times.)

"What are you doing?" I asked as he finally reached the living room where I was curled up with a good book I'd been about to finish before he got home. (So close. Loved him. But. Having another person I had to give my time was seriously crimping my reading style.)

"Just making sure the house is secure," he said.

"Because the hundred-and-forty-pound black dog isn't going to deter someone?"

He glanced at Fancy who was sprawled on her back, one leg sticking up in the air, snoring. She hadn't even budged when he came home. "Not someone who's determined enough."

"Well by that standard what good is a locked window going to do? One big rock and it's all over anyway. Look, if someone wants to kill me they're going to kill me. I long ago accepted that the only reason I'm alive is because there is no one out there who really wants me dead bad enough to make it happen."

"Maggie!"

I shrugged. "What? It's true. Think about it."

"I'd rather not."

"Okay. Don't. Doesn't change the fact that it's true." I put my book aside and stood up. "Now. Why did you just go around the entire house and check that all the windows are locked?"

He crossed his arms and scanned the room one more time. "There was another murder last night."

"Same killer?" I asked.

He nodded.

"How do you know?"

"Well, same method at least. One single thrust of a knife to the right kidney."

I glanced at my bookshelf where I could see the copy of *On Killing* I'd recently finished reading. "Huh. Well, that is one of the quickest and quietest ways to kill someone. But you wouldn't expect the average person to know that."

He frowned at me. "How do *you* know that?"

I shrugged. "I read it in a book about killing people. It stuck with me."

"You read a book about killing people?" The look he gave me said he didn't believe me, but he should have known me better than that.

"Mmhm," I answered happily.

"Maggie…"

"Hey, you chose to marry me, buddy. Which means that you get the whole package, as crazy as it may be. But for what it's worth—because you are a cop after all— I'm not quite sure where the kidney is actually located, so even though I theoretically know that it can be done I wouldn't be able to actually do it, so I'm still not your killer."

"Good to know." He sank down on the couch with another sidelong look my way.

"So who was it? Who was killed?" I asked, thinking of the guy I'd seen at Luke's house before the party.

"That's the weirdest part. It was Agnes Rockmorton."

"But she's like eighty. What does an eighty-year-old woman who goes to church three times a week have in common with a philandering schmuck half her age?"

"Good question." He gave me one of his interrogator looks. "And one that the *police* will find the answer to."

I gave him back my best smile and patted him on the arm. "I'm sure you will, dear. I have every faith in you."

But my mind was already turning.

What did Agnes Rockmorton have in common with Lucas Dean other than living in Creek? And what kind of person would know how to knife someone in the kidneys? There couldn't be all that many people who fit that description could there?

Hmm. I knew Matt had said to leave it to the police, but it wouldn't hurt to poke around a little bit, would it?

CHAPTER 12

Fortunately for me, the perfect opportunity to find out more presented itself the very next day when Lesley called and asked if I'd be willing to help the Ladies' Auxiliary with the annual library fundraiser. She was hosting a lunch meeting at her house and asked if I'd like to come. Everyone was going to bring a salad and we were going to figure out what needed to happen and who would do what since it was right around the corner and not much had been done yet.

I, of course, said yes even though Fancy gave me the absolute saddest look when I blocked her inside. (If I'd been home all she would've done is sleep against the wall in the entryway, but because I was leaving, suddenly I was depriving her of the great outdoors. And I just knew when I came home she'd immediately run outside and stay there until suppertime, asserting her right to be outside no matter how miserably hot it was.)

Ah well, too bad. I didn't trust her and that picket fence. She's not much for jumping, but no point in taking any chances.

So I blocked her in and headed to Lesley's with a

bowl of potato salad as an offering. I'd made it using my grandma's recipe which meant it was a full-fat version of delicious, creamy, tanginess.

By the time I pulled up outside Lesley's two-story home on the edge of town, her driveway and half the street was full of cars. As I walked up the front steps I could see why she wouldn't want to move. My grandpa's house was nice, but hers had gorgeous rose bushes that had probably taken over a decade to cultivate and a unique little rock garden off to the side with delightful gnomes tucked among the flowers.

It was clear to any observer that whoever lived there loved their home very much.

I didn't even have a chance to knock before Jolene Paige opened the door and gestured me inside. She was an incredibly slender older woman who always made me think about a passage I'd once read in a book about a woman who'd chosen, when she reached a certain age, to gain a few pounds to round out her face.

Jolene Paige had clearly never read that book. She was a bit cadaverous.

"What's that you brought? Is it potato salad? Is that *bacon* you put in there?" She looked at me wide-eyed.

"Yes."

"Oh my. Ladies," she turned to the rest of the room, "Maggie has brought the most sinful potato salad. It has bacon in it."

"Bacon?" Patrice Cole asked. She was equally slender and reminded me of some sort of little bird the way she was slightly stooped and always picked at everything she ate. "Oh dear. Well, you may have some leftovers there, Maggie."

"Because of bacon? Are you all vegetarians?"

The two women tittered at each other as I took the bowl of potato salad over to Lesley. "Did I do something wrong?" I whispered as I placed it on the table with all the other food.

"No." Lesley smiled. "Ignore them. Help yourself. We're about to get started."

There was such a wide variety of salads to choose from it was kind of amazing. Some were your standard green-lettuce salads with carrots and tomatoes, but there was also a dessert-style salad that probably had some name like pistachio ambrosia.

Not wanting to be rude—even though I'm really not a salad person and would probably have a snack when I got home—I loaded my plate up with a little bit of each one.

By the time I gingerly piled one of Lesley's chocolate brownies on top, I was wondering if the plate was going to hold up or not. Paper plates are not always the most sturdy and Lesley didn't have those plastic frames you can get to put them in that make them hold up better, but I managed by putting both hands under the plate as I wove my way to an open chair with an empty TV tray next to it.

Only when I had seated myself did I realize I was sitting next to Jolene Paige.

She leaned over and whispered to me, "You know, as you get older it gets harder to keep those pounds off, but I've managed to do so all these years with one very simple little trick."

"Really?" I took a defensive bite of brownie. "And what's that?"

"I never have a meal that's larger than the size of my fist." She proudly displayed her fist for me with a confident nod.

I tried to hide my horror. "Your fist?"

"That's right. My fist."

I looked at my own fist which was about a fifth the size of the plate I'd just sat down with. "So do you have a lot of meals throughout the day then? I've heard that's better for maintaining steady glucose levels."

"Oh no. I only have three meals. And no dessert. Ever." She glared at my brownie.

I took another bite and swallowed. "So all you eat every single day of your life is three fistfuls of food?"

"Yes. And look." She ran her hand down her side where there wasn't a sign of a curve in sight.

"Huh. How interesting. If you'll excuse me? I forgot to grab a Coke."

I left my plate and fled for the kitchen before my face could betray my absolute horror at the thought of living such a deprived life. I didn't care if that fistful of food included lobster mac 'n' cheese and tenderloin steak bites, there was no way on this earth that I would ever be happy eating just three fistfuls of food a day.

I stared at my fist again as I stepped into the kitchen.

"I see Jolene shared her diet tip with you." Lesley handed me an ice-cold can of Coke.

"She did." I shuddered. "I'm glad you don't feel that way about food. It's…disturbing. And now I have to go sit down next to her while I eat that whole plate of food. She's not going to like that very much. But good thing is, I don't care. I like food too much to listen to someone crazy like that."

Lesley patted me on the shoulder. "She means well. But I've had to sit down every one of her granddaughters over the years and explain that's not a healthy way to approach food."

"Glad someone's making the effort. Those poor kids."

I made my way back to the living room and sat down next to Jolene who stared at the Coke in my hand like it was a deadly viper.

"You don't drink diet?" she asked, scandalized.

"No. No, I do not." I took a nice, long sip and settled in for the meeting.

CHAPTER 13

One incredibly painful hour later, the business portion of the meeting was over and I'd polished off every bite on my plate even though a few of those salads had been potentially inedible. And, I am happy to report, there wasn't a drop of my potato salad left. Or any brownies, for that matter, although that could've been because I'd had three myself.

As the ladies sipped coffee and relaxed into casual gossip, I asked Jolene, "Did you know Agnes Rockmorton? Wasn't she a member of the Auxiliary before she passed?"

"Oh, I've known Agnes since we were in school together. I actually dated her late husband Theodore for two years before he went to the war. But by the time he came back I'd met my Charlie and so Theodore and Agnes fell in love. Our kids weren't quite the same age, but mine would babysit hers when they were growing up."

"I can't believe someone killed her."

Jolene gave me a look of surprise and then took a long sip of her coffee. "Oh, yes, right. Neither can I. Can you Patrice?" she asked Patrice who was seated on her other side.

Patrice leaned closer. "Mm. No. Can't imagine. She was always so nice and friendly."

I glanced back and forth between them. Something was off. "But?" I asked.

Patrice scooted her chair closer and made a point of looking around to see if anyone was listening in on us. "Well, my mom told me something very important once. She told me that there's a difference between being nice and being kind."

I let that one stew around in my brain for a minute, but didn't quite get the point. "And Agnes was…"

"She was nice. But she was not kind."

When I still looked confused, she leaned closer and continued, "For example. I never in fifty years had an unpleasant conversation with Agnes. Not once. She was always very friendly. Very cheerful. Never said a mean word about anyone. Always *nice*."

"But not kind?" I asked, still confused.

"No. Not kind. Two years ago my husband, Paul, fell and broke his hip. It made getting around very difficult. We have a side entrance to our house that doesn't have any stairs, and it was much easier for my husband to use than the front porch, which has two. But to access the side entrance required being able to drive across a portion of Agnes's driveway where she normally parked her RV. I went to her house, I explained what had happened, and I told her we'd like to be able to park Paul's van at the side of our house for a few months while he recovered. I even told her she could park her RV at the end of our property if she'd like. An RV I will add, that she had not even used since her husband died."

I nodded, still not seeing the problem.

"She informed me that she really didn't want to park her RV that far away from her house. So I asked her if she could perhaps move it farther up her driveway so that we could squeeze by. She responded that where the RV was parked was the best place for it because it was well-shaded. So I offered to buy her an RV cover. She said she'd think about it. All very nice and pleasant. Not a harsh word from her. But at the end of the day did she move that RV? No. No, she did not. See? Nice, but not kind."

I glanced at Jolene. "She was the same with you?"

"Oh yes. I still remember when we were raising money for the McKenzie's after their house burned down. She was perfectly sympathetic to Mrs. McKenzie and told her how horrible it must've been and how she hoped everything would be okay, but when I asked her to contribute a small amount to the funds we were raising to help them, she refused. Said she already had her charities she supported and couldn't possibly spare another penny."

Patrice barked a laugh. "Is that the same year she bought that absurd fur coat?"

"The exact same."

The two ladies gave each other satisfied smirks.

"Wow," I said. "So she was nice, but not kind. Friendly to someone's face, but never actually cared about anyone. That's probably the type of person who has a few enemies. But would anyone be upset enough with her to kill her?"

Jolene shrugged one shoulder and took another sip from her cup. Only then did I realize she wasn't drinking coffee, she was drinking hot water with a lemon slice in it. I wondered then if maybe she and Patrice weren't the best possible judges of, well, sanity, but hey, they were talking to me about Agnes so I was going to take what I could get.

I leaned closer and glanced around to make them think I was about to share my own big secret. "You know, my husband is working on the investigation of her murder."

"Is he?" Jolene asked as they both leaned closer.

"And he says her murder has something to do with the murder of Lucas Dean." I gave them a significant look.

"Really?" Patrice tilted her head to the side, thinking. "Well, he was doing some work for her last month."

"Was he?" I asked.

"Oh yes." She nodded. "It was quite unusual. Because he didn't have any of his normal work crew with him. It was just him. Well, him and Johnny Duffy. I saw them both there once. But Luke was there by himself every day for at least a week."

"Inside or outside?" I asked.

"Inside. But I notice things. Partially because she moved that RV for him so he could park alongside our house and not be seen from the street. So when I saw that there was a truck parked where she wouldn't let my husband park, I made a point of keeping an eye out to see who it was. And it was Lucas Dean, but not in his normal truck."

"Huh. That's very interesting."

"Isn't it, though?" she nodded.

We all exchanged conspiratorial looks. "I'll definitely have to tell my husband about this," I said.

They both nodded in agreement and the conversation shifted towards Matt's and my wedding and married life, but the whole time I was wondering what secret project Luke could've been working on that had gotten both him and Agnes killed.

Buried treasure? Hidden body? The possibilities were endless.

CHAPTER 14

That night Matt was actually home for dinner for the first time in ages. I'd never really thought before about the challenges of being married to a cop, but it made sense that he'd be at work more during the hours when people generally get into the most trouble.

It was mid-summer and hot enough outside that I didn't want a heavy meal, but I'd had enough of salad to last a lifetime, so I made BLTs with a pesto mayo and added carrots and potato chips on the side. (I was getting fancy with that mayo, but, hey, Matt was home. And I wanted to do something nice for him.)

I tried giving Fancy one of the carrots on her sharing plate and she immediately spit it out. She'd started doing that lately. It seemed she only liked cooked carrots anymore not raw ones. But she was all about the bread and bacon and sat at my feet slowly slobbering a puddle as she waited for me to give her a bite or two.

After we'd settled into our meal and exchanged the normal "how was your day" questions, Matt cleared his throat and looked at me, his expression serious. I thought he was going to lecture me for going to the Ladies'

Auxiliary meeting and asking about Agnes Rockmorton, but what he said instead took me completely by surprise.

"Maggie, I was wondering when you were going to legally change your name. We've been married a few months now and, well…It's time."

I blinked in surprise. "But I'm not going to change my name. Ever."

"We're married now."

"I understand that. But it's a new century and women don't always change their names when they get married." I tensed, realizing this might be our first fight where there was no mutually satisfying solution.

"Is it because you think we won't last?" he asked, softly.

"Oh please. I mean, if there weren't other reasons, that would be a good one. Because I have seen far too many friends think something was going to last and then find that it didn't and have to go through the rigmarole of changing things back or finding a new last name, and that is not fun. And if I were still in the working world I'd most definitely not change it professionally because no one's business what I'm doing in my personal life—especially if I were getting divorced. But that's not why."

"What is it then?"

I shook my head. "See, this is the problem with getting married before you really know someone well. Although, I guess there would be no way for you to really know this because it would've never come up."

"Maggie?" he said, his look telling me to get on with it already.

I sighed. "You know my grandpa is my step-grandpa."
"Yes. And?"
"He didn't actually marry my grandma until after my

dad was grown up."

"What does that have to do with you changing your name?"

"Well…Did it never occur to you that Carver isn't the last name I was born with? Because Lou Carver wasn't my dad's real dad?"

He stared at me in complete surprise. Guess it hadn't. "So how did you end up with the last name of Carver?"

"After my parents died, the only family I had left were my grandma and my grandpa." I looked at the ceiling trying not to cry. "I missed having that family connection. I missed my parents and I wanted some clear way to show the connection I still had to my grandparents. So…I asked my grandpa if I could take on his last name."

Matt frowned at me, still confused. "But what about your original last name? Your dad's last name?"

"My dad's last name was meaningless anyway. I mean, sure, I'd grown up with it, but he'd been adopted when he was little so it wasn't some family name that stretched back generations or anything. It was just the last name of some random dude that my grandma married for a year or so."

"Oh. I didn't know that."

"And you weren't meant to. You were just meant to think that Lou Carver is my grandpa. Because he is." I smiled, remembering. "I can't tell you how proud my grandpa was when I asked to take on his last name. He almost cried and you know Lou Carver doesn't cry much. And I know you and I are married now and that my taking your last name matters to you, but there's just no way I'm changing it. Not a chance in hell while my grandpa is still alive. And probably not after that either, to be honest."

I watched the emotions flit across Matt's face. There was disappointment at first, sure, and some sadness, but then he nodded. "I understand. And I respect that."

So many reasons I loved that man.

"You could change your last name to Carver…" I suggested. "There was a guy I knew in college whose last name was Smith who changed it to some really long, complex German name when he got married because he and his wife both shared an ancestor with that name, so it's not unheard of for a man to change his name."

He laughed. "No. I'm good with Barnes. And Barnes *is* a long-standing family name with hundreds of years of history behind it."

I clasped my hands together, pleased to have that over with. "Okay, then. Let's talk murder. Guess what I found out today?"

"Maggie…" Matt gave me that look that said he wasn't pleased, I assumed with what I wanted to talk about not my changing the subject.

"What?" I looked back at him as innocently as I could. (Which wasn't much.) "I heard some gossip that might help your investigation. Do you not want to know? Do you not want to catch the killer in our midst?"

He leaned back and took a long sip of his beer. "Go ahead. Tell me what you found."

I did. And then I asked, "Who is Johnny Duffy?"

He winced. "A low-life friend of Luke's. I don't know why he would've been at Agnes's house if Luke was doing any sort of construction work. He's not that kind of guy."

"Maybe Luke found something during his work and

he called Duffy over to check it out. Like hidden gold or something."

"And then Duffy killed them both so he could have the gold himself?" Matt asked, his voice full of skepticism.

I shrugged. "It's possible. There was gold mining in Colorado at one point."

"I'm pretty sure people didn't go around hiding gold in their walls, even back then."

"Hey. Don't mock a viable theory. Maybe it wasn't gold. Maybe it was bearer bonds. Or cash. Or a dead body. I don't know. But you have to admit, knowing that Luke was doing work at Agnes's house before they were both killed helps."

He took another swig of his beer. "It does. I won't deny it. But…"

"Stay out of it." I rolled my eyes.

He nodded. "Exactly.

I changed the subject, but that didn't mean my mind stopped working through the possibilities. You can't set me a puzzle and then expect that I won't try to solve it. That's not how my mind works. I'll keep worrying at it like a dog with a bone until I figure it out. Or until someone gives me the answer.

So all Matt had to do was find the killer first and I'd stop trying to solve the murder. But until then…I was going to keep thinking about who the murderer could be and why they'd killed two very different people.

I decided, though, that for the sake of marital harmony Matt didn't need to know I was still *thinking* about it. As long as I didn't *do* anything, that should be acceptable. Right? Right.

CHAPTER 15

Of course, life likes to mock my decisions, so the very next day when I went to the grocery store I saw that jerk who'd been setting off fireworks at Luke's house the week he was killed.

"Whatchoo looking at?" he grunted at me as I studied him from the checkout line.

I pointed at him. "You were at Lucas Dean's house, helping him set up for his party on the third."

"I was. And?"

"We were never properly introduced." I held out my hand. "Maggie May Carver."

He looked at it like I was holding out a deadly snake. "People aren't supposed to be shaking hands anymore. It's not safe."

I raised an eyebrow, surprised to have this Neanderthal of a man telling me about public health and safety. "Fair enough. But you are?"

"Johnny."

"Johnny Duffy?" I asked, suddenly excited.

"Yeah." He narrowed his eyes at me. "What's it to you?"

I pulled my cart out of line and stepped closer to him, but not too close. (Public safety and all.)

"Is it true you were helping Luke out with whatever he was working on over at Agnes Rockmorton's house?" I asked, studying him carefully.

He stepped back as if I'd shot him and glanced around. "I had nothing to do with that."

"With what?" I asked.

"You know."

"No. I'm afraid I don't. I just heard that Luke was doing some work over there and that you were with him one day. What was he working on?" I tilted my head to the side, waiting eagerly for his reply.

Johnny licked his lips nervously and looked around. "Nothing."

"Nothing? He was there every day for an entire week. And you say it's nothing. What did you do over there?" I stepped closer.

He stepped back. "I just helped him move a few things he couldn't move on his own."

"But I heard you weren't the construction type. And, pardon my saying it, it seems to me Luke had a bunch of guys working for him more capable of moving something heavy around than you."

He glared at me, but didn't deny the fact. "Luke and I go way back. He trusted me."

I smiled, triumphant. "So he was moving things around he didn't want people to know about?"

Johnny shook his head slightly and stepped away from me. "I gotta go. I'm gonna be late."

He turned and walked right for the exit, leaving his grocery cart behind, Hungry Man frozen dinners and all. I was tempted to run after him, but instead I got back in line and checked out. But the whole time I was wondering what Luke and Agnes had been up to that had spooked Johnny Duffy so bad he couldn't even talk to me about it.

CHAPTER 16

When I returned home I tried to forget about Johnny Duffy and the murders. I had faith in Matt and his team. They'd figure out what was going on eventually. But, well, you know me. I was home and bored and there was a murderer on the loose. If they'd kill an old lady, who knows who else they'd kill. And I had people I cared about.

(I know. Most murderers don't just run around killing people willy-nilly, so the odds that someone I loved was actually in danger were pretty slim. But they weren't zero. Which gave me enough of an excuse to justify poking around a bit more.)

I figured there was no harm in taking Fancy for her walk the next morning in the direction of Agnes Rockmorton's house instead of towards the ballpark. Variety is good, right? Give her something new to look at. Some new scents to explore.

And give me a good excuse to maybe poke around a bit. That early I didn't expect anyone else to be up and about.

But I'd underestimated the early-bird nature of Patrice Cole, her next door neighbor. Patrice was out in her garden pulling weeds as Fancy and I walked up. The two houses sat side-by-side on twin lots backed up against the side of the mountain, a dirt alleyway running between them and no fences in sight. Agnes's house was painted a brick red, Patrice's a disturbing shade of light green, but otherwise they looked identical—smaller homes on medium-sized plots of land with green lawns and a border of flowers that ran along the street side.

"Morning, Patrice," I called, stopping far enough away Fancy couldn't step on her begonias. (Or whatever they were. I'm not a flower expert. I know a rose and a tulip and a daisy and then after that it's all just one giant blur of "that red flower" or "that purple flower.")

"Morning, Maggie. How are you today?" She was positively radiant, grinning from ear to ear.

"Good." I glanced towards Agnes's house. "I see the RV is gone."

"Well…" She nodded towards the far end of the street where I could see an RV parked. "Paul and I figured Agnes wasn't going to mind if we repositioned it a bit. He can manage the front steps fine these days but that hip still gives him a bit of trouble now and then so it's best to be able to come in through the back."

"You towed it?" I tried to keep the surprised judgement out of my voice, but probably failed.

"Hardly. I knew where she kept the keys, so Paul just borrowed them for a moment." She pulled out another weed with a vindictive little smile on her face and more force than was necessary.

I tilted my head to the side, trying to make sure I was understanding her. "So to be clear. Your husband walked into your dead neighbor's house and borrowed her keys so he could move her RV to a more suitable location?"

"Yes." She nodded sharply, smiling.

"Wasn't the house locked?"

She waved that question away. "Oh, we've had a spare key for a number of years now. Just in case, you know. We were all very close. We'd water their plants when Ted and Agnes traveled. And they'd water ours. Better than relying on our unreliable offspring."

I've always found it mildly disturbing the thought of having someone else in my home when I'm not there. It's why I'd never pay for a house cleaner because the thought of someone else touching my things when I'm not around is more upsetting to me than having a quarter-inch of dust on everything.

(Not that it ever gets *that* bad. But visible dust is not unknown.)

I shook off thoughts of privacy and dusting and focused in on what really mattered. "Patrice, do you think you might be willing to let me use that key to maybe poke around a bit inside? I'm still trying to figure out what kind of work Lucas Dean was doing in her home. I ran into Johnny Duffy the other day and he ran out of the store when I tried to talk to him about it."

She pressed her lips together and studied me while I held my breath and silently prayed she'd agree.

She looked at Fancy with a frown. "We can't take the dog inside. I don't really want to explain to the cops about having that key. They might reach the wrong conclusions."

"Right…"

"But you can leave it with Paul and I'll go over there with you."

"Okay."

I wanted to tell her not to refer to my dog as an "it" but I didn't want her to change her mind, so I just led Fancy after her as she took us in through the back door. Paul Cole was sitting at the kitchen table with a cup of coffee and a copy of the local newspaper. He was a robust man and reminded me of a grandpa-type from a late 80's sitcom, weird mustache and all. Someone with a name like Willard.

Their kitchen was nice enough. Nothing special. Linoleum and wood cabinets, but well-kept, bright, and homey.

"Paul, I'm going to take Maggie next door to Agnes's house. Keep an eye on the dog."

I added, "She might bark a little when I leave, but she's a big fan of bacon and cheese and eggs and bread." I nodded towards his plate. "Hold up a piece of any of that and she'll come right to attention. Just don't do it too long unless you want a giant puddle of drool on the floor."

He eyed Fancy who was standing next to me because I still had her on leash. "Never much liked dogs."

"Well, this one's an exception. And we won't be gone long." I let her off the leash and she made a beeline for the table and started sniffing around. "Fancy, be good."

She glanced at me and then sat down, expectantly waiting, her attention focused on Paul Cole and his plate of deliciousness.

"Be back soon, Fancy" I said as I stepped back outside, following after Agnes.

Fancy whirled around, looking like I'd just told her I was leaving forever and would never ever come back, ever.

"Fifteen minutes, Fancy. Fifteen minutes, that's all." I closed the door and walked quickly away before I could let her heartbroken cries get to me. I couldn't pass up this opportunity. I had to see what Lucas Dean had been working on in Agnes Rockmorton's house and this might be my one and only chance to get inside.

CHAPTER 17

Patrice glanced both ways before quickly opening the front door and letting me in. "Hurry up now," she said, hustling me along so she could shut the door immediately behind us.

"We're not doing anything wrong. You have a key," I said.

"Yes, but I'd rather no one knew that."

I was tempted to ask why, but then I might not get a chance to look around, so I let it slide. Better that than remind her that I was in fact married to a cop.

"So," I said. "You've been here many times before, what looks different? What could Lucas Dean have been working on here for a week?"

Patrice led me through a living room decorated with one too many crocheted doilies. Don't get me wrong, I like a good crocheted doily myself, but when there's one under every single bowl and vase and figurine, it gets to be a bit much. That's why I don't crochet all that much anymore, those things multiply faster than rabbits given the chance.

"She was quite the crafter," I said to have something to say.

Patrice glared at a little table full of crystal figurines and beige doilies edged in forest green. "Mm. She was."

"You didn't like her work?" I asked.

She pursed her lips. "I liked it fine. But every single Christmas the woman gave me something else. And I've known her since the 70's. Fifty years of *this*." She hissed the last word as she gestured around the room. "And if I didn't put them all out, she noticed. *Where's that tablecloth I made you, Patrice? Where's that afghan I made you, Patrice?* Sometimes a woman just wants to use a nice store-bought blanket."

I raised my eyebrows at her vehemence. "It sounds like you guys had an interesting friendship."

She grunted but changed the subject. "Living room looks the same as always."

As we walked through the rest of the main level she confirmed that all of the rooms looked unchanged as far as she could tell. The whole house was decorated in beige, peach, and green; Patrice confirmed that's how it had always been.

"Fifty years and the woman never changed things up."

I bit my lip to keep from commenting again. "If nothing's changed then what was Lucas Dean working on?"

Patrice exhaled loudly through her nose as she stared at a door tucked away at the end of the kitchen, her lips pressed tight together. "Maybe she finally got rid of the fun room." She pronounced the fun in fun room like it was anything but.

"The fun room?" I asked, feeling a little scared about what I might learn.

"Come along. Either you'll see or you won't."

She jerked open the door and led me down a narrow set of stairs into what looked to me to be a very normal and boring basement other than the fact that it was completely empty. There was a long bar at one end of the room with beer steins lined up along glass shelves and stools set up in front of it. But nothing else. No couches, no television. Just bare concrete floor.

It certainly didn't meet my definition of fun.

Patrice looked around and nodded. "Well, that explains it."

"What?"

"She must've had him remove the fun room. She'd want some discretion for that. Probably why he had Johnny Duffy help with the heavy lifting rather than his usual crew. Johnny Duffy is a lot of things, but he's most definitely not one to talk out of turn."

"Patrice, you keep referring to it as the fun room. Dare I ask what that means?"

She crossed her arms and glared at me. "What do you think it means?"

"I don't know. That's why I'm asking."

(I actually had my suspicions, but I wasn't just going to blurt them out. What if I was wrong? This was an eighty-year-old woman we were talking about.)

"Well, do you think we played *Bingo* down here? Because we didn't."

"Okay. What..." I really didn't want to finish that sentence. I really didn't want to know. I understand that everyone has a history and that sometimes that history is quite...interesting. But I prefer to think of my little old ladies as always having been little old ladies and not swinging singles from the 70's, you know?

Patrice stood her ground, hands on hips, daring me to ask. I changed my tactics.

"Um, whatever was down here, would there be anything about it that would make someone kill two people over it?" I asked instead.

"No. Only thing about down here that might make someone kill someone is the memories."

"Uh…what memories?" I kinda winced as I asked the question.

"Where do you think we got her house key from?" Patrice huffed at me before turning and making her way back up to the kitchen.

I did not need that visual in my mind. No, no, I did not.

(Which is not to say that I am judging anyone who has ever participated in one of those key parties. You do you. But it's just so contrary to my possessive nature that I can't go there easily. To think about going to a party with Matt and then…NO. MINE. HANDS OFF. And I'd like to think he'd feel the same way.)

As I followed Patrice back up the stairs I wondered if she was the type of person to hold a grudge over something like that. I knew I was, but was she? Could that initial encounter have led to years of resentment and increasing hostility until she'd finally decided to knife Agnes Rockmorton in the back?

Maybe. But then why kill Luke first? Had he found out about who participated in the fun room? Maybe he'd tried to blackmail Patrice and it failed and then Patrice was so mad at Agnes for giving away her secret that she killed her, too?

Eh. I couldn't exactly picture the bird-like little woman in front of me knifing someone in the kidneys.

Saying something nasty behind their back, absolutely. But killing them? No. That would have to be Paul Cole. And why would he do it? To protect his reputation? Or because his wife told him to?

No. Plus, killing someone to keep a secret has never made much sense to me. What better way for something like that to become public knowledge than to kill two people over it and have it revealed to the world as the motive at your trial?

Then again, not many people think of that sort of thing when it comes to murder. They kill to protect the secret first and only later realize that the murder itself is much more likely to reveal the secret than the person they killed ever was.

Hm.

I wasn't sure it made sense. But I wasn't ready to rule it out yet either.

So good news was I had at least one suspect. Bad news was I was never going to get the idea of Agnes Rockmorton who crocheted beige and maroon dollies but also had a fun room in her basement out of my head.

Or the idea of Patrice or Paul Cole reaching into a paper bag to retrieve a random person's keys and take them home.

Worse yet—because there was nothing left in the fun room anymore—I was left to imagine what had been there before. And I have an unfortunately good imagination...

Yikes.

CHAPTER 18

I thanked Patrice profusely for her help and went back with her to retrieve Fancy who was curled up at Paul Cole's feet, her gaze fixed on the kitchen door just waiting for me to return. Not that she made a mad scramble to reach my side once we walked in the door, she was too annoyed at me for that.

Instead she lay by his side and glared at me until I reached into my bag and pulled out a nice little bribe. I never leave home without copious amounts of treats for Fancy. It's easier to lure her with a tasty salmon snap than rely on her actually obeying me voluntarily.

"Nice dog," Paul Cole grunted as Fancy scrambled to her feet.

"Told you she was special." I nodded at his arm. "Nice tattoo you have there. What is it?"

He glanced at his arm. "From my Army days. Long time ago now. We all got drunk one night and got matching tattoos."

"It's important to commemorate something like that."

He snorted. "Not sure it was worth the lecture we got the next morning. Or how they ran us until we puked our guts out the next three days in a row."

I frowned at his reaction, but didn't say anything else about it, just gathered up Fancy and headed home. It's easy to think that all members of a military service are the same. That every Ranger or Marine or SEAL has the same core beliefs and values. That same dedication to mission and doing what's right. But that's not reality. Different people go into the military for different reasons. And not all of them are because they're good, decent human beings looking to make the world a better place.

And sometimes even the ones that go in good come out the other side broken. Which meant that Paul Cole's military background made him a more likely suspect. Far more likely than someone like Johnny Duffy who could probably fire one of those guns that blow up groundhogs with the best of them but was far less likely to know his way around lethal knife techniques.

I got home and put down Fancy's food for her before picking up my phone to follow-up on the notion that Lucas Dean was trying to blackmail Patrice Cole.

Trish answered on the third ring.

"Hey Trish, how's it going?" I asked.

"Maggie? Why are you calling me?"

It was a fair question. We hadn't exactly bonded when she and Sam were my houseguests. As a matter of fact I might have contemplated certain rash and illegal actions at more than one point while she was staying with me. How can one person watch that much reality television? How can there be that many crazy, trashy shows about people hooking up or trying to hook up? She even watched the UK ones for crying out loud.

"I had a question or two about Luke," I said.

"Ugh. I'd rather not talk about that man ever again. I spent three hours with the cops having my life picked apart. And then I got to go home and spend three more hours talking to Jack about it."

"How are you guys doing with all that, by the way?"

She sighed loudly. "Good actually. We'd never had a talk like that before. Not when we were dating the first time and not this time either. I don't know, we just assumed what the other wanted and turns out we were both wrong. Jack was working second jobs because he thought I wanted another kid, but I don't. Sam is great and I love him, but I'd like to go back to school not get pregnant again. But I thought he wanted another kid so I was gonna go along with it. But he doesn't either. He said you suggested he get a sales job, which I think would be great. So we're going to use our savings to help him start up a sales career. It's not easy those first six months. But if we don't add onto the trailer, we'll have enough to get by even if he doesn't sell anything. Worst case scenario, we can apply for help to the Valley Fund."

(The Valley Fund was the result of Greta and Mason putting their substantial financial resources towards keeping the valley safe and isolated until the current worldwide craziness was over. They were the main backers but we'd all committed to not letting anyone fall through the cracks while the valley was sealed off from the rest of the world.)

I nodded my head even though she couldn't see it. "Glad to hear it. And if I know Jack, he'll definitely make a sale in those first few months."

"I hope so."

She sounded happy about all of it and I was happy for them. Glad they'd worked through their issues and were trying to make it work. Especially for Sam's sake. Jack adored that boy and I think Sam felt the same for Jack.

"You had questions?" Trish prompted.

"Yeah. You were talking to Luke a lot right before everything happened. Did he ever mention to you what he was working on at Agnes Rockmorton's?"

(Yes, I realize I could've avoided an uncomfortable walk through her house if I'd just asked Trish, but, well, my mind doesn't always turn to the easiest solution first.)

"No. I knew he was doing work there, but not what he was doing specifically. Just that it paid well and that he used Johnny Duffy instead of his normal guys to help him move the biggest pieces out. He wasn't exactly thrilled to use Johnny. Guy's a good drinking buddy but not a hard worker."

"Did Jack seem excited to you? Like he thought he was going to come into a lot of money or anything?"

"Come to think of it…He was happy that last night at the party. That's part of why I was surprised when he didn't answer the phone when I called later. Because he told me he had big news he didn't want to share at the party. He said it was huge. Life-changing. But that he'd tell me later."

"Did you tell the cops that?"

"Yeah. But I didn't know what the news was, so I had nothing more to share. Can't really do much with someone was happy they had big life-changing news."

"Fair enough." I thought about it for a moment. "But he wasn't working at Agnes's house that week was he?"

"Oh no. He'd wrapped that up the week before, I think."

"Huh. Alright, thanks. Tell Jack hi for me."

"Will do."

I hung up the phone and stared at the wall.

I shuddered as I forced myself to think about each and every person I knew in Creek who was over the age of sixty who might've attended those parties at Agnes's house. Lesley? My grandpa? The preacher and his wife?

Ugh.

"Don't judge, Maggie," I muttered to myself. "You know darned well when you're sixty you're going to hope you and Matt are still going that strong. Or that you at least have some fun memories to look back on if you aren't."

Still. I didn't like to think about it. I preferred to imagine that all babies were delivered by storks and all marriages consisted of prim little couples sleeping in separate single beds that were made-up each morning with hospital corners.

I know. I'm weird.

The more I thought about it, though, the more the blackmail angle just didn't fit. Because even if Luke had been going to blackmail not only Patrice Cole but every other individual who'd ever used the fun room, I couldn't imagine the amount of money involved would've been enough to change his life. Maybe buy a few kegs of beer…But change a life? Mm. I didn't think so.

Still. Better to be thorough.

Wincing at what I had to do next, I leashed Fancy back up. "Come on, girl. Time to go have the most awkward conversation I have ever had in my entire life."

CHAPTER 19

As I waited at my grandpa's front door I silently prayed that he wouldn't be home. Ever again. Or at least not until after they found the murderer. But he answered almost immediately.

Great.

"Maggie May. To what do I owe the pleasure this early in the morning?" He had his glasses on so I'd probably interrupted him in the midst of doing his morning crossword puzzle.

"Can't a girl just drop in on her grandpa?" I asked, disingenuously, as I let Fancy off her leash and she ran away towards the backyard.

"She could, but she rarely does. Especially at seven in the morning. Are you out of Coke? I should still have one in the fridge." He glanced at his watch. "Is this important? Lesley will be by in a few minutes. We're going out to breakfast in Bakerstown."

Lesley. Just when I thought this couldn't get worse.

It was good for the investigation that she was coming over. But I did not want to be asking my new step-grandmother about her participation in fun room parties at Agnes Rockmorton's house.

"Well?" my grandpa asked.

I nudge my way inside. "Let's wait until Lesley gets here and then I'll explain."

He narrowed his eyes. "Are you investigating those murders? Because you don't need to. That's what the cops do."

"Grandpa."

"Don't roll your eyes at me. You know I'm right. If you are investigating those murders, stop."

I walked into the kitchen and grabbed the Coke he'd mentioned out of the fridge. "I can't just stop."

"Why not?"

I didn't answer until I'd taken a big swig of soda, letting it bite at the back of my throat in that perfect way I love so much. "I can't just turn it off, Grandpa."

"Turn what off?"

"My mind. I can't just start thinking about something like that and then stop. Haven't you ever…?" I glanced around for a good way to explain it to him. "There. Your crossword puzzle. Do you ever have a day when you don't finish? When you just set it aside undone? Like, *'Oh well, I gave it an hour and couldn't finish it, better things to do today'* and then never go back to it and never think of it again? Or do you sit with it until it's done or even come back to it the next day if you don't get a chance to finish?"

He shrugged. "If I can't solve it, I can't solve it. It goes in the trash. Life is too short to keep banging on at something forever. I work the crossword during breakfast and if I'm not done by the time breakfast is over, oh well."

I physically recoiled at that thought. "Really? You can just take a half-finished crossword and throw it in the trash?"

"Yes."

I shuddered. "See, I can't. Once I started that crossword I would have to finish it. Even if it took me four hours. Even if it took me more than a day. And if for some reason I didn't finish it, it would stick with me. My mind would keep thinking about that puzzle until I solved it. And if I never solved it, it would always be on my mind to some little degree. Seriously. Five years later, I'd be reading some book and suddenly think, *'Aha! That was the answer to 42 Down.'*"

He didn't say it, but I knew what he was thinking. That I was crazy. And maybe I was, but that was me. I can't stop trying to solve a puzzle or a problem once I start. Either I have to solve it or someone else does.

"So you're telling me that these murders are a puzzle for you? And that now that you've started thinking about them you will keep thinking about them until they're solved?"

I nodded. "Exactly. Which means the best thing to do is help me solve them so I can clear my mind and move on."

"It's your husband's job to solve the murders, not yours." He gave me his best grandpa glare.

"I know that. But…"

"Maggie May."

I pressed my lips together and stared at him, pleading. I couldn't let it go. "Please, Grandpa. Help me."

He huffed. "Fine. But this is the last one you get involved in."

I didn't answer because we both knew the only way I wasn't going to get involved in the next murder was if I didn't know about it.

Fortunately for both of us, Lesley pulled up just then.

CHAPTER 20

We settled around the kitchen table, each of them with a cup of coffee in hand and me with my Coke.

"Well, out with it," my grandpa said. "How can we help you find the murderer?"

"Did you guys know that Agnes Rockmorton had a fun room in her house?" I asked, not really wanting to.

My grandpa snorted in amusement. "Ah, Agnes and her fun room. Were you there, Lesley? At her sixtieth? When she wanted everyone to line up and…"

"Please, Grandpa. No details. Please."

He smirked at me before taking a sip of his coffee. "What do you want to know then?"

"Did anything ever happen there that was big enough it would be worth blackmailing someone for life-changing money?"

He sat back and thought about it. "There was that one time…But you don't want details."

"Oh, honestly, Lou." Lesley smacked him on the arm before turning her attention to me. "Agnes's parties weren't actually much of anything. Agnes thought she was being very wild with that fun room of hers. And, yes,

I was at her sixtieth. It was nothing more than a bunch of sixty-somethings drinking too much and reminiscing about their wilder days, honestly."

"But I heard something about…keys." I winced.

My grandpa chuckled. "Oh, Agnes's key party…I'd forgotten about that one. It was about ten years ago?" He set his coffee down. "Pretty sure there were only two sets of keys in that bag that night. When Marie and I heard what she had planned we ducked out the back. And we weren't the only ones."

"So did Bill and I." Lesley shook her head. "That was the most transparent attempt I've ever seen by a woman to sleep with another woman's husband."

"Who wanted who?" I asked her.

"Agnes wanted Paul. Had for years."

"And Patrice and Theodore?"

"Went along with it. It was going to happen one way or another. Might as well know when."

I bit my lip. "Do you think they were still…?"

"What, now? No. I always had the impression it didn't go very well. That's why Agnes wouldn't move that RV when Paul was injured. A little bit of payback for leading her on for so long and then not rising to the occasion."

"Do you think Patrice or Paul could've held a grudge this long and finally killed Agnes over it?"

My grandpa answered. "No. No chance."

I finished my Coke and sat back with a frustrated sigh. "Great. I'm back at square one. All I know is that Lucas Dean was excited about some life-changing event but from what you're telling me it had nothing to do with Agnes Rockmorton and her fun room."

"Since you're back at square one, you should let Matt handle it."

"Grandpa. I told you I can't let it go once I get started. But what I can do is tell Matt everything I've learned. Maybe he'll see something I haven't." I stood up. "Thank you guys. Enjoy your breakfast."

Even though it wasn't a part of the investigation anymore, as I left the house I couldn't help but think about what Agnes Rockmorton had asked for at her sixtieth birthday.

My mind, I swear, I'd love to be able to just turn it off some days.

CHAPTER 21

Matt was still sleeping when I returned home so I decided to clean a bit. I know, me choosing to clean voluntarily, something had to be wrong. But see, here's the weird thing. When I was on my own I really didn't care about any mess I made because I knew it was my mess and somehow that made it less of something to worry about.

But now that Matt and I were married and sharing a space, every stain I saw was potentially not my stain but his. And for some reason other people's dirt squicks me out in a way that my own doesn't. It's not rational, but it is what it is.

So I cleaned. Plus, I figured if I felt that way about things then maybe Matt did, too, and I didn't want my "ex-military, lined his shoes up parallel by the front door when he got home each night" husband, to think I was a slob.

Not for the first six months at least. I wouldn't be able to hide it forever, but I figured I could do so for at least the honeymoon period. Let him think he'd gotten a good deal for a few months at least.

When I heard the shower turn on in the master bedroom I set to making him breakfast. Nothing fancy. Just a heated up can of black beans with cumin added in, a couple fried eggs, bacon, some Greek yogurt, and salsa. It was one of my go-to breakfast choices and much more exciting than toast with peanut butter and an apple, which was my other go-to.

By the time he came into the kitchen toweling his hair dry, everything was done and on the table. I'd even put down a napkin for him.

He eyed the table suspiciously. "What have you done?"

"I made you breakfast. Can't a wife make her husband breakfast?"

He stayed where he was, narrowing his eyes at me. "*A wife can make her husband breakfast, I'm just not sure you're that wife.*"

"Hey now. All you have to do is ask and I'll have a hi-ball or whatever it is ready and waiting as soon as you walk through that door each night."

He laughed and sat down. "Thank you."

"You're welcome." I sat down across from him and dropped a bit of yogurt and bacon onto Fancy's sharing plate. "So…How's work going?"

He smiled at me, like *Gotcha, I knew there was an ulterior motive,* but all he said was, "Work's good. You know I thought with the valley closed off we'd have less speeders, but the locals are making up for it."

He then launched into a five-minute-long series of stories about all the various speeders he'd had to pull over in the last few days. The stories were entertaining—I even laughed at a few—but by the end of the five minutes I was glaring at him more than laughing.

"What's wrong?" he asked, guilelessly. "I thought you wanted to hear about how work was going."

"Matt."

"Yes?"

"You know me."

He smiled. "I do."

"So…How is work going?" I stabbed my fork at a couple of black beans on the bottom of the bowl that didn't want to let me catch them.

"Oh, you mean how is the investigation into Lucas Dean's murder going?"

If looks could kill, I would've been a widow in that moment.

He laughed as he set his bowl on the floor next to Fancy for her to polish off the last little bit. When he sat back he was serious and unhappy. "Not well. We know Luke did work at Agnes's house shortly before the murders, but no one seems to know what kind of work he did for her."

"Oh, I know that."

He tilted his head to the side. "Do you now?"

"I just found out this morning, I swear." I proceeded to fill him in on my house tour and embarrassing visit with my grandpa and Lesley.

"Well, at least you got to be the one to talk to your grandpa about that. I'm afraid I'd never be able to look the man in the eye again if I had to talk to him about sex. That's a little too close to reminding him that his granddaughter and I…"

"Whoa, there. No changing the subject."

He winked at me. "Why not? I have a few hours before I have to be back on shift and we are newlyweds…"

"Matthew Allen Barnes. I am trying to catch a murderer here. Stick to the subject. You didn't know what Luke was doing at Agnes Rockmorton's house and I've now told you. Do you have any idea what life-changing news he had?"

"No. A few people commented about how excited Luke seemed that last night. Said he was talking about getting a boat he'd been wanting for ages. Someone said he mentioned sailing around the Caribbean this winter. But no one knew why he could suddenly afford it."

I stared at the ceiling, trying to think what it could be. "Drugs? Smuggling? Did you check that he hadn't established some back way into the valley because that is totally something Luke would do?"

"We're all over that, don't worry. I have no desire to face you if your grandpa gets sick because I failed to catch someone sneaking in here and bringing that illness with them."

"Okay, then. But the life-changing news definitely involved coming into some money?"

He nodded. "Seems so. He didn't tell anyone where the money was coming from or what he was going to do for it. But whatever it was, it didn't sound like a job of any sort. Because all the stories I heard from the few days before he died were that he was talking about taking vacations or buying big toys. If he was going to earn the money through work I'd assume he'd be more focused on the job than the perks."

I put my bowl on the floor for Fancy and took the one Matt had given her to the sink. "Did he have any relatives that died lately? Maybe he was due to inherit and someone killed him to get access to the money themselves. Who gets his house?"

"If someone killed him for his money, that backfired."

"Why?"

He grinned at me.

"What?"

"Luke had a will."

"And? So?"

He crossed his arms and leaned back in his chair looking far too smug. "He left every single penny he had to charity."

I snorted. "No he didn't."

"He did. Split equally between the local humane society, the Red Cross, and some group dedicated to the preservation of the rain forest."

"No. That has to be a joke. Lucas Dean and the rain forest?"

Matt shrugged one shoulder. "He'd also been supporting some charity in Africa every month. Even had a picture of the kid he'd 'adopted' on the wall in his office."

"No." I did not need to hear that at some deep level Lucas Dean was a decent human being. No. No, no, no.

Matt grinned. "Seems you misjudged him."

"I did not. No matter how many kids he saved from starvation in Africa he was still the man who set off fireworks when Fancy was right there and who broke my best friend's heart more than once."

"What can I say? Some people are complex."

I stared Matt down, waiting for him to crack and tell me it was a joke, but he didn't. I shook my head. Who knew that Lucas Dean had a heart hidden somewhere under all those layers of trouble-making jerk?

Still. Didn't make me wish he was alive. It had been far too peaceful without him living next door for that.

I glanced at the clock and then back at Matt. "Well…If there's nothing else to discuss about the case, we do have a few hours until you're due into work, and we are newlyweds after all…Perhaps…"

Matt flashed me his best grin. "Now we're talking."

CHAPTER 22

That night I went over to my grandpa's for dinner and some Scrabble. Lesley was at some sort of event for the library that he hadn't wanted to attend, so he invited me over for his famous stuffed cheeseburgers. Instead of melting the cheese on top of the meat he stuffed it into the center of the patty so that it was all yummy, gooey when I bit into it.

There is no better way to make a cheeseburger in my humble opinion.

When my grandpa played "zebra" to start the game of Scrabble off, I knew I was in trouble. It only got worse from there. By the time I pulled the last tile out of the bag I was down by fifty points and staring at a tray full of consonants without a friendly vowel in sight. About all I could find to play was "by".

But I toughed it out and went down swinging, because even when all the odds are against me I don't know how to quit. I lost by sixty-points. It was a thorough trouncing.

"Rematch?" my grandpa asked as I took a swig of my beer.

"No."

"You okay?"

"I guess. Just wondering what I'm doing with my life, that's all."

He snorted. "You kids these days. I never once stopped to think about what I was doing with my life. I just lived it. There were no plans or second-guessing, it was just life."

"Well, if you hadn't figured this out about me by now I think about everything all the time. If I'm not completely overwhelmed by what's happening, I think. And right now with the barkery shut down and the resort opening maybe never I have lots and lots and lots of time on my hands to think."

"What are you thinking about?" he asked.

"My best friend is having a kid. And…I don't know. I'm happy for her, but I don't want to be fifty-five at my kid's high school graduation, so I'm not really sure I want to follow her down that road. And I don't know how Matt will feel about that. I wish I could go back a decade in time, meet Matt then, and have a kid with him then. But to do so now?" I winced.

"I never had kids," he said with a shrug.

"And? Was that a good thing or a bad thing?"

He shook his head. "It was just life. I told you, I never planned what would happen. I just took life as it came at me and for me that meant not having kids. But I did love being around when you were little. Kids are amazing. They show you the world in a way you'll never see it on your own."

"But they're tiring. It's like Fancy on steroids. I can leave her at home for a few hours and go to the store or whatever, but do that with a toddler they'll throw you in jail. Plus, you put in all that effort and maybe they don't like you at the end of it. Or maybe they never leave. Some kids stay at home until they're like ninety these days. I can't have that."

He chuckled. "Stop worrying about things you can't control and just let it happen."

"No. I have to be in control."

"Maggie May, what makes you think you're in control of anything right now?"

I opened my mouth and then closed it. He was right. Between Fancy, Matt, and random murders my life already wasn't my own. "You are not helping, Grandpa."

"Just calling it how I see it. What else have you learned about the murders?"

"Not much. Seems Luke was talking like he was coming into money. Said he was going to buy a boat and sail around the Caribbean in it. But no one knows how he was coming into that money. Matt said it wasn't drugs or smuggling, but what else could it be? He said the way Luke was talking it wasn't an ongoing job of any sort. Sounded more like found money, like an inheritance or something. Which brings me back to Agnes Rockmorton. Maybe he found something in that basement when he dismantled it. More than just a fun room."

"Maybe. I never heard any rumors about money when it came to Agnes and Theodore. He worked in the forest service most of his life. Wasn't a gambler. Wasn't one to bend the rules in any way. And if Luke did find something there then why was *he* killed first? And why then kill Agnes?"

"To get it back? And then she was killed so she

wouldn't tell anyone and whoever killed both of them could have the money free and clear?"

"Hm." He took a swig of his beer. "Not lining up for me."

"I know. Me neither."

"You sure you don't want a rematch?"

I glanced at the board. Scrabble is definitely a game of skill and my grandpa was a master, but there is that luck angle to it in terms of which tiles you draw and when, and maybe if I tried again my luck would shine through. One thing was certain, if I didn't play him again I'd never have a chance to beat him.

"Alright. One more. But I'm going to grab us both some of that key lime pie Lesley made first."

CHAPTER 23

It was almost nine when I walked Fancy and myself back home. It was a gorgeous night, absolutely still except for the sounds of crickets or whatever they were chirping in the distance. The sky was dark and clear and full of stars. It was that perfect summer mountain cool temperature that I loved. Almost needing a jacket, but not quite.

I tell ya, I'd be happy if it was sixty-five to eighty-five degrees year-round even if I did have to sacrifice the seasons to get it.

Alas. Might take a few months but winter was definitely going to come back, snow and all.

As I opened the gate and walked Fancy towards the front door, I glanced in the direction of Luke's house. Why had he been killed? What did it have to do with Agnes Rockmorton? There had to be something I was missing. What was it?

Fancy tugged on her leash and I let her go to run off behind the house. Matt wasn't due home for a few more hours. Even though we'd walled off the valley from the rest of the world, people hadn't stopped drunk driving and getting into domestic disputes.

At my wit's end, I called Greta.

"Maggie. This is a pleasant surprise. How are you?" she answered, the clipped sound of her German accent more soothing than you'd expect.

"Good."

"You do not sound good."

I plopped onto the couch with a big sigh. "You heard that Lucas Dean was killed?"

"I did. This is very sad. He was not the kind of man you marry, but he was very fun. And he did good work on my house."

"Did you keep in touch with him? After?"

She laughed once. "No."

Her answer made it clear that he'd been hired help and not the type of person she'd choose to associate with socially. I'd been fortunate that not only had she been my best customer when the barkery was open but we'd also become friends at some point along the way.

"So you wouldn't have any idea how he was going to come into a bunch of money? I was thinking maybe drugs or smuggling or something."

"No. It was not that."

"You seem very sure."

"I am. When I agreed to help seal off the valley, I also made certain arrangements to ensure that the valley remained sealed. It has. There is no smuggling. At least not now."

"Was there?"

"Eh. One or two people may have tried. They did not succeed. They are no longer trying."

The way she said that gave me pause. "Are they still alive, Greta?"

"Of course. What do you think of me, Maggie? I was a jewel thief, but never a murderer. No. There were people who wanted to take advantage but they were talked to. Now they no longer want to take advantage. One or two may have been encouraged to leave, but they were not killed."

"Well, that's good at least."

There were more questions I could ask, but I decided I didn't want to know the answers. Those marriage vows might come into play and I did not want to end up betraying one of my best friends in order to honor my marriage.

Instead I asked, "Did you know anything about Agnes Rockmorton?"

"No."

"Any idea how someone could come up with a bunch of money real fast? The kind you spend buying a boat and sailing around the Caribbean?"

There was a slight pause. "Mm. For me it was jewels that I sold, first those I stole then those I was given. Then it was a nice divorce settlement. Another divorce settlement. Another one. Another. Some investments I liquidated. And, of course, being widowed. If Luke were not planning on spending the money on a vacation there are, of course, those people who will loan money quickly and then perhaps kill if it does not come back, but that is not the case here, no? A man does not borrow from that type of person to go on a vacation."

"Anything else you can think of?"

"There is also inheriting money, no? Although Luke did not seem the type to have a rich relative. And there is gambling. Someone local did win the lottery. I do not know that the prize has been claimed. Could Luke have been the winner?"

"Maybe. I don't know. I'll have to ask around. See if he was one to buy tickets. Thank you, Greta."

"You are quite welcome. I will see you soon?"

"Yes, let's have lunch next week. Lord knows there's nothing else on my plate."

"Maggie, tell me, what have you done this week. Work-wise?"

I thought about it for a second. "Let's see…I rebranded our entire product line and updated the website with all the new images. And, of course, had to coordinate that with the drop shippers we use to make sure they had all the new files."

"And you designed these images yourself?"

"Yeah."

"This week?"

"Yes."

"Anything else?"

I wrinkled my nose trying to remember. "I came up with another dog treat, but I don't know what to call it yet."

"And meetings for the resort, no?"

"Well, of course. You were on a couple of them weren't you?"

"I was. So. To summarize. You redid all of the branding for your treat line. You then updated your entire website and made sure the drop shippers had the new files. You also designed a new dog treat and participated in a number of meetings related to the new resort."

I nodded. "Yeah, sounds about right."

"You also were investigating a murder at the same time."

"Yes."

"And yet you think you are bored and have done nothing all week?"

I shrugged even though she couldn't see it. "Well, I am bored."

"Maggie."

"What? I am."

"You may be bored. But you are not unproductive. You must think about this. You do quite a bit while bored."

"Hm. True. Never really thought about it that way before. It's just that I could be doing so much more…"

"Maggie. Enjoy this time while you have it. It will not last. One day you will have kids and then you will never be bored—or sleep—again."

I decided not to dive into that conversation. "Good point, Greta. Thank you."

"Of course. What are friends for."

We hung up and I stared at the wall, thinking. Had Luke won the lottery? Was that the source of his sudden, new-found wealth? But if so, what did Agnes Rockmorton have to do with it? So many questions, and still no answers.

CHAPTER 24

Normally I would've just given up and gone to bed at that point because with Fancy liking to be up so early I need to go to bed early to get my beauty rest. But I was on a roll and I figured it was still early enough to call Jamie.

"Hey, Maggie, how's it going?" she said, sounding slightly surprised to hear from me so late at night.

"Good. How about you?"

"Okay…"

"Jamie, things are never just okay with you? What's wrong?"

She paused and then said, "I may have just screamed at Mason because we didn't have any double chocolate chunk pretzel ice cream in the house. And I may have told him to go to the store and find some or find somewhere else to sleep tonight."

"Jamie!"

"I know. I should call him and tell him to come back. But I really want that double chocolate chunk pretzel ice cream."

I managed not to laugh as I answered, "I've never

seen that kind of ice cream at the store. Who makes it? I've long ago lost track of all the Ben & Jerry's flavors, is it one of theirs?"

Another pause. "Uhhh…Not that I'm aware of? As far as I know, no one makes it? But they should. Because it would be really good. With little chunks of chocolate in there and then crunchy pretzels on a base of dark chocolate ice cream."

"It certainly sounds good. Maybe we can have a line of homemade ice creams at the resort and that can be one of the flavors," I suggested.

"Oh, that's brilliant." I could hear her smiling through the phone. "I'm almost done experimenting with baby foods. Do you know how boring baby food is? Because you're not supposed to put things in it, like salt and sugar. It's just plain fruits and vegetables all mashed up. But ice cream…Now that I could have some fun with. I'm going to call Mason and tell him to pick me up some ingredients. And some samples from the store so I can see what works and what doesn't. But do we have enough room in the freezer…?"

I glanced at the clock. "Just remember that the store closes at ten, so you may have to put this off until tomorrow. No twenty-four hour grocery stores around here, what with wandering wildlife and all."

"Right."

There was another pause and then Jamie said, "Oh no, Maggie, what did I do?" Her voice started to tremble. "I sent Mason out *at night*. Do you know how dark the road can be between here and Masonville? And there are deer. What if he hits one? I mean he has a good vehicle, but what about the deer? And, oh Maggie, I can't handle it if he ends up in the hospital. What if I go into labor early?"

I tried not to laugh. "You're only like five or six months along, aren't you?"

"Exactly. I need him here. What was I thinking?" her voice spiraled as she talked until she was practically squeaking out the last word.

"Jamie," I said, using my parental command voice.

"Yes?"

"I want you to breathe with me, okay?" I continued, keeping my voice level and calm.

"Okay," she said quietly.

"Ready? In…."

I heard her take a deep breath on the other end of the line.

"And out…"

She exhaled slowly.

"And in…"

"Maggie, I can't be breathing right now when Mason is out there possibly running over a deer and I'm at home all alone with no one to help if I go into labor." The words tumbled out so fast I could barely understand her.

Once more I tried not to laugh because I knew she meant what she was saying no matter how absurd it actually was. "Remember those hormones we were talking about?" I asked. "I think they're kicking your butt right now."

"I…Oh. Maybe." She seemed to deflate.

"You okay now?" I asked, letting a hint of amusement finally show.

"I guess. I'd still like Mason to come home. I should call him."

She sounded like she was about to hang up on me, so I interrupted. "Real quick before you go?"

"Yeah?"

"Did Luke ever buy a lottery ticket as long as you knew him?"

"No. He wasn't the type. His dad had a gambling addiction, so Luke never bet on anything, ever. Wouldn't even play penny slots." At last she sounded like her normal self, scarily competent.

"Can't blame him for that," I said. "Sure-fire way to lose money in my book. Unless it's the hundred-play poker machines."

She laughed. "But it's so fun with the little bonus rounds. There was this game I played once that had these cute little chickens that would hatch out of an egg. And another one that had those nesting Russian dolls and each one that opened up gave you coins. I love those games."

"As long as you're prepared to lose the money, I guess." I shrugged. "I don't like being at the mercy of a machine that's programmed to make more money than I do."

"Maggie, you're too serious sometimes. It's just fun. But I should go. Because I want to call Mason and tell him to come home right now."

"Okay. Talk to you later. And if you go into labor before he gets back, you can always call me."

"Good point. Thanks. Bye."

I hung up, shaking my head. Poor Mason. I wasn't his biggest fan, but the man was going to have earned sainthood by the end of this pregnancy.

CHAPTER 25

The next day I tried to forget about Luke and Agnes and just enjoy the mid-summer day that I was able to spend with Fancy. We sat out in the backyard after lunch, her taking a nap, me reading my latest book. I was glad we were still able to get packages into the valley (via helicopter) because I would've died without enough books to read. I'd been consuming them at an unholy rate all year.

Reading is my stress relief. The worse things get, the more I read. I remember one year in college I was working full-time and had five finals in seven days and I somehow managed to read three books that week. (And also miraculously did not fail any of those finals although I do think one of those classes was the one where I got a C+ which thoroughly shocked and horrified me. I was always an A- student which meant sometimes a B or B+ student, but I was never a C student for crying out loud.)

Anyway. I was trying to distract myself with reading. But the book was…not that good. I hate to say that about a book, but it just really wasn't doing it for me. And I didn't have anything else to read because I am still an old-school reader who likes physical books so I couldn't just go online and replace it with something more engaging without having to wait an unknown number of days for it to be delivered.

Which meant my mind started to wander. And when my mind started to wander it landed right back on the murders of Lucas Dean and Agnes Rockmorton.

I was at a dead-end. And I hated that. I didn't want to quit. I didn't want to leave it up to Matt and his colleagues to figure out. I'd solved a number of murders already, there was no reason I shouldn't be able to solve these, too.

I just had to figure out where Luke thought he was going to get money from. If I could figure that out, I'd know who had killed him and Agnes and why.

Unfortunately, the only person capable of telling me that was probably Johnny Duffy. And I had no idea where to find him. Even if I did, he could be the killer so maybe it wasn't the smartest idea to go tracking him down to ask questions.

I was glaring at the book that had failed to capture my attention and contemplating asking around to find out where Johnny Duffy lived when a firework went off next door in Lucas Dean's backyard.

As Fancy jumped to her feet and ran around barking her displeasure, I raced to the fence and jumped up on the little board that ran along the bottom so I could see over the top. I smiled. It was Johnny Duffy. Just the man I wanted to see.

Before he could notice me and run away again, I dashed out the front gate and barged around the side of Luke's house to where an old white pickup with rust over the wheel wells was parked at an angle. The back of the truck already had about a dozen boxes of fireworks loaded up, and as I came around the driver's side Johnny Duffy came out of the back gate of Luke's house lugging another couple of boxes.

"Stop right there," I said.

He ignored me until he'd set the boxes down in the back of the truck and then turned to glare at me, wiping his nose on his forearm like the class act he was.

I placed myself between him and the driver's-side door. "I have some questions to ask you."

"Well I don't wanna answer no questions, so tough." He started to walk past me.

"I'll call the cops."

He stopped, close enough he could grab me if he wanted. "Why would you do that?"

"Because you're stealing from a dead man."

He stepped closer, glaring at me. "I'm not stealing. Luke and I bought these together. He's clearly not going to use them now."

I lifted my chin, holding my ground. "How do I know you're telling the truth? If you bought them together why were they at Luke's house?"

"Because he had the party. But we didn't use them all because he said his little busybody neighbor would probably call the cops if we set too many off after she got back home." He leaned in as he spoke, close enough for me to get a whiff of his tobacco breath.

I nodded. "He was probably right. My husband is a cop after all."

"Big whoop. These fireworks are mine and I'm going to take 'em." He started to walk away.

"Is that all you're taking?" I made a point of peering at the boxes in the truck.

He turned back. "Yeah."

"Why'd you wait so long?"

He spit to the side. "Like you said, they were in a dead man's house. Figured I'd wait a bit in case the cops needed to look through them."

I was honestly glad to see the fireworks go, so really didn't want to stop him from taking them. But I did still need to know if Johnny Duffy had any clues about the murder.

"I'll make you a deal," I said. "I won't call the cops about this if you answer a few questions for me."

He shook his head. "Fine. But let's do this inside. They're mine, but no need to have anyone else come along and start asking a bunch of questions."

"Okay. Lead the way."

He pulled a tarp across the back of the truck before leading me into the house.

(I know. It was stupid to walk into a house no one knew I was at with a man who could possibly be the killer. But, one, I'm not always the brightest bulb. And, two, I really didn't think Johnny Duffy was the killer. A man in need of a good makeover, sure. A killer? Eh. Nah. *Probably* not.)

CHAPTER 26

Based on what I'd previously seen of his backyard, I was surprised that Luke's kitchen was as tidy as it was until I remembered that he'd hosted a party at his house the night he was killed. He must've cleared everything out of the downstairs, which meant that if there was anything interesting to see it would be upstairs.

I immediately headed in that direction while Johnny Duffy shouted at me to come back and stay in the kitchen.

"I'm not that kind of girl, thanks," I said as I headed up the creaky staircase by the front door.

"I didn't say you could go barging through his house. I thought you wanted to ask me questions." He followed me up the stairs, his heavier weight making each step sigh instead of creak.

"I do. But I also want to see if Luke had some sort of office where there might be a clue to where the money he was coming into was coming from."

"What are you talking about?" He caught up to me as I reached the narrow hallway. On the left was a bedroom that was much more typical of how I usually thought of Luke. There were clothes thrown all over the place and the bed wasn't made.

(Not that I ever make my bed either. Why should I when no one else will see it and it's just going to be slept in again that night? Of course, with Matt around now the bed is usually made because he gets up after me and is definitely one to tidy his environment.)

I turned to the room across the hallway. It was a small bathroom with a sink that could use a good wipe down. How can a man shave all the hair off his face and not bother to look down to see that half of it is now in the sink?

I kept going down the hall. The next room on the bathroom side was an office. Clearly everything that had been downstairs had been tossed into it because there were newspapers on the floor with a greasy metal something or other that looked half-assembled as well as random cans of paint and an automatic drill scattered across the floor along with at least three stacks of papers on the desk.

I noted the location of the drill as Johnny Duffy followed me into the room. Never hurts to know where a weapon is, just in case. I wrinkled my nose because he was close enough behind me I could smell the sour scent of him.

"What money?" he asked.

"So Luke didn't mention it to you? That he was coming into some money?" I glanced through the first pile of papers as we talked.

"No."

I turned to study him. "I thought he might've found something at Agnes's house."

"No." He truly looked bewildered by my questions. Clearly that was a dead end.

"Then why'd you get all weird and leave the grocery store the other day?" I asked, leaning against the desk.

He looked away from me, visibly uncomfortable. "Do you know what that place was like before we cleared it out? I didn't want to think about it, let alone talk about it in public."

I was dying to know what it had looked like, but I stayed focused. "Was it weird enough to blackmail someone over?"

"Blackmail? That old bat was proud of it. Tried telling us stories about the parties she'd had down there." He shook himself. "No. Nothing to blackmail her over. Just images I can't bleach out of my mind."

I raised my eyebrows, impressed by his use of imagery. I didn't think he had it in him. "So Luke didn't say anything to you about sailing the Caribbean this winter?"

"Oh, yeah, he couldn't stop talking about that the last week or so."

"How did you think he was going to pay for that?"

He blinked slowly. "I didn't give it much thought. Just figured he had the money."

"Someone said he was going to buy a boat."

He nodded. "That was part of the plan. Even showed me a picture of it. Probably somewhere here on his desk. Give me a minute."

He pawed through a large stack of papers on the corner of the desk. "Here it is. See? Nice looking, ain't it?"

I grabbed the rest of the papers that had been near the photo and glanced through them. "I'd say."

I showed him a print-out that said the boat cost seventy-five grand, new. Below that was a list of expenses for living in the Caribbean. Luke had been planning on a cost of three thousand a month for six months. So about a hundred grand total all told, maybe a little less.

I frowned at the calculations jotted down on that

piece of paper. I thought he'd said it was life-changing money. I mean, don't get me wrong, someone wants to give me a hundred grand, I'll take it and do very nice things with it. And, yes, it would drastically improve my life or the life of most people. But when I think about life-changing money I think a million or more. Because that's enough to put in a bank account and invest and live off the interest. Less than that is just money to tidy things up with and maybe have a bit of fun.

Again, not that I wouldn't happily take any amount of money someone wanted to give me. But he'd said life-changing.

Maybe for Luke it was?

I grabbed the rest of the papers and thumbed through them. On one of the pages there was another series of jotted down numbers. One point five million and then an arrow to a value of seven hundred and fifty thousand. That was more like it.

Below the seven hundred and fifty thousand he'd written his current mortgage balance, what he owed on his truck, the hundred grand for six months in the Caribbean, and then some calculations about investing the rest, which would've been about four hundred thousand. It wasn't quite enough to quit his job long-term but it was enough to ease things certainly, especially with no mortgage or truck payment. With all of that it looked like he could have comfortably split his time between Colorado and the Caribbean and only worked half the year.

But the question still remained: where was the one point five million coming from? And who was he splitting it with?

I snapped a few pictures with my phone and then said, "Thanks" to Johnny Duffy and started back down the stairs.

"Wait. Where are you going? What's going on? What did you find out?" He stomped after me down the hall.

He'd seen the same things I had. Did I really have to spell it out for him? I shook my head as I made my way down the stairs, but stopped in the living room to explain it to him. "From those papers it's pretty clear Luke was coming into about seven hundred and fifty grand. Splitting half of one point five million. But I still don't know where that was coming from."

"The lottery."

When I didn't say anything he added, "It was on the news. Cash payout for whoever won the lottery the week before Luke died was going to be just about one point five million. I remember because I tried to figure out what that would look like in twenty-dollar bills. Like if it was enough to swim in or whatever."

I curled my lip at the thought. "You'd want to swim in money? Have you ever had a job where you handled money before? Because that stuff is nasty dirty. I used to run a cashier's office and by the end of the night my hands were literally black with crud from all those bills."

He hunched his shoulders. "I would've ordered it direct from the bank."

"You would've had to order it direct from the mint."

Before I could get distracted wondering if the mint actually printed currency bills as well as coins, I grabbed my phone and looked up the Colorado Lottery website. Sure enough. The big winner that had been on the news and was still unclaimed had a cash payout value just under one point five million.

I shook my head. "I don't get it. Jamie told me Luke never played the lottery. She said his dad was a degenerate gambler so he never touched any of that."

"Yeah, that's true."

"So how did he end up with half of a winning ticket?"

"And where is it now?"

It was my turn to blink slowly. "Right. Good point. Whoever has the ticket is likely to be the killer."

"Huh? How's that?" Johnny looked at me, clearly confused by my leap of logic.

"Well, it makes sense, right? Why kill Luke if it wasn't for the ticket?"

"But whoever killed Luke also killed that old bat. Why kill her?"

I smiled. "I bet she was the other half. He must've picked the ticket up for her and they agreed to split the money fifty-fifty and then they won. Whoever killed both of them found out about it and wanted the money all for themselves."

He shook his head. "Don't know about all that."

I looked at the corner of the living room where there was still a blood stain on the carpet. "You ever have military training?"

"Nah."

"You know anyone around here who did?"

He grunted. "Lots of guys. Especially the older ones. Most served. You think whoever killed Luke was military?"

"Not exactly common to stab someone in the kidney."

He crossed his arms and rocked back on his heels.

"Huh. Never thought much about it. Won't help you, though. Too many guys around here like that. Plus you got the hunters. All of them know their way around a knife."

"Fair point." I headed towards the kitchen. "Well, thank you. Appreciate the time."

We walked back outside and I winced as the late afternoon sun hit me in the eyes.

"My pleasure." He smiled at me in a way that was almost friendly as Fancy started barking from the other side of the fence.

She couldn't see us, but clearly she'd heard us. "Hush, Fancy. I'll be there in just a minute."

I wanted to immediately go over to Patrice Cole's house and ask her to let me into Agnes Rockmorton's so I could look for signs of the lottery ticket to confirm my newest theory, but it was Fancy's dinnertime and one thing I had learned over the years was that it wasn't wise to delay her dinner.

(Not that Fancy would be destructive or even difficult about it, she'd just give me the saddest, most hurt look in the world, and I'd do pretty much anything to keep that look out of her eyes.)

So home it was. And then…Find the killer.

CHAPTER 27

I was all ready to solve the murder now that I knew where Luke was probably getting the money, but when I really sat down and started to think it through I was still as stuck as I had been before. The "Luke and Agnes buy a lottery ticket" theory was good, but the problem was who else would've known about the ticket? And why kill Luke before they killed Agnes?

It didn't make sense. There was still something I had to be missing. But what?

I tried to do research on who might know how to knife a person in the kidneys, but all that did was lead me down some disturbing internet rabbit holes I would've rather avoided. So, as much as I was sure my grandpa was sick of my doing so, I took myself and Fancy over to his house and invited myself to dinner.

Lesley had made an absolutely delicious lasagna. (And I can assure you that I had more than one fist-sized serving's worth, thank you very much.)

Since my grandpa doesn't believe in talking business during dinner we talked about the fundraiser instead.

"It's too bad Agnes won't be there this year," Lesley said.

"Why's that?" I asked.

"Because she was always the biggest buyer of pickles. Her and Jolene Paige. Between the two of them they'd buy up half our supply every event."

"You're talking about those peel open things you can get that look like a slot machine when you open them up?"

"Yes, pickles."

"I once won twenty bucks on one of those at a little Italian festival in Denver. I think I was like ten. It was probably illegal for me to be playing but no one seemed to mind. So Jolene *and* Agnes bought them? Together?" I asked, taking another bite of yummy pasta, sauce, and cheese.

"Oh yes. They'd pool their money, spend about a hundred dollars each time, and then stake out a table in the corner and go to work."

Lesley took a much more modest bite of her lasagna as I asked, "Did they ever make money off of it? That's a lot to spend if you're not going to get it back."

She nodded as she thought about it. "Yes. I'm pretty sure they did. They also used to go in on buying a lottery ticket each week. Had their lucky numbers that they just swore would win them the jackpot one day."

"You said used to?" I asked, leaning in, sensing a vital clue had just been uncovered.

"Maggie May," my grandpa interrupted. "It's dinner. No murder at the dinner table."

"But we're not talking murder, we're talking lottery tickets."

He didn't say anything, just gave me a look until I turned my attention back to finishing up my last little bit of garlic bread. (Homemade under the broiler and oh so good.)

Only after I'd let Fancy lick the plate clean of pasta sauce and helped load all the dishes into the dishwasher, did I bring the conversation back to those lottery tickets. "So, Lesley. About those lottery tickets that Jolene and Agnes used to buy together. Did they always play the same numbers?"

"Of course. It was some combination of their birthdays and their husbands' birthdays. They played them for years but never won."

"Any chance you know Agnes's birthday?"

My grandpa handed me a small journal with my grandma's handwriting scrawled on the pages. "Probably in here. Marie knew everyone's birthday."

I flipped through the pages. It was a birthday journal with a set of pages for every month. Each day of the month was listed on a separate line with names scrawled on the line for whoever's birthday was on that given day. I blinked back my tears as I scanned the names written in my grandma's once-familiar handwriting.

I missed her.

But there was a murderer to catch, so I kept going. I found Agnes on March 21st and Theodore on August 15th. That gave me 3-21-8-15.

I grabbed my phone and pulled up the winning lottery numbers for the ticket I suspected Luke and Agnes had bought.

Sure enough, 3-8-11-15-21-30. All four of the numbers were included, which made it likely that Jolene or Charles Paige had a birthday on the 30th and either a birthday on the 11th or in November. I flipped through the book, but didn't find entries for either one.

"Why did they stop playing the numbers together?" I

asked, waiting for everything to finish clicking into place.

"I don't know. They'd been a little cold towards one another the last year or so. Might be politics."

"Do you know if either one continued to play those numbers?"

She shook her head. "I don't. Sorry."

I tried not to think about murder for the rest of the night as my grandpa, Lesley, and I played a few games of Scrabble. (I lost. My grandpa is a word-shark and Lesley was far too good at catching even the slightest mistake. Leave one triple-word-score open…) But it was hard. I was so close, but something just wasn't falling into place.

CHAPTER 28

I made it home just before Matt. He looked awful as he came through the door wearing a t-shirt and sweats instead of his uniform. (Not that Matt can ever truly look awful, but he looked like he'd been run through the wringer a few times.)

"Bad day at work?" I asked, dying to talk to him about what I'd found, but trying to be a good, dutiful wife.

"The worst. Give me a second to get a load of laundry started."

"I can do it," I half-heartedly offered while secretly hoping he wouldn't take me up on it.

"No. You really don't want to."

Whatever was going on with the clothes he had in the bag, Fancy was definitely interested. She trotted along next to him, sniffing away, clearly wanting to tear the bag right out of his hands.

As he passed closer, I retreated into the kitchen. "What is that smell?"

Matt didn't answer until he'd thrown his uniform into the washing machine and turned it on. "Do we have beer?" he joined me in the kitchen.

I handed him one and he took a big long swallow and then closed his eyes and just stood there swaying on his feet for a moment.

Noticing that his hair was wet, I asked, "Did you take a shower at work?"

He nodded. "A quick one. At Ben's."

"Why not come home?"

"Because we were only a few blocks from Ben's house when this happened. His wife actually offered to wash my uniform, too, but I didn't want to make her deal with it what with the new baby and all."

"So what happened?" I asked.

"Failed overdose. No good deed goes unpunished. The person we went to help lost their cookies all over me, hence the shower and change of clothes."

"Will they be okay?" I started to heat him up the leftover lasagna for dinner.

"I hope. They seemed stable by the time the ambulance pulled away."

"Who was it?"

He took another long swig of his beer. "Can't tell you. HIPAA rules."

I tried not to roll my eyes, but I probably failed. I knew if it was me I'd want someone to respect my privacy and not go talking about my drug issues all over town, but still. I was his wife and I liked to have a face to put to things.

Ah well. A failed drug overdose wasn't my concern. Murder was.

"I had a break in the case today," I told him as the microwave beeped and I put his plate on the table. (A serving which was most certainly larger than the size of

Matt's fist. Heck, the garlic bread that went with it was larger than the size of Matt's fist.)

When I saw him glance towards the microwave with a slight wince I went back and wiped down the splattered sauce on the inside. (I tell ya, marriage has so many little potholes you can step in.)

"The case? And what case would that be?" He crossed his arms and stared me down.

I pressed my lips together and narrowed my eyes as I looked back at him. He didn't sound happy. Why? What was wrong?

This living with someone thing was weird. Because you were around them all the time, even when they were in a cranky mood and maybe didn't want to be bothered with you.

See, when you're dating—especially when it hasn't been all that long which was the case with Matt and I before we got married—you can manage to only see the person when you're in the mood to see them and they're in the mood to see you.

But get married and suddenly you're spending time together when you're exhausted or cranky or sad or just not in a mood to people. And, sure, for some people that's why they get married—to have someone who will be there for them when they're all those things. But for me…

Well, it was a little hard to realize that sometimes Matt didn't want to hear about something that really mattered to me in that moment because he needed me to listen to him instead.

It seems I'm not good at coddling. But I was willing to try.

I shook my head. "Never mind. Drink your beer, eat your lasagna, get a nice night's sleep, and we'll talk about it in the morning."

"Maggie," he sighed. "Just tell me now."

I winced. "Are you sure? You've had a long day."

"Positive."

He didn't sound positive. He sounded like a parent about to find out his kid had wrecked the car. But he'd asked, so…

As he ate his lasagna I told him about my venture to Luke's house that afternoon and then about what Lesley had told me about Jolene Paige and Agnes Rockmorton buying a lottery ticket together all those years.

When I was done I added, "So see? Luke must've bought a lottery ticket for Agnes and she must've told him they could split it. But Jolene Paige was upset because she'd helped choose and play those numbers all those years, so she must've had them killed so she could take the money instead."

He took another bite of lasagna before saying anything. "You've met Jolene Paige. Did she strike you as a double-murderer?"

"No. But who else could've known about the lottery ticket?"

He rubbed his fingers through his hair and sighed. "I don't know, Maggie. But I don't think it was Jolene Paige. Why would Luke even let her in the door at his party? *After* everything was over? And if there was some sort of rift between Jolene and Agnes, why would Agnes let her in? If the murders had occurred in the opposite order, maybe I'd believe it was Jolene. Maybe. But Luke was first."

I slumped down in my chair. "You're right. So we're looking for someone who knew Luke well enough to be at his party or to go back to his house after the party, and for him to open the door and let them in. And he wasn't wearing his shirt, so it must've been someone who came back. Or who stayed and started something that involved losing bits of clothing…Hm. Not Jolene Paige territory, is it?"

"Nope."

"But the lottery ticket angle could still be valid. Whoever redeems that ticket, you have to check into them. They were almost certainly playing Agnes and Jolene's numbers."

"I'm pretty sure winners can use a corporate shell to protect their identities when they claim their winnings. If that's the case, I'd have to have some very good evidence to pierce that."

I glanced at the fridge. I wanted a drink. But it was too late for me to get started. My days of drinking until two and sleeping until noon had long since passed me by.

I frowned at the table. "Darn it. So I'm back at square one."

Matt finished off his beer. "*You* are not anywhere, because *this* is not your case. But if it were, you're not at square one. We know that Luke had likely purchased that lottery ticket or was splitting it fifty-fifty with whoever had purchased it. And we know that Agnes very likely played those exact numbers every week for years. So the lottery ticket is key to finding the killer. We just don't know who that would be."

"Do you have a list of who was at the party?"

He looked at me, exhaustion in every line of his body.

"Maggie. Not your case."

"I promise I'll give you a really good back massage if you let me see the list of who was at the party."

"Oh good, now my wife is bribing me with sexual favors."

"First, a back massage is not sex. Just like dancing is not sex. People seem to confuse those things often."

"If it's really good it leads to it." He winked at me and grinned.

"Matthew Allen Barnes. Clean up your mind. Second, I'll give you the massage either way because you look like you need it. But I figured it was worth a try to see if I could leverage it to get the list from you. So it's not bribery. It's just…subterfuge."

"Subterfuge?" He smiled and raised one eyebrow.

"Mmhm."

"Well, let's take you, your *subterfuge*, and that promised massage to the bedroom and we'll see what happens with that list come the morning."

I kissed him on the cheek as he laced his fingers in mine. "I love you, you know that?"

"Is that more subterfuge?"

"Oh stop using that word. And, no, it is not. I love you. Pure and simple. No subterfuge about it."

He laughed and pulled on our joined hands. "Well, for what's it's worth, I love you, too. Even if you do keep butting your nose into my cases."

CHAPTER 29

The next afternoon Matt let me tag along to the police station so he could give me the list of everyone who'd been at the party.

"Come on," he said after grabbing the list off his desk. "We'll go sit in the interview room. More space there."

I held back. "Do we have to? It's not exactly my favorite room. We could just go back home."

"Maggie, I'm on duty."

"But it's a block away. If something comes up, they can page you or whatever. Call on the radio. Call your cellphone. Marlene won't mind, will you, Marlene?" I asked the kindly woman at the reception desk.

"Not at all, dear."

"See?"

Matt shook his head. "I have to maintain a professional appearance, Maggie. And solving a murder case at my kitchen table does not do that."

"Don't be silly. Because solving the murder case, period, is far more important than where you're sitting or what you're wearing while you do so."

He shook his head again, crossed his arms, and planted his feet. "No. If you want the list, we look at it in the interview room."

I huffed out an exasperated breath, but I knew that stubborn set to his jaw. He wasn't going to back down on this one. "Fine. Let's go to the interview room."

As we started down the hall, Officer Clark walked through the front door.

"Ben," Matt called, "we're going to go over some evidence in the Dean and Rockmorton murders. You want to join us?"

He looked at me and then Matt, but didn't comment on who the "we" Matt was referring to was. "Sure. Let me get some coffee and I'll be right in."

Once Officer Clark joined us, I explained what I'd learned from Luke's house and from Lesley.

Officer Clark leaned forward and fixed me with a glare. "So you admit Ms. Carver that you were trespassing in the home of a dead man and that you took his property?"

"No. I admit no such thing. I was granted entry to the home of a dead man by a man who told me he had lawful access to that home. And I did not take any documents from the house, I took photos of those documents. Plus, aren't we here to solve the case not arrest our co-worker's wife for…whatever?"

"Meddling."

"I'm not…" I shook my head. "Look. Things just fall into my lap sometimes, alright? And it is my civic duty to share those things with you so that you can find the killer. What kind of member of society would I be if I knew about Luke's lottery win, or potential lottery win, and didn't share that with you? Or about the connection between Agnes and Jolene and didn't share *that* with you?"

"And you being here right now?" he asked.

"I can't know what's important to share with you if I don't have adequate information. The more I know, the more I can tell you what I've stumbled across that's helpful to you. That's all."

He looked at Matt who shrugged and said, "She has been helpful."

He shook his head. "One of these days she's going to get herself into trouble she can't get out of."

I waved my hand in the air. "Excuse me. Right here. In the room. No need to talk about me like I'm not here."

Officer Clark turned his steely gaze on me. "One of these days you are going to get yourself into trouble you can't get out of. You will be alone with someone, like Johnny Duffy, and he'll turn out to be the actual killer and he will kill you. Walk your dog, knit something, read a book, I don't care. But stay out of murder cases."

I crossed my arms and slouched down in my chair, feeling like a bratty twelve-year-old. "It happened right next door to me. I didn't go looking for it."

"You're from DC, right? That's where you were living before this?"

"Yes."

"And if someone next door had been killed in DC, would you have gone investigating it?" He leaned forward like this was an actual interrogation.

"No. You crazy? I had a friend who lived a block from a triple murder but no way if that had been me would I have ever asked questions. I would've been shot."

"And yet here you are."

"But here I know people. I'm part of the community. It's not some stranger killing a stranger over something like drugs that has nothing to do with me. It's someone I might know killing someone I'd known for years. It's different."

He shook his head. "No, it's not. A killer is still a killer. And once someone has killed for the first time it's easier to do it again."

I wanted to ask if he knew that from personal experience because I'm a smart aleck that way, but I didn't. "I promise as long as it isn't my neighbor or someone I directly know and love that is either the victim or the suspect, that I will not investigate any more murders. But for now, I'm investigating this one. And I can do so here safely with you guys, or I can go poking around on my own. Your call."

Officer Clark looked at Matt. "I can't believe you married this woman."

"She keeps me on my toes. And I like her dog." He winked at me before I could pretend to be outraged. Quite frankly, I couldn't believe he'd married me either.

"So? The case? Who was at the party?" I asked.

CHAPTER 30

Matt started reading from a list of attendees that turned out to be three pages long. It seemed half the frickin' county had been at Luke's party at some point. That didn't help.

I asked, "Do you have any times on those people? When they arrived, when they left?"

Matt shook his head. "We tried, but people were fairly vague so I'm not sure it helps."

He slid the list across the table to me and I read through it again. "Anyone on here related to Jolene Paige? A son, daughter, grandson, granddaughter?"

Both Matt and Officer Clark shook their heads.

"Okay….What about…Who on this list is a woman who is attractive enough that Luke would open the door if she came back after the party, and who might also have enough experience with a knife to know how to knife someone in the kidney?"

Matt nodded. "That's a good angle. Let's see." He took the list back from me and he and Officer Clark debated over it, marking the names with little stars for the attractive women and little exes for the ones that probably knew how to use a knife. At one point Officer Clark left the room to ask Marlene about the names, because neither he nor Matt could remember what a few of the women looked like.

They were then able to eliminate most of the names because they had alibis for one or both of the murders which left us with two names: Trinity Jessup and Nicole Grant.

"Those sound familiar," I said. "I think both of their grandmothers were at that Ladies' Auxiliary meeting. Which means they're very likely going to be at the library fundraiser."

Matt, because he knew me too well, said, "Maggie."

"What? Are you telling me they're suspect enough that you can bring them in right now?"

Matt and Officer Clark looked at each other and both shook their heads.

"So let me do what I do best, which is pry information out of people I barely know."

Matt laughed. "Is that what you do best?"

"Matthew Allen Barnes, don't start with me."

Officer Clark leaned back in his chair and muttered, "Still don't see why you married her…"

"I am right here," I snapped. "And for the record, I've met your wife and I don't know how such a sweet, adorable woman found you to be all that. So pot, kettle, back off." I turned my attention to Matt. "Now, do you guys want my help or not?"

"Do we have a choice?" he asked.

"You could solve the murder before the event tomorrow. Then I'd have no reason to try to chat these ladies up."

"Maggie. Be nice."

"Sorry. I was just stating facts. If you solve the murder before tomorrow then there's no reason for me to talk to them. But if it's still open then I will feel compelled to do what I can to close the loop. Because if it doesn't get closed I will be thinking about these stupid murders somewhere in the back of my mind for the rest of my frickin' life. And I don't know about you, Officer Barnes, but I'd rather not have Lucas Dean and his short shorts lurking in the back of my mind for the next fifty years."

"If you put it that way. But I should be there with you. Just in case."

"Oh, hadn't I told you? You were already going to be there. I signed you up for the dunk tank."

"The dunk tank." He didn't sound excited by that possibility.

I shrugged. "They decided not to have a kissing booth this year. Not to mention, had someone actually tried to kiss you I might've had an issue with that, even if it was for charity."

"So instead you signed me up to be dunked in water."

"Well, it has been a year for unhappiness with cops. We figured it might be a big money-earner. And I knew you'd step up and do your part for the library. For Lesley. For my grandpa. And for me."

"Maggie May."

I turned to Officer Clark. "Of course, if Officer Clark here would like to volunteer in your stead…"

"If I volunteer your grandpa will probably throw his arm out trying to dunk me."

"Exactly. Think of all the money that will make for the library." I smiled and batted my eyes at him before glancing away so Matt could silently beg Officer Clark to take his place without losing face with me.

After a moment or two, Officer Clark grunted. "Fine. I'll do it. I'll sit in the dunk tank so Matt can help you interview our potential suspects."

"Thank you," I said, sincerely. "You know, I'm starting to think you're not so bad after all."

He didn't say anything, just glared at me.

"Well, better get going." I flashed both Matt and Officer Clark a grin, lingering on Officer Clark as I added, "I do have a coffee cake to make for the bake sale portion after all. Us married ladies have to keep ourselves busy somehow. Don't want to poke our noses into men's business after all."

(That part was not so sincere.)

Matt stood to escort me outside. "I'd suggest you don't eat a slice if she says she made you one special." He patted Officer Clark on the shoulder before opening the door for me.

As we walked down the hall, I said, "Hey, now. Just because I was slightly miffed that he seemed to imply I should stay home like a good little housewife, does not mean I would bake him a cake with laxatives in it."

"But you thought about it."

"For a second. Maybe two. But I'd never do it."

He kissed my forehead as we stopped outside the entrance. "It's a good thing there are no actual thought police in this world, Maggie, or I'd have to arrest you once a week for attempted murder."

"Once a week? Try once a day. Try once an hour if I drift too close to Twitter. Or the news. Ugh."

He chuckled and pulled me close. "I am so glad I

found you."

"So am I. Because you would've been able to find some cute little Suzie Homemaker with a perky ponytail who bounced when she walked and never said a mean word to anyone, but I would've ended up a lonely spinster if I'd never met you."

I gave him a quick kiss and headed home. Fancy was not going to be amused that I'd left her alone even if it had been for just an hour.

CHAPTER 31

The coffee cake did not go to plan. That's because I was using the recipe off my mom's old Bisquick can and I somehow started making pancakes instead of coffee cake. Don't ask me how I made that mix up, but fortunately I noticed my error before I added any of the wet ingredients. So I was able to sort of scoop out the excess ingredients that didn't belong in a coffee cake and add in the ones that did.

Surprisingly, it turned out tasty enough that three different people asked me for the recipe at the bake sale. Unfortunately, "start making pancakes and transform it into a coffee cake when you realize you've messed up" is not a recipe most people can follow easily, so instead I just played coy and told them it was an old family recipe I couldn't share.

Matt, who knew the truth, gave me a look the first time I said that, but I ignored him. In a sense it *was* an old family recipe—my mom used to make us coffee cake sometimes in the winter for dessert using that very recipe— and I also couldn't share it because I had no clue what I'd actually done to create that particular coffee cake.

I wasn't lying, I just wasn't telling them the full truth. What was so wrong about that?

After the coffee cake discussions I decided it was time to get down to business, but I wasn't sure where to find Trinity Jessup or Nicole Grant.

Fortunately, I knew exactly who to ask: Patrice Cole and Jolene Paige were clustered together in the corner exchanging whispered comments as they picked at their tiny little plates of food. If anyone knew the scoop, it would be them.

"Patrice. Jolene. How are you?" I asked, dragging Matt along with me. "Have you met my husband, Matt?"

Patrice answered for both of them. "I don't believe I ever have. Officer Barnes, a pleasure."

She extended her scarecrow hand in his direction and Matt took it and bowed slightly. "The pleasure is all mine."

(I'd warned him in advance not to say anything about my impromptu tour of Agnes Rockmorton's house. He was as good as his word, chatting casually about the fundraiser and how he was glad to not be in the dunk tank after all.)

Just as he said that we heard a loud splash and I looked over to see my grandpa grinning wickedly as he watched Officer Clark flounder around trying to get himself back on the little dunk platform.

"Aww, look at that. Grandpa's having fun," I said.

Jolene leaned close. "Does he have something against Officer Clark? That's the third time he's dunked him."

"Come now, Jolene. Don't tell me you don't know the full details behind the murder of Jack Dunner? You are far too informed a woman for me to believe that."

"Well, one does hear things. And I guess being arrested for a murder you didn't commit does tend to create some negative feelings, but I thought they'd moved past that."

"Mmm, maybe after today. Speaking of knowing things, tell me, do you know where I can find Trinity Jessup?"

"Trinity? She's right over there in the green dress. Lovely girl. And due any day now which is both exciting and scary in these times."

Sure enough, Trinity Jessup was sporting one very large baby bump. I figured I could rule her out as the killer. I mean, it wasn't *inconceivable* that a forty-weeks-pregnant woman could kill a man with a knife, but it was highly unlikely. Especially since we were assuming that whoever the killer was she'd gone back to Luke's after the party ended and he'd let her in expecting certain things to happen.

Luke was a sleaze, but I wasn't sure he was that much of a sleaze.

"Good for her," I said, mentally dropping her off my list.

"Speaking of babies," Patrice leaned in. "What about you two? You've been married a few months now. Are you pregnant yet?"

Just because we'd been married a few months did not mean we were going to start popping out kids like Tic Tacs. Although a disconcerting number of people seemed to think that's how it did or should work. And even if we were, that did not mean it was some random old woman's business. Didn't she realize that some people have trouble conceiving? And that maybe it's a little sensitive to ask about that sort of thing?

"You know," I answered, squeezing Matt's hand. "There's a lot of uncertainty going around these days, so we're taking our time with that."

"Dear, there's always uncertainty. There will never be a right time to have a kid, you just have to dive in there and do it. Like your friend Jamie did. Look at her. She's glowing with happiness."

And she was. This time in a bright pink dress that accented her adorable bump. I gave her a quick wave and turned back to the ladies, forcing myself to continue to smile and not run from the room.

There had actually been a point where I had this crazy notion that I might have a kid on my own and I'd floated the idea by a handful of mothers I knew. Literally every mother I spoke to with kids under the age of five told me not to do it, and every mother I spoke to with grown children told me it was absolutely worth doing no matter what.

Matt may have changed things—it's theoretically easier with two parents, assuming they're both equal participants—but not that much. Those mothers with young children I'd talked to had all been married and some of them had even had live-in help to go along with it and still there had been a definite trend of "this will cost a few years of your life" in the answers they gave me.

(Two had even told me to never have kids. Ever.)

So, no. Not falling for that one just yet. And we were getting away from the point, which was to find Lucas Dean's killer.

"What about Nicole Grant? Is she here?"

"Nicole…She may be. I don't see her right now." Jolene craned her neck to look around the crowd.

"What does she look like?"

"You know. Average height. Brown hair. Oh, there she is. With her girlfriend. Who is a lovely woman it turns out despite the short hair."

I looked to where she'd pointed and saw two women standing together talking to a young man I also didn't recognize. One was a striking brunette with a gorgeous mane of hair, the other was an average-looking redheaded woman with her hair cut short above the ears.

"So Nicole is the one on the left with the longer hair then?"

"Yes. Exactly."

I pressed my lips together, trying to figure out how to ask the question I needed to ask without sounding like a horrible person. "You know, I believe Nicole was at Lucas Dean's party the night he was killed. Was there ever anything between them?"

"You mean romantic?" Patrice asked with a titter. "Oh no. Nicole has always known what she liked and it was not…men. None of us were surprised when she returned from living in the city for a few years with her friend there. And those two are joined at the hip. If Nicole was at that party, Nat was too."

"Do you want me to introduce you?" Jolene asked.

"Oh no. That's fine. I'm sure I'll meet them later." I tried not to frown. Once more we were back at square one.

"Oh. Look who just waltzed in. Speaking of babies." Jolene nodded knowingly at Patrice.

"Such a surprise, wasn't it?" Patrice nodded back.

"What surprise was that?" I asked.

"Well, I hate to be a gossip," Jolene said, leaning in close. "But it was all quite sudden, wasn't it?"

"Most definitely," Patrice agreed.

"At least Carl stepped up and did the right thing."

"Mmhm," Patrice agreed again.

"Ladies? What are you talking about?" I asked.

Jolene placed her hand on my arm as she leaned in. "Addison West and Carl Rockmorton got married on Wednesday. Must be thirty years between them. He's just turned sixty and she can't be more than mid-30's. Didn't even know they were dating to be honest. And here suddenly they're married. And you just know what had to be behind that. Rushing to the altar. Only one reason to do that sort of thing."

I raised my eyebrows since I'd married Matt the day he proposed to me. "Not really."

"Of course, dear." She patted my hand. "Sometimes you just leave it all too late and can't wait out the niceties."

Matt, probably knowing that I was a step away from throttling her, put his arm around my shoulder and gave me a quick kiss on the cheek. "And sometimes you don't see the reason to wait on arbitrary timelines to start your forever with the woman you love. I know that was the case for me."

Both of the ladies gazed at him with slightly rapt expressions.

"Well, then," I said, taking the slim window of opportunity he'd presented. "We better get going. I think someone needs to stop my grandpa before he throws out his shoulder. Lovely talking to you."

"And you too, dear."

Somehow I managed to keep the fake smile on my face until I was far enough away to prevent anyone noticing the fire in my eyes.

CHAPTER 32

As we approached the dunk tank, my grandpa stood in front of it moving his shoulder around like it pained him.

"Honestly, Grandpa, enough. How many times have you dunked the man?"

"I lost count at five."

"Seven," Officer Clark called.

"You are going to need to ice that tonight and you'll be lucky if you aren't walking around with pain in that shoulder for the next week. Serves you right, really. You made your point, leave poor Officer Clark alone. Plus, we need him."

"You do?" Officer Clark asked from where he sat on the platform.

"We do. Come on. Let's give this a break."

My grandpa grumbled under his breath, but he let us lead Officer Clark off to the side.

Once the three of us were alone, Matt gave him a quick rundown on our suspects. And then added, "We learned something else interesting, though."

"What's that?" Officer Clark asked.

"Addison West and Carl Rockmorton got married on

Wednesday. Unexpectedly. Maggie's friends thought it was because she was pregnant."

"But that can't be. Because…"

Matt nodded.

I looked back and forth between the two of them. "Does this have anything to do with you coming home in a pair of sweatpants the other night?"

He nodded again as all three of us looked over to where the young woman—an attractive blonde with ample curves—was hanging off of the arm of an older, slightly rumpled man. They were not an obvious couple.

"Is he rich?" I asked.

Officer Clark laughed. "No. But he is the only living child of Agnes Rockmorton and therefore likely to inherit everything she had—including perhaps a winning lottery ticket."

"So she's our killer, then," I said. "She found out about the lottery ticket, killed Luke so he wouldn't get half, then killed Agnes so that Carl would inherit the lottery winnings, and then seduced Carl into marrying her so she could get the money."

Matt scratched his chin as he thought about it. "That's a pretty elaborate way to earn yourself a million dollars."

"How else was she going to do it? Not like most people will see that kind of money in a lifetime. I figure opportunity presented itself and she struck."

"I don't know. It seems pretty convoluted to me. Why didn't she just take the ticket?"

"If it was already signed, she couldn't. And if Agnes Rockmorton turns up dead and then Addison West walks in with her lottery ticket—and not just random numbers, but ones Agnes played year in and year out—there'd be a lot of questions. But if Agnes Rockmorton dies and her son happens to find a winning lottery ticket in her house while going through her things, then it all seems reasonable. And if he happens to be married at that point, well then his wife shares in his good fortune and isn't she lucky."

Officer Clark frowned at them. "Why kill Luke?"

"So he couldn't tell on her? Plus, Luke had to die first so all the money would go to Agnes. I mean, maybe that wouldn't hold up in a court of law, but it's how I'd think about it in the moment. Two people have equal interests in the ticket but haven't cashed it in yet, one dies, their interest passes to the other."

Officer Clark and Matt looked at each other. "Worth a conversation," Officer Clark said.

Matt nodded. "Definitely. But we'll do it Monday. In the meantime…" He turned to me. "I think it's only fair that you take your turn in the dunk tank, too."

"Matt! You're my husband, you're supposed to protect me."

"It's for a good cause," he grinned at me, a wicked glint in his eye.

"But…"

"You volunteered me for it."

"Well, yes, but. *Matt.*"

He just looked at me with those oh-so-blue eyes until I finally broke. "Fine. Fine, fine, fine. I will sit in the dunk tank. Probably nobody here that will even want to dunk me anyway."

Officer Clark laughed. "Are you kidding? I'm going to be first in line."

And he was. Followed by Jack and Mason and Johnny Duffy and a few other people I may have ruffled along the way. Even Jamie tried to dunk me!

Good news, most of them had horrible aim, but I did definitely take a dunking or two, which is how I managed to convince Matt that I had every right to be in the observation room when they interviewed Carl Rockmorton and Addison West on Monday.

One thing I've learned about marriage: guilt can be a wonderful tool for getting what you want.

CHAPTER 33

I spent the rest of the weekend unable to sit still because Monday we were finally going to prove who had murdered Luke and Agnes and I couldn't wait.

(Yes, I realize that my excitement over solving the deaths of two human beings was probably not something anyone would consider healthy, but, hey, it takes all types. And if there weren't people like me who got excited about finding murderers, think how many more would go uncaught. Other people can get their thrills from watching football, I get my thrills out of solving things, in this case a double-murder.)

Of course, the reality of police work and the fantasy of police work are two entirely different things. And Carl Rockmorton was, well, to put it politely, a very, very, very boring individual. He had pretty green eyes, I'll give him that, but it was like he had no emotional range at all. Every sentence was delivered in the exact same monotone voice.

There he was, talking about his new, attractive, much younger wife and he could've been talking about car parts for all the emotion he showed. (He owned a local store that carried a variety of automotive and machine parts.)

I won't force you to suffer through the experience of his entire interview. (Because quite frankly I don't want to suffer through describing it. Living it once was enough.) But the gist was that he'd unexpectedly met Addison West when she came into his shop looking for a new gas cap for her car. No one else was in the store so they'd started talking and she'd stuck around and one thing had led to another and they had dinner which led to other things which led to her suggesting that they should get married because why wait when things were so perfect.

And him, being an older, awkward man who'd written off ever meeting anyone, let alone a buxom younger woman, didn't see why not. Not like he had anything of value for her to take. And he figured why not get what he could while the getting was good. Stranger things had happened and he wasn't about to look at that particular gift horse too closely.

Upon further questioning it came out that they had met the day after Luke was killed, so before Agnes was killed.

That put an interesting twist on things until Matt pushed even more and found out that Carl had introduced Addison to his mother just two days later. And that they'd gone to Agnes's house for dinner and Carl had caught Addison in his mother's office when she'd said she was going to the restroom.

And then surprise, surprise, the next night someone had killed Agnes.

It wasn't too much of a stretch to think that Addison had initially slept with Carl to get access to his mother's house with the idea of just stealing the lottery ticket. But when she found it, Agnes must have already signed it, so she had to go to Plan B.

Having already met Agnes, Addison must have gone back the next night with some flimsy excuse or the other and killed her. And then all that was left was to convince Carl to marry her before he found out about the lottery ticket.

It sounded good. Nice and plausible. A believable story about a younger woman manipulating an older, gullible man who didn't even know it had happened.

But something wasn't quite right with the way Carl told his story. It was subtle, but it was there. When Matt didn't quite ask the question that would bring out some critical little detail, Carl found a way to slip it in. It was like he had a mental checklist of things he needed the cops to hear and he couldn't bring himself to deviate from it.

I had a strong suspicion that Matt could wait two weeks, bring Carl back in for another round of questioning, and every single little detail would be the exact same. Because the story Carl was telling was just that, a story. He wasn't remembering events, he was creating them.

Matt, because he's a brilliant, insightful man who is amazing at his job, (why no, I am not biased at all, thank you very much) knew it, too. Instead of ending the interview, he sat back in his chair and studied Carl for a long moment. And then he looked at the mirror where he knew I was and a small smile stretched his lips. Not enough of one to give things away to Carl, but enough of one to let me know that he'd seen it too.

"Well, thank you, Carl. I really appreciate it." He held out his hand and shook Carl's like they were just the best of friends now. "We'll talk to Addison next and then the two of you can be back on your way home. So sorry for the bother."

"My pleasure, Officer Barnes. Always happy to help." As Matt led him out the door I caught one quick glance of Carl Rockmorton's face as it was turned away and the smug little grin he allowed himself before returning to the bovine-like look he'd adopted for the cops.

CHAPTER 34

Just to be sure, before Matt started his interview with Addison I waved him into the observation room.

"You saw it, right? You know he's lying?" I asked.

He nodded. "But I'm not sure how to prove it."

"I have an idea. See, I think we were wrong about the timeline. We thought that Addison found out about the lottery ticket when she went to Luke's house that night. But Luke hadn't even told Trish and supposedly they were really, really close. So why would he tell Addison?"

"He wouldn't."

"Exactly. Luke was keeping it secret. But what if *Carl* told Addison? Before the party. What if she went to the party to find the lottery ticket not to kill Luke? What if killing Luke was just a mistake? Or unplanned?"

Matt rubbed his jaw thoughtfully. "So you're thinking Carl and Addison were working together before the party?"

I nodded.

"And that he sent her in to steal the lottery ticket?"

"Right. But she didn't find it. Or maybe she did. I don't know. But he's in on this somehow." I looked at

Addison where she sat in the interview room, looking nervous, her perfectly-manicured nails drumming on the table.

Matt leaned against the window sill, studying her. "But there's no sign anyone else was there when Luke was killed other than the murderer. And I can't see him opening his door to Carl Rockmorton. Addison has to have been the one who killed Luke. We still don't know how she learned to stab someone in the kidney."

"I have an idea about that one. Jamie texted me this morning and asked if I would be up for taking self-defense classes after she has the baby. There's an ex-Army Ranger offering them and on his website he talks about kidney strikes." I showed him the website on my phone. "What if Addison took his class?"

"That would make sense. Okay. So I need to get her on the record that she took that self-defense class and learned about kidney strikes, and then I need her to admit she knew Carl before she went to that party at Luke's."

"What you really need is a confession."

He nodded. "I know. But all I can do is try to get what I can."

"If anyone can do it, you can." I gave him a quick kiss and pushed him towards the door, eager to see how he was going to pull it off. Because I knew he would.

(Yes, I do have an unwavering faith in my husband. Because he has earned it.)

CHAPTER 35

Matt started off friendly. "Addison, thank you so much for coming to see me today. I hate to bring you in here like this, but you have to understand that we need to cross all those t's and dot all those i's. And since you did just suddenly marry the man who's going to inherit from my murder victim, I needed to talk to you. You understand, don't you?"

"Of course, Officer Barnes." She batted her eyes at him and I glared at her through the window. "I'm happy to talk to you. Whatever you need." She leaned forward, smiling, her low-cut top showing off her available assets.

"That's great. Thank you so much. You graduated from Baker Valley High didn't you?"

"I did. But unfortunately I was a little young to be there when you were. Not that I didn't go to watch your football games when I was in middle school, of course," she simpered before adding, "I was kind of sad to hear you'd gotten married this year."

I glared at her through the glass. Laying it on a bit thick, wasn't she? Of course, I had every faith that Matt knew how to play her right back.

He smiled at her, all warm and charming. "Well, when you know it's right, you know it's right. Was that how it was with you and Carl?"

"Oh, absolutely. I knew from the moment I saw him that my little Carl Bear was the one for me."

"How'd you meet? At work? Maggie and I met when I went to interview her for a murder investigation."

"Carl and I were the same. I went looking for a replacement gas cap and he and I got to talking and…I don't know. We just had so much in common."

Yeah, being murderous greedy psychos.

"When was that?" Matt asked.

"Gosh. The day after Luke's Fourth of July party, must've been? 'Cause I hadn't heard about Luke yet when I met Carl, but I know I hadn't met Carl at the time of the party because Luke and I were flirting a bit and I would've never done that if I'd already met my Carl Bear. We've been inseparable since we met."

"So you'd never met Carl before that day?" Matt asked, his tone suggesting that he knew she was lying to him even though I knew it was a bluff.

"Um." She tilted her head to the side. It was clear she wanted to say no, but she didn't quite have the guts to do it.

"Small town. Wouldn't be surprised if you had," Matt nudged. "You know, like me and football."

"Well, actually, I mean…" She tilted her head to the other side, smiling slightly, trying to be coy. "I guess that's why we knew so fast that we were meant for one another. Because we had met a while back. Even gone out a few times."

"Really? How'd you meet initially?"

She chewed on her lower lip. I'm sure it was supposed to

be adorable, but it came off as nervous. "Ahhh…Online. One of those dating sites."

"Not a lot of local choices on those sites, is there?" Matt asked sympathetically, like he'd ever actually had to use one. The minute he came home every mother in the county with a halfway eligible daughter tried to set him up. "Which one did you meet on?"

"Sugar.ex."

"Sugar.ex? I've never heard of that one. Give me a second, let me pull it up."

She reached out and put her hand over Matt's. "No need. Really. It's, um…" She blushed and looked away. "It's a sugar daddy website? I wouldn't normally date an older guy like that unless, you know, he had something going for him?"

"Ah. A site for older guys with money and younger women?"

She nodded.

"So you thought Carl was wealthy when you met him?"

"He said he owned his own business and all. And the pictures he posted made it look that way."

"But you found out he isn't wealthy. And you ended it?"

She bit her lip again. "Basically."

"But now you're back together. And you even married him."

She nodded.

"What changed?"

She froze, realizing she'd probably made a mistake, but not quite sure what that mistake was.

"Does Carl have money now?"

She nodded again.

"How? Is he selling the business?" Matt asked.

"Mmhm."

"Why?"

"We thought we'd move. Find somewhere new to settle down. A fresh start."

Matt rubbed at his chin, leaning back. "I didn't realize Carl's business would sell for all that much. Masonville Tire has been for sale for a year and I don't think he's had an offer yet. You sure Carl isn't putting one over on you?"

Addison ran her hand through her hair, agitated. "He's not. He has money now. He will."

Matt shook his head. "Hate to break it to you, Addison, but he's probably not going to have anything left after the sale of his business. He played you."

"No he didn't."

"I'm afraid he did."

"No. He didn't. I…" She pressed her lips together, no longer even pretending to flirt with Matt in her agitation. "Look. We weren't going to tell anyone about it because you know how weird people can be when it comes to money, but it turns out Carl's mom had won the lottery right before she died. He found the ticket going through her things."

"And that's why you got back together? Because now he's going to be worth something?"

"You make it sound so horrible. I liked the guy when I met him. I did. But I don't want to be broke my whole life, living in some little town in the backend of nowhere. I needed someone who had prospects." She crossed her arms and leaned back in her chair, pouting.

"And Carl now has those."

"Exactly."

"And you found that out when you went into his shop for a replacement gas cap?"

She nodded.

"What day was that again?"

"I told you, the day after Luke's party."

"So Carl told you he was going to come into a bunch of money because of a lottery ticket the day after Luke's party."

"Yes! That's what I keep telling you."

Matt leaned forward, his gaze intense. I knew that look. I had been on the receiving end of that look. It was like having one of those bright lights they use to interrogate spies shining in your face. "Here's the problem with what you just told me, Addison. That means that Carl was planning on that money being his before his mother was even dead. Which means he told you he was planning to murder her."

"No. What are you talking about? That's not what happened? I had the dates wrong. I must've met him after his mother died."

"That's not what he said in his interview. He agreed that you met the day after Luke died."

"I want to see him. I want to talk to Carl."

"Carl can't help you now, Addison. He has his own problems." Matt was all tough-nosed investigator now. I loved it.

"I want to see him." Her voice quavered, but her eyes were completely dry as she stared at Matt.

It was all just an act and Matt knew it. "No." He leaned forward. "Let me tell you what I think happened, Addison."

She crossed her arms and glared off to the side as he continued.

"I think you met Carl on that website, Sugar.ex, and he told you he was wealthy. Maybe you hit it off. Maybe you thought this was a guy you could like, assuming he really was as wealthy as he said. But then you found out the truth. That he didn't have any money. And you ended things. But then he contacted you. Or maybe you crossed paths at just the right moment. *Before* Luke's party."

Her eye twitched.

"He told you he had a way for you to be together. That if you'd just help him he could give you millions. He told you about the lottery ticket. That his mother and Luke were going to split the proceeds. He asked you to help him get that money. For the two of you. So you could be together."

She continued to glare off to the side, but her leg twitched under the table with each word Matt spoke.

"I bet if I look into your history I'm going to find a self-defense class. One that teaches kidney punches as a way to incapacitate an opponent fast. Am I right?"

A tear fell down her cheek. Finally, some real emotion.

"So what happened? You went to Luke's to kill him?"

"No! That wasn't…"

"The plan?"

She pressed her lips together and stared at Matt, clearly longing to say more, but not doing so.

He switched back to the soft, kind approach he'd started with. "Tell me what happened, Addison. I'll do what I can to help you." He reached across the table and squeezed her hand with his, keeping his attention focused completely on her, willing her to trust him. "I know you didn't want this. I know that's why you took those pills. You felt guilty for what you'd done. Tell me what happened and I'll help you as much as I can."

That finally broke her. She started to cry as she told Matt the truth. "I ran into Carl at the shop a few days before Luke's party. I don't know why I went there. I could've ordered that stupid gas cap online. But maybe I wanted to see him. I'd just broken up with some guy who was a total jerk and Carl had been nice to me. We started talking. And he told me about the lottery ticket and how he could finally give me everything I deserved. He said we just had to wait. His mom was elderly and frail. It would only be a matter of time. A few months? A year or two?"

"But…"

"But he said Lucas Dean had helped her buy the ticket and that she was going to give Luke half just for running to the store for her. That was money that could be ours. And she was just going to give it away to Luke. For what? Ten minutes of effort. He didn't deserve that. Carl said he'd tried to talk her out of it and she laughed at him. Said if he was a better son to her then he could've had it all."

"And then what happened?"

"I told him he should talk to Luke. Ask him to let go of his share. He'd understand."

(Yeah, right. Luke would've given up almost a million dollars because someone asked him to? No.)

"And? Then what happened?" Matt asked.

"We started hanging out. Carl and I. It was just a couple days. And then the day of that party I came home from work and he said he'd tried to talk to Luke. Said he went by Luke's and laid it all out for him. You know, how he was taking advantage of the generosity of an old woman who didn't know any better. But he said Luke just laughed. And said he had far better plans for the money than Agnes did. He said Agnes was going to donate half of her share to the Valley Fund. She wasn't even going to keep it. And if Luke gave up his share to her she'd just donate all of that to the Valley Fund, too." Addison looked at Matt, wide-eyed in disbelief as she recounted what Agnes had planned for the money.

He nodded sympathetically, keeping his gaze fixed on her. "What did you do next?"

She sank further into her seat. "I was…I was drunk. I'd been bartending and sometimes the guys like to buy me a shot, you know? I get better tips that way. And I just…When Carl told me what Luke had said, I got so mad. We were so close and now it was all just slipping away."

"So you went over to see Luke."

She rubbed her hands through her hair and then nodded. "I don't know what I was thinking. I had some notion I'd sleep with him and somehow convince him to give up his half of the ticket. Or…" She looked down at the table.

"Share it with you? Did you offer to leave Carl for him?"

She nodded, chewing on her lip.

"And? What did he say?"

She sighed as if her whole body was deflating. "Luke let me in, offered me a drink. We had a bit of a history, so he wasn't completely surprised I was there that night.

I told him I'd heard he'd hit the jackpot and suggested he take me along. But he laughed at me. Said he already knew who he wanted to take with him and it wasn't some…" She sniffed back tears. "It wasn't some middle-aged washed out drunk. Told me nice try and to see myself out the door because he wasn't even interested in one last, you know."

"That's when you killed him."

She buried her face in her hands and sobbed, nodding her head in answer to his question.

"What about Agnes? Why did you kill her?"

She still had her face buried in her hands, so her answer came out mumbled, but it sounded like she said, "I didn't."

Matt reached across the table and gently tilted her head up.

"I couldn't hear you, Addison. What did you say?"

She sniffed back more tears. "I said I didn't kill Agnes, Carl did."

CHAPTER 36

According to Addison, she returned to Carl that night, freaking out about what she'd done, wanting to go to the cops and tell them. But Carl calmed her down and said it was all for the best. And then to show her that they were in this together he killed his mother.

He had Addison walk him through how she'd stabbed Luke so that he could use the same method. It took a couple days of practice before he was confident he could stab at the same angle that Addison had used.

The next night he waited until Patrice and her husband went to bed—which was sometime around eight-thirty—and then knocked on his mother's door claiming an emergency. When she let him in he killed her and took the lottery ticket.

To cement the deal Addison and Carl got married. The plan was to wait a couple more months before claiming to have found the ticket while organizing Agnes's papers.

Since they'd each killed someone, they were even, bound at the hip for eternity.

"Why tell me all this?" Matt asked when she'd finally

run dry and was just sitting there, slumped in her chair. "You could've gotten away with it."

She shook her head. "I killed Luke in a moment of anger. I'd offered myself to him and he just laughed at me. But Carl…He was meticulous in killing his mom. Cold. He practiced for hours before he went over there."

She shuddered and rubbed at her arms as if chilled. "If I left here with him today, it would only be a matter of time before he decided to kill me, too. I figured it was better to be alive in prison, than dead."

I almost felt sorry for her. Almost. Until I remembered that she'd killed a guy because he didn't want to sleep with her and was rude about it and then helped a man kill his mother.

🐾 🐾 🐾

Carl, of course, refused to confess to his role in any of it. He called her crazy and screamed and ranted. But when they seized his computer they found internet searches on kidney strikes from before the date of his mother's murder. And there was a receipt showing that the date he and Addison reconnected was three days before Luke's party not the day after.

Also, good old Jolene and Patrice were happy to volunteer story after story of the horrible way that Agnes treated her son and how he was a little terror in the making. By the time they were done there was no doubt that Carl had built up years of hatred at his mother's cruel treatment and that he was more than capable of the killing.

🐾 🐾 🐾

I was overjoyed that we'd solved the case, but I couldn't take credit for it. I'd definitely played a part—there's no doubt that my information helped move things along. But it was Matt who was the hero of the day. I don't think ninety-nine cops in a hundred could've gotten that confession out of Addison.

I was so proud of him. And I made sure he knew it. Because that, too, is part of being a good wife.

And one of the few parts that I have no trouble fulfilling. My husband is the best. I wouldn't have married him otherwise.

EPILOGUE

On a gorgeous early August day I found myself at one of the most bizarre womanly rituals that exists on this planet: the baby shower.

Fortunately, Jamie had excused me from all future friend event planning duties after I'd miraculously saved her wedding day so all I had to do was attend. But it was like stepping into an alternate reality. A reality where every woman but me had either a baby bump or a child cuddled in her arms. There was even a woman breastfeeding right there out in the open for all the world to see, for crying out loud.

Not that there was a huge world to see it. Jamie's mom had set the whole thing up in her backyard and there were maybe twenty of us there. But still. I did not need to see that wonderful act of nature, thank you very much. Just like I don't need to see other acts of nature. Pee, have sex, and breastfeed in privacy, please.

The whole backyard was decorated with stork-themed streamers and balloons and table cloths. It was like someone had vomited pastel colors all over the place.

And there were games. *Baby-themed* games. Like Bingo with squares for pacifiers and strollers and teddy bears.

That one I at least had a chance to win. (Although the prize was not a bottle of gin, sadly. It was a koala bib.) But the baby trivia? Oh no. There were literally women shouting over each other with the answers to the average length of labor and average new baby weight.

I suffered through, though, because this was my best friend we were talking about. But I finally hit my limit when a woman passed me what looked like a dirty diaper and asked me to smell it.

Turns out the brown substance in the diaper was melted chocolate and I was supposed to guess what kind it was. But no. No. No, no, no. You do not do that to chocolate. Especially not a *Krackel* bar.

I slunk off and stood at the edge of the crowd wishing I'd spiked my Coke with rum before I left the house.

Jamie found me there. She looked radiant in bright blue overalls over a yellow t-shirt. "Thank you for coming."

"I wouldn't have missed it for the world, you know that. I'm so happy for you." I gave her a quick hug.

She laughed. "I know you better than that, Maggie. This is the absolute last place you want to be."

"But I'm here for you. And I am happy for you. So happy for you. Just please, don't ever expect me to build you a diaper cake. That thing is…"

I glanced over to the side where there was a four-tiered "cake" made completely out of diapers and decorated with little baby toys. Whoever had taken the time to make that needed new hobbies.

(Look, don't get me wrong. I know some women love all of that baby stuff. I've seen them, I've met them. And if you are one of those women, good for you. But if you're not one of those women it's kind of like being surrounded by some baby-craving version of the Stepford Wives. You really are just waiting for someone to sneak you into a back room, knock you out, and inject you with a solution that makes you wake up yearning for a child or, better yet, ten of them.)

Jamie laughed. "It is impressive, isn't it? Maybe we can find a way to create a dog version for the barkery when it reopens. What do you think? Training pads and puppy toys?"

I tilted my head to the side as I studied it. "Actually, that's a really good idea. We could put a few stuffed animals around the base and a few chew toys on the upper tiers…Or dog treats. Ooh! Dog treats would work really well, wouldn't they?"

She grinned at me and I grinned back.

"You're going to have one mocked up before the week is out, aren't you?" she asked.

"Don't you know it. Speaking of, how's the ice cream project coming along?"

"Excellent. I made a pistachio cranberry caramel crunch ice cream that is to die for. You will love it."

As we stood there discussing Jamie's pregnancy-induced ice cream flavors and brainstormed more, I realized that I really, really was happy for her. She was going to be the best mother in the world, I just knew it.

And me? I was going to be the best adoptive aunt who drops by for short periods of time, never holds the baby until it reaches the non-breakable stage, and never, ever changes a diaper. (Because real diapers are not filled with melted chocolate, thank you very much.)

But what mattered was that we were both going to be happy in our own ways. (And murder free. Even if I had to kill someone to make that happen.)

A SALACIOUS SCANDAL
AND STEAK SIZZLERS

A MAGGIE MAY AND MISS FANCYPANTS MYSTERY

ALEKSA BAXTER

CHAPTER 1

I was snuggled up on the couch, my laptop balanced on my lap, clicking away, when Fancy, my four-year-old Newfoundland, came up to me, her rainbow-colored stuffed unicorn in her mouth, amber eyes sad and pleading.

I knew what that meant. The only time she grabbed one of her toys and brought it to me was when she wanted to go outside. Easy enough for her. She was a-hundred-and-thirty-five pounds of well-insulated black fur who could prance around in three feet of snow without batting an eye.

I, on the other hand…

Even with my more-than-normal padding (because it seems I eat my feelings during stressful events that impact the entire world for months on end), I needed about a dozen layers before I'd even dream of stepping out that front door. Colorado winters are no joke.

"Fancy. I'm working." I nodded at the computer, but she wasn't fooled. She can tell the difference between when I'm actually working and when I've gone down a Twitter/Facebook/email death spiral of doom that never ends.

She continued to stare at me with those big amber eyes of hers, adorable toy dangling from her mouth.

"Fancy…It's cold outside," I pleaded.

She settled in at my feet, never taking her eyes off my face, a small sigh of disappointment huffing out of her mouth as she continued to stare me down.

I glanced at her and then towards the door and then at my computer where I'd spent the last fifteen minutes trying to figure out what someone's weird Twitter apology about not knowing they were supporting someone "harmful" was actually referring to.

One of my "favorite" pastimes on Twitter is Guess the Subtweet. Made especially difficult when there's more than one scandal going on at once, or when the keywords behind the scandal lead to other, more dubious tweets.

(Some of the things I've seen on there when searching for the wrong words…My eyes are scarred for life.)

Fancy didn't care about any of that, she just wanted to go outside. She continued to stare me down as I frantically tried to find that one, last tweet that would clue me in.

I was so close.

But what mattered more? My adorable dog, or knowing what random person out there in the universe was considered bad this week?

"Fine," I said as I dumped my computer on the end table. "You're right. I'm sorry. You are far more important than figuring out who said what about something I really don't even care about just because some random person I don't know on the internet definitely does care about it but apparently not enough to actually just come right out and name names. Okay, let's go for a walk."

She jumped to her feet and ran down the hall to my room, waiting for me to catch up because she knew there was a whole process that needed to happen next.

See, it's easy for a Newfoundland to get ready for a walk, even in winter. All Fancy had to do was grab her favorite toy and wait by the door for me to put her collar on.

But me? In the mountains of Colorado? In November? After three inches of snow had fallen the night before? It was a *process*.

First came the long underwear and the sweat pants. Next came the sweatshirt that went over my t-shirt. Then the incredibly warm Peruvian scarf. Then the winter coat. Then the baseball cap and the ear warmer headband. And don't forget the gloves. *Good* gloves when walking a dog in the winter are key. None of those flimsy knitted things that pretend to be gloves but let your fingers turn to ice after five minutes.

Not to mention good socks. *And* winter boots.

Plus I needed to gather up the usual supplies which were always required when walking Fancy, like a phone to call for help if she decided she wasn't going to go home. (That had only happened once or twice, but it's good to be prepared, especially when the alternative is to wait in freezing temperatures until she's sufficiently enjoyed herself.)

And, of course, the most important part of it all: the treats. The only way I ever manage to get Fancy to do anything I ask her to do is with treats. Because for Fancy treats trump everything. For a treat the size of a dime she'll ignore another dog, a rabbit, a deer, and probably a nuclear holocaust, although I have sincere hopes I'll never have to test that.

More importantly, a treat is just enough distraction to get her turned around and headed towards home instead of continuing in whatever direction we're going.

Because if Fancy had her druthers she'd probably keep walking until she collapsed in the middle of the road. At which point she'd take a nap for a few hours and then get up and keep walking.

So treats were a definite must if I ever wanted to see my home again.

Which I did. Because it was cold outside. And cold is not something I enjoy. Which meant that my living in the Colorado mountains didn't make a whole lot of sense. But it was where my grandpa was. And my pregnant best friend. And the man I'd inadvertently fallen in love with and married.

I was stuck. In a good way. Don't get me wrong. I was happy. Very, very happy. Life was good.

And I loved Fancy. (Still do.) Loved her to death. I just wished I could love her from inside a nice warm house.

But since that wasn't possible I'd bundle up and go out in the snow for her, because she was my world.

(Yes, even more than my new husband, Matt. Although please don't tell him that because he's pretty special, too, and I already worry that he'll wake up one day and realize what an incredible fool he was to marry me at which point he will run away and settle down with someone who is actually nice. And sane.)

Anyway. It took a bit to get out the door, but then Fancy, her rainbow unicorn, and I were on our way, me wrapped in approximately eight zillion layers of clothing that still weren't going to be enough to keep me warm, Fancy in her collar and nothing else.

Off to explore the vast reaches of Creek—a town where the trees outnumbered the people by about a hundred to one.

CHAPTER 2

Honestly, it wasn't that bad once I wrapped the scarf around my face so that only my eyes were showing.

I mean, really, there isn't much in the world that is more breathtaking than the Colorado mountains in winter. The way they reach towards a clear blue sky that's dusted with that perfect amount of fluffy white clouds. And the air (when it isn't freezing your nose hairs, hence the scarf) is so clear and crisp and clean. You can't get that in some big city. (I know. I've tried.)

The mountains are special.

And I had Fancy to thank for letting me experience it. Without her I would have been curled up inside with my computer or a book until spring finally arrived. So not only had she brought me unconditional love, but she'd also brought me sunrises and nature. How cool was that?

We made it a whole four blocks before she finally dropped the unicorn toy in favor of sniffing a bright yellow patch of snow.

At least I managed to rescue it before she stepped forward and peed right where she'd dropped it. I'd learned to move fast over the years. Not her fault really. She just gets distracted by an interesting scent and completely forgets that her toy exists and then goes to pee on the interesting scent without thinking about the fact that she dropped the toy where the scent was in order to better smell it.

And, of course, I enable her by swooping in to grab her toy before she actually pees on it so she never "learns her lesson", which, I mean really, she's a dog. That sort of thing doesn't work well with them anyway.

So.

I had just swooped in and grabbed her toy before she could pee on it when I realized we weren't alone.

There was a very shaggy, large, scary man standing about four feet away from us.

"Hello," he said in a deep voice.

"Hello," I replied with false cheer as I casually looked around to see if there was anyone around, anywhere at all. (There was not.)

I tried not to flinch as he took a step closer, holding out a hand for Fancy to sniff, and I recognized him.

Creek is a small town. Even if you don't know someone, you know them. And the man who I was suddenly very alone with, Owen Browers, was someone my grandma and grandpa had told me to avoid from the time I could first leave the house on my own.

Even before that, really. Because I'd never seen my grandpa talk to the man and you have to understand that my grandpa is an ex-con, so he's not exactly the look-down-on-others type. He's seen rough times and is far more likely to put a hand out to lift someone up than to push them down. So the fact that he avoided this man meant something.

I hadn't actually grown up in Creek so I didn't know precisely what he'd done, I just knew he was the embodiment of Stranger Danger and I was suddenly all alone with him.

Fancy, being Fancy, had proceeded from sniffing his hand to licking his beard, which meant there went my "I have a big scary dog you better back off" plan.

He stood back up and stared at me a little longer than was polite. "You're Maggie May Carver."

"I am."

My instincts were saying "run away screaming" but my polite upbringing was saying "that would be an awfully rude thing to do" especially when I didn't even know what he'd done. Maybe he wasn't a killer. Or a rapist. Maybe he was just some weird man with bad social skills who rubbed people the wrong way.

And maybe there was nothing to the fact that he'd randomly chanced upon me when I was all alone. He could be perfectly harmless.

Yeah, right. That was it.

(I was so dead.)

He took another step closer and I could smell a slight whiff of mustiness like he'd put on clothes that had never quite dried out. Eau de backpacker. "I need your help," he said.

It took everything I had not to step back. "Mine? What for? What can *I* do to help you?"

I mean, I was a former barkery owner and future pet resort owner. Not exactly "help someone" professions. And I was pretty sure he didn't need my consulting skills. He didn't look like the type who needed a hundred-page written report with fifty bullet-pointed items for improvement ranked from essential to nice-to-have.

He crossed his arms and rocked back on his heels. "I want you to investigate the murder of Mary Diever."

Oh, that made more sense. I had sort of solved a handful of murders and found a kid's missing mom. And it had been written up in the local paper so it made sense that he'd know about it. Which meant maybe I was going to survive until dinner. How nice.

"Mary Diever? Who is that?" I tried to think if I'd heard of any murders recently, but drew a blank.

"Mary Diever is the woman everyone thinks I killed thirty-six years ago."

"Oh."

Well, that explained why everyone stayed away from him.

"So you didn't kill her?" I asked.

He stared at me for a long moment, but this time it wasn't the stare of a man with bad social skills. No, it was the stare of a man wondering just how stupid I was. "No. I didn't kill her."

"But then…I mean, thirty-six years. Why now?" (And why stop me in the freezing cold of November to ask about it. I mean, seriously. My toes were turning into little rocks.) "And why me? Why not just ask the cops to take another look?"

He shoved his hands into his pockets. "You know what, forget it. I thought you'd be different, not having grown up here. But, just…" He shook his head and started to turn away.

I knew I was going to regret it, but I'm a sucker for people in need. Even big scary men who could snap me in two with half a thought and who I've been warned are dangerous. (I tell ya, I would've so fallen for Ted Bundy's "help me with these groceries" bit.)

"Wait," I said. "Do you want to come back to the house and tell me what's going on? I have coffee. Or tea."

Yes, it probably wasn't the best idea to invite this strange man that no one trusted back to my house when no one would know that we'd even crossed paths and he could easily murder me and be about his day without anyone noticing.

But I go with my gut. And the more I was around the guy I suspected that he was just one of those people who don't interact with others much and so was really awkward when he did. I didn't get that Ted Little vibe off of him.

Plus, Fancy had laid herself down by his side. She clearly wasn't the least bit concerned about him. And dogs are pretty good judges of character in my experience. At least, if a dog doesn't like someone, you should run. They can sometimes like very flawed people, but I've never seen a situation where a dog didn't like a particular person and was wrong about it.

So, yes, it was a risk to invite him into my home. But I lived next to my grandpa, and a few blocks from the police station where Matt was working, and at least I'd be warm if I was going to be brutally murdered.

Plus I was craving some of that peanut butter fudge I'd made the night before. I'd added a dash of red pepper flakes and they'd really kicked the flavor up a notch.

"Come on." I took a step towards my house, but Fancy stayed where she was lying at his feet. (Such a traitor. I swear she loves any man more than me.)

He pressed his lips together and stared at me intently before nodding. "Okay."

As he followed me back towards the house a little voice in my head told me I was going to regret this decision. But that was the voice that had watched too many true crime dramas. My gut was telling me everything was going to be just fine.

CHAPTER 3

"So what would you like?" I asked as I led him through the front room and into the kitchen. "I have coffee, tea, hot chocolate, Coca-Cola, water, or orange juice. And beer, although it's probably a little early in the day for that one, huh?"

He stood awkwardly in the kitchen doorway, his knit cap in his hands. "Um…"

"Sit. Sit, please." I gestured at the small table in the middle of the kitchen area. "Make yourself at home."

The words rolled off my tongue before I even thought about it. That's just what you say to people who are visiting. Make yourself at home. Be welcome.

But I saw him quiver when the words hit him. He stared down at the floor for a moment, his hands clenching and then unclenching. "Thank you," he mumbled before moving forward and pulling out a chair.

It occurred to me then that if you live in a small town where everyone has decided you're a murderer that it probably limits your social options. No invites to come over for a nice meal. No welcomes into anyone's kitchen.

Maybe the local pastor takes some pity on you, because that's what they do. Or the local thugs. (Because there are always local thugs of one sort or another.) But probably not a lot of good, upstanding citizens reaching out to make you welcome.

So if it turns out you really are a nice guy who's just a bit awkward, what does that life look like? Pretty sad and lonely if I had to guess.

As I brought out the container of fudge from the fridge and turned to prepare myself a cup of hot chocolate, I hoped he wasn't going to turn out to be a murderer after all. It would suck to learn that about him now that I'd put myself in his shoes.

"So? Drink?" I asked, trying to restart the awkward conversation.

"I wouldn't mind a hot chocolate."

"Great. And, please, help yourself to some of that fudge or else I'm likely to eat the whole thing myself."

He glanced at the container which probably had a good forty pieces in it. "You'd eat all of that yourself?"

I tilted my head to the side. "Well, maybe not all of it, today, but probably half of it, yeah. I mean, it's rich, so I really can't eat more than one or two pieces at a time. But it's also really good so I keep going back for more. I'd say working from home is bad for my health, but honestly I was even worse at the barkery. Jamie can cook a mean dessert."

"Oh yeah, I heard about that place. Did you really open a bakery for dogs?"

I smiled. "I did. And we were doing well, too. Until someone decided to tear the building we were renting down. But we'll be reopening next summer as part of a whole pet resort. Assuming the world hasn't burned to the ground by then, of course." I grabbed a piece of fudge and savored its creamy flavor as I contemplated the current messed up state of the world.

He took a piece, too. "Doubt it'll get that bad. People always pull through."

The microwave beeped and I poured hot water over the chocolate powder in our cups and stirred each one before handing him his. "You sound like my grandpa. Always looking on the bright side."

"Not surprising. He's seen some things, too. You either look on the bright side or it takes you down."

(He didn't actually use the word *things*, but I'm trying to keep it polite here. Not that I was bothered by that little s-word. I've used far worse in my time. And he was right, my grandpa really had seen some *things* in his life.)

I settled down at the table and took a long sip of my hot chocolate, savoring how the heat spread through my chest and the cup warmed my hands. "So. Tell me why now? Why me? Why not ask the cops to take another look? Why not just let it go after all these years?"

He stared at his cup, his large hands dwarfing the sturdy ceramic as he cradled it between them. "The cops did reopen the case. They took my DNA yesterday. They're going to send it off to a lab."

I set down the piece of fudge I'd been about to shove in my mouth. "And…"

He sighed and finally looked up at me. "And it's going to match. That's why I need your help."

I smiled nervously. Oh, goodie. I was drinking hot chocolate with a killer.

CHAPTER 4

"I'm confused," I finally managed. "If it's going to match, then didn't you…"

He leaned forward, resting his elbows on the table. "I didn't kill her. But the stupid cops are going to think I did. I was just, with her."

"Right. How foolish of them. To think that the man whose DNA was on her when she was found was the man who killed her."

I didn't mean it to come out sounding all condescending, but I mean, come on.

What were they supposed to think? Words are nice and all, but put some good old-fashioned DNA evidence up there on the board and pretty much everyone is going to believe in that result a lot more than someone's word that they didn't do it.

Especially someone without any built-up goodwill who everyone already thought did it.

He glared at me, but not with that quick-spike sort of anger that some men have that makes me want to flinch because I know they're capable of harm.

No, this was more along the lines of my grandpa who

can glare me down with the best of them when I say something particularly ignorant or foolish. So I sat back and took a deep breath.

"Okay. Let's start over here, Mr. Browers," I said. "You obviously knew Mary Diever."

"Yes. And, please, call me Owen."

"Okay, Owen. *How* exactly did you know Mary Diever? You said you were with her, what does that mean exactly?"

Before he could answer, someone knocked on my front door and then opened it. Had to be my grandpa. He was the only one who'd just let himself in like that. Fancy ran to greet him.

"Hey Grandpa, we're in the kitchen," I called

He came through the door from the living room, dressed in work boots, jeans, and a long-sleeved red and black-checkered flannel shirt. He hadn't even bothered to put on a hat or gloves. I should get *him* to walk Fancy. Not that he'd see the point in taking a dog for a walk for fun. Dogs were meant to have a purpose in his world, not be some sort of surrogate child.

At first glance, my grandpa appeared to be about the same age as Owen Browers even though he was over eighty and Owen had to be in his sixties. Part of it was down to the fact that his hair was still a light brown instead of gray and he'd always stayed trim. But the years were there, hiding in the wrinkles around his eyes and the way he limped a bit on really cold mornings.

He turned all of his attention on Owen Browers, but before he could say something cutting, I jumped in. "Grandpa, have you met Owen Browers? Mr. Browers, this is my grandpa, Lou Carver."

Owen nodded to my grandpa. "Mr. Carver. Sir."

"What are you doing here?" my grandpa demanded, not moving from the doorway, his arms crossed across his chest, legs planted shoulder width apart.

That wasn't good. My grandpa had done fifteen years in prison for armed robbery. I'd never seen him be violent, but I knew he was capable of it. You don't survive that long in that kind of environment without learning how to defend yourself, and his stance said he was ready for a fight.

"Grandpa. Back off. Mr. Browers here has asked for my help. He wants me to find who killed Mary Diever."

"I'll give you a clue. You're sitting across from him right now."

I saw that look cross Owen's face, the one that had flashed across it right before he turned to walk away from me outside. "Grandpa! Sit. Give the man a chance to tell his story. Unless you were there? Did you actually see him kill her?"

My grandpa hesitated in the doorway for another moment but he finally joined us at the table, dragging his chair around next to me until he was facing Owen Browers. "Fine. Tell your story. Convince me you didn't murder that young lady."

"Grandpa," I warned.

He raised an eyebrow in my direction, but he didn't drop the menacing glare.

"Mr. Browers, I'm sorry. Please. Tell us what happened back then. And tell us why they're going to find your DNA on her even though that doesn't mean you killed her. I mean, don't they usually send off something intimate in these situations? Not just something a passerby could've touched? And if you were, um, intimate with her, why didn't you tell anyone back then?"

My grandpa snorted in disbelief at my gullibility, but he didn't say anything more, just continued to glare at Owen as the big man turned his coffee cup in his hands and searched for the right words to convince us to help him.

CHAPTER 5

Owen finally looked up and met my grandpa's glare, eye for eye. "I didn't kill Mary."

My grandpa pursed his lips, but didn't say anything.

"Look, I'm not a saint, never have been. Hell, I don't even like most people. But I'd never hurt a woman. And Mary…Mary was an angel. She was my angel."

"Wait one sec." I ran to my room and grabbed a spiral-bound notebook and a pen. "Okay, sorry. Go. You knew Mary…"

He smiled softly. "Yeah, I knew Mary. I was in love with her. Everyone was. But, more importantly, she was in love with me."

My grandpa snorted at that.

"I know. Hard to believe. Me, a no-good loser who'd been in trouble with the law and only got by scraping together the odd job here or there. And Mary, who'd been to college, and whose father was a lawyer, and who lived in a house with more rooms than most hotels. But it's true."

My grandpa shook his head. "She was at least a decade younger than you."

"More. Twelve years."

"But you're telling me she loved you. You got any proof of that?" he asked, not letting up for a moment.

Owen focused on the coffee cup once more. "I have a photo of us. A Polaroid where she was asleep on my chest."

"Mmhm. And why didn't you give it to the cops? Tell them you were involved? Let them know they were looking at the wrong man?"

Owen shoved back from the table and crossed his arms. "Because then they would've arrested me for sure. You know how small a place this was thirty-six years ago. Everybody assumed they knew exactly what was going on with everyone else. They would've never believed me. And her daddy…No way he would've believed it. And him a big lawyer like that? I would've spent the rest of my life in prison."

I leaned forward. "So you lied to the cops when they asked you about her?"

He nodded. "I had to."

"And the DNA?" I asked.

"Well, we'd been together, hadn't we? That morning. She met me down by the river in this little spot we had. And then I left and went about my day, didn't think anything of it. We had plans to meet back there in three more days, but that afternoon someone said she was missing. Didn't take long to find her body."

"How close was it to the spot where you guys would meet?"

He huffed out a breath. "About a hundred feet away. Which is probably why the cops jumped to all the wrong conclusions. They found our spot. And they assumed that what happened there was part of her murder."

I glanced at my grandpa and then at Mr. Browers. I really didn't know how to delicately ask what I needed to ask. And I really didn't want to ask it at all in front of my grandpa. But, I needed to know.

"Um, so, when you two were…together…" I realized I'd intermeshed my fingers as I said the words, blushed deep scarlet, and dropped my hands into my lap. "Um…Were you, by any chance, um, rough with her? I mean, in a way that the cops would mistake for, you know, rape?"

I had to force myself to look at him instead of away. Some topics are so darned awkward. But I needed to see his face and his reaction if I was going to believe what he told me.

He recoiled slightly. "No. I mean…no. We…no."

"So no grabbing her arms too tight or," I cleared my throat, "um, choking, or anything?"

"Maggie May," my grandpa snapped at me.

"What? Some people…enjoy certain things. And maybe in an autopsy they look bad. So if that's the case then we need to know that."

Owen shook his head. "No. Nothing like that. I swear. Just…sex."

"Okay. Good. That helps. I mean, if there were any signs like that then we know the killer left them. And if there weren't then that supports your story. That's good. Either way."

I ran a hand through my hair, wondering why it felt like there was so much of it these days. Getting old is weird. But I put that aside, I had a murder to focus on. "So, if it wasn't you, who do you think it was?"

He turned the coffee cup around and around for a good minute.

"Mr. Browers?"

"Owen, please." He frowned at the table for a moment before saying, "Mary was a good girl."

I tried to catch his eye. "A good girl who was sneaking away to have sex with her much older and rougher around the edges boyfriend. Owen, what else was she into that no one knew about?"

He ran his hands through his hair and dropped them to the table. "It wasn't like that. I mean, it was just a little, a little hash. And maybe she tried cocaine once or twice."

Oh, is that all? I thought to myself. *Just a little cocaine. No biggie.* It always amazes me what vastly different perspectives people have. To me there is no such thing as "a little" cocaine. Or a little hash for that matter. I am such a prude.

"Where did she do this? Who with? You?"

He looked like he wanted to run away again.

"Mr. Browers. Owen. If you want me to find her real killer you have to tell me the truth about her so I can figure out who else might've done it. Did she do these things with you? Or did she do them with others?"

He licked his lips. "With others. I'd...I'd had my party days. I got clean in jail and stayed clean."

"Do you know who these others were?"

He shook his head.

"So how did you know about it?"

"She showed up high a few times. And when I asked her about it, she said it wasn't a big deal. Not something she did often."

"Okay." I jotted that down. "Tell me, how did you meet?"

"I picked up some general repair work around her daddy's house." He shrugged a shoulder. "We met when she came back to live there for the summer. Got to talking one day when he wasn't around. Hit it off. And then, she kissed me."

My grandpa snorted.

"Grandpa."

"What? You never saw Mary Diever. Pale blonde curly hair around these big blue eyes. Soft-spoken. So quiet you had to lean in to hear what she was saying. Couldn't have been an inch over five foot. And this lout wants us to believe *she* kissed *him.*"

"She did."

"Prove it." My grandpa jutted his chin out in challenge as I snagged another piece of fudge and studied Owen Browers.

"I can't. That's why I never told anyone." He glanced towards the door.

"Running won't help, you know," I told him. "It'll just make you look even guiltier."

He smiled at me and I saw a little hint of what Mary Diever might've seen all those years ago. "What are you, a mind reader?" he asked.

"No. Just very good at putting myself in someone else's shoes and trying to think what I'd do in their place. So. She kissed you. And then?"

"And then something started between us. It was…intense."

I jotted that down, too. "How long were you together before she was killed?"

"About six weeks."

"She told you about some of the other things she was

up to, like the drugs. Do you think she told anyone else about you?"

He shook his head. "I don't think so. We agreed to keep it between us. At least until…"

"Until?"

"She was talking about marriage. I mean, can't keep that secret, can you?"

"No, not if you want to actually live together. So no friends she'd confide in?"

"No. None. Look. I want to be clear on something. Mary was a good girl."

It was my turn to snort. "Mr. Browers, I'm not going to judge her for what she did. That's her choice, her business. I've known really decent people who did far worse than that. But, let's be real here. From what you've told me, Mary was sneaking around doing drugs and hanging out with questionable people. Not just you, but whoever was supplying those drugs. That's not a 'good girl' in my books. I've known plenty of women with soft voices and big eyes who were manipulative snakes in the grass."

I held up a hand before he could interrupt and defend her. "I'm not saying she was like that. But from what you've told us it sounds like she was in the midst of a little rebellion and you were one part of how she was acting out. Is there anything else we need to know?"

"No." But he frowned and looked away.

"Mr. Browers? Owen? What is it that you're not telling us?"

He pressed his lips together. "I heard her and her father talking one day. Made me think that maybe there was someone else or had been. She wouldn't speak about it when I asked her, but I know what I heard."

"A jealous ex is a good suspect. Do you think that's why she was keeping her relationship with you a secret?"

"No. That was her father. He'd never approve. He wanted more for his daughter than someone like me."

"But you said she was talking marriage."

"She mentioned it sometimes. Running away together. I didn't really believe her, though." He studied the table, not making eye contact. "I always told her if she found someone better than me she should go for it."

I raised my eyebrows. "I thought you loved her."

He glared at me. "I did. Which is why I knew I wasn't the right man for her. She had so much potential. I was willing to take any moment she'd give me, but I knew eventually she'd wake up and walk away. I didn't want to be the one who tied her to a small life when she could have the world."

I barely managed not to roll my eyes. (It's a personal thing. I'd had a guy or two pull that, "if you find someone else" line on me. But what they didn't realize is that while they were there being all noble I was just left alone because there wasn't anyone else I wanted to be with at the time and they certainly weren't going all in themselves, now were they? Men and their mixed up notions…I was so glad I'd found Matt and would never have to deal with any of that mess again. If he left me I was just going to join a convent, lack of religious calling notwithstanding.)

"Did she have a diary?" I asked.

"Not that I know of."

I drummed my pen against the notepad, trying to think of any other questions to ask, but nothing came to mind.

I took a deep breath and sighed as I stared at what little we did have. "Okay. Let me see if I can sum this up. All the physical evidence will point to you. Most people already think you did it. As far as you know, there's no one else who knows that you two were involved. And even if they did it was a situation where someone could accuse you of killing her when she tried to leave you. Or when you found out that she'd been involved with some other man she wouldn't tell you about."

I took another piece of fudge (only my fifth or sixth) and popped it in my mouth as I contemplated the likelihood that Owen Browers was going to spend the rest of his life in prison even if he was innocent.

I didn't see how he was going to get out of this. Then again, at least there was nothing to lose by trying to help him. I couldn't make it worse, could I?

He leaned forward. "Will you help me?"

I glanced at my grandpa. He knew what it was like to be suspected of a murder or two he hadn't committed. "What do you think, Grandpa? Will you help, too? You probably have more contacts that will be helpful than I do given when it was and the type of folks she was hanging around."

He shook his head. "Maggie May, this is not your problem to solve."

"I know that. But…"

"But you're going to try anyway."

I shrugged. "He asked for my help. And I believe him."

My grandpa reached for his non-existent pack of cigarettes. (He'd stopped smoking a few years before after a lifetime of two packs a day). "Fine. I'll help. But only to get to the bottom of this."

He turned back to Owen Browers. "I'm not as naïve as my granddaughter. I've seen men who could claim they were innocent and be believed while holding a bloody knife standing over a dead body. So if you did this, we'll prove that, too. Beyond the shadow of a doubt."

"I didn't."

"We'll see."

And with that, I was on another murder investigation. My cop husband was going to be so happy.

CHAPTER 6

I walked Owen Browers to the door and then returned to the kitchen. My grandpa hadn't moved an inch. And he did not look happy. "Maggie May."

"What?" I huffed out a breath and sat down next to him, grabbing another bite of fudge from the tray. I knew I was eating too much of it. (Of that and lasagna and all sorts of other comfort foods.) But it made me happy and if 2020 had taught me anything it was that I should let myself be happy while I could, because you never knew when a global catastrophe was going to come along and wipe all of that away.

As I debated making myself another cup of hot chocolate, my grandpa asked, "What are you thinking, telling that man you'll take on his case? You're not a private investigator."

"I know. But who else is going to help him?"

"A private investigator."

"You saw him, Grandpa. He needs help. And he asked me to be the person who does that." I crossed my arms and tried not to pout. "You know, I'm not bad at this."

"You want to be an investigator, become an investigator. But stop poking your nose into other people's business. One of these days someone is going to poke back at you."

I shook my head. "Doubtful. I mean, we're talking something that happened over thirty years ago. The person who did this—let's be real, the *man* who did this—is probably already dead. And if he isn't dead he's in prison somewhere for some other crime. Men who do these things don't usually stop at one. And if he isn't dead or in prison, he's probably old and infirm."

"Like me? Am I old and infirm?" He glared me down from across the table.

There was only one right answer to that question, but I was so tempted to answer the other way. "No."

"Well then."

I pressed my lips together, trying to figure out why I had taken the case. I didn't particularly like the man. Truth be told he was off in some way that made me uncomfortable. One of those people who doesn't quite know how to act normal so always gives people a weird vibe.

And while I did feel sorry for him, I didn't feel *that* sorry for him.

But...

"Look, Grandpa. If he didn't do this then that means there is someone who is part of this community who did. Or who is now part of another community who did. And I don't think it's right that someone can do that sort of thing to a woman and just get away with it and live happily ever after. It's not...fair."

I decided I did want that second cup of hot chocolate and went to make it. After I'd shoved the measuring cup of water in the microwave, I added, "That's not justice. It's not right. That someone can take a young girl's life and then live theirs with no consequences. And back then people weren't as aware of DNA and things like that. So whoever did this is far more likely to have messed up back then than they are now if they're still doing this sort of thing."

I tore open the chocolate powder packet and dumped it in the cup. "So, sure, maybe I'll stir something up I shouldn't. But someone has to. Because that girl was murdered and her killer wasn't caught. The tools didn't exist back then to catch him. But now they do. And we should use them. Every rapist and murderer tracked down and caught is a warning to every other man who thinks he can get away with something like that, that he can't and he'll be caught eventually. It makes every woman that much safer, including me."

"Some things are best left alone, Maggie May."

"Nope. Not this."

He shook his head. "Fine. But promise me you won't interview anyone dangerous without me or Matt there."

"Promise, Grandpa."

He pushed himself to his feet. "I'll let Lesley know, too. She might be able to find something at the library. Or know some of the gossip from back then. You want to come over for dinner tonight?"

"Better not. Matt had an early shift today so he'll actually be home for dinner. I want to fix him something special to soften him up before I ask for access to the case file."

My grandpa narrowed his eyes as he watched me eat yet another piece of fudge. He opened his mouth as if to say something, but didn't. Good thing, too, because my weight is no one's business but mine and I would've let him have it if he'd made any sort of comment.

So I'd put on a few pounds, who cared? No one else had to live in my body but me. And it turns out my body was happier full of fudge than not.

I walked him to the door and then turned to survey the living room where Fancy was snoring away against the wall, ignoring the wonderful, comfortable dog bed I'd just bought her.

I needed to do some internet research. And come up with a fancy meal idea to soften Matt up. No grilled cheese sandwiches for us tonight, no sirree.

Although that sounded really good. Maybe I could have one for a snack before he got home…Grilled cheese sandwich for second lunch and then steak and potatoes for dinner. Mmm.

Maybe I could do cream cheese mashed potatoes with some bacon in them to go with it. If that didn't make Matt my willing slave, I didn't know what would.

CHAPTER 7

Of course, before I could start investigating the murder, I had to meet with Jamie and Greta first. We were trying to run a business after all and we'd agreed to get together to share our latest ideas for the pet resort.

Jamie was in charge of the café for people, I was in charge of the bakery for dogs, Greta was in charge of choosing how to spend the money. It was mostly hers after all. But I could at least provide the place to meet (and the fudge).

Jamie arrived first. She was positively beaming with happiness and so pregnant I wondered how she could even walk with that big belly of hers. She'd cut her long brown hair into a cute bob that hit right at her chin making her look even more adorable than normal.

She gave me a quick hug and grabbed a bite of fudge before putting the ice cream samples she'd brought into the freezer.

"How's it going?" I asked. "The nursery ready yet?"

"No. I've had the nursery re-painted three times so far. I just want the perfect shade of yellow and none of them are quite right. They're either too bright or too pale or too…Ugh. *Green*.”

“You know, I always figured I’d paint my nursery white with black geometric patterns along the top of the wall. Newborns can’t tell colors anyway, but sharp lines and stuff are good for their eyes. So I’ve heard. I’d probably throw in some red shapes, too. Supposedly that’s the first color they can see.”

She looked at me like I’d grown two heads. “That’s not soothing. Or restful. You would really paint a nursery black and white and red?”

“Yeah. I’m surprised more people don’t. It’s psychology after all.”

Before she could say more, Greta arrived with Hans, her Irish Wolfhound. Fancy was thrilled to have the company, which she showed by sniffing him for a few seconds and then lying down nearby.

Greta gave us each kisses on the cheek and then set her fabric samples on the kitchen table. She was her usual polished self with her pale blonde hair pulled back into a chignon at the base of her neck and slim black slacks and a bright purple silk top.

“Jamie, you look wonderful. Maggie, you do as well. What have I missed?” she asked in that wonderful Germanic accent of hers that made everything sound more posh than it was.

“Oh, nothing much,” I answered. “Jamie was just telling me she’s repainted the nursery three times because she can’t find the right shade of yellow.”

“It’s horrible. I think it’s fine and then the sun comes up the next morning and it’s too bright or too dull or too subtle.” She sighed and sat down on the couch, propping her feet up on the coffee table with a wince.

Greta tsked. "This is why you do not paint the entire nursery. You put a small square. You then look at the square at different times of day. You see how it does." She grabbed her phone. "Here. Give me paper."

I handed her a notepad and pen and she scrawled a name and phone number on the page, her Ms looking more like Ws.

"This is my designer. Call her. She will tell you the proper yellow to use for a baby's bedroom."

Jamie tucked the piece of paper away in her over-sized purse. "Thank you. Maggie said she's just going to paint her nursery white with black geometric shapes."

"Ah, so you are finally telling people. Congratulations."

"Congratulations on what?" I asked.

Greta glanced at my belly and back at my face. "On your pregnancy."

"I'm not pregnant. I've just gained a little weight and this type of top makes me look pregnant." Anything gathered below the chest that hangs loose has that effect.

"Hm. Are you sure?"

"Yes, I'm sure. I would know if I was pregnant."

Jamie and Greta exchanged a look.

"I would know."

"Hm. Of course. But you may want to check. Just in case."

"Change of subject, please. Jamie, what do you have planned for the delivery? Can the local hospital do it or are you going to have to go to Denver? If so, I hope there are protections in place to keep you safe."

We'd been happily living in our little bubble while the world around us got scarier, and I didn't relish the idea of Jamie having to leave to go to Denver. Especially to a hospital.

"Actually, I wanted to talk to you about that. I've decided I want to do a home birth. And since our entire house is wood floors, I was hoping we could do it here?" She winced a bit as she gave me that wide-eyed pleading look she'd used to such great effect on all of her past boyfriends.

I stared at her in horror. "A home birth? You're going to shove something the size of a football out of a place much smaller than a football and you would like to do that in my living room? I mean, yes, you are my best friend, but no. I do not need front row seats to *that*. Nnno."

It turned out there were in fact limits to my friendship. I'd kill someone for my best friend or help her bury the body if she needed me to, but I was not going to let her give birth in my living room.

"Wait, you aren't going to be there?" she asked.

"That's what Mason's for. And your mom. They were there at the various beginnings of things; they can be there for the culmination of this particular series of events. *I* will come by the next day when you are all tidied up, and I will bring a balloon and politely refuse to hold something so small and delicate lest I break it."

"It?"

"Well, I don't know the sex do I? Him, her. The child. Lest I break the child."

Greta patted Jamie on the hand as she sat down next to her. "You can have your baby at my house. I will arrange it."

"Are you sure, Greta?"

"Oh yes, my late husband, he was very concerned about his health. We have a full medical suite on the second floor. I will make sure that there is whatever is needed for a baby."

"I want a water birth, not some horrible thing involving stirrups."

"Yes, yes. Of course. We will arrange for that. We will have nice music and a warm pool of water. But the stirrups will also be there. Just in case. And a doctor."

"I was thinking of using a doula."

Greta patted her on the hand once more. "Hm. Yes, well. We will have both, no? Just to be safe."

As they continued to discuss the details of the birth, I stared back and forth at them in horror. These were the types of things people were just supposed to go off and do. No one who wasn't an intimate part of the situation needed to be privy to the actual details.

Just like I hadn't needed the details of the conception, I didn't need the details of the delivery.

"Alrighty, then," I finally interrupted. "Let's get this party started and see what Hans thinks of my latest treat invention, the Steak Sizzler."

Fancy immediately jumped to her feet when I opened the container. If possible, the Steak Sizzlers were her all-time favorite treat. Of course for a dog who would gleefully eat cardboard if it was given to her with enough enthusiasm, (I kid, she wouldn't, not really, I don't think) it was sometimes hard to tell the difference between normal "I will gobble this up" and extraordinary "I will gobble this up."

Hans was more considered in his approach, but once he came close enough to sniff the little steak bite I offered him, he too gobbled it up.

"Looks like we have another winner," I declared.

"Great. Time for ice cream." Jamie lumbered herself up from the couch and waddled into the kitchen, wincing a bit as she walked on her swollen feet.

I shuddered. I was definitely not ready for that, thank you very much. Me, pregnant? Ugh. Some thoughts were just too scary to contemplate.

As Jamie took her samples out of the freezer and I arranged for bowls and spoons, I instead thought about the murder of Mary Diever and what I'd need to do after this meeting to get started on the investigation.

Compared to the horrors of childbirth, that was downright pleasant.

CHAPTER 8

By the time Matt came home from work I had not only whipped up the mashed potatoes and loaded them down with sour cream and bacon, but I also had two juicy T-bone steaks ready to go in the broiler once the roasted Brussels sprouts were done. I'd also prepared a balsamic glaze I found on the internet that I hoped was going to make them so absurdly delicious you could cry.

Seriously, what did people do before they could find recipes online? Crazy to think about.

(And on top of the great recipe I'd also learned that Brussels sprouts hadn't always tasted as good as they do now. Turns out someone revived an old version of them because they'd become woefully bitter over the years. Who knew? The things you can learn from strangers. Hopefully that was actually true. I chose to believe so.)

"Hey, honey," I said as Matt came into the kitchen.

Man, was he beautiful. Six-foot. Dark hair. Blue eyes. And in uniform? Mm, yummy.

Of course, his physical looks had nothing on his heart of gold and his willingness to put up with my you-know-what. I had won the lottery marrying him. And for some crazy reason he thought he was the lucky one. Which, honestly, is how it should work in my opinion. Both people in the relationship should feel just the slightest bit lucky that this amazing person chose them.

And I was. No doubt about it.

He glanced around the kitchen and smiled. "Special occasion?"

"In a manner of speaking."

"Great. Let me get showered and then you can tell me the news."

He rushed off to the bathroom as my timer went off and I busied myself with swapping out the Brussels sprouts for the steaks.

Fifteen minutes later we settled in at the table. Matt smiled at me like a schoolboy. I swear, his eyes were twinkling as he grinned at me.

"Why do you look so happy?" I asked him.

"Well…" He raised his eyebrows like we shared some sort of secret.

"Well, what?"

"I mean, the meal. And you said it was a special occasion."

Had I?

I frowned. "Look, Matt, I'm not sure what you think this meal is about, but I'm pretty sure it's not about whatever it is you think it's about."

His smile dimmed. "It isn't?"

"No. I don't think so. I mean, I made this meal to butter you up so you wouldn't be mad at me." I slipped Fancy a little bit of my mashed potatoes so she'd stop drooling on the floor while she waited for us to start eating.

"Mad at you for what?" Matt asked suspiciously.

"We'll get to that in a minute. First, what did you think this meal was about?"

He crossed his arms and sat back. "Well, I mean…You know. I've been pretty patient. I wanted to give you your space, but I am your husband. And at some point…I mean, we're in this together, aren't we?"

I stared at him, baffled. "I have no idea what you're talking about. What do I need space for?" And then it dawned on me. "Oh not you, too! Matt, I am not pregnant. I have just gained a bit of weight. It's been one of those years. Look, sorry to disappoint, but I made a fancy meal because I didn't want you to be mad that I'm going to investigate another murder, okay? Sorry."

"What? Who? Where? There haven't been any murders around here lately."

I cut a bite off my steak, probably with a little more force than was necessary. "It's not a recent one. It was thirty-six years ago. Mary Diever."

He started cutting his steak just as aggressively. "Mary Diever? But we know who killed her. Owen Browers. We're just waiting on the DNA to prove it."

I rubbed the back of my neck and grimaced. "It's your case?"

"Yes. We got some special federal funding to DNA test old cases and the Chief assigned it to me. I thought I'd told you about it? Anyway. There was a witness that saw him near her house that morning, and we found his t-shirt about a hundred feet from the murder scene. A pretty distinctive one. Even back then everyone knew it was him, but it was all circumstantial so they never arrested him. Give it a week or two, though, and we'll have the DNA to back it up."

He speared a Brussels sprout on his fork. "Why do you suddenly want to investigate this case anyway?"

I bit my lip. "Because Owen Browers asked me to?"

"When?"

"Today. When I took Fancy for a walk." I forced myself not to chew on my thumbnail as I waited for Matt's reaction.

He carefully set down his fork and knife and stared at me very intently. "Owen Browers approached you when you were out alone on a walk?"

"It wasn't like that." I mean, it was, but I wasn't going to tell him that now that I'd decided Owen Browers wasn't a bad guy. "He asked for my help because he thinks you guys won't believe him."

"If he's innocent the DNA will show that. You don't need to get involved."

I wrinkled my nose. "Actually…I'm pretty sure the DNA's not gonna help his case."

"And why's that?" he asked, his voice going flat.

I slipped Fancy a few bites of steak onto her sharing plate before I answered. "Because he told me they were involved? They used to meet in a little spot right by where her body was found. And they'd been together that morning. But she was alive when he left."

Matt sat back, shaking his head in disbelief. "He told you they were involved."

I nodded.

"Then why didn't he tell the police that?"

"Because he didn't think it would help. He thought it would make him look more like the killer. And I'm not sure he's wrong about that. I mean, lying to the police is bad, but sometimes telling the police the whole truth can turn out poorly, too."

Lord knows I'd seen that a time or two.

Matt shoved his plate away, his steak half-eaten.

"Aren't you going to finish that?" I asked.

"Somehow I've lost my appetite."

I frowned at him. Matt is normally a really decent guy, but he has his moments. Everyone does.

"Don't be like that, Matt. The man asked me for help and after I talked to him—with my grandpa present, I might add—I decided I believed him so I'd try to help. I didn't know it was your case. And I had nothing to do with him not telling you the full truth about his relationship with Mary Diever. So, please, eat your steak and I'll tell you everything I know. If it's any consolation, Grandpa thinks he's guilty, too. Maybe we'll find something to strengthen your case for you instead of ruin it."

He frowned off into space, but didn't immediately reach for his plate.

"Plus, if you don't eat that steak, I probably will. And since I've gained so much weight everyone thinks I'm pregnant, I probably don't need to do that."

That got his attention. "You really don't think you are?"

"No! Of course not. I mean it's my body, don't you think I'd notice if I was growing a child inside me?"

"Normally I'd say yes, but…are you sure?"

"Matt!"

"How about you take a test, just to be on the safe side. You don't want to end up on an episode of that show about women who didn't know they were pregnant until it came time to deliver do you?"

A Salacious Scandal and Steak Sizzlers

I rolled my eyes. "Fine. I will pick up a test at the store next time I'm there. It's going to be negative, though. I am not pregnant. Now, about this murder…"

CHAPTER 9

The next day I dropped in on Lesley at the library where she still volunteered twice a week.

She's a lovely woman, but she's always so put together it makes me feel like there has to be a stain somewhere on my clothes even when there isn't. She'd recently cut her hair and was sporting a look that framed her face with soft snow-white curls that curved around her chin. It looked good on her.

Of course, she was one of those people who always look good. Nice clothes, nice tasteful jewelry, and old but still beautiful.

My grandpa was a lucky man to have found a second chance with her. Not that it had been easy to accept when he did, because it was hard to see him replace my grandma, but he deserved happiness and Lesley gave him that.

"Hey, Lesley, how are you?" I asked as I walked over to where she sat behind the circulation desk.

It was still weird to me to walk into the "new" library with all its wide open space and computers and meeting rooms. I'd always have a special place in my heart for the old library that had been an interconnected warren of rooms on the top floor of the court building. That was the library of my childhood summers.

"I'm good, Maggie. Your grandpa told me about the Mary Diever investigation. Looking into another murder are you?"

"That I am. He thought you might know something? Or be able to find some old records?"

"Well, I did make some calls this morning so let me fill you in on what I found out." She pulled a small notebook out from under the counter and scanned through her notes. I couldn't read them. They must've been in shorthand.

She sighed and shook her head. "A tragic story all around. Mary was an only child. Her mother passed away when she was about ten. Official word was that she died in her sleep, but she was a young woman. Thirty-five. Unofficial word was that she might have had other issues that contributed. Alcohol or pills. Mother's little helper of some sort. She wasn't from here and didn't really have any close friends, though, so no push to investigate."

"How'd she end up here if she wasn't from here originally?"

She glanced at her notepad. "Met Roger Diever when he was in law school in Philadelphia. When he came back to take over his father's law practice, she came with him. But she didn't join any committees or participate in any school activities. Kept to herself. Same for Mary."

"That's odd, isn't it?"

The Baker Valley was a small community and it seemed that everyone had been a scout of some sort or other or participated in the annual 4th of July parade or played on the co-ed t-ball team at some point in time.

"Perhaps. The women I spoke to assumed she didn't want to lower herself to associate with them. She was supposed to be from high society. As for Mary, they said the mother kept her away, too."

I pursed my lips. "Was she really that high-class? I mean, she lived here."

"Not a lot of lawyers and doctors in the area, that's for sure. And most people around here didn't go to college. To some people that matters."

I shook my head. Some people are fools. To think the degree on the wall matters more than the intelligence between the ears.

"What about Roger Diever?" I asked. "What did you learn about him?"

"From what I gathered, Roger Diever was a ruthless attorney who'd do almost anything to win. And even though he took over his father's practice, most of his legal work involved Denver clients."

"So why come back here? Why not move to Denver?"

"I presume it was his father. I didn't know the man well, but we did cross paths when I was younger. *He* was cold. Gave me the shivers. Also, not a man to accept anything other than getting his own way. I still remember when he set his sights on my friend, Doreen. It was like a military campaign for him. He lost a few of the battles, but he kept adjusting his strategy until she finally gave in and dated him. And then he dumped her two weeks later for a new target because he'd won."

Sounded like a charmer. Glad I'd never met him.

"Are either of them still alive?" I asked.

"No. They both died shortly after Mary did, actually. Mary's grandfather died about a month later. Brakes failed and he rolled his car off of Elk Road. Mary's father died about a year after that. Heart attack. Some said it was her death that broke him, especially after having already lost his wife. But there were rumors it was helped along by alcohol."

I winced. "What a tragic family history."

"Some families are like that, aren't they?"

Thinking back on my own losses, I nodded. It's like you let in one tragic, unexpected event and more shove their way in after. I just hoped my particular run of bad luck was finally over.

"Did you find anything else out? Any names of friends she had? Anything like that?"

She shook her head. "From everything I could find out, she really didn't have friends. No clubs. No sports. Nothing. Just her family and her studies."

I drummed my fingers on the countertop. This was not going to be an easy investigation. I sure hoped Matt's police file had something more for us to go on or I wasn't going to be able to help Owen Browers after all.

"What about partying? Mr. Browers mentioned she was maybe experimenting a bit with drugs."

"If she was, it wasn't with anyone local. At least not as far as anyone Lou talked to knew. Maybe she was hanging around with folks from out of town. This area wasn't the tourist destination back then that it is now, but there were definitely people who came here for a fun time for a week or a weekend and then left. If she was socializing with them, no one local would know."

I nodded. Made sense. Especially since most of the

people who'd come to the valley on vacation would have more money than the locals, so would be more "acceptable" for her to hang out with.

Of course, if something had happened with one of them, thirty-six years later who would remember some random guy who passed through town for a few days?

I sighed. "Alright. Thank you, Lesley. I appreciate it."

"You're welcome. I hope you can help Owen. I remember when he was just a little kid. Wasn't much of one for big books, but he liked the comic books. He'd come once a week and read them in the corner." She smiled at the memory. "If it's any consolation, I don't think he did this, so anything I can do to help, you just let me know."

"Will do. Thank you." I gave her a quick hug. "I better get going. I need to run by the grocery store before dinner tonight. Matt promised me he'd try to bring home the case file for us to look through."

Lesley shook her head. "I can't imagine sitting down at the kitchen table and discussing a murder with my husband, but to each their own."

I just smiled. Matt was perfect for me in so many ways, that one included.

CHAPTER 10

That night Matt brought home *two* legal boxes full of notes and photos, both from the original investigation and his follow-up. Fortunately, when he'd told the Chief that I wanted to see the files, the Chief had actually okayed it.

Seems I'd done a good enough job helping them out in the past that he was willing to give me that little bit of latitude.

As I reached for the lid on the first box, Matt moved it away. "Uh-uh. Pregnancy test first."

I rolled my eyes and crossed my arms. "I'm not pregnant."

"Good. Then you can go pee on a stick and we'll know for sure and then we can settle in for the night with a nice cozy cold case file."

"Can't I take the test after we look through the files?" I reached for the box again, but he moved it away once more.

"No."

I narrowed my eyes at him. "Let me ask you something. How long have you thought I was pregnant?"

"A week or two. Maybe more."

"And yet not once did you mention it. Even though I drink a ton of Coke and beer and I probably eat things that I shouldn't if I really am pregnant."

"You may not have realized it, Maggie, but you kind of haven't been drinking beer at all. And you've cut way back on the Coke. And you're eating vegetables."

"What does that mean? *I'm eating vegetables.* I always eat vegetables with dinner."

He raised an eyebrow. "But do you normally randomly snack on vegetable trays throughout the day?"

I frowned at him. Just because I'd bought a veggie tray at the grocery store the last couple of times I was there didn't mean anything.

Although, he was right. I had munched on them throughout the day, which was not exactly normal for me. (Of course, that was in addition to everything else I'd munched on throughout the day.)

I shook my head. "That was just from going on the birth control. It makes me crave vegetables. Same thing happened in college."

"And when exactly did that happen? You going on birth control?"

I frowned at him, like how could he not remember. "Right after we got married."

"We went into lockdown right after we got married."

"Yeah. But…" I stopped and thought about it for a long moment.

I'd made the appointment, I remembered that.

But then everything shut down…And they told me I'd have to reschedule…But they didn't know when, so I couldn't…

And I was going to call them back…

But then I got distracted with my grandpa and his friends deciding to blow up part of the canyon to keep us all safe and isolated from stupid people who wanted to treat lockdown like a road trip vacation permission slip.

And…

I stared at Matt in horror. I'd never actually made the appointment.

How could I forget that?

"Oh no."

He nodded. "Wanna pee on that stick now?"

"Why didn't you say anything?"

He shrugged. "You knew I wanted to have kids as soon as possible. I just figured you'd changed your mind and wanted to, too. Or were going to leave it up to fate. I've heard you mention often enough how hard it was for some of your friends to conceive, and you are in that age range."

If Matt hadn't been Matt I wouldn't have trusted his explanation. But I suspected that's exactly what had happened. He'd just shrugged it off as no big deal. Let me be in charge of the entire direction of our lives without so much as a worry.

I grabbed the box and raced to the bathroom, suddenly desperate to know whether I really was pregnant or not.

All I can say about what happened next is it's a good thing they give you more than one of those things, because I didn't quite pull it off correctly the first time around. What can I say, I'd never had to do one of those before. (Never expected to ever do one, to be honest.)

And they're not exactly straight-forward. At least not the brand I bought, which was not the one with the cute baby on the box. It was the one that promised fast and accurate results. You know, for the woman freaking out that she might be unexpectedly pregnant.

Anyway.

Ten minutes later, after the peeing and the crying and the hyperventilating, I walked back into the living room where Matt was sprawled on the couch, a beer in hand, Fancy snoring at his feet.

"Well?" he asked.

I handed him the stick, my hand trembling.

He looked at it and let out a big whoop. "Yes! We're going to have a baby!" He jumped up from the couch, picked me up, and spun me around, startling Fancy into a barking fit.

Fortunately, his enthusiasm was contagious, because inside I was freaking the frick out. I was not ready to be pregnant.

There are women—Jamie is one of them—who have been talking about wanting to be mothers and how many kids they'll have since high school. *I* was not that girl. I was *never* that girl. Marriage, babies, they weren't exactly on the priority list.

Oh sure, I figured they'd happen someday. I wasn't opposed to the idea. Not a hundred percent. But maybe sixty percent. And whatever day I'd expected them to happen it was a day far in the future.

As much as I loved Matt, the whole marriage thing had been enough of a shock to the system, I wasn't exactly ready to go plunging into the next "this is how life works" stage.

Honestly, I'd kind of been planning to spend a decade or so married and then go, "Oh, golly gee, those eggs are all gone, so sorry" and live a happy life of quiet peace with just Matt, me, and Fancy.

But it seemed life was determined to shove me into that traditional path whether I was ready for it or not. And don't get me wrong, I knew I'd love the kid to pieces just like I loved Fancy to pieces. That was never in question. It was just…holy shit scary.

And yes, I just cussed. But, it was a cussable moment if there ever was one. I was pregnant.

Holy #@&!

CHAPTER 11

In my opinion the best thing to do when you find out that you are unexpectedly pregnant is to read an old murder case file and try not to think about it.

Matt on the other hand wanted to talk about our plans and whether we should buy our current house, which I didn't really like because it had stairs, or move elsewhere.

The house was conveniently located next door to my grandpa who I had moved to Creek to look after. But he didn't really need the help. Then again, maybe he and Lesley could help us with the kid. More Lesley, I assumed, since she'd actually raised kids whereas my grandpa had entered the picture after my dad was grown.

The other option, of course, was to move. But then the question was where to. Not like there were a lot of homes for sale in the area.

And if we were going to move that put Bakerstown on the table because we could be close to the pet resort and the auxiliary police station, which might even mean a promotion for Matt and would certainly make for an easier commute, especially in the winter.

So there were good reasons to stay and good reasons to go. But I had to finally, gently, tell Matt to please, shut, up. I was a little overwhelmed by the news and if he didn't want me to start hyperventilating into a paper sack we needed to leave that discussion for another day.

"Maggie, you do understand that we only have so long before that kid is here and the next five years of our life become a whirlwind, don't you?"

I reached for the crime scene photos, refusing to look at him. "I'm trying very hard not to think about that, thank you very much."

He laughed and I looked up in time to see him grinning at me, flashing the dimple in his cheek that only makes an appearance when he's really, really happy. "I can't believe we're going to be parents. I'm so excited. When should we tell everyone?"

Never probably wasn't an option, so instead I said, "Not yet. Not until after I know how far along I am."

(And could confirm this turn of events with a more reliable test than one that depended on my ability to properly use that stupid stick correctly.)

As I reached for another file out of the case boxes, Matt asked, "What do you want to name her? Or him? I guess it could be a boy, but I kind of hope this first one is a girl."

First one? Wasn't he getting a little ahead of things?

I shook my head. "Sorry, but we are not naming the baby until it's born."

"Can't we at least put together a shortlist?"

"No."

"Why not?"

Ah, this poor man. He did not know what he had married.

"Because things go wrong in life. And while I don't personally have some huge, strong belief in a higher power that takes a direct interest in my life, I do have this weird belief in fate and luck and jinxes. So we will not be naming this child until he or she is in our arms alive and well."

He looked at me with a sad understanding, but just gave me a kiss on the forehead. "Okay." But then that grin came back. "This is going to be such a fun adventure. I'm so happy."

"Right. Now, if you really are my loving, adoring husband who is going to support me through this mess, you will drop the subject of babies and futures and everything that's coming our way like a freight train, and will instead sit down and help me look through this case file for any clues as to who could've done this to Mary Diever." I flashed one of the crime scene photos at him.

As he took it he asked, "Other than Owen Browers?"

"Yes. Other than Owen Browers."

"Fine. But I won't promise not to think of baby names while I'm doing so."

I sighed. "Fine. Just don't share them with me, please."

🐾 🐾 🐾

An hour later we'd looked through the whole case file. It was not good. At least, not for Owen Browers. There were no notes about Mary's friends or another love interest. There was an investigative note that she'd had sex shortly before she was killed, but the autopsy report was missing entirely.

From the photos it was pretty clear she'd been bashed in the head with a rock, but if they'd found it, there was no record in the file. And no other obvious signs of trauma other than that, so chances were the DNA was going to only tie back to Owen Browers.

Also, as Matt had already mentioned, there was a witness who'd seen Owen Browers coming out of the woods that morning near where everything happened.

I sat back and frowned at the table. How do you prove that someone didn't kill someone thirty-six years ago when there's nothing to go on?

"Right. So. What are the angles?" I grabbed my notepad and started jotting down ideas.

"What about the father or grandfather," Matt suggested. "Either one could've discovered what she was doing with Owen that morning. There's a fight, it gets heated, and bam, she's dead."

"Could explain the tragedy of the next year, too. Grandfather kills her, father finds out and cuts his brakes, and then drinks himself to death." I wrinkled my nose. "Of course, that's a little too pat don't you think?"

I went to the fridge to grab more fudge, and then remembered I'd already eaten all of it the day before. Easy enough to make more. The recipe only required about 90 seconds in the microwave and then some time in the fridge. But I hesitated. Was I allowed fudge anymore? It was peanut butter not chocolate, but still.

Luckily I'd cut way back on the Coke because I'd been feeling a lot of indigestion. (I can't believe I hadn't noticed all the little signs of pregnancy before that…There were so many once I thought back on it.) But what about sweets in general? And weren't there certain cheeses I wasn't allowed to eat, too? And something about tuna fish maybe? And folic acid?

Jamie would know. She probably had a frickin' meal plan I could borrow. But if I told her she'd get all excited and I just couldn't do that yet.

"Who else?" I asked as I grabbed an apple from the fridge instead. I was pretty sure I'd never heard anyone say pregnant people can't have apples. "Someone in from out of town?" I added that to the list.

Matt nodded. "What about a drug dealer? If she really was doing drugs she might've gone direct to get them."

"Yep. Or what about a complete random stranger who just happened upon her in the woods, but didn't sexually assault her?"

He gave me a skeptical look.

"Yeah, I know. Not likely. But better to throw the net wide and narrow it down from there, right?"

"Well if you're going to do that, was there a money motive? Someone who wanted to inherit and took out the whole family?"

I wrote it down, but it also didn't seem likely.

"What about jealousy or lust?" I asked. "Those are always classics. Maybe she had a stalker. Or Owen Browers had someone he'd broken up with who was jealous he'd moved on. Maybe she had an ex who didn't take it well. Or another guy she was seeing, too."

He nodded. "It's easy to assume it's a man in these situations, but it doesn't have to be. Could easily be a woman, especially since it doesn't look like there was a sexual component."

"Right." I scrawled woman on my notepad to remind me not to assume it was a man, but I still believed it was a man. "What else? What other reasons do people have to kill someone?" I asked.

"Power."

"How would power play into it? She was a college student."

He shrugged. "I don't know."

I wrote it down at the bottom of the list. Just because I couldn't think of anything right now didn't mean I wouldn't later as I learned more about her and her life.

I glanced at the two boxes once more. "No offense, but I wish the original investigators had done more work than they did."

"If you're going to blame them, you have to blame me, too. I didn't do much more."

"I wasn't trying to criticize you, Matt, I promise."

He held up his hand. "No, it's a fair assessment. As a new investigator I have to constantly remind myself not to jump to conclusions about who is guilty. It's too easy to fixate on an obvious suspect and be blinded to the other possibilities. Of course, it doesn't help that outside of books and movies and real crime shows that a lot of murders really are that obvious. It usually *is* the husband or boyfriend."

"And, see, since all of my experience is from watching shows and movies, I'm pre-conditioned to look for some twisty motive when in real life it's usually just Person A knew Person B really well and something made them decide to kill them. Like a huge life insurance policy."

I wrote that down.

"Exactly." He glanced at the notepad and then at me. "So are we done? Can we eat and talk about babies now?"

I flinched. "Do not say that."

"Say what?"

"Babies. As in plural. Twins run in my family, Matt. At least on my dad's side they do. Maybe. My dad was an only child and his dad only had brothers, but the two or three generations above that? All had twins."

He grinned. "Really? So maybe we could have a boy and a girl right from the start?"

"Matt!"

"What?"

"No."

"Maggie, it's too late. If you're having twins, you're having twins. Which would be great, wouldn't it? That means we could maybe have six kids before you get too old for more."

"Six kids?" I curled up in horror. "See, this is why you date someone for years before you marry them. So you know that they want six kids and you can say no, sorry, you better find someone else."

"Would you have really told me that? Is six kids a deal-breaker?" He mooned at me with those gorgeous blue eyes of his, but I wasn't having it.

"Yes! Six kids is a deal-breaker."

"What about three?"

"Can we just get through one? I have more than one friend who had that first kid or, more often, that second kid, and was like, oh hey, I'm good. No more. So let's see where we're at after this first…one."

He grinned again. "Twins."

"Shut up. We don't know that yet."

"But, maybe…"

As he went to the kitchen to whip something up for dinner my mind started to cycle through everything I was going to have to take care of before the kid or kids were born. It was not a short list. And I did not have the time to get it all done.

Which meant by all rights I should call Owen Browers up and tell him I couldn't help right now. But I'd promised. And if I didn't help he was very likely going to be in jail by the time I gave birth.

Plus, I was enough of an independent woman that if I hadn't had a murder or crime to investigate I would've probably gone out looking for one just to prove to myself that I was not going to let motherhood consume me. Which meant it was good, actually, that I had a case to solve. One less thing to put on the to-do list.

Now if I just had a snowball's chance in you-know-where of actually solving it. That would help.

CHAPTER 12

The next morning as I stood in my kitchen and tried to figure out what to make for breakfast, I realized I had two choices: I could call up Jamie who probably had a pregnancy meal planner that optimized for nutrition at each stage of pregnancy and ask her what I was allowed to eat, or I could wade into the realms of pregnancy forums and websites to figure it out for myself.

Since I didn't want to accidentally go down some weird pregnancy conspiracy theory black hole, I decided Jamie was the safer option. Not that her whole home birth idea was something I was on-board with, so I'd approach it with a bit of skepticism still, but I'd known her for years and found her generally intelligent and level-headed.

Far better getting my information from her than listening to some rando who believed who-knows-what. (The internet is a blessing and a curse. As nice as it is to find information at your fingertips, sometimes that information has absolutely no connection to reality.)

Of course, that meant telling her I was pregnant. And I just…I wasn't quite ready for other people to be happy about my being pregnant. I know, that's weird. Everyone wants you to believe that being pregnant is this wonderful, glorious, life-affirming process that any woman should want to rush into head first and with bells on.

But it's actually *a lot*.

It's hormonal changes and physical changes and lifestyle changes. And not all of those changes are good ones. Maybe it was my worst-case-scenario brain working on overdrive, but I'd noticed those formerly-pregnant women on the "I have a weird medical issue" shows where things were not right after the fact, you know? Birth is a violent act.

And because I hadn't planned it, I was having horrid thoughts about birth defects and what does folic acid even do and should I be shoving handfuls of it in my mouth now to make up for not taking it in the months before I got pregnant.

To calm myself down I turned my attention to the murder investigation. Maybe Jamie's husband, Mason Maxwell, would know more about the family. He was rich. And a lawyer.

He answered on the second ring.

"Mason Maxwell, Esquire, how can I help you?"

Seriously? He said the esquire part? Who does that?

"Mason, it's Maggie. How are you?"

Fancy, noticing that I was on the phone and thus vulnerable to her antics, started crying until I slipped her a few steak sizzlers.

"I am doing well, Maggie. Surprised to hear from you, though, on my business line."

Even though he was married to my best friend and I'd come to accept him, I'd never come to adore him. He was just a little stick up the you-know-what for me. But he was a very handsome (older) man who had more than enough money to provide a good life for my friend and her child, and he treated her right, which was really the most important thing. It was clear he adored her and for that I was willing to forgive the fact that he seemed to not understand how to use contractions.

I left Fancy in the kitchen before she could start crying at me again. "I know. I'm not much of one for random social calls. So let me get right to the point. I'm investigating a murder and thought you could help with some background information."

"A murder? Whose?"

"Mary Diever. My understanding is her father and her grandfather were lawyers and she'd just returned home from her first year at college when she was killed."

"That was a long time ago."

"Thirty-six years."

"And why are you investigating it now?"

I settled in upstairs where I knew Fancy wouldn't follow me, although I could hear her crying from downstairs. "Owen Browers asked me to. The police took his DNA and he thinks they'll arrest him when it comes back, but he said he didn't kill her."

"Why would there be a DNA match then?"

"They were involved."

"Interesting. That does explain a few things."

"How so?"

"As you probably surmised, Mary's family and my own moved in similar social circles. Her father and grandfather both belonged to the country club and would golf on occasion. That summer, when Mary returned from school, her father tried to set us up."

Interesting.

"And?"

"I was willing. She was an attractive young woman, good family, similar backgrounds. There were synergies there. But she was not. I asked her to join me for lunch at the club, but she refused. Same with playing tennis or golfing. I thought maybe we could chat casually at the Fourth of July party, but she was not in attendance."

"Did you see any signs she was a drinker? Or into drugs? Or maybe was more friendly towards others at the club who were, um…a little more…?"

"Were a little more fun?" he asked, with a slight chuckle in his voice.

"Uh, yeah, that."

He thought about it for a moment. "No. There weren't many of us around that were that age and of that," he cleared his throat softly, "social standing. As far as I know she stayed away from all of us. Most of her time was spent at home."

"And what about the father? Or the grandfather? What did you know about them?"

"A little before my time. I was just getting started in practice when they both died. I know my father was not sorry to see either one of them go. I was not privy to the details but there was a case where my father was on one side and her grandfather was on the other. My father believed her grandfather had violated his duty in some way, perhaps by letting a client perjure himself on the stand to win. It was never clear to me what exactly had happened only that my father did not approve."

"And yet they would've been okay with you marrying Mary?"

"My family? No. It was her father and grandfather who wanted the match. Their family had been in the valley two generations but were still considered outsiders. Mary marrying me would have solved that. Well, at least for our children."

I thought about what that meant for Jamie's child or children. Would they associate with my little brat or brats or would we be too far beneath them? I knew Jamie. She'd never cut me off. But for kids it's hard. Life forces them to choose and in the ugliest ways possible. It's like a little Lord of the Flies at every middle school.

"Alright, so, they wanted social standing. But then I don't understand why the women kept themselves apart the way they did."

Mason was silent.

"Mason? Do you know something?"

"I am not one to gossip."

"Look, I'm trying to clear a man's name in a thirty-six-year-old homicide. If you know something, please share it. It could be the difference between his going to prison for life and his being able to live out the rest of his years as a free man. Please, Mason, tell me what you know even if it's conjecture."

He inhaled deeply. "Very well. My mother made a comment once. She stopped by their house to visit, because my mother will recruit anyone to her pet causes, and she at least did not believe that Mary's mother was too far above her."

"What was the comment?"

"That in her experience women who wear long sleeves in the middle of summer usually have something to hide. Obviously there was more to it than her choice of attire, but it was my mother's way of saying she suspected Mrs. Diever was being abused. It was never proven as far as I know. And if the rumors about her alcoholism were true, then that could have just as easily been the cause of any bruises she was trying to hide."

"But you don't think it was alcohol abuse? Having heard about her husband?"

"I do not know and could not give any testimony related to the matter."

I laughed softly. "You're such a lawyer sometimes, Mason."

"Thank you. I take that as a compliment."

I shook my head. I could never be married to Mason Maxwell. But to each their own. Jamie was happy and that's what mattered. "Alright, thank you for the information. If you think of anything else, please let me know."

"My pleasure."

"Also, is Jamie around today, do you know?"

"She just stepped into my office. Do you want to talk to her? I can give her the phone. I have to join a Zoom meeting in a moment anyway."

"Um, yeah, that would be great, thanks."

As I waited for Jamie to pick up the phone, I glanced down the stairs to where Fancy had settled herself, watching and waiting for me to come back downstairs. She wasn't crying anymore, but she was not resting either. That silly dog…

"Hey, Maggie, how are you?" Jamie asked.

I closed my eyes. I was dreading this conversation, but I figured it's like pulling off a Band-Aid, you just have to get it done as fast as possible and try not to scream when it hurts.

CHAPTER 13

Where to start when you have to tell your best friend you're pregnant…

"I'm good, but um…I could use your help." I paced down the hallway, wincing at what was going to come next.

"Sure, what with?"

"I, um, I'm, uh…"

"Oh! Did you finally take a pregnancy test? You're pregnant aren't you?" She didn't have to sound so excited about it.

"How did you know?" I stopped and glared at the wall, exasperated. Was I the only one who hadn't known?

"What else would it be? I've been waiting for this call every single day for the last month or two."

"Month or two? I've probably only been pregnant for a couple of weeks. Or like six weeks if you factor in the first month that doesn't really count."

"Oh, Maggie, no. It's been longer than that."

I sank to the floor. "Don't tell me that. I didn't take folic acid. I didn't eat the right things. I probably ate things that were bad for me. Like cheese. I love cheese, Jamie. I eat it every single day."

"But you don't eat fancy cheese every single day. You're fine. Look, if I'd seen you eating something that was truly terrible for the baby I would've probably said something."

"I've had beer. And Coke."

"It's fine. You're fine. Look, let me give you the number of my doctor. She's great and she promised me she'd squeeze you in as soon as you called. And I'll email you over my meal lists."

"I knew you'd have those." I rested my head against the wall, part of me relieved that she'd gone through this before me so she could help and part of me panicked that I was maybe further along than I'd thought.

"I'll also include my own personal list of what to expect so you can prepare. Are you still going to paint the baby's room white with black patterns on the walls now that you know you're actually pregnant?"

"I don't know, maybe. Although, there is some weird instinct that has me suddenly thinking about soothing pastels. But there really are psychological studies behind the black and white thing. Plus, I probably won't know the gender until the baby is born. And white will make the room much easier to use later."

Jamie laughed. "Use later? Like when the kid goes off to college?"

I sighed, the reality of what was happening finally hitting me smack in the face. "Oh no. This is eighteen years of my life growing in my belly."

"Eighteen years?" Jamie laughed again. "No, this is the rest of your life. Unless something really goes wrong somewhere down the line."

"Great, thanks. That really helped. I think I'm going

to go put my head in the toilet and cry.”

“Don’t be silly, Maggie. Eat a Saltine for the nausea. I’ve had a few friends who only felt fine if they were snacking all day long.”

“Hm. Maybe that explains my current fascination with peanut butter fudge…”

“Probably. I’ll send over the lists right now. I’m so happy! We get to raise our kids together.”

I let out a deep breath. “That is the silver lining to all of this. Although, I was kind of hoping for the free babysitting. You know, let you get about four years ahead.”

“Nope. Sorry. We’re going to bumble through this together. It’ll be good, Maggie, I promise.”

“I hope you’re right.”

“I am. You’ll come around, don’t worry.”

After I hung up the phone, I stared at the ceiling. How? How had my life so drastically transformed in such a short period of time? All I’d wanted to do was move to small-town Colorado and open a little business with my best friend.

But now, marriage? And kids? And the business had morphed into something so much bigger than my little cheesy idea…What was all this mess?

I went to the kitchen and opened the fridge. At least I now had an excuse for eating my feelings. Good thing there was still some lasagna leftover from the other day.

Fancy had followed me to see what I was up to, since she knows she always gets a little bit of whatever I eat. She crowded closer as I peeled back the cellophane. I sniffed at the lasagna to see if it was still good and Fancy’s eyes widened in horror. She immediately ran out the doggie door and disappeared outside.

I shook my head as I searched for a fork. I had the weirdest dog. I could inhale deeply and she was fine with it. But one little double sniff and she went into immediate panic mode and had to leave the room.

What traumatic moment in her past had brought that on? It was probably something I'd done.

As I poked violently at the lasagna I thought about how if I could turn a sweet, adorable dog into a neurotic mess that was scared of the sound of sniffing, what damage was I going to do to a living, breathing child who could actually understand what I said?

Oh, dear.

Matt could save for our kid's college fund. I was going to save for their therapy fund. Because with me as mom, that kid was going to need it.

Mom.

Me. Holy…I shuddered and shoved more lasagna into my mouth.

Murder. Better to focus on murder.

CHAPTER 14

I decided the first thing I needed to do was track down the autopsy report. Assuming there was one. Small town, thirty-six years ago, there were no guarantees. But my grandpa would know who at least had been in charge of that sort of thing. And if he didn't, Lesley would.

I leashed up Fancy and we strolled next door. Even though I knew the front door would be unlocked, I still knocked. I don't care how old they are, a newly-married couple is not to be walked in on without permission.

Lesley answered the door wearing the cutest embroidered apron I'd ever seen. (Then again, it's quite possible it was the only embroidered apron I'd ever seen, but it was still cute.) It had prancing reindeer along the border with a jolly Santa in the middle.

"Baking?" I asked as the smell of warm sugar and pumpkin filled my nose.

"You guessed it." She stepped back so I could follow her inside.

"It smells delicious. What is that?"

"Pumpkin bread. And after that some pumpkin cookies. I'm visiting my daughter tomorrow and wanted to make sure I brought along enough goodies for the grandkids. Plus it gets me in the holiday spirit. You and Matt are coming over for Thanksgiving?"

"I think that's the plan. You're okay with Jack and Trish and Sam coming, too, right?" We were lucky to be walled off from the insanity of the rest of the world so we could safely gather.

"Absolutely."

I rubbed carefully at my back, trying not to make it obvious. How had I gone from not realizing I was pregnant to wanting to be off my swollen feet in a day? Probably psychosomatic.

Lesley gave me a shrewd look. "It was the worst with my first one. The back pain."

"I…You knew I was pregnant, too?" I asked.

"You didn't?"

I shook my head. "Not until Matt forced me to take a test yesterday. Here I am, priding myself on solving these various mysteries that have come my way over the last year and a half, and I somehow missed the fact that I was pregnant."

She smiled. "The mind's a funny thing. Come on. Have a seat in the kitchen and I'll get you some tea and a slice of pumpkin bread."

"Am I okay eating that?"

She patted my shoulder. "Yes, you'll be fine. Plus, remember, when I was having kids none of us knew all these rules and for the most part it turned out fine. You're not a closet alcoholic or drug addict are you?"

"No!"

"Well, then, you're probably just fine." She bustled around, preparing the tea and bread for me as I sat down at the kitchen table.

"I'm scared," I told her. My mom and grandma were gone, which made Lesley the closest thing I had to a mom.

She nodded in understanding as she settled into the chair across from me. "And you should be. It's a big change. To your body, to your life. I loved being a mother, every minute of it from poopy diapers and colic to first grade musicals and high school graduations. But that doesn't mean it was easy. Or that it didn't change my life in ways I'd never anticipated. And you're one for using that mind of yours. I'd expect nothing less than a bit of panic."

I took a bite of the bread and mmm'ed in pleasure. It was delicious. "Twins run in my family, you know."

"Ah, that would add an extra level of concern, wouldn't it?" She squeezed my hand. "Don't worry. We'll be here to help."

"What if we move? Matt thinks we should move to Bakerstown. And I really don't like our house, but I do like being near you guys."

"We'll still come by to babysit when you need it, even if you move. Maybe not quite as often. But you won't be alone with this, Maggie. We'll be there. Now, is that why you came by? To tell us?"

I cringed. "No, actually, I was going to wait until I saw the doctor to confirm it. I was still kind of hoping it was a false positive. I know that's horrible, but I just wasn't quite ready for this."

"If you waited to be ready, you'd never do anything in life that's worth doing. Or so the old saying goes."

"True. I guess. I did sort of jump into owning Fancy and marrying Matt and both of those have turned out alright so far."

"See, there you go. Now. The reason for your visit."

I finished the last of my pumpkin bread before answering. "I'm wondering if you know who the medical examiner was thirty-six years ago? Or if there wasn't one, who would've looked at Mary Diever's body?"

"There's no record of it in the file?"

I shook my head. "I know they probably didn't have someone fulltime to do that sort of thing, but no mention of it at all."

"Hm. Maybe check with the lead investigator on the case. Who was that?" She put another slice of bread on my plate. I would've felt guilty for eating up her bread, but there were six loaves cooling on the counter.

"Adam Ripley." I took another bite of bread, savoring all the yummy spices, and slipped Fancy a little bit, too.

"Oh, Adam. Nice man. He's retired now. Has been for quite some time. But still comes into the library every couple of weeks. We have a nice chat when he does. He's living with his grandson out on a ranch property near Masonville. I'd start there if you can. Let me see if I have the address. He usually sends a Christmas card."

She pulled out an address book and flipped through it. I was amazed at the neat little listings on each page with checkmarks for cards sent and received for the last few years.

Who is that organized?

I usually forget to send any cards and then feel bad and send a group email on the day after Christmas when I realize that I'm not going to get any cards out for the year. And that's in a good year. In a bad year, I don't do anything and then feel guilty. (But not guilty enough it seems to do better the next year.)

"Ah, yes. Here you go." She wrote out the address for me on a slip of paper and handed it across.

"Thank you. I appreciate that."

"You're welcome. And, here, let me send you with a couple slices of bread for him. Help you warm him up a bit." She winked at me. "He can be a little crotchety with people he doesn't know well."

I stared at the Tupperware container, wondering if the slices of bread would still be there by the time I reached his place or if I'd succumb to the temptation to eat them myself. (I wasn't proud of the thought, but pumpkin bread was a lot more tasty than Saltines and it really did help to keep snacking on something throughout the day.)

She caught my look and laughed. "And, here, another slice for you for the road. Do you want to leave Fancy with me while you go out there?"

"Is that okay? I mean, I know it's silly to worry about leaving her alone, she literally spends eighty percent of her day sleeping, but I also know that she's far more content when she can do that near someone."

"Of course. Dogs are social creatures, too. Plus, I like the company. I assume she can have a little bit of pumpkin bread?"

"Pumpkin is one of her favorites. Absolutely. Thank you so much, Lesley."

She walked me to the door and Fancy watched me leave with a look of absolute betrayal on her face, but I'm pretty sure she forgot who I was as soon as Lesley offered her that bite of pumpkin bread. At least I hoped so. There was a lot coming up in our lives that was going to require me to leave her behind more than either one of us was ready for.

CHAPTER 15

It was a nice day for a drive. Most of the aspens had already changed, but that's the beauty of evergreens, they stay ever green. And the Baker Valley has its own special beauty with the big mountains framing it in on all sides and the sprawling farmland. Not that anyone actually farms in the valley. Maybe hay. Lots of cattle, I think.

That's one of those things I don't pay much attention to. (Just like the fact that evergreens are not actually a specific type of tree even though that's what I'd always called them my whole life until I walked through an arboretum and realized that what I think of as evergreens are actually pine and spruce trees…Oops.)

It's funny the things you don't give much thought to if they don't directly impact you. And I'm the type to only keep the information I need in my brain and let everything else wash its way back out. (This would be why I have the lyrics to probably a thousand songs memorized but miss on details like that. Priorities. And really even there I'm not sure I know all the lyrics, more the shape of the song.)

Anyway.

The Ripley farm was down two dirt roads, tucked against the base of a mountain. There was a rusted blue pickup truck parked out front right next to a shiny new Ford F-250. It's easy to think about folks in rural areas being poor, and then you park your cheap as van next to their eighty-thousand-dollar vehicle and it puts things in perspective.

That was not a typo, by the way, with cheap as. I spent a little too much time around some New Zealanders back in the day. Learned to say sweet as and cool as and cheap as. At least I think it was the New Zealanders who said it. Could've been the Americans who brought it back when it turns out only five New Zealanders ever spoke like that. Language is funny that way.

I set aside my deep thoughts and parked my beat-up van that was probably going to require an actual back seat before the baby was born next to the shiny new truck and got out. Luckily, before I had to decide if I should look in the house or out in the barn or out in the field, a middle-aged woman came bustling my way from the barn. She had her hair pulled back in a long braid and was wearing jeans, a long-sleeved shirt, and work gloves.

"Can I help you?" she asked, all brisk efficiency.

"Looking for Adam Ripley? My…" What was Lesley? My step-grandfather's wife? That was a mouthful. "Uh, Lesley Pope told me I could find him here."

"Yeah, he's inside. What do you want with him?" She took off the gloves and tucked them into her back pocket.

"To talk about an old case he worked on."

She eyed me up and down. "You a cop?"

"Nope. But married to one. And he got the Chief's permission to let me see the file I was interested in."

She crossed her arms. "And what file was that?"

I wanted to say it was none of her business, but I figured that wasn't going to get me inside where it was actually warm. "Mary Diever. Old case. Thirty-six years ago. But they just ran some DNA on it, so it's back in the spotlight."

"And your involvement?"

I raised my eyebrows. "There any chance we can have this interrogation inside where it's warm? And where I won't have to repeat myself because I'm sure Mr. Ripley will have the same questions."

"Oh, you won't have to repeat yourself. Come on."

She led me through the front door, depositing her work gloves and boots just inside. When I went to take off my boots, too, she waved me off. "Unless you've been mucking stalls?"

"No, can't say I have."

"Then you're fine."

She led the way down a narrow hall to a large kitchen. "Hey, Pop. Visitor for you. Says she's looking into the Mary Diever murder and has the Chief's permission to look at the file. Wanted to ask you some questions."

A large, bald man looked up from the table, setting aside his newspaper as he assessed me. "Heard you'd been poking your nose into this case."

"Have we met?"

He leaned back, crossing his arms and giving me the once over. "No. But Maggie May Carver has a certain reputation amongst my fellow officers. None of us take kindly to civilians thinking they can do a better job than we can."

Even if I had?

"The Chief said it was okay for me to look into this one."

He snorted and took a sip of his coffee.

As the silence started to stretch into something awkward, I figured I'd try small talk. "So, how long have you been retired for?"

"Twenty years."

"Any chance you know my grandpa, Lou Carver?"

"Yep."

Well, this was fun. About like pulling teeth out.

"Um, oh, I almost forgot. This is for you." I handed across Lesley's pumpkin bread. "Lesley thought you'd like it."

He opened the container and smelled the bread suspiciously, but then smiled and nodded. "Pumpkin. One of my favorites. Tell her thank you for me."

"I will. Can I…sit?"

He shrugged as he broke off a small piece of the bread and munched on it. I sat and watched in envy, but didn't say anything, hoping he'd maybe participate in the conversation I was trying to have with him. No dice.

"Um, so, yeah, the reason I came by was because there was no sign of a coroner's report in the file."

"Didn't have one." He took another bite of bread, not even bothering to look at me.

I sat back. "No one looked at the body?"

"Someone looked, but no report needed. We weren't paper-pushers back in the day."

It felt like there was a dig somewhere in that sentence but I couldn't figure out where. "Do you remember what the findings were?"

He closed the Tupperware container and shoved it aside, finally looking at me once more. "Likely hit in the head with a rock. No signs of other violence. Had sex shortly beforehand."

I nodded. "We did see that part in your notes. Nothing else?"

He leaned back and crossed his arms, glaring at me. "What do you think you know?"

Until that moment, nothing, but the way he'd reacted made it pretty clear there'd been something else found during the examination. But what? Drugs? Would they have tested for that? Mary Diever being such a good girl and all? Not likely.

So what then?

I tilted my head to the side. Maybe…

Should I take that gamble? If I was wrong it was going to be ugly. But then again, this was already the most awkward and uncomfortable interview I'd ever conducted. "I was wondering if whoever looked at the body discovered her pregnancy," I said, trying not to show that it was just a guess.

He leaned forward, planting his elbows on the table. "Mary Diever was a good girl."

"So I've been told."

"What makes you think she'd been pregnant?"

Been pregnant, not was pregnant. Interesting. If he hadn't just misspoken that was.

I tried to keep it casual, just tilting my head slightly. "A little word here or there. Nothing specific. Why didn't you note it in the file?"

He sat back, crossing his arms once more. "Like I said, Mary Diever was a good girl. No need to ruin her name over something that wasn't relevant to the investigation."

"Even if the father could've been the killer?" I asked.

"He wasn't."

"How do you know?"

He glared me down. "Because it happened months before and the father didn't know about it."

"How do you know that?"

"Her father told me." He reopened the Tupperware container and started in on the last slice of bread, clearly agitated.

"What exactly did he tell you?"

"That Mary got in the family way with a boy she met from out of town. The boy never knew. He was gone before Mary even knew she was pregnant."

"What happened to the baby?"

He finished the bread and shoved the container back at me. "Adoption. Out of state. Her mother's cousin. Philadelphia I think it was. Father didn't know until it was all over."

I thought it through. "Was this the year she was supposed to be in college?"

He nodded.

"Did you confirm it with anyone? Other than her father, that is."

"I didn't need to. Roger Diever was a well-respected member of this community. I trusted his word."

"And the reason it wasn't in the file?"

"The fact that Mary Diever gave birth to a child out of wedlock had nothing to do with her murder almost six months later. That was over."

"Are you sure of that?"

"Positive." He planted his hands on the table and glared at me. Speaking slowly and clearly, he said, "Owen Browers was seen leaving the woods shortly before Mary Diever's body was discovered. His shirt was found near her body. He killed her."

I leaned back, studying him carefully. "But you didn't arrest him. Why not?"

"We had no murder weapon."

"And? Was that it? Just the lack of a murder weapon?"

He lifted his chin. "It was an election year. The DA at the time didn't want to risk such a high profile loss. He refused to take the case until we had more evidence."

"And her dad was okay with that?"

"Of course not. Why do you think he drank himself to death? But he was a lawyer. He knew there was room for doubt in what we had."

I nodded, thinking. "Okay. Thank you for your time."

I stood to leave, but his words stopped me. "Owen Browers killed that girl."

I nodded again. No point in arguing with him. "If he did then maybe we can find the evidence to prove it this time around. Give Mary the closure she deserves."

I grabbed Lesley's Tupperware container and left.

As I pushed my way back out the front door, my gut was jumping, but I couldn't tell whether it was excitement because I finally had what felt like a good development in the case, or because I desperately needed to eat something to settle my stomach back down.

Either way, I had a mother's cousin in Philadelphia to find. But first, time to circle back to Owen.

CHAPTER 16

Owen Browers picked up on the first ring. "What have you found out? Do you know who killed her?"

"Hold your horses there. I just got started. You're lucky I've found anything out."

As I navigated my way back to the main highway, I gave a small nod of thanks to wireless ear buds that let me safely talk in the car. I love Fancy, but she's not very accommodating when I need to be on the phone.

"But you do know something," Owen said, undeterred.

"Perhaps."

"What is it? What did you find?"

I took a moment to collect my thoughts as I turned back onto the two-lane highway that led to Creek. Was there a delicate way to ask this? Not really. "Owen, did you know that Mary had a kid?"

"No. Are you sure?"

"Pretty sure. The original investigator on the case just told me about it. Said she gave birth about six months before she was killed. Turns out she didn't go away to college; she went away because she was pregnant. So you didn't know?"

"I had no idea…But that explains a few things."

"Like what?" I glared at the slow-moving truck in front of me, resigned to going under the speed limit for the rest of the drive because it just wasn't worth it to try to pass him.

"Well, we weren't together all that long. Just six weeks or so. But Mary kept bringing up getting married and having kids. I liked her. I mean, she was Mary Diever, I couldn't hope for anyone better than her. But it seemed very rushed. Especially the part about kids."

(I knew exactly how that felt.)

"Huh. Interesting. But you thought she was talking about future kids that the two of you would have, not one she'd already had?"

I finally gave up and passed the truck, remembering to smile and wave as I went by in case it was someone I knew. Living in the valley, the odds were pretty high, so I couldn't be as rude as I wanted to be to someone who clearly thought speed limits were not in fact a target but instead something to avoid at all costs.

"At the time I definitely thought it was about kids we'd have in the future. But given what you just told me…There was one time that she asked if I thought I could love a kid that wasn't mine. I assumed she meant adoption, but now…"

"Now you think it might've been about this kid she'd had? Raising it."

"Him."

"What?"

"She always talked as if we'd have a boy."

That was interesting. I wished I wasn't driving so I could be sure to make a note of it, but it wasn't something I was likely to forget. "So somewhere out there was a boy child that Mary Diever gave birth to and maybe wanted to get back."

"Maybe. If what that detective told you was true."

"Oh, I'm pretty sure it was. And you know what that sounds like to me?" I smiled even as I pulled up behind yet another too-slow vehicle.

"What?"

"A motive for murder. Did she ever mention a prior relationship to you? One that would've been the summer before she met you?"

"No. Nothing."

Fortunately this time the too-slow vehicle turned before I had to pass them. I waved as I gunned it past. Almost home. If I was lucky the road would be clear the rest of the way.

"The detective said it was some random stranger passing through town," I said. "Does that sound like Mary to you?"

"Not at all."

"Even though you said she kissed you right when you met?"

"She did kiss me pretty fast, but she was shy about the rest of it." He cleared his throat, clearly embarrassed. "It took about a month for that to happen."

"Interesting. So did she lie to her dad or did her dad lie to the cops?"

"I'd bet she lied to her dad. She was definitely scared of him. I'm actually surprised she told him about the pregnancy at all."

I pulled into the driveway and turned off the car. "Hm. Me, too. I wonder why she did that? Then again, can't exactly hide a baby if you decide to raise it." I pursed my lips, trying to think of next steps. "Well, sounds like I need to see if I can track down this cousin she supposedly stayed with. She mention anything about that?"

"Nope. No family other than her dad and grandpa that I knew of. She hardly even talked about her mom, though."

"What did she tell you about the year she was away?"

"She didn't. She mostly wanted to talk about me and my life or about our future. When I tried to bring up her past, her friends, any of that, she shut it down. I didn't think anything of it at the time, because she did it with a laugh and a smile, but looking back now, I clearly didn't know her that well, did I?"

"Ah, well. New relationships can be like that. Sometimes it's just nice to be with someone who doesn't know all that baggage, you know?"

He chuckled. "Yeah. I can see that."

"Okay, well thanks for the help. At least we have something to go on now. I'll let you know what I find out."

"Please, call any time. And thank you."

He hung up and I went into the house, ready to find what I could find on Mary Diever and her family.

CHAPTER 17

You'd think that everyone is online these days. And that tracking down someone's family is as simple as finding the right family tree on Ancestry. Sadly, that was not the case with Mary Diever. At all.

Three hours later, I had nothing. I hadn't even been able to prove that Mary's mother was from Philadelphia. Or find a wedding certificate for her parents.

I had nothing. Zilch. Nada. Squat.

So when Jamie showed up and informed me that she'd made me an appointment with her doctor and we had to leave immediately to make the appointment in time, I figured, why not? Time to put the nail in the coffin, so to speak.

(Yes, yes, having a child is a wonderful, glorious experience that no one should ever question or doubt. And if they do they must be a horrible aberration that probably shouldn't reproduce. Might I remind you that I am the same person who found a dead body and wanted to just leave it there rather than go through the hassle of getting involved? So, yeah, I am possibly one of those aberrations. Hate to break it to ya.)

The doctor's office was not located in the one medical center in the valley, but was instead in a converted single-story home at the edge of Masonville that was painted bright yellow with white trim. It even had a yard surrounded by a white picket fence. Talk about cheerful and happy.

It felt a little forced, to be honest. Like some intro to a horror movie or something. Happy splat horror. Or maybe it was just my state of mind coloring things a little dark.

"You will love Dr. Dillon," Jamie said as we walked up the two steps to reach the front door. "She is the best. She's about our age, actually. And just so nice. And understanding. And competent. I love her."

I almost turned around and walked back out. One, because cheerfulness overload. But, two, because sitting in the waiting room were Abe and Evan. I adore them, they are a wonderful couple and some of my favorite people in the valley. But that meant the inevitable, "what brings you here?" conversation and I was not ready for people to know just yet.

Unfortunately, they spotted me before I could run, so I made the best of it. "Abe. Evan. What brings you here?"

They grinned at each other. "It's our first ultrasound today," Abe said.

I must've looked puzzled, because they didn't wait for me to ask my stupid question before Evan gestured to the tall woman sitting next to him. "This is Amy. She's our surrogate."

"Ah, that makes more sense. I mean, modern day, gender, had me going for a second there, but yeah, a surrogate makes a lot more sense. Hi, nice to meet you.

So. You're a surrogate?"

She nodded, smiling with deep contentment. "Yes. I've had three kids of my own and now I try to help other couples find their joy. This will be my third surrogate pregnancy."

I blinked hard. "This is the *sixth* time you've been pregnant?"

"Yes. It's such a wonderful experience. To carry a life." She ran her hands along her belly which was just slightly visible.

"But the swollen feet and ligaments stretching and hemorrhoids and morning sickness and…"

"Oh, but it's worth it. To feel that life growing inside you. And to know that you were part of the creation of a living, breathing being. The fact that I can give a couple like Evan and Abe this gift. It's…special." She was so serene about it.

I just nodded and smiled. It was better than every spoken response that came to mind. I'd once had someone describe the passing of their grandmother in terms like that right after I lost my parents.

How it was so special and magical to be there by her side for those final moments. Whereas my personal experiences of death had been more like, "I'd really like to never repeat this experience again, thank you very much."

Fortunately, I had grown enough since then to acknowledge that we do not all experience the world the same way, so there was no point in my stomping on this woman's joy just because I thought she was crazy for going through childbirth *six times*.

I forced myself to smile at Evan and Abe. "That's fantastic you guys. I'm so happy for you. When are you due?"

"We'll figure that out today, but in about eight months. So, June or July?"

They were so happy I couldn't help but be happy for them. And July seemed so far away. That was manageable. It was more than midway through another year entirely. I could get on board with a July due date.

"What brings you here?" Abe asked with a sly grin.

(I had a feeling that whole, ooh you're pregnant look was going to get *real old* before I finally delivered.)

I waved in Jamie's direction. "Oh. I'm here because Jamie's thinking of doing a home birth and wanted to use my living room for it. So I thought I'd chat with her doctor and see if we could inject a bit of sanity into her thinking."

Jamie laughed and came back over to join us. "I do want to do a home birth. The idea of giving birth in some sterile medical environment just doesn't work for me."

From there the conversation devolved in ways I tried not to pay attention to. I settled instead for pacing what once was someone's living room, looking at all of the framed pictures on the walls of happy smiling babies dressed as flowers.

In the corner was one of those thumb boards, covered with photos of smiling moms with newborns in their arms. Hard to believe how many people did this thing every single day.

Jamie came over to join me when the conversation wound down, smiling at the photos with a peaceful anticipation that frightened me. I waved to Evan and Abe as they and their surrogate were led down the hallway for their appointment.

"By the way," Jamie said, "I told the receptionist to call for me not you, so don't worry that they'll find out before you're ready to tell them. Although, you are going to have to tell everyone at some point. Being pregnant isn't something you can hide."

"Wanta bet?"

"Maggie."

"What. Mary Diever hid her pregnancy. Although I'm not sure for how long. Seems she went away to have the kid so maybe she was gone before she started to show."

"Really?"

I nodded. "Yep. According to the original investigator. Gave birth about six months before she was killed. Supposedly she went to Philadelphia to stay with some cousin of her mother's, but I can't find any sign of the mom before she arrived here, let alone the cousin."

"Interesting."

I nodded, but before we could talk about it further, Abe and Evan were back with photos from their ultrasound. I honestly couldn't tell what I was looking at except it was black and white, but they seemed very excited.

Fortunately for us the receptionist waited until they'd left before she looked at me with a knowing smile. "Ready to see the doctor?"

Since "no" wasn't an acceptable answer, I nodded and followed her, Jamie at my side. Truth time.

CHAPTER 18

The receptionist led us down the hallway and to a room on the left. There was a room on the right, too, but that door was closed. As we waited for the doctor to join us, I looked around the examining room.

It's weird to have a doctor's visit in what once was someone's bedroom. It wasn't unprofessional in the least, but there was just this strange disconnect in not having the sterility I was used to in a standard doctor's visit. I think it was the colors. They were warm instead of cool because she'd left in the brown wood paneling on the walls. I'm used to white walls, you know. Bright, glaring, white walls. Clean walls.

(Not that these were dirty, but they could've been and I'd never have known it. I like that in my own home, hides the dust, but not in the doctor's office.)

At least the floor wasn't carpet. That would've been a step too far for my secretly germophobic soul. I may not like to clean, but I very much do not like smells and I can imagine in a doctor's office things would accumulate in carpet. (And now that we've had that unpleasant thought together...)

There was a light knock at the door and a woman with dark hair streaked the slightest bit gray stepped into the room, smiling. "Hi. I'm Dr. Dillon. You must be Maggie." She held a hand out to me and I took it. She had a firm grip, but soft hands. "Jamie's told me a bit about you."

"Why, because she's known I was pregnant this whole time even though I didn't?"

She laughed as she washed her hands in the sink. Her laugh was warm like the room. "No. I was curious about the barkery and café and the plans for the pet resort. I love to cook, but the thought of turning that love into a business is a daunting one. Not that I would, mind you. I didn't attend all those years of medical school to become a baker. Although, there are days when that seems very appealing."

"Oh, that makes sense."

She smiled at Jamie. "But she did make me promise to fit you in as soon as possible if you ever asked."

I rubbed at the back of my neck. "I didn't realize I was pregnant, you know. I just figured I was stress-eating."

"It happens."

"I haven't been taking folic acid. And I drink Coke. A lot."

She squeezed my shoulder. "There's actually not as much caffeine in a Coke as there is in a cup of coffee. Which means you're probably better off than a coffee-drinker who doesn't know they're pregnant." She smiled at me. "Let's make a deal. We won't worry about the baby's health until there's something to worry about. Your body and mind are going to have enough to deal with in the next little bit without adding in additional concerns."

Clearly this woman did not know me well, but I just nodded.

"Now. First things first, let's get you to pee in a cup so we can confirm this pregnancy, and then we'll see what we can see with an ultrasound."

"Okay."

Jamie laughed. "You're going to be fine, Maggie. Trust us. It's…it's great."

"For you, maybe. You wanted all of this. I wanted to live a life that involved curling up on my couch with a good book and a dog at my feet."

"And you will have that. You'll just also have a gorgeous man who adores you and adorable little kids that have his eyes and your spirit."

I flinched. "Can we flip that around? Let them have his calm demeanor and my eyes instead?"

Her laughter followed me down the hallway.

🐾 🐾 🐾

Five minutes later it was official. I was in fact pregnant.

"Congratulations," Dr. Dillon said. "Now let's see what there is to see."

She had me lie down on the table and lift up my shirt and unbutton my jeans so she could get to my belly.

"We'll start with this type of ultrasound. But if you're not that far along then we'll move to the other option."

Since I really didn't want to know what the other option was, I just nodded my head and closed my eyes.

"Don't close your eyes. You'll want to see this. Trust me."

She dimmed the lights. It was all oddly peaceful and soothing. The gel she used on my belly was warm and smelled like baby powder. She ran the little transducer firmly along my belly, her eyes focused on the black and white monitor we could all see.

"Ha. Look. Right there."

I stared at the screen. There were two large dark spaces, each filled with a white blob. Kid-shaped blobs.

Tears filled my eyes. Not because I was sad. But just because it's an overwhelming moment to see that you're carrying two living, breathing beings inside of you. (Don't worry. I cried plenty later over the idea of twins, trust me. But in that moment it was awe overwhelm not freaking out panic.)

"Twins," I managed to say.

"Yes."

I glanced at Jamie who was crying in happiness.

"Don't. You're going to make me cry, too." And then it hit me. "Oh no. Matt should be here for this. Oh no. I've messed up, haven't I? He was supposed to be here. And I can't fake it if we do it again. You only get that overwhelmed feeling once."

I'd been so concerned with whether I really was pregnant I hadn't even thought that this was one of those big moments you share with your spouse. And now it was too late. I could try to schedule another appointment and lie to him, but then I'd be lying to him. And he was my husband. I didn't want to lie to him, not about something as important as this.

I really did cry then.

"Don't worry, Maggie. Matt will forgive you. Here. Call him. Right now. You can FaceTime."

So I did. Lying there in the doctor's office with our little twin terrors on the screen, I made a video call to my husband.

"Maggie? Is everything okay? You never call me at work." He was standing on the side of the road somewhere, the wind audible through our connection.

"It's fine. I just…Um, Jamie was able to get me a last-minute appointment at the doctor and I went with her without thinking about it."

"You're there now?"

I nodded.

"And?"

"And we're pregnant. Twins. Do you want to see? Jamie can hold the phone and it'll be just like you're here," I said, hopefully. Matt had been so great up until that moment that I really shouldn't have been nervous about his reaction, but I kept waiting for that one thing that he'd get really mad about.

"Of course. Give me a minute." He set the phone down and I heard some grunting and muttering and then a slamming door.

"What were you doing?" I asked when he picked the phone back up.

"Oh, arresting someone. But he's in the back of the squad car now. Let me see that ultrasound."

Jamie took the phone from me so he could see everything at once.

"Twins!" He laughed and did a little jig (at least that's what I think he did from the movement of the image on the screen). "Do we know the sex yet?"

Dr. Dillon answered, "If I had to guess, I'd say girls. But it's a little early yet."

"How far along do you think I am?" I asked.

There was a part of me that wanted to be a week from delivery just so I didn't have to think about it all. But the other part of me wanted something like five years to prepare.

"I'd say you're right around the fourteen week mark."

"So, forty weeks, minus fourteen, I have about twenty-six weeks to go? So like six months?"

She shook her head. "Actually, most twins deliver early. Generally around thirty-six weeks. Which means you have more like five months."

Matt cheered. "That's the best first-year anniversary present I could imagine. Twin baby girls."

I sighed. "And here I was hoping for a luxurious weekend at a resort where we never got out of bed all weekend and drank champagne and ate steak and chocolate until we were ready to burst."

"We'll do that for our ten-year anniversary. Or maybe our twentieth, depending on the kids and who we can get to watch them."

"Or twenty-fifth or thirtieth if you convince me to go through this more than once."

We smiled at each other, both thinking about spending that many years together.

Matt glanced away. "I better go. Guy I just arrested isn't exactly happy about me leaving him sitting in there."

"Love you."

"Love you, too. And love those little bumps."

Jamie hung up the phone for me.

"Well, what now?" I asked.

"Now we keep a good eye on things," Dr. Dillon replied. "You're what we used to call a geriatric pregnancy, which comes with some additional risks for both the babies and you. We'll want to test for birth defects, which fortunately we can do with a blood test for now. We can follow that up with amniocentesis if we have to later, but the blood test is always where I prefer to start. Less invasive."

"Geriatric pregnancy? I'm only thirty-seven." I sat up and tugged my shirt back into place.

"Any woman over thirty-five is considered a woman of advanced maternal age."

"Seriously?"

She smiled at me as she put away her equipment. "It's not a judgement. It's just the body. These things work a lot easier when you're younger."

I shook my head. "Lovely. Just lovely. Although I will point out that my body seemed to do an absolutely swell job of conceiving despite my advanced maternal age."

She laughed. "It happens that way sometimes. The ones who desperately want to get pregnant struggle and then someone who wasn't planning for it at all gets pregnant after one night. But it doesn't change the fact that being older and pregnant comes with some added risks."

"Yeah, fine, whatever."

We wrapped up the visit with a blood draw (not my favorite, but better than a giant needle going into my belly) and then Jamie and I headed home, her chatting the whole way about all the *things* I was going to need for the babies.

At some point I tuned her out for my own mental health. There was so much involved in bringing a kid into the world, let alone two at once, I just couldn't handle it yet.

All I wanted was to solve a murder and take a nap. And maybe eat a big greasy plate of French fries smothered in red chili and cheddar cheese. With a little extra hot sauce thrown on top for an added kick of flavor.

CHAPTER 19

The next day I'd just returned home from showing my grandpa and Lesley the ultrasound when Jamie called. "You free this afternoon?" she asked.

"Of course, I am. I have no life, Jamie."

"Maggie, your definition of no life and everyone else's are worlds apart. But be ready for me to pick you up at one."

"Why? What's up?" I pinned the ultrasound image to the fridge with an "I Love My Newfie" fridge magnet. If I was going to be one of those parents with the cluttered fridge, might as well start early.

"Mason's grandmother has requested our presence."

I shuddered. "Why?"

"Well, yours actually, but I'm to deliver you."

I shook my head even though she couldn't see it. "That woman scares me, Jamie. Why would I agree to meet her?"

"She said she has information related to your investigation."

"Really? How'd that come up?"

Jamie cleared her throat. "Mason and I had dinner with her at the club last night, and I may have mentioned what you told me about Mary Diever being pregnant and going away to give birth. I wondered out loud who the father was. At which point Mason's grandmother shot me a look of pure venom and told me that idle gossip was the Devil's work and to shut my trap about things I didn't know about."

"Ouch. That woman is not subtle."

"No, she is not. But then after dinner she pulled me aside and told me to bring you by today. So maybe she knows."

"Do I have to go? She scares me. Couldn't you just go and find out what she knows and then tell me about it?"

"No. She definitely wanted you. Plus, I kind of like her. She has spunk. Even when she's telling me I'm doing the Devil's work. So, one o'clock?"

I sighed. "Fine."

I had an hour to get ready. But what do you wear to go visit the matriarch of the valley? Do you try to dress up to her standards? To pretend that you can fit into her upper-class domain?

Or do you do what I did which is throw on a comfortable pair of jeans and a t-shirt that says Book Nerd on it in big bold letters because there's simply no point in trying to pretend that you belong somewhere you really don't?

My lack of dress-up meant I had plenty of time left to call Owen before I left. I figured maybe he'd know why Mason's grandmother had information on Mary Diever.

But the phone went to voicemail. Odd, considering how fast he'd picked up the last time I'd called, but I shrugged it off. People can't always answer the phone immediately.

Still. I flagged it for follow-up later. Now was not the time for Owen to decide to go on the run or something equally foolish.

🐾 🐾 🐾

Jamie glanced at my outfit when she came to pick me up, but she didn't say anything about it. She was in an adorable purple dress that accented her baby bump. She also had full make-up on and her hair was curled and styled, something that had probably taken twenty minutes to get looking so carelessly cute.

To be fair to me, I had at least thrown on some mascara and lip gloss. But any make-up routine that would require more than a minute of effort was beyond me and had been even when I was in a corporate job.

We chatted about more baby stuff as we drove to the house which was set halfway up a mountainside outside of Masonville, only reached along a long, winding road through the trees.

I don't know why, but the whole time we were driving up that road I kept thinking about Medieval times and how you'd enter a castle that had murder holes where if the person didn't like you they could shoot you or drop something on your head.

"She's actually pretty nice, you know," Jamie said as we pulled up outside a large but not overly ostentatious home.

"Jamie, you'd say a wounded pit viper was pretty nice as it tried to strike you."

"Don't be silly. Come on. She doesn't bite at least."

"Well, that's one plus," I muttered as I reluctantly followed her to the front door.

A woman in a maid's uniform met us at the door and led us into what could only be described as a parlor.

There were floral couches surrounded by small tables, each with one incredibly delicate and breakable item on it.

Mason's grandmother was seated on one of the couches, her wheelchair discretely placed behind it.

"I'd rise to greet you, but these legs are not cooperating today."

I hadn't realized that some wheelchair users can actually walk on a limited basis until I had a co-worker who was in a wheelchair my first job out of college. It seemed Mason's grandmother was like that as well.

"It's good to see you Grammie," Jamie said, bending down to give her a kiss on the cheek.

Mason's grandmother caught my surprised expression and cackled. "I let her call me that because she's nice. And she's family. *You* call me Mrs. Mason. My husband's been dead twenty years, but I earned it."

"Of course, Mrs. Mason. Thank you for seeing us."

I wondered if I was expected to step forward and kiss her hand or something, but she waved towards the couch. "Sit. Jamie tells me you're poking into the Mary Diever murder."

I nodded. "Owen Browers asked me to. He said he's innocent, but he thinks they're going to charge him because he was involved with her and they were together that morning."

"Fool boy. Getting mixed up with that girl."

"Everyone says she was a good girl," I responded, curious how she'd react.

She harrumphed. "Any women say that or was it just men who didn't know her well?"

"Men."

"Figures. A woman bats her big eyes at a man and

suddenly she's the best of all girls. I'm sure you've seen that one yourself."

Pit viper, I tell you. I cleared my throat and decided to come back swinging. "The original investigator said she might have left town to give birth to a child the year before she was killed. Maybe stayed with a cousin of her mother's, but I can't find any record of her mother or this supposed cousin. You know anything about that?"

She cackled again. "You have moxie. I like that."

"Thank you. But you didn't answer the question."

The maid came in to serve us tea just then and we sat in silence until she'd left again. Mrs. Mason studied me as she sipped her tea, her pinky finger raised slightly. "Mary's mother, Genevieve, wasn't what she seemed. The Dievers would have us believe that she was part of society. A real blue blood. A debutante. But I had family who were part of society in Philadelphia and they'd never heard of her."

"Just because *your* relatives hadn't…"

"My relatives knew every family worth knowing," she snapped. "If Genevieve Diever grew up in Philadelphia and they didn't know her, then she wasn't someone worth knowing." She took another sip of her tea, studying me, clearly waiting for my comeback.

There were so many things wrong with what she'd said that I didn't know how to respond. Finally I said, "I've heard that gossip is the Devil's work."

"Ha. So it is. But what I know is not gossip. I hired a private investigator."

I choked on my tea. "Really? Why?"

Back then that had to have been pretty expensive.

She raised her chin. "Because a woman I didn't know

showed up in my territory and tried to put on airs that she was too good to associate with me. I didn't like that. I wanted to know who she was that she thought so much of herself."

I narrowed my eyes. "Did she actually try to put on airs? Or did her husband and father-in-law try to do so on her behalf?"

"Ah, very good. It was her father-in-law. But I couldn't let the insult stand, so I looked into it." She sipped at her tea again, a small smile on her face.

"And what did you find?"

"That Genevieve Diever had been a dancer at a men's club in Atlantic City. Not a drop of society blood in her veins. Not only that, but she married Roger Diever when she was already six months pregnant."

"I don't understand. Why did Roger Diever marry her then? From what Mason said, he was a social climber. He could've just walked away from her and the kid. And nothing I've heard said he was such a loving father that the existence of a baby would've changed his mind."

She nodded. "I don't know for sure, but I suspect it was because it put him in control. That man was cold and mean and any woman who could would've avoided marrying him. But a woman in a bad circumstance? Who saw him as some sort of savior? And saw Colorado as a chance to wipe the slate clean? She'd take that chance. And because he knew her secret he'd always have the power. She could never leave him. Not without losing everything."

I set down my tea and grabbed my notepad to jot down a few notes. "It seems plausible, but how can you be sure that's what happened?"

She smiled and I wondered exactly who was calling whom cold. "I'm positive about *her* motivations and how he used her past against her, because after my investigator returned with his information, I confronted her with it. Over tea. Right here in this living room."

"What did she do?"

"Cried. Confessed it all to me. Told me about how he hurt her. About how she wanted out, but didn't know how to leave and not lose her daughter."

I stared up at her, suddenly cold. "When was this?"

She took another sip of her tea before answering me. "About a month before she died."

"And you didn't tell anyone? What if he killed her? What if her death wasn't from natural causes?"

She set the cup aside. "Oh, I'm quite certain he did kill her."

"But…Why not tell anyone?"

"Because I had something much bigger to protect." She folded her hands in her lap and sat up with perfect posture. "Since I was a young woman I have been a part of a network that stretches across the entire country that helps abused women flee their abusers. When they're ready to run we pass them along, find them new identities, new jobs, and new lives. We make it so their abusers can never again touch them. If they have kids, we include the kids."

"But then…"

She took a deep breath and stared me down. "We can't jeopardize what we do for one woman. Which is why when we lose one before she can escape, we have to let it go."

"But that left Mary…"

She nodded. "Alone with her mother's abuser. Yes."

I swallowed heavily. "Did he…?"

"Hurt her? Not that I'm aware of. I would have done something if I thought he had. No. He spent a lot of time in Denver and he kept a woman there who I am certain he did hurt. Even so. When Mary was old enough that I thought she'd keep the secret, I told her about her mother, and I told her that if she ever was in need of my help to let me know."

"Which is why she came to you when she got pregnant."

"Yes. I don't know who the father was before you ask. All I know is that she was scared, very scared that he would find out. She came to me and asked me to help her. Told me she couldn't have anyone know about the pregnancy. Asked if I could send her somewhere until it was time to deliver."

She pressed her lips together. "I told her it would be easier if she didn't have the child at all, but she insisted. I think she loved the man, whoever he was. So we arranged for it to look like she was going away to university, but she actually went to stay with someone I knew until the baby was born. She came home a couple months after that when the school year would have ended. No one but the two of us knew."

"Her father did. He told the investigator about it"

She shook her head. "Not beforehand, he didn't. He believed she'd received a scholarship and was attending classes. The woman she stayed with was in the same city as the university she was supposed to be attending. And she was accepted at that university. She planned to return and attend the next year. If she could finish her degree in three years, no one would ever be the wiser."

"Which means her father found out at some point *after* she returned."

She shrugged. "Most likely. I wouldn't know. We didn't speak after I arranged for her to go away. It wouldn't have been safe to do so."

"Did she try to speak to you at any point after she returned?"

She nodded sharply. "She came by the house the week before she was murdered. But I had my maid send her away. Like I said, it wouldn't have been safe for us to speak."

I chewed on my lip, thinking. "You said she was scared of the baby's father finding out."

"Yes. Very."

"But you didn't know who he was. Could the woman she stayed with know?"

"It's possible. I have the contact information for her. She's still part of the network." She took out an address book and jotted down a name and phone number.

When I reached for the slip of paper, she didn't release it right away, instead staring at me intensely. "Some things are best left in the past. If it was this man who killed Mary and not Owen Browers, then he killed the woman who gave birth to his child. He won't take kindly to you resurrecting the dead."

I snatched the piece of paper away. "I realize that. But he also shouldn't be allowed to live his life without any consequence for what he did. If he killed her, he should pay for that."

She raised one eyebrow, but didn't say more about it.

The conversation then turned to Jamie's pregnancy and her plans for the nursery. At least she'd finally found the right shade of yellow. But as they chatted about that, my mind was focused on who the mysterious father could be and where Mary Diever's child was now.

🐾🐾 340 🐾🐾

CHAPTER 20

The first thing I did when I returned home was call the number Mrs. Mason had given me.

"Margie Price," the woman on the other end of the line said, her voice thick with, of all things for someone living in Philadelphia, a southern accent.

"Ms. Price. I was given your number by a Mrs. Mason in Colorado. She sent a young lady to live with you about thirty-six years ago, Mary Diever."

"Was that her last name? I never knew. We try to keep these situations as protected as possible. I only knew her as Mary Smith."

I settled onto the couch and put my feet up. "So you remember her?"

"I do. Sweet young lady, but scared of her own shadow. I suspect the men in her life had not been kind."

I reached for my notepad. "She talked to you about that?"

"Mm. Well, not exactly, but one can always tell these things. My now-husband would come by every few days and Mary always hid away when he did. Shied away from men at the grocery store as well. Kept to herself, poor thing."

Interesting. I tapped my pen against my lips, trying to think what to ask next. "I don't know if you're aware of this, but Mary Diever was killed the summer after she stayed with you."

"She was? Oh dear. That poor child. I really shouldn't call her a child, she was eighteen at the time. But there was always something very young and innocent about her."

I frowned, because that didn't seem in line with some of what Owen Browers had said. "Did you see any signs that she was a drinker or into drugs?"

"Oh, that."

"So you did?"

She huffed in annoyance. "That only started after the baby was born. She found it very hard to let go and needed an escape. Poor thing had to stay with me four months after the baby was born so her daddy wouldn't know why she'd come here. And there wasn't much else for her to do. So, yes, she did start drinking and doing some drugs. But nothing too bad. Just a kid trying to cover her pain."

"You said she found it very hard to let go? Did she want to keep the baby?"

"Not initially. The day of the birth there was no problem at all. She gave that little boy up as quick as you please. But then she had all that time to think. I know it weighed on her. She didn't say anything then, but you could see it in how she looked at other babies and how she cried sometimes."

"You said she didn't say anything then. Did she say something later?"

"Why yes she did. She called me about a month or two after she'd gone back home and asked me if I knew where the baby was and if there was any way she could change her mind and get it back."

I sat up straighter. "When exactly was this?"

"I don't know. July maybe? She'd been gone for a bit by then."

"Did she tell you why she wanted to try to get the baby back?"

"Um. Well. Not sure how smart it was, but she said she'd met a man who loved her very much and she thought he'd be a good father and might be willing to raise her child with her."

I scribbled that down as I asked, "And what did you tell her?"

"That it was too late. That she should marry that man if he loved her, but to let the baby go. Her only chance of reversing the adoption at that point was having the father come forward and challenge it. They'd just started allowing DNA paternity testing, but it wasn't very common yet, so even that wasn't a certainty."

I nodded to myself, thinking it through. "I bet that's when she told her father. He was a lawyer. Maybe she thought he could challenge the adoption for her. But he obviously didn't."

"Not that I know of. That call was the last I heard of it."

"Do you know where the baby is now?" I asked, just in case, because I suspected we were going to need to prove who the father was at some point and DNA was our best hope.

There was a long silence on the other end of the line and then she finally said, "It was a private adoption."

"Yes, but, do you know where the baby is now?"

Another long silence.

"Look, Ms. Price. Someone killed Mary Diever. And if it wasn't the man who was going to maybe marry her and help her raise that baby, then it was very likely the man who fathered the child. If we can get a DNA sample from the child, then we can maybe figure out who that was."

She sniffed. "Oh, I'm pretty sure I know who the father was."

"You do? How?" And how did she remember after all these years. It's nice to have the information you need fall into your lap and all, but color me skeptical that she'd remember the name of some random baby daddy thirty-six years after the fact.

"He came to visit while she was here. He was quite memorable."

"How did that happen? He wasn't supposed to know she was pregnant."

"Oh, he didn't. Not until that visit at least."

"What happened?" I asked, thinking about how horrible that must've been for Mary to have the man show up on her doorstep like that.

"Well, as you know, Mary was supposed to be here for school. That's what her daddy believed. Now, she told him she couldn't go back for the holidays because of the travel time and all. Truth being she was about to pop. That girl gave birth in January. But about a month before that, I'd say early December, her daddy called and told her that a friend was going to be in town and had a few Christmas presents for her that he was going to drop by."

"Couldn't she refuse? Or just be out when the man dropped by?"

"That's what she tried to do. Hid in her room as soon as he showed up here. But it didn't work."

"Why? What happened?"

"Well, the man came by, and I told him Mary wasn't here, but he insisted on staying until she returned. Sat in my living room for four hours. Finally, I suggested he just go on now because I really wasn't sure when she'd return, but he said he was prepared to stay there all weekend if he must."

"That's strange, isn't it?"

"It would be, if he weren't the father of the baby. At least, that's what I figured after his reaction when he finally did see her."

My stomach grumbled, but I didn't dare move to get something. I was too fascinated by her story. "So Mary finally gave up and came into the room?"

"Oh my, yes."

"And what happened then?"

"He grabbed her by the arm. Shook her. Got in her face and demanded to know what she was doing pregnant. Hissed under his breath, asking her why she hadn't gotten rid of it." She made a disgusted noise before she added, "And then that man had the audacity to suggest that she get rid of it right then even though a fool could see it was too late for that. Poor girl. She started sobbing, telling him she was sorry, begging his forgiveness. I honestly don't know what would've happened next because he was fixing to take her away from there."

"What did you do?"

"I told him I was fixing to call the cops and that he better get the hell out of there right then if he knew what was good for him."

"Did you?"

"Yes, ma'am. Soon as I started dialing, he took off. But when the cops arrived, Mary refused to speak about it. Wouldn't even give them his name." She tsked, still clearly annoyed after all these years.

"So how do you know who he is? If you just saw him that one day and then he ran off and Mary wouldn't name him."

She took a deep breath. "Oh, well, see, I've seen his face on TV. He's a senator. That mouthy one with too many opinions."

"He's a *senator*? Really?" I tried to think about who I knew from the Baker Valley who'd run for the Senate. There was only one.

"Well, at least he was. I believe he was just defeated in the latest election. Good riddance and God speed. Your voters finally got a bit of sense."

I covered my mouth with my hand for a moment, horrified by what this could mean if the father of Mary Diever's baby really was who Margie thought he was.

"Just to be clear, you're saying the man who hurt Mary and was likely the father of her child was Senator Quentin Baker."

"Yes. Although he obviously wasn't a senator back then."

"Oof."

Senator Quentin Baker was one of the most well-respected and well-known men in the valley, maybe even in the state. A man who lived and breathed family values. And had to be seventy-five now?

Seventy-five minus thirty-six was thirty-nine. Which meant that upstanding, very married father of three Quentin Baker had been involved with a seventeen-year-old and not in a nice, loving supportive relationship either.

But that might explain why everyone was so determined to sweep things under the rug back then. Because if he wasn't the DA at the time, then he was probably the judge. I wrote the name on my notepad and circled it three times.

Quentin Baker. Yikes.

"Did you ever see him again?" I asked. "Did he try to come back after the cops were gone?"

"No. I was worried about it for a bit there. Had my boyfriend stay over just in case and didn't let Mary go anywhere alone until after she'd delivered. But I never saw hide nor hair of him again. A few hang-up calls, so he may have tried to get through, but that was it. She told him before he left that she was giving the baby away, so maybe that was enough once he got cooled down some."

"And what about the baby? Are you sure he didn't go after the baby?"

"The baby was fine."

"How do you know?"

She paused.

"Ms. Price. Please. How do you know the baby was fine?"

"Because I was a nurse at the hospital where he was born. And that dark hair and those gray eyes were very distinctive. He also had a birth mark on his neck, one of those wine stain ones."

"So you know his name?"

"Yes."

"And do you know where to find him now? If we needed to get a DNA sample, could we?"

She didn't answer.

"Margie? It may be the only way we can prove who killed Mary Diever. Will you tell me how to find him if I need to?"

She sighed. "Yes. But only if you need to. He is a good man who does not need to find out that his mama was killed so soon after he was born."

It wasn't ideal, but it would have to do for now. "Thank you. I appreciate it."

"You're welcome. Just watch yourself. That Quentin Baker was one of the scariest men I've ever crossed paths with. Meet him on the street and he'd seem like the nicest man in the world, but he is not. I am telling you, steer clear of that man if you can."

"I'll keep that in mind. Thanks again."

I hung up the phone and stared at the wall.

Senator Quentin Baker. A man at the start of an illustrious career. A man with a lot to lose if Mary Diever came forward about having his baby…

Definitely a motive for murder in my book. Of course, I had a feeling no one was going to want me to pursue this one step further once I told them who the new suspect was. Which meant maybe I should just keep that to myself for a bit longer.

CHAPTER 21

I was trying to figure out how exactly to pursue this new lead without bringing the world down on my head when my phone rang. Caller ID said it was Matt, but he never calls me when he's at work, so I answered immediately.

"Matt, what is it? What's wrong?"

He hesitated for an extra second. "It's Owen Browers."

"What happened to him?"

"We don't know. They found his truck at the west end of the valley, abandoned. There was a note on the seat."

My stomach clenched. He better not have given up on me just when I was starting to make progress in his case. "What kind of note?"

Matt hesitated again. "It was a confession, Maggie."

"A confession to what?" I stood and started pacing the room.

"What do you think?"

"Mary Diever's murder? No. Why on earth would a man ask me to investigate the murder and then turn around and confess when I'm finally starting to make progress on the investigation?"

"Because you unearthed the secret that made him kill her. According to the note, he killed Mary in a jealous rage because he found out she'd had another man's child."

I shook my head even though he couldn't see it. "That doesn't make sense. She had that child before they even met. And he didn't know about the baby until I told him, I'd swear to it. Plus he still loves her even now."

"People do strange things for love."

"No."

"I'm just telling you what the note said, Maggie."

"So it was a suicide note?"

"No. He's on the run."

I scoffed. "That makes even less sense. Who tells the authorities they're going on the run? If you decide to run you hide the fact as long as you possibly can so you can get a good head start."

"Thought about that a lot have you?"

I glared at the wall because I couldn't glare at Matt in person. "Don't be smart with me. You met Owen, did he strike you as that stupid? To confess to a murder and then tell everyone he was running away?" I shook my head. "No. It doesn't make any sense. It's a set-up. You have to find him, Matt. He's in danger if he isn't already dead."

He sighed. "Sometimes people do things that don't make sense."

I shook my head again. "If you won't look for him, I will. I'm going to his place. See if there are any signs of foul play."

"Maggie. This is not your job."

"No, it's yours. But if you aren't going to do it, then I am."

I could almost see him frowning at me through the phone. "Maggie, please. If you're right about Owen then going to his place could be dangerous."

"Then come pick me up so we can go together."

He didn't answer, so I added, "Fine. If you don't want to come with me then you can sit there and nervously wait for me to contact you and tell you everything's okay, not knowing if I'm alive or not for the next hour."

(I didn't get out of my high school curfew by playing nice.)

He sighed, a deep heavy sigh full of defeat. I crossed my arms and waited.

"Okay. I'll be there in a few minutes. Do not leave until I get there. But you have to understand that whether he wrote that note or not, it may be impossible to clear his name at this point."

"Why? It's just one piece of evidence."

"That the press were tipped off to. They found the truck first. Owen Browers' confession is going to run on the evening news tonight. Oh, and the DNA results came back today with a match to Owen. Those leaked as well."

I glanced at my notepad where the name Quentin Baker was circled.

"Matt, think about what you just told me and ask yourself if you really think there isn't someone behind those two leaks who's trying to frame Owen Browers. Someone who's very media-savvy and somehow knew I was getting too close."

"Maggie, no one thinks like that in the real world."

I laughed, once. "Politicians do. Like Quentin Baker, the likely father of Mary's baby."

"What?" he snapped.

"Yeah, that's the phone call I just had. The woman

Mary stayed with was pretty sure Quentin Baker was the father. He showed up before she gave birth and was furious to find out she was pregnant."

"Maggie, you need to step back from this right now. Quentin Baker is not someone you want to mess with." He'd gone from casual to full alert.

"But if I don't, who will? I mean, look at poor Owen. Thirty-six years of being a murder suspect and then framed for it when someone actually gets close to the truth? I can't step back because no one else will step forward."

"Look, I'll tell the Chief. Let him figure out how to proceed. He won't go after Owen with what you've found."

"Come on now, Matt. You know that isn't true. Between that note, the abandoned vehicle, and the DNA match, do you honestly think Owen Browers is going to get a fair trial? Actually, do you honestly think he'll be alive to go to trial? Much cleaner to get rid of him. A nice little staged suicide and it's all wrapped up with a bow."

I shook my head. "No. We need to pursue this right now. If we wait for some bureaucrat to make a decision, it could mean Owen's life. So, are you going to pick me up so we can go over to his place together? Or am I doing this myself?"

He let out a deep, exasperated breath. "I'll be there in twenty. Wait for me."

"Okay. Love you."

"Love you, too," he muttered.

(It was the type of love you, too, that a man says when he really does love you but there's a part of him that really wishes you had an ounce of sense or had taken up macrame as a hobby instead of murder.)

CHAPTER 22

Owen Browers' house was actually nice. I don't know why that surprised me so much, probably because I can be as narrow-minded and biased as the next person, so I'd assumed that a man who was basically shunned by everyone and was big and scary looking would live in some run-down dump of a place with rotted out car parts littering the front lawn.

But it wasn't like that at all. There was enough snow on the ground I couldn't see the yard, but it was pretty clear he put a lot of effort into his home. It was freshly-painted a soft shade of blue with white trim and all of the windows and doors were well-maintained. It wasn't a big place, but it was nice.

Matt tried the door and it opened for him so we carefully walked inside, looking around for any signs of foul play. (I watch too many true crime shows, sorry.)

Everything seemed in order. There was a small table with two chairs in the kitchen that had a stack of business papers tucked against the wall. The fridge was full and was another surprise. Owen Browers hadn't struck me as the type to like organic yogurt and fresh vegetables, but that was what was in there.

(The large freezer in the garage full of hand-labeled portions of elk meat that we found later eased my mind a bit. At least I hadn't been completely off about the man.)

There were two bedrooms, one with a small bed tucked into the corner. That room had the cold, dusty feel of a room that wasn't used much. The other bedroom had a large bed, perhaps even custom built, that dominated the space.

The living room, hallway, and both bedrooms had wildlife photos hung on the walls, each framed in an identical simple black frame. The photos were really good. The type that make you feel like you could reach out and touch the animal in the photo.

"What does Owen Browers do for a living?" I asked Matt, studying an image of a bear about to eat a fish.

"Wildlife photography. He posts to stock photography sites mostly, but also sells prints off his website."

"So these are all his?"

I looked at the pictures more closely. Impressive. It's one thing to know that someone out there has that kind of skill, but another thing entirely to realize that the strange man you just met has that kind of skill.

"He's exceptionally good," I said.

"I know. I almost bought one of his prints. He has one that's of a deer in a meadow just as the sun's coming up. It's stunning. But I figured buying artwork from a man you're going to arrest for murder was poor form."

"I don't know about that. Could've helped the man eat for a few days in the meantime." I stared at the photos on the wall again. "You know, if we get through this and he's not arrested or killed for some fool reason, I'm going to ask him to do a series of photos of Fancy, Lulu, and Hans. I think it would be really neat to include their photos somehow at the new pet resort. I'm not sure how yet. I'll know once I see the photos. If he's willing that is."

"I like that idea. Maybe you should have a local artists gallery, too. Let visitors buy artwork while they're there."

"Ooh, I like that. We could have Owen's photography and I know Melinda Nederland does some gorgeous pottery and Paul Barlin does acrylics that are just stunning." I smiled up at him. "You are a genius. I knew there was a reason I married you."

"Thank you. But that still doesn't tell us where Owen is."

I glanced around. "No, it doesn't, does it? Where do you think he develops his prints? Or stores his equipment? It has to be somewhere here, you'd think."

"Good question."

We poked around and started opening what we'd assumed were closet doors until we found a small walk-in closet off the hallway. It must've been custom-built to take a corner of the garage and turn it into his darkroom.

It was a very tidy, organized space. There were shelves along the back wall where Owen's cameras were stored in a neat row, each one labeled carefully, all of the special lenses and attachments placed beside them.

"Hey, Matt."

"Yeah?"

"If Owen went on the run like the note in his truck implies, don't you think he'd take his cameras along, too? I mean he's clearly used to hiking with them given some of the photos he's taken. And if they're his livelihood I can't imagine him just abandoning them here. And I don't see space for more of them."

He nodded. "Good point."

"See? Someone really is trying to frame him."

"That's what it's starting to look like."

"You've gotta find him, Matt. Before whoever left that note does. I mean, assuming they didn't already and that the note wasn't just covering their tracks."

He pursed his lips. "I don't know that we've found enough for the Chief to change direction on this. But let me call my buddy Paul, see if he's willing to bring his tracking dog out. Do this off the books for now. He owes me one."

"Thank you."

I glanced around the place one more time. I really hoped nothing had happened to Owen. He was a man dealt a bad hand by life who'd somehow found a way to carry on and survive despite it. I hated to think that after all this time trying to find out the truth about Mary was going to ruin everything for him. That would be too bitter a pill to swallow.

CHAPTER 23

While Matt worked on getting his buddy Paul to help find Owen Browers, I went to talk to my grandpa.

He answered the door with a big hug and a smile. He was so excited about being a great-grandpa it was kind of funny. "Maggie May, come in. Lesley and I were just about to play a game of Scrabble. You want to join us?"

"Sure." It was not easy to beat my grandpa at Scrabble, but it was always fun to try.

We settled in around the dining room table and each drew our first tile. I got A so was able to play first. I almost played GNAW but I knew I'd regret wasting an N and G at the beginning of the game when I could save them to form a word with -ING at the end at some point later. Instead I played WAR.

My grandpa was not impressed. "You know we all have to play off of that, don't you?"

"Sorry, I had bad letters."

Lesley smiled at both of us and turned my WAR into BEWARE. "Better, Lou?"

"Better playing options, but a horrible use of your Es."

I suspected Lesley had made that play just to make him happy. "Grandpa, it's a game. Games are supposed to be fun."

He snorted. "Games are played to be won. Now. What brought you over? Pregnancy or murder investigation?"

"Murder investigation. Although, I was wondering, if it's not too much effort, could you build a crib for the babies? Or a rocker or something? I'd love to have something you made in their room."

My grandpa is an amazing carpenter. Some of the work he's done over the years is absolutely stunning. Multiple types of wood used to form beautiful patterns and designs. He's a master craftsman.

He gave me a shrewd look. "Are you sure that wouldn't violate your rule about jinxing the pregnancy?"

I'd told him and Lesley about not discussing baby names until our little bumps of joy were born and he'd laughed at me.

"I hope not. If I thought you could whip something together in a weekend, I'd probably wait to ask, but I know some of the things you do take a lot longer than that."

He smiled. "Just so happens I was working on some sketches of that very thing today. As long as you're sure you don't want some new-fangled creation that does ten things at once?"

"No. I'd much rather have something that reminds me of family."

"Consider it done. Now, what've you found out in that murder investigation of yours?"

I chewed on my lower lip, desperately wanting a Coke or ten but knowing I shouldn't. "Promise this stays in this room for now?"

He turned his full attention on me. "Why? What did you find out?"

I rubbed my chin. Where to start? "Mary Diever didn't go away to college. She went away to have a child."

"Was that nonsense still happening in the 80s?"

I shrugged. "It seems so. If you were a girl from a good family who didn't want your dad to know that you'd been knocked up, but also wanted to actually have the kid."

He took a sip of his coffee. "So she'd had a kid. How does that impact the murder investigation?"

"Well, she hid it from her father but he somehow found out right before her death."

He crossed his arms. "So you want to know if her father was the type to kill his daughter for shaming him?"

"No...Although, was he? Especially if she was thinking about reversing the adoption and raising the kid herself? Would he have tolerated something like that?"

He blew out a breath. "Her dad and her granddad were hard men. But I don't think either one would've killed her for something like that. Maybe very strongly encouraged her to change her plans. But not murder. I can't see it."

"That's what I kind of figured."

"So then why the visit?"

I gave him a sideways glance as I shuffled my tiles. "Because I think it's likely the baby's father killed her."

"And who was that?"

I laced my fingers together and pressed them to my mouth, still not sure telling him was a good idea. My grandpa sometimes has notions about the risks I should be taking.

"Maggie May. Who do you think was the father of the baby?"

I scrunched up my face. Best to just get it over with. "Looks like it was Quentin Baker."

He pushed back his chair and stood. "Drop this. Right now."

"Grandpa."

"I mean it Maggie May. Quentin Baker is a dangerous man."

"He's a senator."

"Exactly." He pressed his finger down on the table as he made his points. "Some men get that far because they have no major skeletons in their closet. But others get that far because they're ruthless at hiding or eliminating those skeletons. Which do you think he is given what you're investigating?"

When I didn't say anything, he shook his head. "You have to drop this. Quentin Baker is a man with money, power, and a lot to lose if this should come out."

I knew he was right, but I couldn't help arguing about it. "He's not even going to be in office anymore come next year. What does he really have to lose?"

"His reputation. All he has now is who he once was. If this comes out, he loses that." He stared me down. "Drop it."

"I'm not a dog grandpa. And Owen Browers will go to prison if I don't help him."

He reached for his non-existent cigarettes and then cussed under his breath when he was reminded once more that he no longer smoked.

I knew he wanted to tell me that Owen Browers didn't matter. But my grandpa also knew what prison was like, and he'd never wish that on anyone, especially an innocent man.

Well, at least not on anyone that didn't really deserve it.

"Let the police handle this, Maggie," he sank back in his chair.

"I can't."

"Why not?"

Reluctantly, I told him about the note they'd found in Owen's abandoned truck and the fact that he was missing.

"That is exactly why you need to drop this, Maggie May."

"But don't you see? No one else is going to believe Owen now. I'm his only hope."

My grandpa looked at me like I'd lost all my marbles. "Maggie May. Who exactly do you think arranged for Owen Browers to go missing and leave behind a confession?"

I hunched my shoulders. "Quentin Baker."

"My point exactly."

"But…"

"No buts, Maggie May." He shuffled his tiles so aggressively I expected one to fall off the rack. "You need to start thinking about your family. About those two little babies in your belly. Matt does, too. This isn't about you anymore. This isn't about your principles. This is about your family."

I pressed my lips together and shook my head. "But don't you understand? That's how the world goes to shit, Grandpa. People prioritize their own concerns at the expense of the greater good. Of the community. Of justice. And before you know it, we're living in a corrupt, cruel world where everyone justifies their most selfish instincts because everyone else is like that."

"You're damned right people prioritize themselves. Because most people are smart enough to realize that all championing the greater good does is gets them a whole lot of nothing. You try to do the right thing and you lose it all while the powerful still don't face any consequences. You can't win this fight, Maggie May. You have to focus on what matters." He glanced pointedly at my belly before he played his next word. "It's your turn. Play your tiles."

I fumed silently through the rest of the game. But surprisingly it either made me a better player or my grandpa a worse player, because for the first time in what felt like ages I beat him, by thirty points.

CHAPTER 24

Matt had a late shift that night, but I stayed up and waited for him to come home. (Well, actually, I took a bit of a nap on the couch while I waited to be honest. Pregnancy is hard.)

"Maggie, you waited up." He gave me a kiss on the cheek before removing all of his winter layers.

I nodded. "I needed to see your face."

He collapsed on the couch and rested his head on my lap, smiling up at me. "You know, pretty soon I'm not going to be able to do this. The bumps are going to take over and you're going to be as big as a house."

He looked so happy about it, I had to laugh.

I sighed. "Twins. Someone up there has a sense of humor."

"Twin *girls*. We both got hit on this one. I wanted a girl, but two? We're in trouble." He smiled again. "They're going to wrap me around their little fingers. How do you feel about pony ownership?"

I laughed. "Fancy is as close as they're going to come to pony ownership. They may wrap you around their little fingers, but I will have final say on all dream vacations and purchases of live animals."

I ran my hand through his hair as we sat there in companionable silence. I was scared on so many levels, but so content, too.

Finally, I said, "Do you ever think about how if a murder isn't solved right away and you don't have anyone out there advocating for you then the person just gets away with it? I mean, I watch all these cold case shows and each time there's some mother or brother or father behind the case that called the police station every year on the day of the anniversary of the murder. Or hired a private investigator. Or did something else to not let the police forget. But if you don't have anyone to advocate for you, the person just…gets away with it."

He cupped my face in his hand. "We don't want to let the murderers go, but there's always a new one. Or if there isn't a new murder then there's other police priorities. We're starting to see an uptick in fentanyl deaths right now. Resources have to be used the most effective way they can."

I nodded. "I know why, but it's hard. To think of some poor girl like Mary Diever who no one fought for. Or Owen Browers. Have you found him yet?"

He shook his head. "No. Good news is there was no trail from the truck, which means it was a plant. Bad news is there was also no trail from his place. So wherever he went missing from, it wasn't home.

"I was hoping for better news."

"I know. So was I."

I nudged him off my lap. "Here, let's get you fed while we talk about what to do next."

He scarfed down leftover turkey casserole while I filled him in on my conversation with my grandpa. (I always go a little wild around Thanksgiving and buy myself a turkey even if I'm not hosting that year and then have to find some time to make the turkey before or after the actual day. This time I'd chosen before),

He didn't say anything until he was done eating and then he carefully set down his fork and sat back in his chair. "I hate to say it, but I agree with him, Maggie. Look what happened to Owen Browers. It would kill me if something happened to you, too."

Before I could object, he held up his hand. "I'm not going to let it go, I promise. I just want *you* safe."

I pressed my lips together. I trusted Matt. Not only with my life, but with my heart and my insecurities. And I didn't want to doubt him, but I wasn't sure he could pull it off. The Chief was a political man. And Matt had other more pressing priorities. I was the only one who was focused solely on this case.

At the same time, maybe I should play it a little safe. I mean, I was growing two little lives inside. But did backing off make me a coward?

Of course, was being a coward such a bad thing to be?

"Maggie," Matt squeezed my hand. "I'll take care of it, I promise."

After a long moment I said, "Okay." Part of being married is trusting your partner, so I decided I'd let it go.

For now.

(Because you don't tell a competent woman you'll take care of something if you aren't going to see it through. That's just an invitation for her to get angry and do it herself.)

I resolved to give Matt a chance to show me that he really would pursue the investigation. But if he didn't…Well, I wasn't going to sit around and watch some innocent man convicted for a crime he didn't commit if I could do anything about it.

CHAPTER 25

Over the next few days I tried not to think about the case. I really did. I threw myself into baby research instead. Being older and having twins, there was a lot to know on top of all the regular baby stuff.

Of course, all that made me do was pray daily that by the time I gave birth there'd be no risk in going down to Denver to deliver in a nice, big, sterile hospital that had a well-respected maternity ward and lots of medical supplies. That whole "let me float in a pool of warm water while soothing music plays in the background" approach to delivery was not for me, thank you very much.

Nope. Fill me up with drugs and use every trick in the modern medicine playbook to move things along, please.

So I really was trying to be good and forget about the case. Even when they finally found Owen Browers holed up in an abandoned cabin and arrested him for Mary's murder, I still kept my nose out of it. Barely.

But then the case came to me.

Because I bumped into Quentin Baker at the grocery store of all places. Granted, there's only one grocery store in the whole valley and with the entrances to the valley shut down there was no easy way to go elsewhere to shop, so it wasn't completely unexpected that we'd run into one another.

Then again, it had never happened in the year and a half I'd lived in Creek. And I certainly would've never expected him to turn in my direction when he saw me. It's not like we were on a wave-at-one-another-in-the-grocery-store basis.

"Maggie May Carver. Or is it Barnes now?" he asked as he walked up to me.

He was one of those politicians that embrace the good ol' boy look. He had on cowboy boots and jeans and a button-up denim shirt with one of those bolo ties that were probably never actually worn by any real cowboy.

The only part of the cliché he'd left off was the cowboy hat and the aw shucks attitude.

I casually moved so that the cart was between us. "It's Carver still. I kept my last name."

"Interesting choice, to continue to associate yourself with a known felon. I'd think you would've dropped your last name as soon as you could."

I met him eye-for-eye. I knew he was dangerous, but no one insults my family. "I chose that last name. And my grandpa may be an ex-felon, but he's the most stand-up man I've ever known. As a matter of fact, he has far more character and moral fortitude than most."

"Is that so?" His smile was positively smarmy.

"Yes. It is."

He studied me with cold gray eyes. "I heard you were looking into the Mary Diever murder."

"Who told you that?"

"I hear things."

"Then you probably know how far I got in that investigation, too. And know that I identified another suspect in her murder."

He stepped closer and I was glad for the cart between us. "I might have heard that. But of course, you've stopped that investigation now that the police have arrested Owen Browers, haven't you?"

I didn't answer him immediately, but finally I said, "Why did you do it? Why kill her? Was being powerful more important to you than that young girl's life?"

He forced a hearty laugh. "Is that what you think? That I'd dirty my hands that way? On a little bit of fluff?" He studied me for a long moment before placing his hands on the other side of the cart and leaning in. "You've lost a lot of people in your life, haven't you, Maggie? Your parents? Your fiancé?"

I didn't answer him. It took everything I had to stand there and not run. Never run from a predator. Rule one.

He gave me a big, hearty smile. "It's good that you've found someone now. Someone who makes you happy." He glanced down at my belly. "And that you're going to add to that. Children are priceless."

I crossed my arms against the shiver that ran up my spine. "Yes, they are. All children. Even Mary's."

He shook his head and laughed softly. "You know, I have a certificate on my wall that says the Bakers were one of the first families of Colorado. We have a long, proud history in this state. And I will do whatever it takes to ensure that history is not tarnished by some upstart nosy little busybody who came from nothing."

I held his gaze even though I really wanted to run. Or hit him. "You know what's funny? I've got one of those certificates, too, somewhere in a drawer. Because while your family was busy with their proud history of living off the backs of others, mine was down in Trinidad working the coal mines and cleaning the houses of rich folks like you. And if you think that puts you above us, you're wrong. My family has a proud history here, too. One where we don't bow down to the likes of you just because you tell us to."

He stepped back, still smiling his politician's smile. "We'll see about that. Be careful, Mrs. Carver. Hate to see you lose anyone else you love, but life can be tragic sometimes, can't it?" He winked as he turned away.

Only after he was out of sight did my brain catch up to my mouth. What had I just done? I knew better than to poke a bear.

CHAPTER 26

By the next day, I'd almost convinced myself that I'd overreacted to the conversation with Quentin Baker at the grocery store. I mean, really, he was a senator. Senators don't threaten people's families, do they? I'm sure I'd just imagined that. He was simply a man with a bad past who didn't want it brought up, that was all.

But then Matt didn't come home on time.

And when I called to ask where he was, the dispatcher couldn't reach him.

These things happen. A man needs to use the facilities, maybe he turns off his radio for a minute or two and forgets to turn it back on. Or he finds himself stuck in an area without reception.

But after twenty minutes, I started to panic. Fortunately, I was able to get Officer Clark on the line. I didn't like the man because he had it in for my grandpa (or at least he had), but he was a decent friend of Matt's. I knew he'd take it seriously.

I didn't tell him who had threatened my loved ones at the grocery store—I knew that would make him less likely to help me—but I did tell him that I'd been threatened the day before.

"Maggie, why do you always get involved in things you shouldn't?" he asked.

"Is this really the time for that conversation? Just find my husband, would you? Please. I need to know he's okay."

"Alright. I'll put out an alert for his vehicle, see if anyone can find it. Don't worry, it's probably nothing."

I paced the living room for the next thirty minutes as Fancy eyed me from her dog bed in the corner. She is not a fan of movement. She likes me to settle in one place so she can settle in a place nearby and snore. She probably would've fled to the backyard to get away from my pacing, but I'd blocked her in with me, just in case. A man who'd go after a pregnant woman's husband likely wasn't above going after a dog.

I almost jumped out of my skin when someone finally knocked on the door. It wasn't Matt, he would've just walked in. So who was it? I flung it open to see Officer Clark.

"What's happened? Where's Matt?"

He held his hands up like he was trying to calm a horse. "We don't know. We found his vehicle, abandoned. It was on the side of the road outside of Bakerstown."

"And? Why are you here? Why aren't you looking for him?" It took all of my self-control not to grab him and shake him.

"They're looking, don't worry." He licked his lips. "But I wanted to let you know as soon as possible. There was a bullet hole in the windshield."

Before I could faint, he grabbed my arm. "It was on the passenger side. No blood. We're pretty sure he wasn't hit."

Tears filled my eyes. "I can't lose him, Ben. I'm about to have twins and he needs to be here. He's gotta be the good parent. I'm…I can't…I can't do this. Not without Matt. You have to find him. I can't…"

I couldn't do any of it. Not just parenting, life. Getting through every day. I don't know how he'd done it but that good-looking, likeable, kind, intelligent, funny, you-know-what had made himself absolutely essential to me and I could not envision a life that didn't include him.

Ben stood there awkwardly, not quite knowing what to do in the face of a desperate, crying pregnant woman. You'd think they'd train cops to hug someone who's all distraught, but I'm pretty sure they actually train them to keep their distance and their hand on their weapon instead, which was the exact opposite of what I needed. It made me want to scream.

"Is there someone you want me to call?" he asked.

"My grandpa. Can you bring him over please? I don't want to leave in case they find Matt."

I could see that he didn't want to deal with my grandpa, but all he did was nod. "I'll go get him for you. Be right back. You'll be okay until then?"

"Yes. I'll be fine," I gritted out, directing all my fear into anger at men who treat women like breakable little dolls.

I swear, completely melt down in front of someone once and they never forget it.

"Okay. I'll be right back." He looked at me again like he wasn't sure I'd be okay for the amount of time it took him to go next door and come back, and I almost slammed the door in his face for it. But instead I nodded and smiled calmly back at him, trying to appear serene and calm so he'd get my frickin' grandpa already.

🐾 🐾 🐾

It took another thirty minutes to locate Matt. Thirty of the most nerve-wracking, heart-wrenching moments of my life. I sat on the couch, chewing my thumbnail down to the quick (something I never do) while Lesley rubbed my back and told me it was going to be okay and my grandpa paced back and forth, clearly struggling not to tell me he'd told me so about Quentin Baker.

When they finally found Matt he was just fine. Seems when someone shot at my ex-military husband he took it personally and turned soldier. Which meant he'd parked his car, calculated an estimated trajectory for the bullet, and then went after the shooter, turning off his radio so the sound of anyone trying to reach him wouldn't give his position away.

The shooter had fled as soon as he realized what Matt was doing, but Matt grew up hunting and tracking in those woods, he wasn't about to be deterred. It just took him a little longer to catch the kid than he'd expected.

Yes, kid. Quentin Baker's sixteen-year-old great-nephew who insisted that he hadn't meant to shoot anyone. He'd just been playing in the woods and made a mistake. No intent to harm, especially not a cop.

Didn't even know who my husband was or I was. Just a weird coincidence that I was the one who wanted to accuse his great-uncle of murder and that said great-uncle had made veiled threats to my family the day before.

(Yeah, right.)

His very high-priced lawyer was all over things almost immediately. No way the kid was going to be charged with anything close to attempted murder which was very, very annoying.

But at the time I was a little more caught up in the realization that I was married to a cop, a man who risked his life at work every single day of his life. And not just because of me, either. Matt dealt with drunk drivers, drug users, abusers, fighters, killers. You name it. Each day there was a chance he wasn't going to come home to me.

As much as I wished it were the case, my husband wasn't out rescuing kittens out of trees and walking grandmas across the street.

Which is why I sobbed my little heart out on his shoulder when he finally got home to me. Seriously, you should never, ever mix life-threatening moments with pregnancy hormones.

Poor Matt. I'm pretty sure he did not know what on earth had happened to his competent, put-together wife. I mean, I'm normally solid when things go wrong. But it was just too much. All of it. Everything.

Fortunately, I was lucky enough to have married a man who was there for the tears just as much as he was there for the good parts. He sat with me on the couch and held me until I finally wound down. And then, bless the man, he offered to fix me whatever I wanted for dinner.

"You know what I really want?" I told him, still sniffling.

"What? Name it and it's yours."

"I'd really like a grilled peanut butter and jelly sandwich."

He chuckled. "I offer to fix you anything in the world and you ask for a grilled PBJ?"

"Please."

"Done." He kissed my forehead and went off to make

me the most perfect grilled **PBJ** in the world. I was so lucky to have him in my life.

CHAPTER 27

The next morning I woke up angry. You do not threaten my husband, I don't care who you are, and think you can get away with it. I'd thought about it most of the night as I lay in bed staring at the ceiling. There had to be a way to strike at Quentin Baker. And to do so in such a way that he never acted against my family again.

That meant exposing his secret.

As soon as it was a decent hour, I called Mason. I told him everything I'd found out about Mary Diever and Quentin Baker. And I told him how Quentin's great-nephew had shot at Matt. And how I wanted to make Quentin Baker pay for threatening my family.

"I don't care if he goes to jail for Mary Diever's murder, Mason. I want him ruined. How do we do that? How do we prove that he was the father of Mary's child? Publicly."

"Hmm. Good question."

I wanted to jump through the phone and throttle the man for sounding so coolly competent, but I needed him so I clenched my hand in my lap and waited while he thought it through.

Come on, man, figure it out, I silently fumed. *You're a sharp legal mind, you have to know how we can expose this. Get it together already.*

I didn't say any of that, though. I just calmly waited and practiced counting backwards from a thousand.

Finally, Mason spoke. "I think I have a possible solution. You said the woman Mary stayed with knows where to find the child?"

"Yes."

He thought about it another long, excruciating moment during which I refrained from screaming at him. "Hmm. Yes. I think it could work."

"What?" I finally snapped.

"Of course, the statute of limitations has passed. However, the case does not have to succeed to serve our purposes. We simply need a plausible reason to file."

"Mason. What case? What are you thinking?"

"Oh. I was thinking I can file suit on behalf of Mary's child to establish paternity. Usually the court only allows cases like that until the child is twenty-one. However, they have allowed cases in other states that were past the statute of limitations where there was a medical need to know. Which means I can probably make a general argument that the child needs to know paternity because he needs to know his medical risks. Although it would help if the child actually has a medical reason for pursuing the paternity case. At a minimum the filing will make public the fact that Quentin Baker may have been the father of Mary Diever's child."

I nodded. "Okay. Let's do this. And the initial filing will be public, right? If they somehow want to suppress the case, they have to counter-file to do so?"

"Yes. It will be a public record when it is filed. But I cannot guarantee it will stay public. Or that anyone will see the filing."

"But if we tip off the media about the filing they can find it before it's suppressed."

"Mm. Well. That can be a slippery slope. As an officer of the court…"

"Which I'm not. Look, no need for you to walk down that slope. As soon as you tell me you've filed, I'll find the filing and forward it to every investigative reporter I can think of. How will Senator Baker ever know that they didn't have a keyword search set for his name. He is a senator after all."

He hesitated for a moment and I thought he'd refuse to go through with it, but then he said, "What you do with knowledge of the filing is not my concern."

"Great. So what do you need to make this happen?"

"The name of the child. The child's agreement that I should make the filing. And a signed affidavit from the woman that Mary Diever stayed with about her encounter with Quentin Baker and her suspicion that he was the child's father. Get those for me and I'll make the filing."

"Done. I hope. How much do I owe you for this, Mason?"

Mason Maxwell was a very good lawyer, which meant he was not cheap. The only reason he wasn't already in possession of my entire life-savings was because he'd been sweet on Jamie when I needed his services last.

"Nothing. I never did like Quentin Baker."

"Excellent. I'll get the information today."

"I'll be ready to file as soon as you get it to me."

I hung up and smiled. Quentin Baker had messed with the wrong woman. And as soon as Mason made that filing everyone I loved would be safe again. Now I just had to convince Margie to tell me how to find Mary's son and had to convince the son to agree to file the suit. That should be…easy. (Or not.)

CHAPTER 28

At least I was calling Margie at a decent hour since Philly is on the east coast so a couple hours ahead of Colorado. After we exchanged the typical set of pleasantries and I filled her in on what had happened and why I was calling, I jumped right in.

"So you really thought you recognized Mary's kid? You know his name?" I asked.

"I did," she answered, wary, like she was regretting that she'd told me that and trying to figure out how to back away from it without lying to me.

"Could you give me the name, please?"

She was silent for so long I thought she might've walked away from the phone.

"Margie? We're trying to catch a killer here. Confirming that Quentin Baker was the father would help with that."

"I just, the scandal of it all. I'm not sure Mary's child deserves to go through that. He's happy. He has a good life. This could ruin all of that."

I sat up so fast, I startled Fancy who glared at me and took herself outside. "Wait. You know where he is *now*?"

"Well, of course. He did his residency at the hospital where I worked. We're connected on that Facebook thing. I doubt he sees any of my posts, he's a busy man. But I see his."

So Mary's son had become a doctor? Good for him.

"Do you happen to know if he's had any medical issues? Genetic ones? Or have his kids? Because that would be a legitimate reason he might want to track down his biological parents."

She sighed. "Yes, he has. He's actually been trying to find out who his parents were for about two years now."

"Really? Why?"

"Well, it seems during the genetic testing for his first child, he found out he was a carrier for Tay-Sachs disease."

I frowned. "That usually occurs in the Jewish population doesn't it?"

"Yes, ma'am. Which made him a little curious about his ancestry. Because the parents who raised him were definitely not Jewish. And it seems they had not told him he was adopted, bless their hearts. Of course, he obviously knows now after that whole Tay-Sachs scare. But he's had no success finding anything." I could almost hear her shrug through the phone. "Last I heard, he was going to try that DNA tracing through one of those national databases. Find his parents that way. Of course, from what you've told me, Mary and her whole family were dead before that became a possibility so I doubt he found anything useful. Maybe there was something that pointed towards his daddy, though…"

I stood up and paced the living room. "If there was, that would be perfect. Anything that points this direction adds to the case that Quentin Baker is the father. And the fact that he was already looking means he's more likely to be on board with our plan. It's perfect."

She was quiet on the other end of the line.

"What am I missing, Margie?"

"Well, it's just that…" she sighed. "I like the boy. But you have to understand that you contacting him like this is going to be a bit awkward for me."

"How so?"

"I told you, he's been looking for his parents for two years. And I knew all about Mary all that time. He may not take too kindly to finding out that I could have solved his issue long ago and I didn't say anything."

"Mm. Fair point. How about you give me his name and phone number and I keep you out of it?"

"But you said you're gonna need that affidavit from me about what I saw between Mary and Senator Baker."

"True. But maybe we can list you as a Jane Doe due to your ongoing involvement in helping battered women flee their partners. It's worth a shot. And it'll at least give you time to figure out how to square things with him."

"That might work. I still feel bad for the boy. Looking for his mama only to find out she was murdered and his daddy might have been the one to do it."

I nodded. "It's definitely not the end he would've hoped for, I'm sure. But then again, this is someone he never actually knew. He has no emotional connection to her like you or I might to the mothers who raised us."

"True…" She sighed again.

"Margie. I need him to file this case so I can protect my family. Can I please have the name?"

"Fine. Might as well. It's in God's hands now."

CHAPTER 29

I was lucky. It was Dr. Brian McKendrick's day off. (That was the name of Mary's son.) So when I called his cellphone he actually answered. Which was another small miracle, because there is no way I am answering my phone if I don't recognize the number. But as a heart surgeon it seemed Dr. McKendrick was a little more open to calls from strangers.

There was no easy way to start the conversation I needed to have, so I just went right for it.

"Dr. McKendrick, my name is Maggie Carver, I live in Colorado, and I believe I know who your parents were. I'd like your help in proving that."

"How did you get my name? Or my number? This is a private number."

"I was given them by someone who knew your mother. And recognized you as her son. Can I have a minute to explain. Please?"

He hesitated for a moment, which I can't blame him for. Someone calls you up out of the clear blue and claims to know who your mother was, it has to set off about a million alarm bells. Either that or you're the type of person who falls for every "free trip" scam there is.

"Dr. McKendrick. Please. It's important that I get your help on something related to all of this. Don't worry, I don't want money. It's…Just let me explain?"

I could hear his wife in the background asking what was going on, but he must've waved her off because soon it grew quiet. "Okay. You have five minutes. Go."

I took a deep breath. Where to start?

"Alright. As I told you, my name is Maggie May Carver. I live in Creek, Colorado. Recently a man asked me to look into a thirty-six-year-old murder where he was the accused. The woman who was murdered is the woman I believe was your mother. As part of the investigation I found out that she went away to Philadelphia to give birth to you and then gave you up for adoption."

I paused, waiting for the inevitable questions.

"So you're an investigator?"

"Not exactly. I just happen to have gotten involved in a few investigations here or there and it made the paper so now other people ask for my help, too, sometimes."

I doodled on my notepad, giving him time to absorb all of this and ask more questions.

"Who was my mother then? And how can you be so certain?"

"You have a port-wine stain on your neck, right? And fairly distinctive gray eyes?"

"Yes."

"Well, the woman that Mary stayed with when she was pregnant was a nurse. And she saw you at your birth and then she saw you at the hospital after you'd been adopted. And later she worked with you when you became a doctor."

"Who?"

"I'm not at liberty to say. She's helping me out by putting me in touch with you and I need to respect that. Hopefully she'll tell you herself at some point since Mary did live with her for about nine months."

"You keep saying Mary. Is that my mother?"

"Yes, Mary Diever."

"What was she like?"

"Everyone said she was very nice. Very pretty. Quiet. Kept to herself. A good person." (I decided he didn't need to know the rest of it.)

"Do you have any photos?"

"Only one or two. Unfortunately, shortly after she died, her father and grandfather also died and her mother had passed away years before so there really wasn't family left to keep things like that."

"And you said she was murdered?" he asked, tentatively.

"Yes. About six months after you were born."

"Why call me? You said you needed my help. This isn't just you being a nice person." It was clear he still didn't trust me, which was fine. I wouldn't have trusted me either.

I bit my lip. Moment of truth time. "True. I called you because I suspect that your biological father is the one who murdered Mary because she changed her mind about giving you up for adoption."

"What would he care?"

"He was married at the time." I cleared my throat. "And had kids and political ambitions. He was about twenty years older than her. I don't think those ambitions could've survived the scandal."

"So he killed her?"

"Maybe. Yes. If nothing else, it's another suspect for the cops to look at other than the man who loved your mother and would've helped raise you if she'd been able to get you back."

He was silent for a long moment. "This is a lot to take in. And I still don't understand what you want from me."

"Well…" I took a deep breath. How to explain this in a way that would get him on board? "I would like you to file a paternity suit to prove that the man is your father."

"Why? Can't I just reach out to him and ask if he's my father? Why do I have to file a lawsuit?"

"Because the fact that he is the father would still be a scandal. And I think he would want to hide that and is willing to hurt people to do so."

He scoffed at that. "Look, lady, I don't know you. And I don't believe you."

"Someone shot at my husband the other day. After this man threatened me and told me to drop my investigation."

"And you want me to prove this man is my father?" He laughed once. "Why? He doesn't know who I am, I'm safe. Filing this lawsuit will risk my family. And for what?"

"To help get justice for your mother. A young lady who was scared as could be, but still chose to give birth to you even though she knew it would upset the father of her child."

He didn't respond.

"Please. The only way I can protect my family is by making this public. Until it's public, I'm a danger to this man and he will try to stop me. Once it's public, there's nothing to hide anymore."

"I'm not a lawyer, but I'm pretty sure something like this will get squashed pretty fast."

"Not fast enough. Your dad is a public figure. We're going to…*I'm* going to, make sure that the news knows as soon as the filing hits. It will be out there before they can suppress it."

"Who is my dad?" he asked, suddenly wary.

I grimaced, but he'd have to know sooner or later. "Senator Quentin Baker."

"That man is my dad? He's vile."

"Well…yeah."

He was silent for a long moment. "I need to think about this."

"Please don't think too long. We're in danger until you make that filing. And I…I just found out I'm pregnant? With twins? I really don't want anything to happen to us or to the babies' father. Or to my dog. Or my grandpa. I mean, I'm not giving this up. I'll find a way with or without you to bring your mother justice, but I'd really like the people I love to be safe while I do so."

Another long stretch of silence. "What would I have to do? How much will it cost?"

"It's free because I have a lawyer-friend who really doesn't like the man. All you have to do is agree to be part of the suit. And provide your DNA if it comes to that."

When he didn't immediately respond, I added, "My nurse friend said you'd tried posting your DNA to some of those sites? Did anything point to Colorado?"

"Yeah. But it was fourth or fifth cousins. Nothing too close."

"Well, the family has been here for over a hundred years. The other side, your mother's side, was actually

Philadelphia."

"There were results for Philly, too. But again, only fourth or fifth cousins."

"I think your mom was an only child of an only child, so makes sense."

I didn't want to end the call, not without him agreeing to help. But I'd stretched things as far as I could. "Do you mind if I get those DNA results from you? And I can send you the pictures I do have of your mom if you want."

"I had a private lab do the sequence so I can send that to you. Police should be able to use it. And, yeah, I'd appreciate the photos."

"And you'll think about the case?" I didn't want to beg, but I would've if I thought it would help.

"How certain are you that he's my father? This isn't some stupid political stunt is it?"

"No. Not at all. That nurse friend who gave me your name saw them together shortly before you were born. She was pretty convinced he was the father. And you guys have the same eyes, according to her. But that's all I have, which is why the DNA is so important."

"So we could be ruining some man's life for nothing?"

"He did also threaten me at the supermarket and his great-nephew did put a bullet through the windshield of my husband's car. I mean, it's circumstantial, but there are some clear signs there I think."

He was quiet for another long, long moment.

Finally, he said, "Okay. Fine. Let's do it. We'll find out one way or another. And if he isn't my father, maybe this will make someone come forward with new information on the man who really is."

"Thank you. Thank you so much." If we'd been in person, I would've hugged him.

"I just hope you're right."

"Me, too."

I jotted down his email and got off the phone as fast as I could before he changed his mind.

CHAPTER 30

My next call was to Mason Maxwell, but that's where we hit a bit of a snag.

"Mason Maxwell," he answered, clearly distracted and not wanting to be on the phone.

"Mason, everything okay?"

"Maggie. Right. I was supposed to call you. You need to get to Greta's."

"Greta's? Why?" I stood up, looking around for I wasn't even sure what.

"Jamie went into labor."

"Already? But it's too early. Are you sure it was labor and not just those fake contractions pregnant women get sometimes?"

That seemed to settle him because the note of panic left his voice. "Positive. She gushed all over the foyer when her water broke."

"Well where is she now? Why aren't you with her?" I barely refrained from adding, *What kind of husband are you to be telling me to get over there when you're not there yourself?*

He calmed even further. Seems my being obnoxious

is sometimes a good thing. "She's at Greta's. I took her over there but then we realized we'd forgotten everything. Our go bag, my computer, her phone, her purse. Everything. We ran to the car without even thinking. So I had to come back here."

"Mason, you don't need your computer when your wife is in labor."

"You do when you're an attorney who has a hearing at ten."

I let my silence speak for me.

"Jamie is the one who told me to come back home and get it. She said she's fine."

"This is Jamie we're talking about. She'll probably say she's fine right up until the baby pops out. I bet you money if her water hadn't burst she would've waited until the last possible moment to go over to Greta's."

"You're probably right. Which is why you need to get over there right now. Because that hearing is in ten minutes and there's no way I'm going to make it back to her before it begins."

"Mason!" I had really been hoping there'd be a snowstorm or something when Jamie went into labor that would let me politely decline having to be there for the big event. And now I might be there but Mason wouldn't? "What is wrong with you?"

"I do not want to miss the birth of my first child. But I have to attend this hearing. I will try to get it postponed and will hopefully be there within the hour, but right now if you can get there, please do."

I really wanted to make up excuses for why I couldn't go, but I also didn't want Jamie to have to give birth without her husband or her best friend there. "Fine. I will get in my van and head right over to Greta's. By the way, I have a name for you for the lawsuit against Quentin Baker."

"Good. If we have time between when I arrive and the actual delivery I can get that filed while we're waiting."

I wanted to tell him to wait, that Jamie was more important, but at the same time…Labor can take *hours* and it was my family's safety on the line. The sooner Mason managed to make the filing, the better.

"Okay. See you at Greta's."

I hung up, grabbed a change of clothes, food for Fancy, food for me, and Fancy and I were out the door in five minutes flat.

My best friend was having a baby. Holy…

CHAPTER 31

I desperately wanted a Coke to accompany me on my drive to Greta's, but I was a good girl and took a water bottle filled with mint tea instead. (It had that same bite to it that I liked in Coke so it made my lack of my favorite beverage more manageable.)

Fancy stood at my shoulder the whole drive, staring out at a sky that threatened snow. It wasn't clouded or anything, but there's a certain cold haze that develops sometimes right before a snowstorm. So we had blue sky but misted, like seeing it through a frosted glass pane.

I pulled up in front of Greta's mansion (it's very Italian-feeling with its circular driveway and central fountain and two wings leading off of the main entranceway) and took a moment to breathe. I could do this. I needed to be strong for Jamie. She couldn't see me freaking out or else she might freak out, too.

This was normal. Women had babies all the time. It was no big deal. Haha. Right. The lies we tell ourselves.

I might've stayed in the van for another hour or ten, but Fancy started crying her head off, demanding to be let out.

Jamie met us at the door with a big smile. She grabbed my hands. "I can't believe it's time already."

"Neither can I. Are you sure? I mean, don't they sometimes try to just put you on bed rest or whatever if your water breaks early? I thought that's what I read the other day."

(I'd been doing far too much reading up on early deliveries since finding out about my own little bumps of joy.)

"They can, yes. Especially if the baby won't do well being born too early. But Dr. Dillon thinks I'm close enough to term not to worry about it. She said it might be a different story if they had to induce contractions, but no need there." She sort of grimaced. "This little guy is determined to come out today."

She stepped outside. "The doctor wants me to walk around for now. Will you walk with me?"

"Outside? Shouldn't you stay close to the delivery room? Because I am not prepared to help you give birth in the woods."

She laughed and then winced, bending over in pain. "Ooof. Those things are painful."

"Was that a contraction?"

She nodded and slowly stood back up. "They're still pretty far apart. We have time. Come on."

"If you say so…"

As we walked down the path that led around the side of Greta's mansion, I added, "You know, I kind of think Evan and Abe have the better end of this one. Hire a surrogate, let her sacrifice her entire body for ten months and go through the pain and risk of delivery, and then voila, baby in hand. Easy peasy. I really think that's the optimal way to do this thing."

Jamie laughed and shook her head. "Oh no. You just wait until you feel that first little kick. Then you'll understand how the pregnancy portion is just as magical as the parenting portion."

"If you say so." Me, I personally preferred the idea of parenthood without life-threatening risk and intense pain. Ah, to be a man.

I glanced up at the leaden sky, wondering what we'd do if Jamie went into labor before anyone could arrive to help. Because once that storm closed in, we were probably on our own.

"By the way," I said, "Doctor Dillon is here already, right? This isn't a 'call me when we get closer' situation is it?"

"Yes, Doctor Dillon is already here. Along with my doula, Ruth. And a nurse. Unfortunately, there's no birthing pool. Greta didn't get it in time. And, given the fact my water burst early, no one is comfortable with my taking a non-standard approach. So I'm stuck with the whole feet-in-stirrups thing."

"What about an epidural?"

"Nope. Don't want one."

"Jamie…"

"I don't want one."

She stared me down until I changed the subject. As we wandered our way around Greta's backyard for the next half hour we talked about the pet resort and my idea to use Owen Browers' photography. Jamie suggested we could maybe do Colorado wildlife-themed menu items both in the barkery and the café although we'd need to make sure it didn't tip over into too kitschy given our target clientele. We wanted upscale hunting lodge not theme park.

(You can charge twice as much that way for the same thing.)

She also knew a ton more local artists who could be part of the art gallery. The more we talked about that idea the more excited I was for it. That would definitely be upscale if we set it up right.

As we turned for another loop of the backyard, a police car with flashing lights and Mason's black Lincoln pulled into the driveway. Matt and Mason hopped out of their respective vehicles, both grinning.

Mason made a beeline for Jamie. "Are you okay? How far apart are the contractions? Have you been doing your breathing? How long until the baby is here?"

Jamie laughed. "Maybe you should practice your own breathing, babe. I'm fine. We have time. Go file that case so Maggie and Matt will be safe."

He hesitated.

"Go." She shoved him away, laughing.

"Don't worry," I said. "I'll bring her inside so you won't be haunted by worries about her giving birth in the woods." Like I was.

He stared at me. "That would be horrible."

"I know. That's why I'm going to bring her inside. Right now."

Jamie laughed. "I'm fine you two. I am not going to give birth out here, I promise. Now, go."

As Mason turned back towards the house, Jamie sucked in a breath through her teeth.

"Another contraction?" I asked as we both smiled at Mason as he glanced back at us.

"Yep."

"How many have you had while we were walking around out here?"

"A few."

"So we really should get you inside, then?"

"Mmhm. Yeah, that would be good."

Matt who'd been on his phone, joined us just then. "Can I help?"

"Yes. We need to get Jamie inside. You walk on one side, I'll walk on the other. Just in case."

As he took his position on Jamie's other side, he grinned at me. "This is going to be us soon, you know."

"Do not remind me."

I glanced at Greta's house. I was sure she had state-of-the-art facilities, but giving birth in a room of my friend's house was not something I wanted to experience. Ever. Ah well, at least it wasn't the good old days when women gave birth in their marriage bed. Ugh. That didn't even bear thinking about.

CHAPTER 32

We escorted Jamie upstairs and down the hall to the delivery room. It was very nice. There was everything you'd expect to see, including what I presumed was a baby warmer in the corner. Dr. Dillon was there and smiled at us as we came into the room.

"Contractions getting closer together?" she asked.

Jamie nodded through one. "Yes. I'm thinking it might be time."

"Well, climb on up on the table and let's see."

"I'll just go get Mason," I said, trying to make my escape.

"No." Jamie grabbed my arm with so much force I was pretty sure I was going to lose it if I tried to pull free. "Don't leave me alone. Matt can get him."

I turned to Matt, silently pleading for him to rescue me, but he nodded instead. "Will do. I'll be right back."

"Matt…" But he was gone. Nothing to do but tuck myself away at the head of the bed where I wouldn't have to see any of…whatever was going on down below. There's being friends and then there's things you just don't need to see.

I appreciated that Jamie thought I should be there in that moment. And that I *could* be there for her in that moment. But delivery is not something you really want to be present for, you know?

I mean, even cheery, happy types like Jamie crack under the pressure. And to know that I was going to have to go through that in a few months? Yeah, not something I wanted to witness.

But Jamie wasn't letting go. And by then my trying to run for the door meant running past whatever Dr. Dillon was up to in the baby area. So I sucked it up and tried to keep a never-ending nonsensical conversation going with Jamie instead.

I was about to bolt and drag Mason into the room by his ear when he finally arrived. "It's time?" he asked.

Uptight, buttoned-up, never-a-hair-out-of-place, Mason Maxwell, looked nervous.

Dr. Dillon smiled at him. "It's time."

Now, let me tell you that when they say, "it's time" they don't always mean what you think they do. Because, me, I think, okay, we'll be done with this in about five minutes or so, right? Just push a few times and there's the baby.

Oh no. That is not how it goes. That just means the straining, pushing, gasping cacophony has begun.

Don't ask me how long it actually took. But it was no five minutes. Or if it was five minutes it was some purgatory-style version that never ended.

Lucky Matt got to hang out somewhere with Greta. Me, I got to have my hand nearly torn off by Jamie. Mason did, too, except he was grinning like a happy fool the whole time.

At the end Jamie was a red-faced, sweating mess and I'd learned a few new, highly creative and definitely not realistic phrases to use when I was mad at someone.

I would tell you the baby was beautiful when it was born—and ultimately he was, Jamie and Mason make very good-looking kids—but fresh out of the womb? No. Not so much.

That whole expelling a child from your body thing is very messy. And that boy was a squaller. Had some lungs on him. And a face as reddened as his mama's was at that point.

Not that Jamie or Mason noticed, not one bit. The adoration on their faces…It was like someone had slipped them both the best drug in the world and they were flying high as high could get.

I freed my broken hand and stepped outside to let them have their moment. I was so happy for them. But, wow, what a process.

I found Matt snoozing in a chair about ten feet down the hall. I kicked his foot. "Wake up. It's over."

"Yeah?"

I nodded.

"What do you think?"

"I think someone better invent a magic technology that transports these two out of my belly without any of that or I'm not going to make it."

He pulled me onto his lap and kissed me. "You'll be fine."

"Says the man who does not have to do this."

"No. Worse. I have to stand there helpless while you perform a miracle."

I side-eyed him. "I should call you on that worse part,

but the rest of it was pretty good." I rested my head against his shoulder. "You want to see the baby?"

"In a minute." He cuddled me closer and I closed my eyes, so glad to have him in my life.

🐾 🐾 🐾

When we finally walked back into the room, the baby had been cleaned and bundled up. Mason was holding him, a dopey smile on his face.

"You want to hold him?" he asked, looking at me.

I held my hands up to keep him back. "Oh no. I wouldn't want to break him. Me and babies, you know."

He laughed. "You sure you don't want to practice now before you're trying to juggle newborns?"

I stared at him. He was right. *I* was going to have to juggle *two* of them. Two, tiny, small, fragile, breakable little babies. How was I going to do that?

"Any chance you'd like to raise three kids instead of one?" I asked, only half-kidding. "We'll take the twins back when they're about, say, nine months old. That's a fun period with kids, I think. Right?"

Matt laughed. "I'll hold him."

And he did. Frickin' natural. Didn't even need to be told what to do, he automatically had one big hand cradling the head and the other cradling the body. That little baby snuggled up against his chest like it was home.

"See? Not too hard," he said.

"Yeah. Not too hard at all," I mumbled semi-hysterically. "I'm just gonna…Go down the hall…Find Greta…Tell her about the baby…Yeah. That. I'll, I'll be back."

I fled.

CHAPTER 33

We all ended up crashing at Greta's that night because the snowstorm moved in and it was a doozy.

Fancy had managed to find the baby, who Jamie and Mason had named Mason Maxwell, Jr. (Max for short). She posted herself right in front of wherever Max was and kept a careful eye on anyone who approached. It was a bit awkward, but definitely cute.

I finally had to lock her in our room when it came time to go to bed or I think she would've stayed there the whole night.

The next morning the paternity filing against Quentin Baker was all over the news. Mason had managed to get his filing in before Jamie went into labor and Matt had conveniently sent a copy of it to every major news outlet in the state while he was waiting in the hallway.

By the time we all gathered in Greta's kitchen for a breakfast casserole, fresh orange juice, and coffee it had hit the national news. Mason's phone was blowing up. He ignored most of the calls, but then he flashed us all a smile and answered.

"Mason Maxwell."

I could hear the sound of someone screaming on the other end of the line.

"Quentin, there is a very easy way to prove you are not the father. Simply submit your DNA. Then you can call the press and tell them we had it wrong, that this was just a political witch hunt meant to smear your name."

There was more shouting from the other end of the line.

"You can try that, but I should tell you that it is only defamation if it is not true."

He set the phone back down, smiling. "He hung up. Don't know why. Must have been something I said."

Matt offered to take Max while Jamie and Mason were eating. They already looked exhausted and it was only the first day. But they were both so clearly happy, leaning into one another with soft little smiles on their faces, too, that I couldn't help but smile at them.

I nudged Matt with my hip. "Well, at least one of us will be able to hold our children without breaking them in the first few months," I quipped. "All we have to do is teach you how to nurse and we are set."

He smiled at me, his expression all soft and warm. "I can do the night feedings. Although, juggling two might be a bit of a trick. But you give me a bottle, I'm happy to help."

"And you'll do diapers, too?" I asked, skeptical.

"Of course. They're our children, aren't they? It's as much my responsibility to raise them as it is yours."

I kissed him on the cheek, careful not to disturb the baby. "I picked well when I picked you."

He chuckled softly. "I'm the one that did the picking, not you. You were just smart enough to succumb to my charms."

I laughed. "Well. Not sure smarts had anything to do with it. You overwhelmed me with your…regard."

I rested my head on his shoulder, watching the baby sleeping peacefully, his little face scrunched up. "So, what happens now? With the Mary Diever case?"

I knew he'd talked to his Chief earlier.

"Good news is the paternity suit cast enough doubt on Owen Browers being the killer that the Chief has agreed to release him and hold off on anything further with respect to him for now. We're filing today to compel Quentin Baker to give us a DNA sample. The paternity suit gave us enough probable cause to ask for it."

"I'm surprised the Chief backed off so easily."

He smiled and moved the baby around to make him more comfortable. "It probably helped that I told him Mason Maxwell was going to be the attorney representing Browers if he went forward."

"Is he?" I glanced across the table at Mason who was looking at us in surprise.

"Probably not. But it worked." Matt's phone started to ring.

"Here. Take the baby." Before I could stop him, Matt turned and nestled the baby against my chest, placing my hands for me. "Officer Barnes," he said, answering the phone as he abandoned me.

The baby started to fidget and I froze. What was I supposed to do? What if I tried to adjust my grip and dropped him? Mason and Jamie would never forgive me. And somehow I didn't think offering them one of my twins would fix it.

(I'm kidding. Obviously only a psychopath would even think about trying to give away one of their children, and I'm clearly not that, right? Ahem. Right.)

"Jamie," I called out softly, trying not to move. "You should probably take him back now."

She laughed. "Okay. Give him over." She held out her hands.

"Uh…Can you…I'm not sure what to…"

Greta reached over and plucked him out of my arms. "You are so funny, Maggie. Have you never held a baby?"

"No, not really. I never had siblings. And I've managed to avoid holding my friends' kids until they were older."

"This must be fixed. You must be ready when the twins come, no?"

I sighed. "Yeah. That's probably a good idea. Maybe I can get one of those fake babies from the high school. Do they still do that sort of thing?"

Jamie shook her head. "You don't need a fake baby, Maggie, you can hold Max."

Before I could say "do I have to", Matt hung up the phone and I desperately transferred my attention to him. "Any news?"

"We've been getting some interesting phone calls this morning since the paternity story broke. Seems there might have been a couple of witnesses who didn't realize what they saw at the time. Chief wants me to go interview them." He kissed me on the forehead. "And, sorry, but this is now police-only. Too high-profile to have you involved."

I wanted to object, but it made sense. "Okay. See you at home tonight?"

"See you then."

CHAPTER 34

Once the dominos started to fall, they really started to fall. But not exactly in the direction I thought they would.

The court compelled Quentin Baker to submit a DNA sample that same day. His lawyers fought it, but they only bought an extra two days for him and then the crime lab put a rush on the results because it was such a national story.

By the end of the week the results were back. Quentin Baker was in fact Brian McKendrick's father. The source of the Tay-Sachs, though, had to be Mary Diever because there wasn't a trace of it in the DNA for Baker.

Further digging by McKendrick unearthed the fact that his grandmother had very likely been from a Jewish family in Philadelphia but had run away when she turned eighteen. She'd been the only child of an only child so it wasn't definitive, but it made the most sense family tree-wise.

And those calls that started pouring in shed a whole new light on Senator Baker. Seems he'd made a pattern of targeting the quiet daughters of men he knew. Mary

Diever was not the first nor was she the last. By the end of it all, sixteen women had come forward.

All said he had a temper. All felt they couldn't tell their families about it because he had one form of leverage or another over their families that he threatened to use.

There were no other illegitimate children, though. Brian was the only one.

Where things got interesting was when it came to figuring out who the killer was. Likely even with the testimony of those sixteen women, Mary Diever's murder would've remained unsolved. It's a big jump to make from aggressive ex-lover to murderer especially without physical evidence or witnesses.

But it turned out the murder weapon was in Senator Baker's office. At that point it looked like a slam dunk case. Use Brian's DNA to match to Mary's blood on the rock, tie it via circumstance to the senator, and all done. Except…

Senator Baker hadn't been in town when Mary Diever was killed. But his wife had. His wife who then gifted him a big, ugly rock as a book end and informed him he needed to do a better job of cleaning up his own messes next time around.

He, of course, threw her under the bus the minute the police found the rock. (Why he hadn't disposed of it when I started snooping around, I do not know, but maybe thirty-six years without being caught had made him sloppy. Or forgetful of what that rock might reveal.)

But he didn't get off. He'd known who killed her after all. It was all very headline-worthy and scandalous, but I was just glad that my family was safe, including my not-quite-as-little-as-they-had-been bumps of joy.

EPILOGUE

Thanksgiving Day is my favorite holiday. I know it has a fraught history in this country and that's why some don't like it, but for me personally it was never really about any of that. I identify with the Pilgrims about as much as I identify with that patch of something behind the fridge that really needs to be cleaned up if I ever get around to it, which means not at all.

For me Thanksgiving is about two things: spending time with the people I love and good food.

Let me tell you about the food we had first.

There was a turkey with its crispy, golden skin and juicy flesh stuffed with stuffing made using my super-secret recipe that had come down through my mom's side of the family. It involved giblets. Which meant hours of preparation just so those little suckers could be diced up and thrown in with the usual bread and celery and onions and what-not to give it that extra-rich flavor.

I know they don't think you should stuff a turkey these days, but I'm about as on board with that notion as I am with the idea that you can't taste-test chocolate chip cookie batter as you're preparing it.

Yeah, yeah, salmonella, food poisoning, blah, blah, blah. I didn't care. I wanted my stuffed turkey. And of course I snuck off the crunchy bit at the end when it was all done just for myself. (Which I shared with Matt, that's how strong our love is. Some people may be willing to die for their spouse. *I* am willing to share the crunchy bits of the turkey stuffing.)

We also had green bean casserole. Not the fancy kind that people try to create and ruin the whole thing. No, we had the real deal. The good old-fashioned, cooking with canned products version. Dump in two cans of green beans, follow that with some mushroom soup, make sure you have plenty of crispy fried onions mixed in there, and…Perfection.

And there were mashed potatoes. So simple to create, but oh so good.

And gravy. Lots and lots and lots of gravy to smother it all with.

And cranberry sauce. Again, nothing fancy. No homemade mess. Just that smooshed-up, canned version that plops onto a plate.

(Truth be told, I could easily eat an entire can of cranberry sauce all by myself which is why I had four extra cans of it at home.)

That right there was the core of my Thanksgiving meal. Trish had made sweet potato pie and Lesley had made a macaroni bake and there was bread, of course. And deviled eggs. And stuffed celery. And pie. So much pie. Pumpkin and pecan and lemon chiffon.

(Don't ask about the lemon chiffon. Not a traditional choice, but some sort of joke between Matt and Jack that dated back to their childhood. They'd both brought one, so it must be a good joke, but neither would say more about it.)

Of course, it wasn't about the food (even though I love the food). I've had other Thanksgivings where we had ham instead. Or pork roast. And once I even went out with a friend for a fancy French meal where we ate duck. Those were all good Thanksgivings, too.

Because they had the part that really matters. The people.

Some years it's family, some years it's friends, some years it's both. But it's companionship and laughter and joy that we're all here for another year. All able to be together. (Sometimes just in spirit and that's okay, too.)

My grandpa and Lesley were there. And Jack and Trish and Sam. And Matt. And Fancy.

And Owen Browers. Because that man deserved a new start. My grandpa pressed his lips together when I told him I'd invited Owen, but he also took him aside after the meal and they had a good long talk. My grandpa knows all about giving people second chances.

I knew he'd opened up to Owen when he invited him to a friendly game of Scrabble.

Thanksgiving is about seeing what you have and appreciating it for what it is. It's not a day for regrets or wanting something more.

It's about being in that particular moment with those particular people and being grateful to be there.

Life never works out the way we want. That year was certainly testament to that fact, for us and for the world.

But I couldn't see the point in looking at what we hadn't had—like the long, luxurious honeymoon to some exotic locale that I'd dreamed of—when I had something far more important in my life. Love. Acceptance. Community.

And a chance to make it even better the next year.

I looked around that table at all those smiling faces and I was content, if just for a moment.

A PUZZLING POOCH
AND PUMPKIN PUFFS

A MAGGIE MAY AND MISS FANCYPANTS MYSTERY

ALEKSA BAXTER

CHAPTER 1

Do you want to know the worst words in the English language? Bed rest. Bad enough that I was the size of a small house and had all sorts of things going on with my body that I had never wanted to experience thanks to the two bumps of joy I was incubating inside me.

But now…

Now my doctor, Dr. Dillon—an attractive middle-aged woman who was way too pleasant even when delivering bad news—had just told me that I had to go on bed rest.

I stared into her sympathetic eyes and wanted to do violence.

Instead I took three, deep, calming breaths, and reminded myself it wasn't her fault. Really. It wasn't. Truly. Not her fault. Not anyone's. Just…biology. Sometimes these things happen, especially when you're pregnant with twins.

Finally, when I thought I had calmed down enough not to scream, I asked, "For how long?"

"Until the babies come."

No. Not possible.

"That could be another two months."

"Hopefully." She smiled and it took every ounce of reserve I had not to tell her to stop being so frickin' calm and cheerful already. She squeezed my hand. "Every single day we can get is a day closer to those babies being just fine when they're born."

Right. It was all about the babies now. I was just an incubator trying to get them across the finish line.

Nobody talks about that part of having kids. The worry that they won't turn out all healthy and perfect. That there might be weeks or months at the hospital after the birth.

At least not much. It's like this collective forgetfulness that constantly happens.

I had one friend who had a kid with a collapsed lung in utero. The doctors had to go in there with some sort of needle and inflate it while she was still pregnant. But did anyone mention it after the procedure? Noooo. All good. Just a minor collapsed lung. No biggie. Carry on.

Gah!

I stared at the monitor with my two little girls on it and sighed. "Fine. Bed rest. Do I get to pee on my own at least or is there something fun I get to use for that?"

Matt, my tall, dark, and gorgeous husband who I wanted to strangle for being half of what got me into this situation, kissed my forehead. "It's okay, Maggie. Two more months and then they'll be here. You can do this."

Easy for him to say. He wasn't the one going to be stuck in bed for the next two months and then have to get them out on top of that. He just had to show up and cut the umbilical cord and show the babies around to everyone.

Must be nice.

(I know, I know. I wasn't being fair to him. He had to stand by, mostly powerless, for nine months while I grew two little lives inside me. Honestly, that lack of control would've upset me more than everything I'd already been through and was about to go through. But still. I had to have some sort of target for all of my anxiety and he was right there.)

The doctor smiled and nodded her head slightly. "You can pee on your own. Just try, as much as possible, to rest and stay calm. Every moment you can do that is better for the babies."

I glanced at my very, very large stomach. "You two hear that? I'm doing this for you. So when you're fifteen and try to sneak out of the house and I'm too darned tired to stop you because I'm *old*, you think about your poor mother and what she sacrificed to get you here. And then you turn yourselves around and go back to bed. I couldn't even do all-nighters in college, I'm definitely not doing them for two little hellions who've snuck out of the house for some stupid boy or party."

Matt chuckled. "Don't worry. I think that falls under dad duty. I'll be sitting on the porch waiting for them."

"Good. Because I will need every minute of beauty sleep I can get by that point." I sighed and glanced back to the doctor. "I assume this means I can't walk my dog anymore?"

"Absolutely not. No dog walking."

That was not going to go over well. Fancy, my almost five-year-old Newfoundland, loved her walks. And she was quite vocal about when she needed one.

Matt rubbed my shoulder. "I'll walk her. Or your grandpa can."

I laughed. "My grandpa? I can just imagine that conversation right now. *What do you mean she needs a walk? She has a yard already, why would she need a walk on top of that? You spoil her.*"

"He'll do it for you, though. You know he will. And you know he'll probably enjoy it. He tries to hide it, but he has a soft spot for Fancy."

"Yeah, you're probably right. But what about the resort? We're finally gearing up for opening. I was going to do things."

"Leave that to Jamie. And Greta. And Mason. And me if it comes to it. You're not alone in this Maggie."

Thankfully. I'd at one brief point in time before I met Matt thought about having a kid on my own. I was my parents' only child and it was all down to me to pass along their genes so I felt this sort of weird guilt that I hadn't yet.

But…doing it alone?

Hahaha. Oh hell no.

I mean, yes, of course, it was amazing and wonderful to bring beautiful children into the world and having a child is one of the best things most people have ever done in their lives. And women make it work on their own all the time. Yadda, yadda, yadda.

Let's not pretend any of it is easy.

Ask a mom of a two-year-old if you should have a kid on your own and she will laugh hysterically while trying not to fall asleep mid-conversation.

I was so glad to have Matt and everyone else around to help. And even then…bed rest. And who knew what would come after that. No one could help with that part. It was all me.

Yes, yes, I know. Negative Nelly. But better to think the worst and get the best than think the best and get the worst. That's my motto at least.

I prefer to be pleasantly surprised when life doesn't turn out to be a dumpster fire. And when it does, like when your doctor puts you on bed rest for two months, well, you figure out the best path forward and roll with it because you were never expecting it to be smooth sailing anyway.

Might not make me a good party guest or person to have a conversation with, but at least I can roll with the punches when they inevitably come.

CHAPTER 2

As we took our papers and Matt helped me navigate the waiting room like some sort of tanker ship at risk of blocking half of the world's shipping supply, he said, "Maybe we should move down to Denver until the baby's born. Stay somewhere near a hospital. It's probably safe enough to do so now."

He had a point. I mean, living in small-town Colorado is great. Clean air, beautiful mountains, quiet. But when there's a medical issue…That helicopter flight to Denver could be the difference between making it and not.

Assuming the flight could even go, because April in Colorado is not always bright and sunny. We've had snows as late as June, although May is much more likely to be the last month of snow.

Either way, chances were, whenever the babies arrived it would still be snow season, which meant regardless of my own preferences I'd probably be giving birth at the local hospital unless we stationed ourselves down in Denver.

And I might not even make it to the local hospital. It was a solid twenty minutes from Creek in good weather.

Did I really want to be at home, realize I needed to get to the hospital NOW, and not be able to get there? When something as delicate and precious as my two babies was at risk?

I shuddered as Matt helped me down the two steps on the front porch. (The doctor's office had at one point been a small house that was then converted over to medical offices. It still had the white picket fence, which was just weird in my book. I like my doctor's offices sterile and unfriendly, not a cheery bright yellow. But it was what it was.)

I sighed.

The stress of it all was overwhelming. I'd thought taking care of a dog was hard. Being pregnant was a whole new level of anxiety involving weird bodily changes and hormone surges. But it was too late to turn back now.

(Not that I would want to. Babies. Yay.)

"What about your job?" I asked. "You can't just not go for two months."

"I'll take the time off."

"Will they let you?" I couldn't imagine a small-town police force had paternity leave. Not like we lived in Sweden.

"You and these babies are more important to me than anything, Maggie."

He helped me into the back of the minivan we'd bought the week before. My van without any backseats and his truck weren't exactly ideal vehicles for transporting kiddos around after all. (Or hugely-pregnant women for that matter.)

It was awkward sitting in the back like some sort of celebrity with a chauffeur, but I'd hit the point where a normal front passenger seat could not accommodate my very large belly. Not to mention all the lovely statistics Matt had shared with me about people in front passenger seats and car wrecks. Something I could have gone my whole life without knowing, thank you very much.

As he drove us back towards home, I picked up the conversation once more. "I know you want to take care of us, but I don't want you to lose your job over it. Maybe my grandpa and Lesley could come down to Denver with me. Or…well, not Jamie. She's hip-deep in the resort preparations. And she has Max to worry about. Same with Greta. At least as far as the resort is concerned. Plus, being away for two months…Ugh. Also, are we really sure it's safe now? I mean, things certainly seem safer…"

"If you go to Denver, I go with you."

"But work. You can't just take off like that and expect to come back. You know that."

He drummed his fingers on the steering wheel. "I've been meaning to talk to you about that, actually."

I tensed. "Talk to me about what?"

He stared straight ahead, not glancing in my direction as he turned onto the two-lane highway towards home.

Uh-oh. This was going to be bad.

He didn't say anything as we accelerated down the road, the snow-covered mountains rising up on either side of us, covered in evergreens, the sky a pure, soft blue with no sign of a storm in sight.

Finally, I couldn't stand the silence anymore. "Matt, I am a hormonal pregnant woman who has just been told she's going to have to lie in weird positions for the next two months so she doesn't accidentally drop her babies out before they're due. It would be a good idea to get to the point and not spike my blood pressure any more than it already is."

"I'm thinking of quitting my job." The words tumbled out so fast I barely understood what he'd said.

"What? Why? I thought you liked it? I mean, I know it was hard at first having to arrest people you grew up with, but I thought you'd moved past that. I thought you were angling for a promotion even."

He nodded. "I did. And I was." His fingers clenched the steering wheel until his knuckles turned white.

"But then I got pregnant."

He shrugged one shoulder. If he hadn't been driving a motor vehicle at sixty miles an hour down a two-lane highway and I wasn't the size of a large walrus, I would've grabbed his chin and forced him to look my way.

"Matt, talk to me. Do you want to quit or do you think you have to?"

He sighed and finally glanced my way in the rearview mirror. "A little of both."

"Explain."

He let a deep breath out before he answered. "I talked to the Chief about that promotion. I couldn't be based out of Creek, which means a longer commute unless we move."

"Which we've discussed. Moving would put us closer to the resort, too, so it makes some sense to do it."

"But it puts us farther away from your grandpa and Lesley. The Chief also said if I wanted more responsibility then I'd have to be prepared to give more at work. Longer hours, filling in unexpectedly when someone's sick or a situation requires extra staff. As a supervisor I'd be that go-to person. Lots of late-night call outs. Leaving you home alone with two babies."

I won't lie. The thought of being alone in the middle of the night with two screaming babies scared the you-know-what out of me.

But Matt was my husband and life is never perfect. You always have to make some compromise or another. Always.

"We can make it work, Matt. If that's what you want. The promotion, all of it. We'll find a way. If we stay in Creek my grandpa is right there. He can always come over and help if I need it."

"He's not young, Maggie."

"No, but I don't think he's leaving us anytime soon either. Knock wood. He's gotten his shots now and he's as protected as he can be at this point. Plus, you know he's an ornery bugger who'll probably be here until he's a hundred. We can make it work, Matt, if that's what you want."

He clenched his jaw. "My dad wasn't really there for us, you know. He provided, we always had a roof over our head, but he wasn't there. I don't want to do that to my kids. I want to see their first steps and hear their first words."

"Oh, Matt." I would've squeezed his shoulder, but I couldn't move far enough to reach him. "Okay. I get it. If you want to quit, we'll figure it out."

Of course, I was panicking inside. I was about to bring two little lives into the world and we were going to need to feed them, which meant income. You can't exactly live outside in the Colorado mountains even if I were so inclined.

So, you know, we needed a plan. I just hoped he had one. Because I was supposed to not be stressing. "Do you have any idea what you want to do instead?" I asked, hopefully.

I winced as the words left my mouth, because it was not the most diplomatic thing to ask, but I had to ask or else my mind was going to spiral out of control with doomsday scenarios of my supporting two babies and a husband on the income from a pet resort that could very well fail.

He was back to not looking at me. "I thought maybe the resort could use a head of security. Mason mentioned something about it the last time I saw him."

I opened my mouth and closed it again. If Matt went to work for the resort, too, and it failed…Then we'd have nothing.

I drummed my fingers on the armrest.

Nothing.

But I couldn't say that. Matt clearly didn't need to hear that right then.

Marriage is so darned hard. Being supportive when you are a practical person is not always easy, especially when your life is not yet settled into a steady track.

"Do you want to call him about it?" I asked. "Or I can."

Secretly I was screaming for him to please call now so I knew that he'd have a job for at least the first three months of the babies' lives.

"I'll do it. And if that doesn't work out, I'll figure something else out. Don't worry." He flashed me a quick grin over his shoulder. "We won't starve, Maggie, I promise. We might not be eating steaks off of china plates, but as long as you're okay with the occasional hot dog off of a paper plate, I'll always provide for you."

I forced a smile when he glanced back at me even though I was silently cataloging everything I owned and how much it could be sold for and how long our savings would last on one income and what we could do if the resort failed and how likely it was I could get some consulting work if I needed it.

But all I said was, "I know you will. I trust you."

Because *that* is love. Smiling at your husband when all he can provide is hot dogs on paper plates even if you'd prefer steaks on china. Because you can't imagine anyone else you'd rather spend your life with and all you want is to see him happy.

And, really. In the grand scheme of things what are steaks and china next to a life partner you wouldn't want to live without? Right?

Right.

CHAPTER 3

Within days Matt had it all sorted. It was kind of amazing really.

We decided not to go down to Denver. That was a little too far from our support system and Matt had agreed to keep working as a cop until the babies were born so they could find a replacement for him. As you can imagine, cop wasn't the most in-demand job in early 2021.

By staying in the Baker Valley we could also arrange for a rotating set of people to drop in and check on me on a regular basis when he had to work. And there would actually be people I could call in an emergency other than him.

We did move into one of the cabins at the resort that had already been completed, though. Partially to be closer to the hospital, partially to let me do some work and meet with at least Greta and Jamie when needed.

Also, because I was a little freaked out about living in a home with stairs being as pregnant as I was. I'd had a pregnant friend I'd made online fall down the stairs the week before. She was fine—just a quick trip to the ER and some pain for a few days—but that was it for me.

Stairs and I have never been friends to begin with. Add in a huge belly that didn't let me see my feet and there was no way I was going near them again until after I'd given birth. Add bed rest into the picture on top of all of that and I was just done with that place.

The cabin was located about a mile from the main resort buildings and nestled amongst the trees around a small pond along with about a dozen other cabins. Each one was fully-furnished with a good-sized bedroom, bathroom with both a tub and a shower, a small combined dining and living room area, and a full kitchen.

It actually reminded me a bit of some of the cabins I'd stayed at when backpacking through New Zealand, with the exception of the kitchen and bathroom. Most of the ones in New Zealand had a communal kitchen and bathroom area, but we'd decided that wouldn't work as well with the high-end resort feel we were going for.

(I say we, but I mean the people who were actually high-end in our little venture, namely, Mason, Greta, and Jamie. Me, I was a little bit closer to being trailer park trash than a denizen of a high-end luxury accommodation.)

Because our property was a pet resort the cabin also had a back porch and small fenced-in yard that Fancy could reach via a doggie door. I'd insisted that the doggie doors be large enough for a dog Fancy's size even though everyone had argued with me that with bears and mountain lions and what-not in the area that it maybe wasn't the best idea.

Ultimately, I'd pulled pregnant hormonal woman privilege and gotten my way, but we'd compromised and only three of the cabins had the extra-large doggie doors. Also, visitors had to sign a waiver that they understood the risk of actually using the doors.

(Mason being a lawyer there were lots of waivers for guests to sign. I swear, he'd probably included a waiver for staying at high-altitudes in there, just in case. I miss the days when people were expected to know the risks they were taking rather than go through life mindlessly until something bad happened to them and then find an appropriate party to sue for not telling them that life ultimately ends in death, and that that death can arrive in about a million different ways on any given day. But America being America I was also glad to have someone like Mason on the case. Better to cover too much than too little when it comes to potential lawsuits.)

Even though I was close enough for meetings, we limited my visitors to my grandpa, Matt, Jamie, Greta, and Mason, all wearing masks. That's because we'd been forced to remove the barriers to the valley the week before and none of us were sure what that would mean for case counts.

As soon as the barriers came down the valley was immediately flooded with the "this was never a big deal, you joy killers just wanted to keep us from our lives" crowd, so those of us who did think it was a big deal were being forced to be careful.

My grandpa and Lesley were fully vaccinated and the rest of us had managed one shot so far, but the last thing I wanted when I was two months from delivering twins was to get a respiratory illness that was best treated by putting patients on their bellies. I was pretty sure that wasn't going to work all that well in my case.

So, yeah, my life was a lot of "fun" between bed rest, limited visitors, and masking. Good times.

Of course, me being me, I'd done my own research about bed rest and come to a slightly different conclusion than the doctor.

After careful review of numerous sources, I had decided to take into account the spirit of the recommendation from my doctor— to take it easy, don't stress out, and don't take undue risks with my body— without actually spending twenty-four hours a day in bed—which would have spiked my anxiety levels so high I would've probably gone into labor within a week.

In my defense, it turned out not every doctor agreed that bed rest actually did anything useful for prolonging a pregnancy. In fact, some thought it made things worse because the forced inactivity led to blood clots.

I wanted to listen to my doctor, I did, but sometimes with medicine you have to find your own balance, you know? And sometimes doctors are so busy being doctors and trying to squeeze in personal lives on the margins that they don't have time to keep up with all of the latest research.

(Although, as the world had so recently shown, not everyone is qualified to make their own medical decisions. Because sometimes when people take medical decisions into their own hands they end up taking horse dewormer for no good reason. Seriously, people. Learn how to figure out when you're being scammed.)

Anyway.

I was staying at the cabin full-time and no walks for Fancy to be safe, but I'd decided I could at least make myself meals and sit at the dining room table or on the couch if I wanted.

A Puzzling Pooch and Pumpkin Puffs

I actually didn't mind being isolated at the cabin. It had the nice side benefit of keeping me away from weird-ass strangers who wanted to touch me all the time. And, yes, I did just cuss, but I mean, what is it about a pregnant woman that people suddenly think they have the right to *touch* her?

"Oh, look. You're pregnant." Hand on stomach.

Do not do that to me. Do not touch me. I am a person who hurts first and asks questions later.

Which is why it was probably a very good thing I was restricted to the cabin for the rest of my pregnancy, since I was pretty sure Matt would not want to arrest his very pregnant wife for slugging some old lady in the grocery store.

(You should've seen the death stare I gave some woman who told me I wasn't allowed caffeine when she saw me drinking a Coke. Lady, mind your own. I talked to my doctor about it, thank you very much.)

Anyway. Being away from the stomach-touchers and this-is-how-you-should-do-pregnancy-opiners was very soothing in and of itself. Brought my blood pressure right down.

But poor Fancy was completely lost.

She's a champ, but the last two years had been a lot of change and stress. The cabin was her fourth home in that time and then there I was suddenly growing this huge belly and acting weird. It was a lot.

She wouldn't let me out of her sight. It was all I could do to get her to go outside and do her business. The rest of the time she spent within about three feet of me.

Which I appreciated, I did. I liked the company. Especially with Matt doing so many double shifts and being gone most nights. (He was doing the double shifts partially from guilt over quitting his job and partially in an attempt to build up a little extra money before the babies came, since we didn't know what challenges that might bring.)

So I liked the company, I did. It's just that Fancy's really big. And sometimes she would position herself so that I had to try to maneuver around her and, well, I was big, too, and the combination did not work out well. I almost tripped on her at least a dozen times the first two weeks we were there.

Anyway.

That's all a long explanation of how I found myself awake in the dark at midnight in an isolated cabin listening to the sound of the over-sized doggie door thwack back and forth as something or someone pushed through it.

CHAPTER 4

At first I thought the noise I'd heard was Fancy going outside in the middle of the night—she'd definitely done that at the old house—but no. Fancy was snoring away on the floor right next to me.

Soooo, not Fancy.

Which meant…

A bear?

A mountain lion?

A scary serial killer stalking hugely pregnant women?

Probably not that last one. Of course, that still left the bear or mountain lion options. I winced, thinking about how my grandpa was going to tell me he'd told me so, because he'd warned me it wasn't a good idea to have a doggie door in the mountains and now here he was, proved right.

Fancy, through some miracle, was still snoring as I heard nails scramble on the kitchen tile. I froze, wondering what to do next.

I didn't want to wake Fancy. If it was a bear or a mountain lion she wouldn't have a chance against it. I mean I've heard of Newfies that defended their owners against wild animals like that, but Fancy was not going to be one of them. She's a marshmallow.

I did have a steak knife somewhere on the dresser, but I wasn't sure what good it would do me.

(Yes, I'm weird, thank you very much. But I'd spent most of my life as a single woman living alone. And it's comforting to have a random sharp object you can scramble for in the dark should the worst happen. Not that I'd be able to use it effectively if it ever came to that, but it did at least let me sleep better at night.)

Well. I figured a knife in hand was better than nothing, so I patted around trying to find it hoping that Matt hadn't put it away—he was not a fan of random sharp objects in the bedroom, don't know why.

I couldn't see anything and didn't want to turn on a light, so it was not easy to find the knife. Also, my gaze was fixed on that dark doorway just waiting for whatever it was to make its appearance.

A floorboard creaked in the living room and Fancy snorted and sat up.

Crap.

She jumped to her feet and ran out of the room, barking, before I could stop her. I heard nails on the kitchen tiles and then the doggie door flapped. Once. Twice.

Great. Now Fancy was outside with whatever it was.

At least that meant I could turn on the bedside lamp without alerting the creature to my presence. I did so and carefully levered myself to my feet, cussing the whole time about how awkward it is to move when you have a gigantic mass sticking out from the middle of your body that no amount of widening pelvis can account for.

Once I was sure I wouldn't fall back onto the bed, I grabbed the knife in one hand and my cellphone in the other, and took a step towards the doorway.

The doggie door flapped again, once.

"Fancy?" I called as I hit the speed dial option for Matt.

She didn't come into the room, but the doggie door flapped again. Were both of them inside now? Or had the one that had come back, gone back outside?

"Fancy?" I asked more hesitantly, taking another step towards the doorway.

"Maggie?" Matt answered the phone, sounding breathless. "Everything okay?"

"I don't know."

"Are you in labor? Do I need to get home?"

"No…Not in labor…" I finally made it to the doorway but everything was dark. I really had to pee, too. That was not helping.

"Maggie. What is it then? I'm…in the midst of something here."

"Fancy?" I called again as I heard movement from the living room.

I stopped next to the door. Should I close it? That would lock Fancy outside the bedroom with whatever it was and I didn't want to do that. But I also didn't want to meet a deer or bear or mountain lion or…whatever. Me and my little steak knife weren't exactly going to do anything useful against it.

"Maggie," Matt snapped. "What is going on?"

I continued to peer into the darkness. "Something came in the doggie door. Fancy went after it. And now I think they're both in the living room. Either that or they're both outside. I don't know what it was. I'm gonna go see."

I took another step forward.

"No. Don't. Stay in the bedroom, Maggie. I'll be there in five minutes."

"It's fine. You're busy. Fancy isn't crying out or anything. I'm sure it's just a…I don't know. But I'm sure it's fine. Go back to work."

"Stay in your room, Maggie. I'll be right there." He hung up.

I stood there, desperately needing to pee, wondering where Fancy was and what was out there with her, and wondering exactly how long Matt was really going to take to arrive. Because I was pretty sure he was not five minutes away.

Probably more like ten.

And I couldn't wait that long. I needed to pee. And I was not going to just casually pee when I didn't know what was in my home.

Steeling myself against what I might find, I tightened my grip on the knife, groped around on the wall until I found the switch, and flipped on the light.

CHAPTER 5

I didn't realize I'd been holding my breath until I choked on it.

I'd been so ready for a bear, or a moose, or a mountain lion. What I had not expected was a little fluff ball of a dog. It was pure mutt. All multi-colored black, brown, and white, with floppy ears.

And probably not exactly small to anyone else, but Fancy is a hundred and thirty-five pounds and this little guy was half her size.

He saw me and his whole body started vibrating with excitement, but he didn't move because Fancy was there between us.

"It's okay, Fancy." I stepped closer and rested my hand on her back. "You're fine. Let him be. Hi there, fella." He wiggled his whole body even more as I talked to him.

But now that the threat was past, I really, really needed to pee. "Be right back," I told them.

I know, I should've blocked them in different parts of the cabin or something. But right then all I could think about was the intense pressure on my bladder. Sorry. TMI.

I ran into the bathroom. I figured they'd stay where they were until I came back. At least Fancy would. And I was right, she was still there when I emerged a couple minutes later.

But our visitor was gone.

"Where'd he go, Fancy?" I asked. She looked at me with those intelligent amber eyes of hers, but didn't move. "Where's the dog?"

She ran around the living room, sniffing, but then came back to me.

"You understand that didn't help, right? I could've done a lap around the living room myself, you know."

I winced. I'd been trying to only be loving and affirmative with Fancy since I'd found out I was pregnant. I figured it was good practice for when the babies came and they could actually understand what I said and hold it against me when they were older.

Seriously. It's not like every single off-hand comment has to be taken literally. Come on. But with kids…Yeah.

As you can see, I wasn't doing well with my attempts to limit my sarcastic nature which is why I figured I'd just have to start putting a dollar away towards the kids' therapy fund every time I said something less than perfect.

I figured with interest and compounding it would hopefully be enough to get them started with therapy at least.

Plus, the good thing about those sorts of comments is they would probably drive my kids to be relentless overachievers, so they'd have some funds of their own to work from which I could indirectly claim credit for, thereby creating yet another therapy spiral where they questioned their entire existence and whether their personal success was in fact a direct result of their overly-sarcastic mother and her comments.

I would've probably stood there having an existential crisis for the rest of the night, but Matt arrived. He dashed through the door looking all adorably frazzled. "I'm here."

"I see that."

"Are you okay?" He grabbed my arms and looked me over.

"I'm fine. Go back to work. You were in the middle of something when I called. I'm sorry to pull you away for nothing."

"Just some kids spray-painting a few stop signs. I almost had one of them, but then the phone rang."

"And you stopped to answer it?" I teared up at the thought. Pregnancy hormones, I tell ya. "You didn't need to do that for me."

"You could've been in labor."

"Oh, yeah. True…Okay, fine. Sorry. Always answer when I call."

"I do." He kissed me on the forehead. "So where's the intruder?"

"Gone. It was a dog. A very cute dog. Some sort of mutt. But it left when I went to the bathroom."

Matt glanced at the doggie door. "We did tell you…"

"Yeah, yeah. Mountain lion. Bear. Blah, blah. But Fancy likes to be able to go in and out. And it's a lot easier than me having to get up to let her out each time." I patted my belly. He'd watched the conniptions I went through each time I had to stand up. He knew.

But…

We both stared at the doggie door.

I really didn't want a bear to come inside. But I also didn't want to deal with a Fancy who was blocked in. She's very high-pitched when she wants to be. And relentless. She'll make a sad little cry in the back of her throat every ten seconds until she gets her way.

Matt slid the cover in to block the doggie door. "Just for tonight."

"But what about the stray? Now it can't come back."

"Did it look like a stray? Maybe it just ran away from home and has now run back."

I chewed on my lip, thinking about it. "I don't know. I didn't get a very good look. It definitely wasn't starving, but it didn't look like it just came from someone's house either."

He squeezed my arms. "It'll be fine. Dogs are good at finding their way home. And this way you aren't waking up to a dog fight in the yard in the middle of the night."

I looked at Fancy who had sprawled by the front door. Yeah, dog fight. Right. Only if it could be done while lying down in a comfortable position.

(Although, Fancy has had her moments. She has a one-handed takedown I've seen her use on other dogs before, but then she doesn't really know what to do from there other than stand above them and growl the dog-equivalent of "leave me alone you annoying little dog". I don't know what she'd do if a dog actually tried to attack her…Then again, I didn't want to find out either.)

I glanced at the closed doggie door. That dog had looked harmless. And it was cold out. But…

One of the twins decided to kick me in the kidneys. Ow.

I was worried about that dog, but not as much as I wanted to go back to bed. "Okay. Yeah, fine. Thank you for running home to protect me." I kissed him on the cheek. "Love you."

"Love you, too."

Fancy followed me into the bedroom and curled up at the end of the bed while Matt let himself out the front door.

As I listened to the sound of his police vehicle driving away and tried to find a comfortable position around my absurdly-shaped but oh-so-necessary pillow, I wondered who the dog belonged to and if Matt was right that it would find its way back home.

I sure hoped so. But before I could worry about it too much I fell back asleep.

CHAPTER 6

The next morning I couldn't stop thinking about that poor dog. What if he hadn't found his way home? What if he'd spent the night shivering under a bush somewhere because he hadn't been able to get back inside the cabin?

I decided I could at least look around the yard and see if there was any sign of him. That shouldn't be too risky for me and the babies. It was just the yard. And it was small.

It had snowed a bit overnight so I had to bundle up. Since I couldn't manage boots I had gone down the dreaded Crocs path. I'd somehow avoided that particular awful fashion trend the first time around, but with my feet so swollen and not being able to put on shoes that tied or slipped over my heel, they were a blessing.

They even had lined ones. I had a pair of blue, green, and purple ones that had a black lining that didn't look too old-lady. (Although they were definitely, "I've given up on being fashionable and just want to be comfortable", which I had decided was my new fashion aesthetic.)

At least they weren't as bad as the ones Matt had bought me for inside. Those I was embarrassed to wear around anyone I didn't know well, because they had multi-colored puff balls on top in pastel colors.

Horridly embarrassing. But they were so comfy…

Anyway. I threw on my outdoor Crocs and as many layers as I could up top and went out to the yard to find where the dog had gone. But because it had snowed there were no prints, so I started a board-by-board check of the fence to see which one might be loose.

That's where Jamie found me. She of course was looking fashionable and adorable in a fur-lined coat that matched her fur-lined boots, her brown hair curled to just below her chin. If I hadn't known that she'd given birth less than six months ago I wouldn't have been able to tell from her slim figure. Some people, I swear, they make the rest of us look bad.

(Still my best friend and love her to death. I'm just sayin'. Some people make it look easy when it is most definitely not.)

"Maggie? This doesn't look like bed rest."

She had Max in his carrier. He was sound asleep like the perfect angel he was, his long black lashes visible against his plump little cheeks. I spared him a quick coo and waved her off as I finished my fence inspection.

"Oh, the Mayo Clinic thinks bed rest is a crock anyway."

"What are you doing?" she asked, running a hand through her curls to fluff them back up.

I shook my head. There she was, the mother of a newborn, and you couldn't even tell. No frizzy hair. No bags under her eyes. I'm pretty sure she was even wearing makeup.

Meanwhile, I hadn't even given birth yet and I couldn't quite remember the last time I'd taken a shower. I was pretty sure it was the day before, but maybe not. And there was a stain on my shirt that was *probably* from breakfast but could've been there for longer.

It was the second (?) day I was wearing that shirt. (Maybe the third? No. Not the third…I didn't think. Although it was possible. Eek.)

Fancy who'd been sprawled in a snowbank taking a nap started in Max's direction, but I called her back to me.

I knew she wouldn't do him any harm, but no one wants to wake up to a big black furry head in their face either. And I was pretty sure Fancy wouldn't enjoy when he grabbed at an ear or a lip. Babies are curious. They explore their world through touch. And putting things in their mouths.

Last thing we needed was Max to try to eat Fancy's ear. Or to get a handful of her slobber. Ew.

"I had a visitor last night," I told Jamie as I led the way inside.

"A bear?"

"No, not a bear." I filled her in on my midnight panic as I made us some tea.

She offered to make it, but I waved her off. I wasn't ready to sit down just yet. Being comfortable was not easy at that point in my pregnancy and in that moment standing felt better than I figured sitting would.

I described the dog for her. "You don't know who he belongs to do you? If so I could at least call and make sure he got home okay. Or let them know I'd seen him here last night if he's still missing."

She shook her head. "No. But…Let me see your laptop for a minute."

Her fingers flew across the keyboard as she muttered to herself. "No. Not that. No. And why are there so many ads on this site? Go away."

"You're starting to sound as cranky as me. Still not getting a lot of sleep I take it?"

She shook her head. "You just wait. With two of them you may never sleep again."

"You know, I was thinking I might just share one of them out to someone else for the first year or so. Maybe Evan and Abe would like the practice until their kid is born?"

She frowned at me. "You're not funny, Maggie. And one day someone is going to think you mean it and you'll be stuck in interviews you don't want to have."

I took a sip of my tea. "I know. But this is how I handle stress. I joke about it."

"Ha! Here it is. Was this him?" She turned the laptop in my direction.

On the screen was a picture of a young couple crouched down with a multi-colored fluffy mutt, his tongue lolling out of his mouth.

"I think so. Who are they?" I quickly scanned the article she'd found. "Oh, that's not good. They're missing?"

She nodded. "Yeah. Went backcountry skiing with their dog, but no one knows exactly where they went and their car hasn't been found so no one knows where to search. And since there were a few avalanches this weekend…Well, it's not looking good."

I scanned the article for more details. They'd been missing for two days already and the family thought they'd disappeared near Breckenridge, but weren't certain.

"How far do you think a dog can travel in two days? Not that far, right? I mean, Breckenridge to here? With mountains in between? And in the winter? It's not like dogs take the highway."

She typed some more and showed me a map. It was almost two hours by car. Could a dog really travel that far on foot? He'd have to climb a couple mountains or find a way through a few snow-filled valleys. And I'd watched enough of those lost in the wilderness shows to know that when you don't know the path you don't always get it right the first time, which would mean lots of false starts and backtracking.

Hm.

I shook my head. "I don't think they're in Breckenridge if their dog is here. I bet they used one of those trails up behind the ski resort. Can you pull that up?"

It took a few minutes, but Jamie finally found a map of backcountry hiking trails.

I leaned forward. "Where do you think people park to reach those trails? Maybe here or here? I bet no one goes up there this time of year...Which means...If we..."

"No."

I stared at Jamie. "No, what?"

"No. You, a heavily-pregnant woman who is supposed to be on bed rest and I, a woman with a newborn, are not going to go out and try to find this couple's car on some remote back road that isn't used in the winter."

"It's not like we're going to try to hike into wherever

they're stranded. I just want to drive up a few roads and see if we can find their car. According to that article they're looking near Breckenridge which is all wrong if that's their dog I saw, which I'm pretty sure it is. Without us they may never be found."

"No."

"But…"

"No."

I glared out the window, regretting that we'd very deliberately chosen not to bring my van to the cabin so that I wouldn't be tempted to drive.

I bit my lip. "They're looking in the wrong place."

"Then we call and tell them."

I rubbed at my belly, feeling a little heel poke into my palm. (Which really is kind of cool when it happens.)

"We could call. It's just that…"

That was boring. And then I'd have to watch it all play out on the news while I was stuck in bed being fat and awkward.

I gave Jamie my best pleading look. "That dog and I have a bond. It wiggled when it saw me. I think it would come to me if we found it again."

"It ran away from you, Maggie."

"Technically. But I think it was running away from Fancy more than me. I'm sure if we went out there and found it again…"

"No." She stared me down. "Do you *want* to give birth in the woods?"

"Of course not. We never even have to get out of your car."

"Do you want to give birth alone with only me to help on some remote backcountry road?"

I sighed. "Noooo."

Jamie didn't say anything more, just raised her eyebrows and stared me down.

"Can't we just drive around a little bit? Look for signs that someone ran off the road somewhere? I bet they ran off the road after they'd finished skiing. Let their guard down and whoosh, there they went."

"Maggie. Bed rest."

"But Mayo…"

"Mayo nothing. Your doctor ordered it."

I tried to cross my arms but there was too much in the way between my boobs and my belly. "Sometimes doctors are wrong."

"Fine. Let's say that this individual doctor was wrong about bed rest. Science as a whole, though, rarely is. And science says that when a woman is pregnant with twins they're usually early. Which means it doesn't matter about bed rest or not I am not going to drive you into the twisty, turny side roads around the valley looking for a dog and some lost couple. Not when you could go into labor at any moment."

"I am not going to go into labor right now. And Jamie, they have a baby with them. What if…" My mind started to spiral around where they could be and what could be happening and my eyes filled up with tears.

"All the more reason to leave it to the professionals." She closed the laptop with a definitive snap. "Now. Let's talk about what really brought me here. I brought you more pregnancy ice cream to try. Sriracha and plum."

She grabbed a small container from the freezer as I said, "Sriracha and plum? What is wrong with you?"

She scooped up a big bite of the ice cream and held it out. "Try it."

I wrinkled my nose. "Do I have to?"

"Yes."

(She was going to make a very good mother with that tone.)

I took a very, very small taste. It was…not exactly bad. Actually, it was kind of good?

"How do you do that? How do you take these weird flavors and make them taste good together?"

She shrugged. "Spicy and sweet work well together."

"But in an *ice cream*? Huh." I took the spoon and container from her, plopped down in a chair, and kept eating. I glanced towards the closed computer. "Jamie…"

"We're not going to drive around trying to find those people. But I'll call it in. There's a number for any tips in that article."

"Fine." It wasn't what I wanted, but it was better than doing nothing.

CHAPTER 7

Jamie called the tip line and told them everything we knew as I continued to eat the surprisingly good ice cream.

"The man on the line was very nice. He said they'd bring a tracking dog by in a little bit to see if they can find a trail to follow."

I scraped the bottom of the container for the last little bit of ice cream. "That's good. Maybe they can at least find the dog today. Poor thing. Out in the cold, alone. I bet he came back and couldn't get inside because Matt blocked the doggie door and now he's probably out there somewhere frozen to death."

Jamie gave me a look. The type that says stop being an overly-dramatic pregnant person. "Animals are smarter than people when it comes to that sort of thing. I'm sure he found somewhere else to shelter for the night. Remember, this wasn't the first day he was missing. He had to have made it through the night before, too."

"Maybe. Maybe he stayed with the family the first night and then they sent him off for help. Like Lassie."

She shook her head as she made another cup of tea. "Would you send Fancy off for help? Because I certainly wouldn't send Lulu off and expect her to ever come back."

I glanced at Fancy who was sprawled on her back against the couch, all four feet up in the air, snoring. "Fair point."

I drummed my fingers on the table. There had to be something more we could do. "Will you do me a favor? And put some dog food out on the back porch, just in case?"

"No."

"Jamie." She'd really taken this whole setting boundaries thing to heart since she'd become a mom. Not that Max was anywhere close to needing those yet. "Why not?"

"You, city girl, did not grow up here. So you have never had a bear in your kitchen. But it happens. Which is why I am not going to put food out on your back porch."

I pouted at her. "But how do we get him to come back if we don't tempt him with food?"

"We could call for him."

"Right. Because we know his name now. You're a genius!" I levered myself back onto my feet. "Come on. We can do it now while we're waiting for the rescue folks."

Jamie and I spent five minutes walking around the backyard of the cabin shouting "Dodger" and shaking bags of treats. But all it did was excite Fancy to the point I had to start shoving treats in her face because every time I shook the bag she'd move to sit in front of me, a small line of drool running from her jowls down her chest.

Our shouts also woke Max from his nap. While Jamie was busy breastfeeding him to calm him back down—she had this under the sweater trick that was thankfully quite unobtrusive—the rescue folks arrived.

The main guy was named Parker and was sexy in a *I wouldn't actually date you because of the facial hair, but I might want to fantasize about you* sort of way.

(What? I was married and pregnant, not dead inside. I can always appreciate a little rugged sexiness.)

But his enthusiasm for our tip wore off as soon as he saw that he was dealing with a new mother and a pregnant woman.

"You're sure you saw this dog?" he asked, holding up the picture from the news. "It couldn't have been another dog that looked like him?"

I threw up my hands. "I'm pretty sure it was that dog. It was the middle of the night. I was a bit startled that some strange dog was in my living room. But, yes, when Jamie showed me that picture this morning it looked an awful lot like him."

"I can't be wasting resources on a dog that looks an awful lot like this one. I need to focus resources where they'll be the most use."

I pressed my lips together. Suddenly Mr. Ruggedly Handsome had morphed into Mr. Know It All Jerk. I glared at him. I bet he'd come over to the cabin so fast because he'd thought Jamie would be attractive. But now that he saw she was a mother with a kid he wasn't interested.

I hate men like that. Who only want to talk to a woman if they think she's attractive. Granted, when you are *not* massively pregnant or carrying around a newborn, that sort of guy can be very useful if manipulated properly.

(Nothing extreme. I'm not a lean on the table and show off the girls sort of person. But a smile and appeal to his kindness can do wonders when a man finds you attractive.)

Of course, it only works if they think you have a certain sort of potential which it seems neither of us did anymore.

(A fact that hit Jamie harder than it hit me. I was eagerly awaiting the day I turned into an old hag that men would overlook. I'd seen enough dirty older men to know that just aging wasn't going to do it, so I was planning on striving for witch in the woods energy when I got old enough. I just had to get Matt on board first which was probably not going to be easy since he'd have to live with me and my rat's nest of hair and saggy clothes and permanent snarl.)

Anyway. Hot ranger dude was not buying my story. But he was already there with the tracker dog so he let the young woman with the dog take a turn around our yard.

"Sorry. I didn't catch any sign. It could be the snow covered the scent." She at least pretended to believe us and for that I gave her my best smile.

"Thank you for trying," I told her. "If the dog comes back I'll try to keep him here this time."

"Good idea."

The ranger dude just rolled his eyes. "Come on. Let's move out. We have a ton of leads to follow-up on today and this one took us out of our way." He shot a nasty look at my belly before walking out the door.

If I'd had the ability to burn literal holes in peoples' backs, he would've been on fire. The young ranger woman gave us an apologetic shrug as she followed him out the door.

After they were gone, Jamie turned to me. "Take a few deep breaths, Maggie. Calm down. *Think of the babies.*"

"Don't even get started with me on that line. Think of the babies. How many times have I heard that in the last couple of months?" But I did take a few deep breaths and sit back down and force all of my annoyance at the ranger dude out of my mind.

Jamie sat down at the table with me. "I'm sure they'll find that couple eventually."

"Yeah, come spring. I mean, really, if you've got a little kid and a dog and you're going to go out for some fun in the snow, why not just join the slew of tourists on the normal ski slopes? Doesn't Winter Park still have that boring-as-can-be trail for cross-country skiers down the backside of the mountain? Why not just take that?"

"It is not boring. It is beautiful. And it's a great trail for cross-country skiing."

I didn't say anything to that. The one time I'd taken that trail it was boring. Then again, I am not a winter sports sort. The closest I get to skiing is hanging out in the lodge with a spiked hot chocolate. And even then I'd rather be curled up at home with Fancy and a book.

Jamie stood up. "Well, I better get going. You're going to rest now, right? For the rest of the day?"

I rolled my eyes and smiled sweetly at her. "Yes, mom."

"Maggie, I mean it. I don't care what some website says about bed rest, you should listen to your doctor. And stop taking on the problems of the world. You've got your own to deal with."

I smooshed my face up at her. "Thanks for the reminder."

"Go on. Go. I'm not leaving until you lie down."

"Really?"

"Really."

I shuffled off to the bedroom. I had every intention of getting right back up after she'd left, but by the time I laid down on my side and arranged my pillow and pulled up the covers and she turned off the light…

I decided a little nap wouldn't hurt. I'd conquer proving that man wrong later.

CHAPTER 8

I woke up to Fancy leaning against the edge of the bed making sad little noises. When I flipped my phone over to check the time I understood why. It was thirty minutes past her dinner time.

"I'm sorry." I rubbed her ears as I tried to force myself awake. They were so velvety soft, I loved them. "Thank you for letting me sleep." I would've kissed the top of her head, but there was a gigantic belly that wouldn't let me bend in half or do anything else for that matter.

Of course, as soon as I moved, my bladder made its needs known, so when I finally did manage to get upright I immediately headed for the bathroom instead of the kitchen, which made Fancy very unhappy. She stood there lecturing me in a high-pitched whine until I was done.

"Sorry, Fancy. But that took priority. Trust me."

She looked at me with the most wounded expression on the planet.

"I know. I know. You did not ask for any of this. Moving cross-country. Changing homes multiple times. Matt. Babies. Murder. Mayhem. I'm sorry."

Her sad but patient look made me feel so guilty I added a couple of Pumpkin Puffs to her bowl. I would've probably given her a spoonful of peanut butter, too, but the vet had informed me on our last visit that Fancy needed to lose weight.

I'd debated having a discussion with him about how research on humans had shown that diets don't really work, but then I realized that I am one hundred percent in control of what Fancy eats and that if I stopped giving her things like treats, peanut butter, and helpings of everything on my plate that she probably would lose weight, so I kept it to myself.

That vet was still a jerk, though. What kind of person walks into the room and immediately says, "It looks like somebody needs to lose weight." Too bad he was the only vet in the valley.

Anyway. To Fancy Pumpkin Puffs were just as yummy as peanut butter, so it all worked out. She was almost done with her dinner when Matt walked in with two pizza boxes.

"There're my girls. All four of you." He kissed my cheek and ruffled Fancy's ears before setting the boxes on the table.

"Four? Oh dear, you're right." I laughed. "You poor man. You're going to spend the rest of your life surrounded by women. Can you handle it?"

"Absolutely."

"And you brought me pizza." I reached for the topmost pizza box. "Have I told you how much I love you lately?"

I opened the box to see a massive heap of sausage, onions, and green peppers. It gave me heartburn just looking at it, and I bit my lip to keep from taking back what I'd just said.

Matt grabbed the box and slid it to the side. "That one is for me. The bottom one is for you."

I opened it. Cheese, tomatoes, and basil. Much better.

It probably still wasn't great for me, but I'd take the hit for that yummy melty cheese and crunchy crust. I grabbed a slice and took a big bite as Matt went to the kitchen for plates.

"What did you do today?" he asked.

I told him about Jamie's visit and the ranger who ignored us. "Do you know if they found them yet?" I asked.

He shook his head. "I was swamped all day. Now that the valley's opened back up to tourists it's non-stop craziness."

"Really? Most people haven't even gotten their shots yet."

He snorted. "Like that'll stop a certain type of person who never took it seriously in the first place? And the worst part is that that's ninety percent of the tourists right now, so there's no buffer between the different groups. I never realized how much my job relied on regular, normal people giving a rude look here or there to keep others in check. Now that those folks are hiding away at home for the most part and people are feeling the need to get out and live…It's bad."

"I'm sorry." I gave Fancy a bite of pizza before she drooled a puddle on the floor.

"That's alright. At least the end is in sight. My days of dealing with drunken fools are almost over."

"Are they, though? Because you'll still be dealing with all of that at the pet resort. We all will." I sat down at the table and let Matt serve me up another slice of pizza. "I may not be working the barkery counter myself at the new resort but if I have to stand by and listen to some woman criticizing every single treat in the display case because she wants a discount, I will scream."

I dropped a bite of pizza on Fancy's sharing plate as I added, "I don't like people, Matt."

He laughed. "I know."

"I mean, that's not exactly true. I like you. And Jamie. And my grandpa. And Lesley. And Abe and Evan. And…others who I can't think of right now. But there are so many people in this world I really don't want to be around." I sighed. "Does that make me a bad person?"

"Would you care if it did?" Matt popped open his beer and took a sip.

I gazed at it longingly. I'd never been much of a drinker, but having to give up alcohol for so long made me realize I did like the occasional drink here or there.

I thought about his question for a moment. "No. I don't care. Because I'm still not going to force myself to like that sort of person who's just a jerk. Or so self-absorbed they can't see how they treat others. Or so arrogant they think their you-know-what doesn't stink."

He shrugged. "Well then. Don't worry about it. If it's not going to make you change, worrying about what kind of person it makes you just wastes precious time and energy you could better spend elsewhere."

"Like on finding that poor couple. I can't imagine what they're going through. Do you mind if I turn on the TV?"

"No. Go ahead."

Fortunately, the news was just getting started and the missing couple was the third story. They interviewed the sexy-yet-hairy ranger who grinned at the attractive young reporter before putting on his serious face and turning towards the camera.

"We've focused our search in the Breckenridge area. That's where Zoey's mother thinks they were going. We made progress today, but no sign of them yet. When someone disappears in the backcountry there's a lot of ground to cover, but we're hopeful we'll find them tomorrow."

I set down my pizza and glared at the TV. "I told him they're not in Breckenridge. There's no way the dog could've shown up here if they disappeared in Breckenridge. Stupid man who won't listen to a woman just because she's pregnant."

As I was muttering at the TV they once again showed a picture of the Niels family looking very wholesome and All-American.

"No other leads?" the reporter asked. "Are you sure you're looking in the right area?"

"No. He's not," I said.

"Yes, we're quite sure," he answered. "I mean, obviously, in situations like this you do receive a number of tips from people who want to help and think they've seen something, but we're quite confident they'll be found in the Breckenridge area."

"I saw the frickin' dog!" I shouted at the TV. "I didn't *think* I saw him, I did see him."

"Maggie, calm down."

"I saw that dog. It was here. In this very living room. They are looking in the wrong place."

"You need to be calm. Think about the babies."

I glared at him. If one more person told me what I

needed to do for the babies, I was going to kill someone. And then what was going to happen to the poor babies? Born in prison. Adopted by strangers.

Tell me to think about the babies…Seriously. What else was I thinking about twenty-four hours a day? They had taken over my body like some sort of alien predator. How could I not think about them?

(And yes, yes, it was all so adorable. The sight of a foot thrusting against my skin like some sort of horror movie with a trapped alien trying to escape its fleshy prison. Just adorable.)

I took three deep, calming breaths. For the babies.

"I saw the dog, Matt. I was not mistaken."

He squeezed my hand. "I believe you."

"But they don't. Which means they are looking in the wrong place." I glared at the TV. "He thinks I'm wrong because I'm pregnant and hormonal. *Crazy pregnant lady can't know what she saw.*"

"He could just think you're wrong because you're a woman."

I inhaled through my nostrils and turned to glare at Matt, ready to release all my fury on him, but he was trying so hard not to laugh that my anger fizzled out.

He grinned at me. "It's fun to rile you up sometimes. It's so easy when you're pregnant."

"Matthew Allen Barnes, do not make me divorce you and leave you with custody of our kids."

He chuckled. "Yes, ma'am. I'm sorry. You want some ice cream?"

"Maybe. Did Jamie leave an extra container of that sriracha and plum?"

"Sriracha and plum?"

"Don't look at me, she's the one that came up with it. It's actually really good."

"Huh." He grabbed the container and two spoons. "So now what?" he asked as he took a bite for himself before handing the container over.

"What do you mean?"

"Maggie. I know you. What are you going to do about the missing couple and the dog?"

I took a bite of ice cream before I answered. I knew what my answer would've been before babies and bed rest. I would've been out driving down every one-lane dirt road I could find looking for their vehicle and shouting for Dodger.

But it probably wasn't a good idea to do that. Knowing my luck I'd get stuck on some rutted backroad and go into labor.

"I don't know yet. I was going to put food out so the dog would come back, but Jamie told me that was a bad idea."

"She's right."

"She also said I shouldn't go driving around backroads looking for them."

"Also right."

"But Matt…They're out there somewhere. For the third night. They have to be getting desperate."

He grabbed a handful of cookies out of the panda cookie jar I'd made in ninth grade that was misshaped and poorly painted. I'd brought it with us because (a) we needed a cookie jar and (b) it reminded me of my childhood.

(Matt hadn't said a word about it. Love is living with your significant other's sentimental claptrap, because that thing was fugly.)

He handed me a cookie and sat back down at the table. "Okay. You can't go for a drive or put out food. What can you do from here to help find them?"

I glanced towards the television where they'd now moved on to the weather. Two more days before the next snowfall was expected.

"I wish I knew where they were actually going. How do you go skiing in Colorado in the backcountry in the middle of winter and not tell anyone where you're going?"

(Ignore the fact that I have never once told anyone where I was headed when I went out for a hike. Even in dangerous countries when traveling alone.)

"Good. Go with that. How can you find that out? Sounds like the rangers have already talked to her mom. I bet they've also talked to other family members and neighbors and friends. Who else would know? Where else could you find that information that they haven't already looked?"

I thought about it as I nibbled on the cookie. No friends. No family. No access to phone records. Or email. But…

"Social media. If either one of them had an account, maybe they said something about it. I know more about some people's personal lives because of what they post online than their family does."

"There you go. Track it down. Find their accounts. See if there's a clue about what they were planning."

"But shouldn't the cops have already checked that?"

He shrugged one shoulder. "Only so many hours in the day and so many available resources. If the family is saying Breckenridge and the first few posts don't say anything different, they might not have dug deeper. Or they might have stopped at Facebook and never found Twitter or a blog."

I nodded. "Okay. Makes sense. Thank you. For humoring me."

He kissed my cheek. "I'm not humoring you. You're a force to be reckoned with when you set your mind on something. And I want to see that family found just as much as you do." He stood up. "In the meantime, now that I'm home, we can leave the doggie door open and see if Dodger comes back."

I blew him a kiss as he walked towards the back door. "I love you."

"Come here and give me a real kiss then." He winked at me.

I was tempted. He's a good-looking man. But…

"Sorry, I love you, but I do not love you enough to move from exactly where I am right now. Nothing hurts, the babies aren't kicking, and I don't have to pee. I am going to hold on to this state of bliss for as long as I possibly can."

I batted my eyes at him. "Which means I need you to go get my laptop, please."

"Yes, ma'am. Will do. And then I'm going to grab my service revolver from the lockbox in the car. Just in case we do attract a bear or mountain lion."

"No. No guns in the house. Ever."

"Maggie…Be reasonable. What if whatever comes in that doggie door isn't a dog?"

"Then you find some other way to deal with it. Look. I trust you. I love you. But the statistics are the statistics. No gun in any house I live in. Ever."

He frowned at me. "You can sleep with a knife on

your bed stand, but I can't sleep with a gun in the drawer?"

"Exactly. I am very unlikely to in any way harm anyone with my knife even if I need to. But a gun?" I shook my head. "Too easy to use."

"I am trained, you know."

"I don't care. Chalk it up to my mom's pacifist nature that she passed on to me. No guns in the house. Especially not for the next eighteen years."

"You're being silly."

I shrugged my shoulders. Maybe I was, but that was one topic I was not going to cave on. Ever.

He pursed his lips. "Fine. But I am going to put my baseball bat near the bed."

"Feel free. Now can I please have my laptop so I can get to work?"

As Matt grabbed the laptop for me I realized that was probably as close as we'd ever come to a deal-breaker kind of fight. Odd all the little landmines that exist in a relationship that you never see coming until you step on them. I was just lucky he let it go, because I wouldn't have, and I did not want to do this whole babies thing on my own.

CHAPTER 9

Lucky for me, Zoey Niels lived her entire life online. I swear that woman didn't take a bite of food that wasn't posted to Instagram or Facebook or both. And the videos on TikTok…Oh my.

That woman had cutesy opinions about everything. And little hacks for how to clean this or repair that. (Walnuts to fix scratches in your cabinets? Who knew.)

And the lunches she made for her husband? Hm. Let's just say I didn't let Matt see those. Loved him, but I was not going to hand-draw love notes for him every day of his life while putting gourmet food into little cutesy containers. The 50's ended for a reason, thank you very much.

It was wild. But the real substance was on her blog.

She posted every single day. Even when all she had to share were pictures of her sleeping child. Every. Single. Day. That woman did not miss.

I was in awe of her dedication. I knew more about her life after three hours than I did about the lives of my three best friends combined, and I was married to and living with one of them.

"Find anything useful?" Matt asked after he'd finished watching whatever hockey game had been on.

(I don't watch hockey. To me the Avs are that team we bought from Canada so we could win whatever trophy you win when you're the best hockey team in North America. They aren't a *real* Colorado team like the Broncos. And, yes, I realize how absurd an opinion that is since they've been in Colorado for twenty-plus years, but it's still the way I feel about it.)

I stared at the notes I'd taken before answering him. "Depends on what you think is useful. I know her food allergies. I know she struggled with postpartum depression and that it freaked her out because she'd dealt with some serious depression in college. I know the names of all of her dogs, ever, including the one she had when she was two years old. It was a golden retriever. I know that Dodger was a rescue they adopted last year. I know that she one day wants to go to Paris. And that she's written a novel. But none of that is going to help find them."

"Nothing about where they were headed then?"

"Nope. Just a mention that she was feeling a little stir-crazy and wanted to get out and that maybe it was time to try some backcountry skiing. I guess they'd done it a lot before the baby came, but not since."

"Where did they like to go?"

"No idea."

It's crazy how someone could live that much of their life online and still not mention something so obviously important. Just goes to show, that even when you think someone is sharing *everything* about their life, that they're really not. There is no substitute for a good face-to-face conversation.

"Could there be another blog?" He sat down across from me and pulled my notes over to scan through them.

I shook my head as an uncontrollable yawn overtook me. "Maybe? Probably. I went back six months on all of her socials, but it looks like I'll have to go back even further. Ugh." I set the laptop off to the side. "Tomorrow, though. I am wiped out."

"You don't have to do this, you know. It's enough to be working on the resort and taking care of Fancy and being pregnant. You don't have to try to find a couple of complete strangers."

"I know. But…I feel obligated."

He raised one eyebrow. "Because the dog found you?"

"Exactly. And I can't just leave it alone now knowing that they're looking in the wrong place." As I stood up and shuffled towards the bathroom, I asked, "Can we drive around tomorrow? Just a little bit?"

"Maggie…"

"I'm not going to go into labor. I promise."

He laughed. "I don't think that's something you can promise. Especially when the doctor has already put you on bed rest and twins come early."

I gave him my best winning smile. "Worst comes to worst, you can deliver the babies, right?"

He laughed, a full-throated roar of amusement. "No."

"But you're trained in emergency situations."

"I am not about to try to deliver my own children. I would be too nervous. About you. About the babies. No. Not going to happen."

"Right. Because I'm not going to go into labor unexpectedly. But if I did…You could handle it. I have faith in you."

He came over and kissed my forehead. "No."

I sighed deeply. "Fine. I guess we just sit around and hope that Dodger returns then."

"I guess so."

I gave him one last glare before I toddled off to the bathroom. It was good I'd married a stubborn man. But there were moments…

CHAPTER 10

I woke up in the middle of the night and struggled out of bed, careful not to step on Fancy who was sleeping pressed up against the side of the bed mere inches away from me. I had to be careful as I scooched down the bed and moved around her to not step on that one back paw she sprawls out from her body. You can never see it, but it's lurking, just waiting to be stepped on.

Pre-pregnancy it was easy to maneuver around her, but almost eight months into my pregnancy, not so much. Somehow I managed, though.

The whole time I was shuffling around and getting up, Matt snored away contentedly on the other side of the bed. My big, brave protector.

I swear, he'd sleep through an earthquake. Fancy on the other hand is always on a hair-trigger where I'm concerned, so her breathing immediately shifted from deep, deep breaths to alert and poised to act.

"It's okay," I told her. "I just need to pee."

But of course Fancy doesn't understand English or the concept of time quite as well as I'd like. So my getting out of bed was the equivalent of "time to be up" in her world. Anything within about three hours of normal wake-up time means she's up and ready to go and expecting attention.

I tried to get her to go back to sleep, but she stood in the living room and cried softly at me until I finally threw on a heavy winter coat and stepped outside into the cold, cold night air with her. I wasn't letting her out alone in the middle of the night, not after all that talk of bears.

It was peaceful out there. I could see the shape of a few of the other cabins amongst the trees. Somewhere an owl hooted. But other than that it was just me shivering on the porch and Fancy crunching through the snow as she went to pee.

It was dark out there. Darker than I ever remember it being in DC or Denver. Light pollution they call it. Big cities are always too lit. But up in the mountains, tucked away on the back corner of a resort, that was not an issue. It was so dark Fancy blended right in. My little spot of blackness in the blackness.

I heard a rustle somewhere off to the side.

"Come on, Fancy. Come back inside," I called.

No response. Knowing Fancy she'd laid herself down in a snowbank. Forget that it was cold enough you could see your breath. This was her happy place. Silent, cold, dark. Outside.

It was not mine.

"Fancy. Come on. Come back in. It's the middle of the night."

Still nothing.

I didn't know where a flashlight was or if we even had one to use. And I wasn't about to go stumbling around in an unfamiliar yard trying to find her. But I didn't want to leave her out there either. All that talk of mountain lions and bears had made me a little paranoid, you know?

I mean on one level I was sure there wasn't some predator out there stalking me or my dog. Bears and mountain lions tend not to want a big hassle. If you're a predator who has to kill to eat, you choose the path of least resistance. Why go after the challenging target when you can find the quick bite instead?

But still.

"Fancy. Come on."

A shuffling noise off to the right made me whirl around. I'd forgotten I was an ungainly beast with a weird center of gravity, so I almost knocked myself on my butt before I managed to grab the railing.

"Fancy? Is that you? Come on then."

Two eyes stared at me out of the darkness.

"Fancy?" I said, softer. Was that really how tall she was? Were her eyes really that big? And did they glow like that when it was dark?

The eyes blinked and whatever it was came one step closer.

I laughed nervously. "Come on now, Fancy. Time to go in. Treat?"

Treats always work with Fancy. And it did that time, too. She came lumbering up from my *left* and looked at me attentively. I nudged her through the doggie door and then slowly turned my head back towards where I'd seen those shining eyes.

They were still there.

"Dodger?" I asked, my voice squeaking higher at the end.

I'd been able to convince myself the eyes might be

Fancy's. Maybe they were a little big and a little high in retrospect, but it was at least possible. Dodger on the other hand…

Yeah, no.

As whatever animal it was took a step closer, I reached for the door handle, still trying to block the doggie door with my body so Fancy wouldn't come back out.

There was a railing around the deck. It would stop whatever it was.

I hoped.

I groped around for the door handle, never turning my back on those very big, very still eyes until my hand finally closed over the handle and I could open the door and step inside. Quickly. Well, as quickly as an ungainly pregnant woman can step.

As soon as I was inside, I slammed the doggie door cover back into place, my heart racing as I tried to look through the window. It was too bright inside and too dark outside to see anything.

I turned off all the lights, but I still couldn't see anything. Hopefully, whatever that had been was gone, but I was not going to take any chances. I wanted to help Dodger but I was not going to leave the doggie door open anymore. No siree. Not at night.

A ripple of pain spread across my belly and I sat down at the kitchen table, taking the type of calming breaths I'd learned during that one summer of Ashtanga yoga. Ujjayi breathing. I figured they'd helped with skydiving panic, they could help with this, too.

But they didn't. My heart was racing. My body hurt. And Fancy was sitting there with a sad look that darted back and forth between me and the treat container.

"Sorry, Fancy. I did promise, didn't I? Just give me a minute here, okay?"

She stared at me with those sad amber eyes of hers. Unblinking. Judging. Demanding. (Sweetly, of course. That's why I always feel so bad if I neglect her in any way. Because she's so accommodating and accepting when it happens.)

"Okay. I think…I think I'm okay now." I shoved to my feet, gave her a treat, and went to the door one more time.

No eyes. Just darkness. Lots and lots of darkness.

"Well, Dodger, I'm pretty sure that wasn't you. And I really hope you don't run into whatever it was."

I made my way back to bed, Fancy at my side. As I snuggled in with my pillow and Fancy sprawled on the floor next to me, Matt continued to snore away softly, completely oblivious to our little mid-night adventure.

CHAPTER 11

The next morning on the news they still hadn't found the missing couple so I went back to my social media snooping. It took some digging, but I finally found a small blog from a few years before that the couple had devoted to hiking and hiking pictures.

That's the thing about the internet. All the information you need is probably there somewhere, but finding it…that's a completely different story.

The blog had only been used for a year right after they started dating and then for some reason they'd abandoned it. The only reason I found it was because she'd linked over to it when she started her new blog. Which had meant going through so, many, posts. Oh my gosh. So. Many.

She hadn't (thankfully) posted on the hiking blog daily. But it did seem to document every single hiking trip they took that year. Not just Colorado either, but Moab, too.

I once went hiking in Moab. We were going to camp out in the wilderness for three nights as part of a school trip. But we couldn't find water. So we ended up at a hotel instead. Which is one of the many times I did not become some tragic story on the news. Glad the teacher wasn't foolish enough to assume we would eventually find water and have us push on.

Anyway. There were about forty posts on the blog, each full of gorgeous photos. The Niels were so young. And happy. And full of energy.

Just looking at the pictures made me feel old and boring. Then again, at their age I'd been spending my weekends shopping or sitting on the couch watching DVDs, so I guess I'd always been boring.

I know that we're all humans and supposed to be alike because of that, but it occurs to me sometimes that humans are as diverse as dog breeds.

Everyone is trying to pretend we're all just "dog" and fit us all into the same little bucket of behaviors and beliefs. But really some of us are Newfoundlands who want to sleep all day and love water and good food, others are labs who want to be out in the wilderness hunting or hiking with their people, some are golden retrievers who love literally everyone and just want attention, and some are Chihuahuas who are full of anxiety and ready to throw down with the biggest baddy around to show they're not actually as scared as they are.

It fascinates me that we all understand those differences when we look at dogs, but then we turn to one another and are like, "What's wrong with you that you don't like almond milk soy protein shakes and going for a run first thing in the morning? You just need to try it and you'll love it."

Yeah, no. Never. But nice try.

Anyway. I digress.

A Puzzling Pooch and Pumpkin Puffs

While I was tracking down her social media, Matt, being the saint he is, made me yummy breakfast frittatas.

They're not really frittatas in my opinion because they go in a muffin tin and frittatas are flat, but that's what the recipe called them, so that's what Matt called them, so that's what I reluctantly call them, too.

Whatever they were, they had all the yummy goodies you want in a breakfast. Eggs, ham, cheese, spinach, and mushrooms.

Okay, so maybe you don't want that in your breakfast, but I did. Pair that with some hashbrowned potatoes, an apple, and some orange juice and you've got a good meal. Oh, and salsa. Never forget the salsa.

Matt even did the dishes when we were done. But then he had to leave for work.

It took me another hour to parse through all those posts and mark each location I could identify on a map. I was so thorough I even marked every location someone in the comments mentioned. (To be fair, there weren't many. That's the sad fact of social media. Lots of great content out there, but most people have five followers or less and that's including family.)

When I was done I spread the map out on the table and stared at it, waiting for it to reveal its secrets. I don't know what I was expecting. Some great big arrow from on high saying, "Here. Right here. They are here."

That did not happen.

I rarely get lost, but at the same time geography is not my strong suit. So I knew where we were and I knew where all the little marks on the map were, but what I was missing was that sense of how they fit together. Which of the spots on the map were close enough to the valley geographically for them to have gone to and for Dodger to have then made his way to my cabin.

I had no clue.

Luckily for me, my grandpa dropped by before I could tear the map up in frustration.

"Maggie May, what are you doing out of bed?" he asked as he opened the front door.

"You could knock you know," I told him as I stood up and went over to kiss his cheek.

He'd aged in the last two years since I'd moved to the valley. He still looked twenty years younger than he was with his faded brown hair and flannel shirt and jeans. But there was more weight on his shoulders.

He was happy, don't get me wrong. But life's hard, you know? Bodies wear down. And the world was…a lot.

Not just the lockdowns and fear about getting sick, but that January mess had really thrown him for a loop, too. We didn't talk politics because I still wanted to love him and certain beliefs and behaviors get so ingrained you can't argue them away easily, but I figured he'd voted for a certain person and seeing that January thing made him finally realize that maybe that person wasn't who he thought they were.

The world he'd grown up in—which had not been an easy world as evidenced by the time he spent in prison because he'd been too poor to think of any other solution to life than bank robbery—had changed.

And I think he knew it wasn't going to change back.

That comes with a certain dose of fear. And a feeling like, *I am too old for this, I do not have it in me to adapt to whatever THIS is.* Heck, I wasn't even forty yet and *I* felt that way.

But he was still there despite it all. Carrying on, holding his head up high, and keeping all the rest of us on our toes.

He took off his jacket and hung it by the door. "If I knocked you'd just run off to bed so I wouldn't know you were disobeying doctor's orders."

I laughed. "I'm afraid running is beyond me these days. Coffee?"

"Sure. You sit. I've got it." He made his way towards the kitchen. "Easy enough to pop one of these little things in the machine."

He took a minute to figure it out, but he managed.

"So what brings you around?" I asked.

"Mason asked me if I could do a bit of woodwork in the reception area. He wanted some flourishes to make things look fancy."

"Oh."

I pursed my lips. It seemed Mason and I needed to have a bit of a chat. I didn't mind him including my family in the resort, but it would be nice to know when he was going to do so. "Let me guess. Does he have Jack working around here, too?"

(Jack is Matt's brother, a reformed hellion with too much charm for his own good. But he's a good general contractor and maintenance guy.)

"As a matter of fact. Jack is doing the base work and then I'm doing the fancy work. Problem?"

I shook my head. "No. I'm glad he's using you guys. I just wish I'd known. It seems odd is all. Didn't he have anyone else he could call?"

My grandpa plopped down in the chair opposite me. "You spent too much of your life in the big city. Here there are only so many choices when you want something done. Plus, why wouldn't you call on the people who are friends and family?"

I thought about it for a second and winced at my answer. "It's harder to yell at friends or family if the job isn't done well."

He leveled a look at me that made me feel two inches tall before pointing his chin at the map. "What's this mess you've got spread out on the table here?"

I told him about the dog that had been in the cabin and the missing couple and how I was sure they were near us but how the rangers thought they were in Breckenridge. And I showed him her blog and the map I'd put together from it.

"Hmm." He studied the map. "It's possible if they went to one of these three locations here that are north of Breckenridge that the dog could've made his way along here and reached the valley."

He tapped his finger on the map and sat back. "But not likely. Are you sure the dog you saw is this couple's dog?"

"Grandpa."

"It was the middle of the night. You were wound up. You didn't have the picture with you at the time. Are you certain it was the dog?"

"What other dog could it be?"

He shrugged and took another sip of his coffee. "I don't know. Lots of cute fluffy mutts that look alike out there."

I felt tears starting in my eyes.

"Now, now, Maggie May. No need to get upset. Come on now." He brushed a tear off my cheek.

"It's just…" I sniffled. "I hate this. I hate not being able to do things. And…being forgetful. And tired. And having people not listen to me anymore."

I stared at a small scratch on the table and ran my finger over it. "And worrying that I'm going to screw it all up once the kids are born. I don't think mother instincts just kick in like everyone wants you to believe they do. What if, what if I'm a bad mother?"

He squeezed my hand. "You are not going to be a bad mother. Look how you are with Fancy. And you had some of the best parents around to set a good example. And that man of yours is a good man, too. Plus you have a whole community that will support you when you need it. You'll be just fine."

Fancy came over and leaned against my chair and I ruffled her hair as I sniffled and tried to control myself.

My grandpa leaned closer. "It's okay to be scared. We all are at one point or another. The key is to not let the fear shut you down."

I nodded and stared at the map once more. "Maybe you're right. Maybe it wasn't Dodger I saw. In which case…" I spread my hands apart in defeat. "I just wasted an entire morning on some stupid map that no one needs."

"Tell ya what. I have a few friends who are rangers and involved in this search. Let me reach out to them and share what you put together here. Even if the dog you saw wasn't that couple's dog, that doesn't change the fact that you've identified some likely spots to find them." He lifted my chin. "Sound good?"

"Yeah, I guess."

"It wasn't wasted time, Maggie May."

I nodded, reluctantly.

"Now. You go lie down for a bit and rest."

I rolled my eyes. "I'm so tired of resting." (And yet, a good nap sounded kinda nice right then.)

"I know. But I need enough time to finish that crib for you so you can't go into labor just yet, you hear me?"

I nodded. "Okay. I'll do it. For you."

"Good." He kissed my cheek and took his cup to the kitchen while I shuffled off to sleep, yet again.

CHAPTER 12

I woke up from my nap just in time for the twelve o'clock news. Fancy of course really didn't care that the news was on or that there might be a story I wanted to watch. She had patiently slept next to my bed for most of the morning and now wanted to go outside.

She picked up her stuffed snake with all the squeakers and took it to the front door.

"I can't, Fancy. I'm sorry."

I was willing to push the doctor's orders a bit, but not enough to take my dog for a walk. Fancy's a good walker, don't get me wrong, but when a hundred and thirty-five pounds of dog wants to chase a squirrel or cross the street to say hi to another dog, that requires strength to hold her back. And balance. The last thing I needed was to lose control of her and fall and go into labor and…

No.

"I'm sorry. I am. Come on. We'll go out on the back porch."

The small cluster of cabins with fenced in yards on the edge of the resort property had been one of my brilliant ideas. I loved to travel before I got Fancy but afterward it became much trickier.

Staying in a hotel room with a dog is always a bit hit and miss. There was the time the room didn't have carpet and Fancy wouldn't set more than a foot inside. And the time we had to use an elevator. And that really long hallway with multiple barking dogs behind doors that scared her so bad she wouldn't move.

A small little cabin with a fenced-in yard for her to go in and out as needed? Perfection.

I would've paid a premium for something like that when I was traveling with her. I just hoped that others felt the same. If our bookings for the summer were any indication, they absolutely did.

And in these plague times being able to stay in a standalone unit without shared air? Even better.

Fancy dropped her toy on the floor and followed me outside. If she'd been a toddler—which dogs kind of are—she would've been dragging her feet the whole way and pushing out her lower lip in a disappointed pout.

"I'm sorry. I am. I know I keep saying that, but I really am."

I could just imagine what she was thinking. *Fat lot of good saying you're sorry is when you still go ahead and do whatever it is anyway. Just like when you tell me you love me as you do something I really don't like you to do, like trim my nails.*

Sigh. Puppy parenting is hard. *Life* is hard.

Fortunately, Fancy can always be brought around with a treat or two, so I fed her about five Pumpkin Puffs and then she was content to lie down on the porch in the shade.

I sat in the sun, because it was frickin' cold out. I also wrapped myself in the big heavy blanket I'd pulled out of the closet. That made it just bearable enough to stay out there with her for a little bit.

Since I am completely incapable of just sitting somewhere and doing absolutely nothing, I ran back inside after about a minute.

"I'll be right back," I promised Fancy, because otherwise she'd follow me.

As I grabbed my laptop and a cup of tea I continued to tell her that I'd be right back, it was okay, stay where she was, don't worry. She was alert to the fact that I was not there, but she waited patiently until I returned at which point she gave a deep sigh, closed her eyes, and promptly fell asleep.

As I sipped my cup of tea, I navigated to the website for one of the local news stations down in Denver. I debated between clicking on the linked article about the Niels or just watching the live coverage, and finally opted for the news article.

(It looked like they were covering sports on the live segment anyway which meant it was too late for any of the news that actually mattered.)

(To me. Yes, I know, for some sports are important.)

The news article didn't really say anything new, just that they were missing and people were searching. But just as I was about to click away from the news site and get lost in my email/Facebook/Twitter death spiral for an hour or so, they interrupted the live broadcast with breaking news.

I unmuted my computer and clicked on the video.

"This just in. Authorities have located Zoey and Trevor Niels. The Niels, their baby, and their dog are all safe. We go live now to the scene."

The footage cut away to one of the fresh-faced newbies the station had recently hired. I know the old-school anchors who've been there forever, but I can never keep track of all the shiny new faces who will soon leave for jobs in Miami or LA or New York or whatever the bigger markets are.

This one was a young woman with dark hair and warm brown eyes and honey-colored skin. She pointed to an ambulance behind her where Zoey and Trevor Niels were seated, paramedics checking them over. Zoey was holding the baby and leaning against her husband. They looked tired but happy.

Their dog was barking and running around their feet. He seemed to have an overabundance of energy.

Fancy heard the barking and lurched to her feet. She ran off into the yard barking in all directions.

"Sorry, Fancy, it's just the computer," I called after her.

I used the distraction as an excuse to go inside where it was actually warm. I should've probably called her in with me, but there was no one around to be bothered by her barking and I was too tired to multitask.

I turned my attention back to the screen just in time to see my not-a-very-nice-guy-after-all-but-still-sexy-in-a-hairy-way ranger step up to give a statement.

He rattled off the details of when they'd found the couple and what state they were in.

It seems they'd been fine on their skiing outing, but then run off the road on a narrow turn as they were headed home at the end of the day. (I knew it.) They'd assumed someone would come by to find them so had stayed in their vehicle, but no one had.

Mr. Niels had spent the daytime hours that first day

putting a bright orange tie on the tree next to where the car had slid off the road and building a big SOS on the ground for anyone doing a flyover to find, but then they'd just hunkered down and hoped.

Fortunately they'd had enough water and food to last for a week.

(You might think they should've tried to get out, but really I think what they did was the best call. It's easy to get lost wandering the woods and end up in a stream or caught out without shelter at night. I once read this book, *Deep Survival*, that was really good and talked all about how adults sometimes have the wrong survival instincts. It's also I'm pretty sure what would explain how they were fine when they were skiing because they knew that was risky, but then ran off the road when the "danger" was past. Maybe not, though. It's been a decade since I read that book.)

The ranger smiled into the camera. "The real breakthrough in this search came this morning when someone who'd taken the time to track down the Niels' old hiking blog gave our rangers a map of all of the locations they'd mentioned. The Niels weren't in any of those identified locations, but it gave our rangers an idea of another location to try. And, as you can see, we sent a team up there, and found them."

I smiled. I had actually helped. Take that Mr. Too Hairy Who Doesn't Listen To Smart Women.

My grandpa opened the front door just as the ranger was finishing his statement. "You're up."

"Just got up a few minutes ago, I promise."

Fancy ran to the front door with her stuffed snake in her mouth and looked imploringly back at me.

I sighed. "I'm sorry, Fancy. I can't. I really can't."

"What're you apologizing for?"

"She wants to go for a walk. But I can't. I sat out on the porch with her for a bit, but clearly it didn't work."

He pressed his lips together. "It's too cold for you to be sitting out there."

"I was fine. But you know what would really help me…" I batted my eyes at him. "If someone were to take Fancy for a walk. She really loves you, you know."

"You want me to walk the dog? When she has a perfectly good backyard right there?"

"It's not the same." Fancy and I both looked at him, begging. "Would you? Please? It doesn't have to be far. Just a little walk. Just down a trail or two."

He frowned down at Fancy as she stared up at him, all patient hope. "Fine. But I came over here for a reason. They found that couple."

"I know. I just saw it on the news. Thank you. For giving them my map."

"Happy to do it. You saw that the dog was with them?"

I nodded.

"And?"

My shoulders slumped. I hate being wrong. "And it wasn't the dog I saw the other night."

"So there's still a mystery to solve then. Assuming you did see a dog."

"I did, see a dog. I am not losing it that much. It was in the living room. I promise you it was a real, live, flesh and blood dog."

"Well, then. You'll have to figure out whose dog that was, won't you?" He winked at me and I smiled back.

"I will. After lunch. You want some? Leftover pizza."

He nodded. "Love to. Right after I walk this mutt. And maybe we can play some Scrabble. I brought it with me."

"Sounds good."

Fancy wagged her tail as she stood at the door and patiently waited to get leashed up.

I rubbed at my belly and smiled as I watched them, realizing how much better my life was now than it had been five years ago.

It wasn't perfect, nothing ever is. But all in all? I had it pretty darned good and was definitely glad I'd thrown my old life away.

(No matter how much I might sometimes worry that I'd made a giant bank-account-emptying mistake. What was money next to family and Fancy, right? Right…)

CHAPTER 13

Of course, me being me, that pleasant little interlude of contentment lasted about five minutes and then I was back to picking at everything in my life that wasn't perfect.

Like that dog I'd seen.

Clearly it hadn't been the dog that belonged to the Niels. But that meant it was someone else's dog. And that it was running around loose in Colorado in the winter. Although, maybe it had found its way home? It didn't look particularly neglected so it hadn't been lost for long, maybe it had wandered away for a few hours and then wandered back.

I wanted to pace the living room while I thought things through, but have you ever been pregnant? Have you ever had ankles so swollen they hurt? No socks are comfortable. None. But I couldn't go without something covering my feet either because it was Colorado in winter and I'm not a particular fan of chilblains.

So I lay down on the couch, tucked the big blanket around my feet, and stared at the floor while silently giving thanks that the cabin was new and I didn't have to stare at some gross stain that would make me worry about black mold or what the prior occupants had done while they were there.

I closed my eyes. The dog was probably fine. It had probably found its way home. (Or already been caught by whatever that big scary thing in the yard the night before was.)

I yawned.

I could let it go. I had babies to worry about. I needed to focus on resting up, staying calm, and letting my body do this crazy weird thing where it took a couple little bundles of cells and turned them into living, breathing people without any conscious effort on my part.

But…

You know me. I can't leave well enough alone. I needed to know about that dog.

Which meant I was going to have to brave the wilds of Nextdoor, that lovely neighborhood forum where people show their weirdness.

I'd once lived in a neighborhood where the posts alternated between "please stop setting off fireworks" and "please keep your stupid dog from barking". Hmm. Wonder what those two things had to do with one another.

But Nextdoor in the Baker Valley was something else. It was usually nature photos, like "see this beautiful deer in a meadow", followed by hunting posts, like "see the buck I got last weekend", with the occasional hot-headed debate over things like fence lines and private property thrown in for spice.

It was a place to start, though. I could check if anyone had posted about a missing dog. And then I could call animal control and the pound, see if they had any reports or had found the dog already.

First, though, lunch with my grandpa. He and Fancy returned about twenty minutes after they'd left looking all red-cheeked (him) and happy (her).

"Good walk?" I asked.

My grandpa grumbled but I could see he'd enjoyed himself. As we ate lunch we talked about Lesley's family and the upcoming t-ball season and everything normal. It actually felt like the world was returning to what it was before, but there was that lingering question of whether we'd really manage to turn the corner or not.

Rather than think about that, which would not be good for my stress levels, I turned my attention back to the missing dog.

"Hey, Grandpa?" I asked. "After lunch will you drive me around?"

"Where? The store? I can pick up whatever it is you need."

"No. Just around the resort. We didn't bring the van so I don't have a vehicle or else I'd do it myself."

My grandpa gave me one of *those* looks. "Maggie May…"

"It's winter, Grandpa. And somewhere out there is a cold, lost dog. I can't put food out for it because everyone tells me that might attract a bear. I can't walk around looking for it because…you know. I can call the pound and animal control and check Nextdoor, but if they don't have anything, I want to go look around. Please?"

He shook his head.

"Grandpa!"

I was not used to being told no. (Actually, people told me no all the time, it's more that I was used to being able to work around them and do it anyway. One more annoyance of pregnancy if there weren't enough already.)

He shook his head again. "Sorry, but Matt would never forgive me for that one. Sometimes you have to be protected from yourself."

"It's just driving around in a fricking car."

"On icy or snow-packed roads. And is that really restful? Would your doctor be happy to hear that you're driving around in the middle of winter looking for a dog?"

"The Mayo Clinic…"

"I don't care about the Mayo Clinic. I care about what your doctor told you. Now, if you want some company I will stick around and we can play a few games of Scrabble before I head back home. But I am not going to drive you around looking for a dog that may not even be lost. Your call."

I pressed my lips tight together. Being pregnant was so damned inconvenient. I was too frickin' selfish for this nonsense. I wanted control of my bladder and my ligaments and I wanted my time back already.

(I didn't want the babies to actually come out yet, of course. I wasn't a fool. I just wanted to somehow miraculously fast-forward to the end already.)

I took three deep, calming breaths. "Fine. Fine. Let's play Scrabble. Who cares about some poor, lonely lost dog out there on its own."

My grandpa didn't say anything, just shook his head and went to grab the Scrabble board.

CHAPTER 14

After my grandpa beat me at Scrabble twice and left, I made my calls. It felt weird, calling to ask about a dog that wasn't even mine, but I had to know.

Neither animal control nor the pound had received a missing dog report and they hadn't seen the dog either. Animal control promised to keep an eye out for it. So did the girl at the pound.

"If you find him, will you call me and let me know?" I asked her.

"Uh, yeah, sure, I guess. But it's not your dog, right? Why do you want to know?"

"So I can stop worrying about it."

"Oh. Guess that makes sense."

"Plus, if you do find it and no one else claims it, I…" I paused for a minute. Did I really want to say what I was about to say? I'd only seen the dog for half a minute and Fancy was probably not going to like it, let alone Matt.

But, yeah, I kind of did. "I'd be interested in adopting it. If you can't find someone else, of course, or the original owners, obviously."

She perked right up at that. "Right. Of course. We'll

absolutely let you know. In the meantime, if you're looking for a dog…"

"I'm not. I'm very pregnant with twins. The last thing I need is another dog."

"But you just said…"

"I know. And in this one particular case, if you find this particular dog, and if you can't find its owner, and if no one else wants it, well, then…I would probably adopt it." I winced, thinking how that conversation was going to go over with Matt.

"Ok-ay…" the girl said, clearly thinking bad things about my mental health.

"Look. Chalk it up to pregnancy hormones, alright. Just call me, please, if you find the dog? Even if you find the owners. Just let me know it's safe."

"Yeah. Sure. Will do. Buh-bye now." She hung up.

I hate being written off as some sort of crazy person. I was going to have to call daily if I ever wanted to find out about the dog.

Then again, to be fair, I kind of was crazy. What was I thinking saying I'd maybe adopt that dog? I had enough going on in my life, I did not need to add a rescue dog to the mix.

I mean, all dogs are great. All of them. But adding a new dog into the house. One with an already developed personality and training and everything else? That's… hard.

Fancy was so good with her sharing plate, but I'd once had a dog her size when I was growing up that would jump up on the counter and snatch a roasted chicken if you weren't careful. And some dogs chew things up. Or bark incessantly. Or have separation issues.

What was I thinking wanting to add a new unknown into the mix? Especially with babies on the way?

Ah well, it didn't matter. I was sure that dog had owners that it had already found its way back to or that would come and pick it up from the pound as soon as it was located. Which meant I was not going to be springing a new dog on Matt at the same time I sprang two babies on him.

It was just words. Meaningless words.

It was fine. Really.

But I did want to find that dog. And I was not going to rest until I did.

Or so I thought. I laid down for just a few minutes to take some of the pressure off my back, fell asleep, and didn't wake back up until Matt came in the door three hours later.

Too bad you can't bank sleep in one period of your life for when you need it in another period of your life, huh?

Alas. None of that sleep I managed pre-delivery was any help post-delivery.

When he came home Matt gave me a kiss on the forehead first thing and gave Fancy a good ear rub. He held up a snazzy plastic food container, the type that has a snap-on lid with an actual seal around the perimeter. "Lesley came into the station today and brought some leftover casserole for dinner."

"Bless that woman. I was not looking forward to a dinner of chips, chicken, cheese, and pickles, which is what we were going to have if she hadn't intervened."

Matt grimaced. "Neither was I. I would've run to pick something up if it came to it. Or we could've had leftover pizza."

"Pizza's gone. My grandpa was here for lunch and I was hungrier than I realized." I slowly levered myself to a sitting position. "I hope you still love me when I'm the size of a house."

"I'll always love you." He helped pull me to my feet.

"You say that now…"

He tilted my chin up and gave me a soft kiss on the lips. "I will say that always. Because what I love about you is that feisty spirit and sharp mind. I mean, don't get me wrong, I like some of the physical things to. Your smile. Your eyes. Your hair…[A few things I'm not going to repeat here for you, dear reader.] But I can't imagine a day will come when you lose every single thing I love about you."

"Well, I can. You need a better imagination."

He laughed. "Maybe, but you need to anchor yourself in the present. Tomorrow will bring what tomorrow brings and nothing that can be done about that."

I rubbed at my lower back. I was so tired of aching everywhere all the time.

Matt handed me the casserole container. "I could use a shower. Are you okay with getting dinner ready?"

I nodded. "Absolutely. But first…" I handed the container back.

"You need to pee."

I nodded. It was a miracle I had any moisture left in my body the number of times I had to pee with those babies those last few weeks.

As I made my way to the bathroom I grumbled to myself about how Matt got to take nice, long, luxurious hot showers anytime he wanted and I was stuck with tepid water until I gave birth. *Tepid*. Miserable. There's nothing soothing or comforting about *tepid* water. The word itself made me want to gag.

I patted my belly. "You two better be worth it, you hear? I want some Nobel Prize-winning efforts out of you." I winced and added, "But, honestly, you can be whoever you want and I will still love you. I promise. Find your bliss."

(Yes, I was a bit back and forth on my parental expectations. I wanted big things from my girls. But I also wanted them to be happy. So I wanted them to live up to their potential while also not pushing themselves so hard they were miserable, anxious, and unhappy all the time. Not too much to ask, was it? Ha.)

As I did my thing I resolved to throw another ten bucks into their therapy fund. They were going to need it with a mom like me.

CHAPTER 15

Dinner was delicious. Some mixture of sour cream and chicken and breading and vegetables. I know a lot of people like that fresh and healthy thing, but for me you just can't beat old-school recipes that involve things like condensed cream of chicken or cream of mushroom soup and a bag of frozen vegetables.

(Although, I am glad the days of my grandma making the frozen vegetables that included lima beans are gone. I have never been a lima bean fan. Ever. Not even when there are equal amounts bacon involved.)

But I digress. (Always.)

Matt and I had finished dinner and I was resting with my head on his lap as we watched some cooking show on the TV when I told him about my day.

He rubbed my shoulder and smiled. "That's my girl. Helping solve a disappearance. You think you'll still get involved in things like that after the babies arrive?"

I sighed. "I don't know. I mean, part of me hopes so because it means my life will not have become consumed by being a mom, worker bee, and wife. No offense. But at the same time, I never really wanted to get involved in half the cases I did, it's just that someone had to. So I kind of hope there aren't any more situations like that. I mean, someone involved in the search for that couple could've easily done what I did."

"Hm."

"What do you mean, hm?"

He thought about it for a minute and I could see he was trying to figure out the right way to frame what he wanted to say. "In my experience, people who are really good at things rarely realize that they're as good at them as they are. I played baseball with a guy in middle school—he moved away after that and made it to the minor leagues, actually—and he used to say things to me like, 'All you have to do is focus on the ball hitting the bat and it's easy to connect.' And for him it was that easy. But for me the ball came so fast I never saw it leave the pitcher's hand before it was in the catcher's glove."

I pressed my lips together. "I guess I get what you're saying."

He chuckled. "No you don't. You're just being polite. So what I will say is this. You have an ability to see what could be done that most people do not. You recognize patterns and put together information that's not even connected as far as the rest of us are concerned."

Before I could argue with that, he added, "To you it's all connected. Just not to the rest of us. I imagine that living in your head is like having one of those conspiracy theory boards with multi-colored lines connecting all the unrelated events to form some bigger picture that no one else believes in until they see what you've put together."

I shifted to make myself more comfortable. "It's not that crazy in here. Anyone can do it if they try. It's just patterns and connections. You hold two things up next to each other and see how they match."

He chuckled and shook his head. "Did you know that there are some people who when they aren't talking or interacting with others have completely blank minds?"

I stared at him. "What do you mean, completely blank minds?"

"I mean that there are some people who when they lie down to go to bed, have nothing in their minds."

"No music?"

He laughed. "No. No music. Which is probably most people, by the way. But also, no thoughts. No memories. No stories they spin to put themselves to sleep. Just…silence."

I sat up. "No! I don't believe it. I mean I met a girl once who said she wasn't thinking of anything at all when she was sitting there quiet, but there can't be more of her in this world than that. Can there?"

He raised his eyebrows and nodded.

"No. I have to look this up."

I tried to find it. I really did. But I couldn't.

"It exists. I promise. People's minds are always functioning because they keep breathing and circulating air and blood and all that, but some people's minds can be absolutely blank otherwise."

I refused to believe him. It just wasn't possible. And I hadn't found it on the internet, which, I mean, the internet has everything.

Then again, I'd once tried to confirm the definition of a heuristic online and had never been able to find a good source for it, but then a year or two later ran across a discussion of exactly what I remembered it to be in a book.

So the internet doesn't always yield its secrets.

Still. No thoughts? None? Just blankness.

I shuddered at the thought.

Matt kissed my forehead. "Regardless. My point is that what you think is easy for others to do maybe isn't. Which is why I suspect that even juggling me and babies and the resort and everything else you will still get drawn into the occasional investigation."

"Maybe. I won't have you as an inside source anymore, though, so chances are I won't even hear about cases except a little blip in the newspaper."

"No, but you'll have an entire pet resort full of interesting mysteries instead. The first dognapping we have, you will be all over it."

I opened my mouth to disagree, but stopped myself because he was right. "Fair enough. Speaking of…"

Matt raised one eyebrow.

"That dog I saw the other night is still missing. I called around to the pound and animal control but they haven't seen it and no one has filed a report."

"It probably found its way back home then."

"Maybe…But."

"You want to track it down."

I nodded. "Can we drive around tomorrow before you go into work? See if it's in a yard near here somewhere maybe? Ask around a bit? It'd really help with my stress levels to know it's safe."

I gave him my most sincere look but he just responded with a look my grandpa would've been proud of. "Maggie."

"Please. Indulge your pregnant wife."

"By risking her health and that of our babies?"

I frowned at him. I had spent over thirty-five years of my life with no one the least bit concerned about my health, but get pregnant and suddenly my health was everyone's business.

"Maggie. It's winter. You are very pregnant. I know you want to find this dog, but driving down a bunch of small mountain roads looking for it doesn't make a lot of sense."

"Fine." I grabbed my laptop and moved to the table. "Plan B. Or C. Or D. Whatever we're up to now."

"What're you gonna do?"

"A little social engineering, but for a good cause." I opened Nextdoor and typed up a post as Matt watched over my shoulder and read it out loud.

"Hey everyone. Please help me out. I am stuck at home on bed rest and feeling bummed. Will you please post pictures of your favorite furry friends to cheer me up? Let me know names, how you found them, and why they're the absolute best pet in the world. I'll start. This is my girl, Fancy, who has been with me through it all and is right here by my side through this, too. Thanks!"

He shook his head.

I shrugged. "You never know. That dog was adorable. I can't imagine its owner doesn't love it to pieces and wouldn't be proud to post a photo."

"Not everyone is online, you know. Or on Nextdoor."

"True. But what else can I do when my family won't let me leave the house."

He smiled and shook his head. "Do you want ice cream?"

"Does the sun shine?" I flashed him my best smile. "Yes, please. Have I told you you're the greatest husband in the world yet today?"

"No."

"Well, you are."

As Matt went to grab me ice cream (because he really is the best husband in the world), I watched the posts start to come in.

There were an inordinate number of cat photos shared. One lady had six of them and each had its own very unique story. And rabbits, too. Big ones.

Another person shared a photo of a lizard of some sort. Not sure how that qualified as furry, but hey, if it made them happy, which it clearly did, more power to them. Just, you know, read the room, buddy. Soft and fuzzy not scaled and cold, please.

Surprisingly, even though no one had posted about my particular dog by the end of the night, seeing all those cute, fluffy pets and their adoring owners really did cheer me up.

That's the thing with life. There's always going to be some challenge or other or something going wrong, but there's usually also a cute kitten or puppy or beautiful sunrise to balance it out if you look for it.

CHAPTER 16

I'd like to say I slept through the night, but who are we kidding. Between the three trips to the bathroom, the challenge of getting anywhere close to comfortable, and the fact that I was on a hair trigger waiting for that dog (or something else) to come through the doggie door, I did not sleep well at all.

Fancy ran outside barking her head off sometime around two, but when I finally managed to join her outside I couldn't see anything. I knew I should look for the missing dog but I was honestly more worried about the silent predator that had stared me down the other night, so I immediately brought her in, blocked the doggie door, and went back to sleep.

(Yes, it does sometimes take me more than once to learn caution.)

The next morning, after another yummy breakfast courtesy of my yummy husband, I decided to check my Nextdoor post.

And…It was the dog!

Someone had posted a picture of that little fluffy mutt I'd seen that night. His name was actually Spots. He was even more adorable than I remembered. And he had someone who loved him enough to tell strangers about it!

I was all ready for it to be done and over, but then I read what the person had written.

"This is my grandma's dog, Spots. He was there by her side every day for three years and was the best dog in the world. But she lost him on a trip to Denver two years ago. We found him, but that's when we realized she had memory issues. A year ago she needed to go into a care facility and none of us could take Spots, so we gave him to a rescue in Denver who found him a new home. I hope he's out there living his best life. Love you buddy."

I teared up. I really did.

One of my greatest fears is not being able to take care of Fancy for her whole life. No one will love her and care for her the way I do. And think how confused she'd be to suddenly lose her person.

And then to be surrendered to some strange dog rescue. I mean, I know they do amazing work and they mean so well and they really do help dogs, but have you ever been to one of those places? All the cages and concrete and noise?

Fancy would be so miserable.

And she's big, you know? Not everyone wants a big dog. The thought of her just sitting there day after day surrounded by barking, crying dogs wondering what happened that she ended up there…

That's when the waterworks really started.

I was sitting there on the couch, sobbing, Fancy sniffing at my face trying to make it better when Jamie knocked on the door and came in.

(I'm not normally one to just let people walk into my

house, but with the bed rest and all I'd given my grandpa and Jamie permission to come in without knocking. Plus, I was expecting her for a meeting.)

"What's wrong? What happened? Did somebody die?" Jamie rushed to my side.

"No. No one died, at least, I hope they didn't."

Between choked sobs I told her about the post I'd made and the responses and showed her the one about the dog and the grandma. "Isn't that just the saddest? I mean, losing your dog like that. And the poor dog."

"Well, if she couldn't take care of it anymore, it probably was the best thing."

"But to lose everyone you know. How could her family not take him in? And then bring him by for visits?"

"Maybe they had other dogs. Or traveled too much."

I stared at her. I love Jamie. She is my best friend. But we are not identical and our views towards our dogs is one example of that.

Jamie is good to Lulu, don't get me wrong. She pets her and feeds her and gives her treats and takes her places. But at the end of the day Lulu is just a dog to Jamie. Which, fair enough, that's probably the more rational approach to having a dog.

For me Fancy is my partner in crime. She's a living, breathing creature with her own thoughts and feelings that I try to take into account.

I once had her work with a dog trainer after she got scared of going to the groomers, and that guy wanted me to teach her to stare at me our entire walk.

Don't sniff the grass, don't look at other dogs, just watch me for any command I might give.

He wanted to make paying attention to me her entire

world. Which, if you're training a police dog probably makes sense, but I wasn't training a police dog. I was just trying to help my poor dog get over what turned out to be a justified fear.

I handed the guy a check for that session and told him to go away and never come back. For me taking Fancy for a walk is as much about her personal enjoyment and development as it is about mine.

Granted, ultimately my choices are what win out. She didn't have any say in Matt or where we live or the babies. At the end of the day I make the decisions that work for me first and foremost.

But if she'd met Matt and hadn't liked him? No way I would've forced her to share a home with him. And no way I would've given her up for him either, because I took responsibility for her and it is on me to give her a good life.

Not just a "you're a dog so I'll feed you and house you" life, but a *good* life that honors the fact that she deserves comfort, companionship, and enjoyment aside from any pleasure I get from her presence.

So Jamie was absolutely right in what she said about that dog from a practical, reasonable, logical standpoint. But I gave her a death stare anyway.

Because if someone did something like that with Fancy I would've been livid. Or broken-hearted.

But there was no point having that argument. She'd be calm and reasonable and I'd be emotional and hysterical and neither one of us would change our opinion.

Instead, I said, "I bet that dog came back here looking for its owner. She's in a home of some sort now, so he wouldn't find her, but I bet that's what happened."

"From Denver? You said he didn't look that bad."

"Well, I only saw him for a minute or so in the middle of the night."

"Maybe his owners brought him up here and he got away from them."

I nodded. That made sense. "Maybe. Which means they should be looking for him. I wonder…If they brought him up to the mountains, but not the Baker Valley, then they might've called a different pound or animal control looking for him, which is why I didn't find anything when I called the local ones…"

"Easy enough to check, right?" Jamie smiled at me. "This is great news. Now we know he has owners and we can let them know where we spotted him and he'll be reunited with them in no time."

I felt a little sad thinking about that. I mean, I'd literally only seen the dog for a minute at most, but some weird part of my brain had already spun out a tale of us finding him again and adopting him and Fancy getting a friend to keep her company during the upcoming chaos.

Sigh.

At least now the dog had a name. And owners that were probably missing him.

"I need to call around and find out where he was lost. Maybe I can reach out to this person on Nextdoor to find out where they surrendered him. Or call animal control in nearby counties to find out if they've had a report."

Jamie nodded. "Good idea. But first, we have our business meeting."

"Ugh. Right. Business meetings are so much fun. I can't wait."

She laughed and headed to the kitchen to grab some

drinks while we waited for Greta and Mason to arrive. I couldn't believe after all this time that we were mere weeks from opening weekend. There was so much still left to do…

CHAPTER 17

Greta was the next one to arrive, looking as classic and put together as ever. Jamie is always fresh-faced and full of energy so you think she's ten years younger than she is whereas Greta is always so contained and polished you assume she must be ten years older than she is.

I think it's mostly just being a certain type of European. And having a good, classic sense of style. She was wearing an emerald green silk top and black slacks. It worked well with her pale blonde hair and tasteful yet expensive jewelry. I didn't even want to know what the small emerald and diamond earrings she was wearing probably cost.

She kissed me on the cheek. "You are coming along nicely."

"That's one way to describe it."

She patted my hand. "It will be over soon. And then you will wish you were still pregnant."

"Greta, I know it's rude to ask, but with all of your marriages, you never wanted to have kids?"

(Greta had been married something like ten times. Mostly to very wealthy men which had made her very wealthy in her own right.)

She tilted her head to the side. "I have a son. He is twenty. At university in Dusseldorf."

"You have a son?" I looked at Jamie. "Did you know she had a son?"

She shook her head. "Never thought to ask."

"Oh yes. Here. Here is his picture." She showed us a picture of a very handsome young man with a ski slope behind him. "This was taken in Austria on a ski holiday last year."

"He's never been here to visit has he?" I thought we were friends, but maybe I'd been wrong and she'd snuck in a visit with her son without ever mentioning it.

"No. It is…a complicated situation. My seventh husband? He was Spanish. Aristocracy. He wanted my son to go to boarding school. My son was ten at the time?" She huffed. "He was unhappy. He did not like Spain. He did not want to learn Spanish. He missed his friends. So I agreed."

I stared at her. She'd sent her son away to school when he was ten? Rich people are weird sometimes.

"Was that, the last of it? He never came home for the holidays or anything?"

"He would come home in the summer. But when that marriage ended, things were unsettled. My son stayed with a school friend." She shrugged her delicate shoulders. "By the time things were settled and I wanted him to come home, he was thirteen and he did not want to come."

"So you're estranged?"

"No. We talk once a week. And before, I would visit him when I was in Europe, which was often. Or he would visit me." She shrugged again. "We are cordial, but he does not need a mother so much."

I couldn't imagine. If my parents were still alive I'd like to think I'd speak to them more than once a week.

Then again, at twenty maybe I wouldn't have. At that age I had been pretty caught up in my own little world. Still. I hoped my girls were more attached to me at twenty than Greta's son seemed to be to her.

Mason arrived then carrying three large bags of food. He was a good-looking man. Reminiscent of an older but not old Sean Connery. And I'd come around on liking him for the most part. He was a great dad to Max and good husband to Jamie.

Of course, he still sometimes had a stick up his you-know-what. He hadn't changed, I just liked him more than I had initially.

I flashed him a smile. "Mason. I hear you've been hiring all of my family to work for the resort."

"Have I?"

I ticked them off on my fingers. "My grandpa. Jack. My husband."

"Oh. Yes. I have hired all of them." He set the bags of food down on the table and gave Jamie a kiss on the cheek.

"It'd be nice to know you were going to do that before you did it, you know."

He frowned at me. "Why?"

"Because…I don't know. They're my family. Maybe I didn't want that."

He gave me a weird look but didn't answer as he started removing takeout containers from the bags and placing them on the table. "I figured we could sample the food from the on-site restaurants during the meeting."

He glanced at me. "Of course, if I am also not allowed to hire your friends to work for the resort, then I guess we will be starting over and no point tasting the food."

I glanced at the others. "What do you mean by that?"

Jamie patted my hand as she sat down next to me. "Well…You know that Mason and Greta took point on staffing the on-site restaurant."

"Yes."

"As it turns out…"

I glared at everyone. "What?"

"Abe and Evan decided they would like more regular income now that they have a baby on the way, so they're going to be running the casual dining restaurant for us."

"What about the Creek Inn?"

Abe and Evan had been running the Creek Inn just outside the valley from Creek until we shut down the valley by bringing some boulders down across the road just this side of the inn. They'd chosen to close down the inn and move into the valley where there was a better chance of being safe. No point in running an inn at the end of a dead-end road. But I'd always assumed they were going to go back when the valley reopened.

"They sold it. To Sally Broykes."

I looked around the table. This was clearly only news to me. "Why didn't they tell me?"

"When's the last time you saw them?" Jamie asked.

"At the doctor's office when they were there with their surrogate."

"And do you chat with them on the phone? Or otherwise keep in touch?"

I frowned at Jamie. "No. But…"

"Well, then. I'm sure they would've mentioned it next

time they did see you. So that's what these are." She set aside six takeout containers that looked like they had sandwiches or burgers in them. "And these," she pushed three more containers to the other side of the table, "are from the new high-end restaurant that's going to be located up the side of the mountain behind the resort."

"When did we add that?"

She smiled. "When a certain Michelin-starred chef decided to move here."

I threw my hands up in the air. Did I know nothing anymore? "Are you talking about Jean-Philippe? He's moving here permanently? Since when."

Greta smiled serenely. "Since I asked him to. This will be good for the resort, no? Attract a higher-end clientele."

"And you guys? Are you still together?"

She shrugged one shoulder. "We are what we are."

Jean-Philippe had been my freshman-year mistake and Jamie's freshman-year amusement. When he came to rescue Jamie's wedding he and Greta had formed an unlikely connection. As far as I knew his situation with Greta was the longest he'd ever stayed interested in one woman.

"Okay. Wow." I turned to Mason and asked sarcastically, "Is Elaine going to be our accountant?"

"As a matter of fact."

"And Lesley? Did you find a way to rope her in, too?"

"She might be making some pies for us."

I glared at him. "I was joking."

"I know. But I was not. Just so you know, Trish is going to be heading up our housekeeping and Jack is staying on to do general maintenance."

"And Sam?" (He was only nine-years-old, I couldn't imagine they'd found a use for him.)

"Will be around and I am sure will help out from time to time. His parents have permission to bring him to work if needed."

I shook my head. "Good thing Lucas Dean is dead or you would've had him here, too."

"True. The man was a cad, but he was also a very good general contractor."

Without even realizing I was doing so, I'd started snacking on the various containers of food while I glared everyone down. It was good. Really good. Homemade potato chips. Fresh guacamole. Corn salsa. Thick-cut fries with the skin still on.

I shook my head. "I don't like it. Aren't there any other people you could hire?"

Jamie frowned at me. "I don't understand why you're so upset about this."

I tried to think of a way to explain it that didn't sound horrible.

"Look, I love the fact that I'll have everyone I know and like around and that we'll all benefit together if the resort does well. But…I…have been disappointed in the past when I tried to rely on others to do things for me. And I worry that because these people are my friends and family that I won't be able to say anything when they fail at their part of things. I realize that sounds ridiculous, but it scares me to rely on people I like because if they don't come through then I'm not allowed to be angry at them. Or fire them."

Mason popped a fry in his mouth. "I have no problem telling people when they have failed me. Even people I like. Rest assured, I will handle any performance issues just fine." He glanced at Greta as he put some steamed mussels and skinny fries on his plate. "Even my co-investor's lover, if needed." He winked.

Greta raised her chin. "No. *I* will handle any performance issues Jean-Philippe may have myself. I too have no problem telling someone when they have failed me, even someone I like quite a bit. And with Jean-Philippe he is quite used to my corrections."

Jamie laughed. "Well then. If that's settled. Let's talk about the daycare."

"The daycare?" I asked. "I thought we'd already settled that."

"We had. For the pets. But I want to talk about adding a daycare for children. You will have the twins, I will have Max, and Evan and Abe will have their baby soon. Not to mention anyone else who works for us and has a kid too young for school. That's at least five years of having kids to worry about."

She cut a juicy cheeseburger topped with barbecue sauce and onion rings into fourths and took a piece before offering it to me. "As much as I'm okay right now with keeping Max in the back room while I work, I expect he'll outgrow that box of printer paper at some point and also need a little more hands-on management."

"You put Max in a box of printer paper?" That sounded like something I'd do, not Jamie.

She shrugged. "He needed a nap and a box was a better choice than his carrier. So. Daycare? Yes. Where should we put it?"

As they debated the best location for the daycare and whether it should just be for employees' kids or whether it should be large enough to accommodate guests' kids as well, I sat back and enjoyed the food and contemplated where my life had led me.

I couldn't believe my little dreams of what my life would be like living in Creek with my lonely, widowed grandpa and running a small little café and barkery with my best friend had morphed into this. I would've never imagined it the first day I moved to Creek.

My grandpa remarried. Jamie married. *Me* married. Both of us having kids. The resort. Never in a million years.

But there we were. And it excited and scared me in equal measure. It was everything I never knew I wanted, which is why I was so worried that it would be taken away somehow.

Once more I took three deep, calming breaths. (Yes, I was doing that a lot. Because, really, on a daily basis I was about two steps away from needing to breathe into a paper bag.)

Everything would be fine.

Time to take Matt's advice and live in the moment. Life was good *now* and that's all that mattered. No point borrowing trouble from the future. Or so I told myself, but you know me, it didn't work.

CHAPTER 18

After the meeting I took a nap. It's hard creating life. Kudos to every woman who keeps on going like it's nothing until the day they go into labor. I do not know how they do it. I stand in awe.

I have had friends like Jamie for whom pregnancy seemed like this glowy miracle of happiness the whole time, so maybe that's how. But whatever good hormones those women's bodies produced to let them feel that way, mine did not.

So I took a nap with Fancy snoring away at the side of the bed thinking how lucky I was that I had a dog that slept most of the day.

I was sort of drifting in and out of sleep when I heard the doggie door flap and figured Fancy had gone outside. But then I heard her move. Which meant Spots was back!

Or so I hoped.

I dragged myself out of sleep. You know how sometimes if you awake when you're not ready to it's like wading through sludge? It was like that. I sleep best in either three and a half or four hour segments, but this had been something like two hours and I'd been deep in REM sleep and my mind did not want to snap into focus.

When I finally managed to open my eyes Spots was standing in the doorway. Now that I had a better look, he was in pretty rough shape. Pine needles caught in his coat. A bit of a gash on his nose. Mud on his paws.

"Hey there, buddy," I called softly as I tried to sit up.

Unfortunately, my voice woke Fancy and she jumped to her feet as soon as she saw him and he bolted. They both went racing outside as I "scrambled" to follow. I say scrambled because I wanted to hurry after them—the intent was there—but my actual movements were more of an awkward sort of thing where I slowly lurched after them.

By the time I joined Fancy outside, Spots was gone again.

"Spots. Come here, Spots. Come on. Good boy. Come on," I called.

He appeared in the trees a few feet from the fence and Fancy ran over there to bark at him. I swear the only time she has real energy is when she's barking at someone or something through the fence. Even non-pregnant I can't get ahold of her while she's like that. So I ignored her because there was absolutely no chance I was going to corral her as I was.

"Do you want a treat? Let me get you a treat." I went back inside for some Pumpkin Puffs as Fancy continued to run and bark along the fence.

When I came back out she was still barking and he was still lingering there in the woods. As soon as Fancy saw that I had treats, she stopped and turned her attention on me.

"Hey buddy," I said as I approached the fence, holding out one treat for Spots and one for Fancy.

He wouldn't move from his shelter in the trees, so I tossed the treat at his feet. He cautiously sniffed at it and then gobbled it up. Meanwhile Fancy was circling around me trying to get another treat.

"Fancy, stop."

She didn't. Treats are a great way to get her to do pretty much anything but unfortunately that means that she becomes relentlessly focused when she sees them.

I threw all but one of the remaining treats out into the yard for her to find, which bought me about a minute to try to lure Spots closer. He almost came to the fence, but she's fast when she wants to be and was back before I could get him to trust me.

"You stay there, okay? I'll be right back," I told him.

I led Fancy inside with my one remaining treat and blocked the doggie door behind her. She immediately started crying so loud I could hear her outside—she is not used to being blocked away from me—but it was the only chance I had of luring Spots closer.

Unfortunately, he was gone when I turned back around.

"Spots. Come here boy," I called over and over again, but he didn't come back.

I debated following him into the woods, but the pain shooting across my belly warned me that maybe it was time to take it easy.

Sighing, I reluctantly went back inside. At least I knew he was still around. And safe. But I was more determined than ever to find him and reunite him with his owners.

Of course, that meant I needed to know who his current owners actually were.

I stepped back inside, ignoring Fancy's pouting look

of absolute betrayal. She'd laid down two feet from the door in her platypus position (hands sprawled to the sides, chin flat on the ground) and wouldn't take her eyes off me.

"Sorry. But you know I had to do it."

I grabbed my laptop and sat down at the table.

First step was to message the person on Nextdoor who had posted Spots' picture and ask if they'd call me. (Ironically, *I* would not have called some rando who messaged me from Nextdoor, but I was hoping the person was more trusting than I am.)

My phone rang only a few minutes later, showing a call from an unknown number. Which was a bit surprising. I mean, who hangs out on Nextdoor?

"Hello?" I said, waiting to hear about how my car warranty was expired and it was time to renew it.

"Hi. Is this Maggie? From Nextdoor?"

I smiled. "Yeah. Is this Alex?"

I couldn't tell if the person on the other end of the line was a young woman or a man with a high-pitched voice. Didn't really matter I guess, but it's something I think we all try to do subconsciously. Put people into known buckets as soon as possible.

"Yep. You wanted to talk to me about my grandma's dog?"

"I did. I think he's running loose in the Baker Valley. I've seen a dog twice now that looks just like him. We're staying in a cabin on the new Baker Valley Pet Resort property. Is that by any chance near where your grandma used to live?"

"Yes." They suddenly sounded very cold and I wondered what I'd done wrong to upset them.

"Whereabouts?" I asked

"Probably right about where you are now. My parents sold my grandma's place off when we moved her into the care home and those [redacted] developers were going to level it for their [redacted] pet resort."

"Oh. I'm sorry."

I hadn't realized that Mason or Greta had purchased private homes as part of the pet resort development. I obviously knew they'd purchased retail space since the original site of the Baker Valley Barkery & Café had been leveled as part of the work.

That had hurt enough. I couldn't imagine what it would feel like to lose a family home.

Alex answered with a verbal shrug. "Yeah. Well. Nothing to be done about it now is there?"

True enough. And I needed to find that dog, so no point dwelling on it or telling them exactly who I was in relation to the resort.

"So that means Spots came back here but had nowhere to go back to."

"Sounds like it."

They were not warming back up to me, but nothing to be done about it so I just plowed on. "Okay. So if I can find him, I need to reunite him with his owners. What shelter did you leave him at?"

Alex rattled off the information. "That all you need?"

"Actually…While I have you on the phone. If I can't locate the new owners for some reason, would you want him back? In your post you seemed to really love him."

"Can't. I'm at school. No room for a dog. I'm never home. I work two jobs on top of class. And my parents are not dog people. Don't like the mess."

"Okay. Fair enough. Thanks for the information."

"Sure." They hung up.

Not the most pleasant call ever, but at least I was one step closer to locating Spots' new owners. That was a positive. I just hoped they wanted him back.

CHAPTER 19

Before I could make my next call, Elaine stopped by. She'd changed a lot since I first met her that day at the YMCA when I was scoping her out as a potential wedding saboteur. Then, she'd been very plain and mousy and mostly forgettable.

But Jamie had taken her under her wing and taught her a few things about hair and makeup and fashion. She hadn't transformed into some tarted up mess, but thanks to Jamie's guidance Elaine had started using a bit of mascara and some lip gloss and making better fashion choices.

(Me, personally, I am all for the no makeup, sweats for life club, but if you actually have to interact with the rest of the world it is good to know how to present well to others.)

"Hey, Maggie. I hope it's okay that I came by. I was bringing some masks for the resort and Jamie mentioned you were staying here until the delivery."

"Absolutely. Come in."

She stepped into the living room area and glanced around awkwardly, but then Fancy made herself known and Elaine immediately relaxed as she said her hellos to Fancy and gave her a few good chest and chin scratches.

"So you're still doing the accounting?" I said. "I figured after news broke of how talented you were as a dress designer that you'd be quitting your job and taking on a bunch of fancy, high-end wedding projects."

She ducked her head and blushed. "I have had a commission or two, but sewing is what I love. I didn't want to turn it into a business venture. Especially since the Mason Foundation provides very good benefits. Better to be able to pick and choose what I work on."

"Oh, that makes sense. Everyone's so ready to rush to turn their passion into a business it never occurs to me that some people might want to just keep their hobbies as hobbies and enjoy a nice steady income. So how've you been otherwise?"

"Good. I'm dating Dennis Clay. I don't know if you knew that?" She sort of winced as she glanced at me.

"Dennis, huh?" I'd interviewed him during Julie Lewis's murder investigation. He was an attractive guy, seemed nice enough. But…

"I know about what happened in college. He explained it to me. And, I actually called the woman up who'd filed the restraining order. Talked to her about it for a long while. I can see why what he did scared her, but even she agreed now looking back on it that it was probably mostly just different interpretations."

"Hm."

I do believe in listening to women when they come forward with their stories. And filing a restraining order is some serious business. It's more than "Hey, there was a rumor about this guy."

But I had also had a situation at my job in college where I would've sworn that some dude I worked with was stalking me because he followed me everywhere. I found out years later that yes, he had been following me around the store, I was not wrong about that, but it wasn't because he was interested in me. It was because his sister the manager thought I was stealing. (I wasn't, obviously.)

Regardless of why he was doing it, it made me ill to go into work with him and deal with that for eight hours a day. Eventually I said something not so nice about him in a very public way and got fired.

The feelings I had about that situation definitely existed and were real. But at the same time I was wrong about what had happened.

So…

If that woman had talked to Elaine and had a similar epiphany, I guess I was willing to give Dennis the benefit of the doubt. I guess. But.

I held Elaine's gaze. "Okay. I will trust that you know what you're doing on this. But if he gives you any trouble, any trouble at all, call me and I'll put Matt or my grandpa on it. I don't need to tell you that a man should never hit you or call you nasty names? Ever. Walk if that happens. Okay?"

"Okay. He doesn't though, I promise."

"He also shouldn't follow you around or check up on your movements."

"And he doesn't. It's fine, Maggie. It is."

"If you say so." I gave her one more long look. She seemed fine. So. "I'm glad you're happy and doing well. I'd offer you food or drink or something, but…" I gestured towards our masks. "I'm trying to keep it safe here."

"Understood. And, just so you know, I didn't randomly drop by to chat, I actually had a reason to come by. First, here are some new masks for you guys to wear. Jamie wanted me to bring them by."

(This was back when cloth masks were still the accepted thing. Ah, the good old days…)

I spread out the masks. They were great.

"Look at this one. It has little dancing Newfies on it!"

"I thought you'd like that one. I did a whole bunch with different dog and cat breeds on them for the resort to sell."

"Do you think we'll still need them this summer when we open? I thought things were turning the corner."

Elaine shrugged. "Mason's hedging his bets. All I care about is they're bought and paid for."

"Fair enough. If you're getting paid for them, that's what matters. These are great, Elaine. Thank you so much."

"You're welcome. But that's not actually all of it. I'll be right back." She ran out to her car and came back with a beautiful quilt with turquoise and white panels. When she unfolded it, there were actually two smaller matching quilts. "Jamie said you like blues and turquoises?"

"I do. Oh my gosh. Are these for me? Elaine, they're stunning. These are heirloom pieces."

She beamed at me. "I'm glad you like them. See, by keeping my sewing a hobby I had the time to make them for your girls."

I ran my hand over the panels. They were exquisite. The level of detail work was amazing.

"Elaine…"

She held up a hand. "You saved my life. And more than that, you're a friend. I wanted to do this for you. The quilts are for when the girls are a little bigger, after they're past the sleeping with no covers to avoid SIDS stage. Once they have their first real beds."

I nodded. "I…I don't know what to say. Thank you. We will treasure these forever."

She smiled. "You're welcome. I'm glad you like them. I better get going. We've got some month-end entries that aren't going to do themselves. But I hope to see you again after the babies are born?"

"Absolutely. We'll figure something out. Thank you again."

I walked her to the door and then went back to stare at the quilts. I was so lucky to have found all these people who made my life that little bit better.

I of course then needed to have a bit of a cry, because pregnancy, hormones, and all that jazz. But once I sniffled my way back into shape it was time to turn my attention to finding Spots' owners once more.

CHAPTER 20

My next call was to the dog shelter down in Denver. The lady on the other end of the line was incredibly nice but absolutely refused to give me the contact information for whoever had adopted Spots.

"But I've seen their dog now. Twice. Don't you think they want him back?" I said.

"Ma'am, I don't know you from Jesus. You could be lying to me right now. You could be telling me you've seen this poor lost dog up in the mountains when what you really are is a stalker trying to get the contact information of some pretty young lady you saw in the park."

"I'm a married woman who's about to give birth to twins. I assure you I have no time for stalking anyone. I just want to return this dog to whoever adopted it from your shelter."

"So you say. Maybe some strange man hired you to call on his behalf to lower my suspicions. I don't know."

I counted to five, slowly. "Look. I am as suspicious as the next girl, so I appreciate your fervent protection of the owner's information. Any woman who has been harassed by some overly-involved weirdo would appreciate what you're doing here. But I would also like to reunite this dog with its owner. So can I maybe instead leave my contact information and ask that you pass it along to whoever adopted the dog?"

"I'm sorry ma'am, but no. For all I know you kidnapped the dog in the first place and this is an elaborate ruse to lure the individual who adopted this dog into meeting you in a remote, lonely location."

"Lady. Either you watch too many true crime shows, read too many crime books, or need some better medication to control the voices. I don't know which it is, but this is absurd. You really won't have them contact me?"

"No. I won't. And if you'll excuse me I have things to do." She hung up.

(Yes, I know the dig about her medication was not nice. I am a work in progress and I was pregnant, tired, and worried about that poor dog, so I was not at my best. People are human, you know, which means not perfect.)

That woman, though, I mean, come on. She was a bit much.

I shook my head. I spent most of my adult life living alone as a single woman. I get it that there are weird men out there.

(My least favorite being the guy who sits close to you on public transport and then proceeds to make a lot of loud noises and move around in a ploy to get you to look at him, so he can then start talking to you because you guys made casual eye contact. See also, the reason someone could literally be choking to death next to me and I'd never once look at them.)

So I get it. But that woman…She took it to a whole new level. She needed to be a writer with an imagination like that.

It left me with a dilemma, though. If I did manage to find the dog, how was I going to get it back to its original owners? Maybe it was microchipped. That would help. Or maybe I could just drop it off at the shelter. Would she find that suspicious?

Since I still didn't know where the dog had been lost or where the owner lived I decided to call all of the animal control offices within a hundred miles of the Baker Valley and of Denver.

Nothing. None had received a report of a missing dog named Spots or one that fit the description I gave.

At that point I was so tired I laid down for another nap.

What? I was pregnant with twins. Give me a break.

CHAPTER 21

I woke up to find a note from my grandpa on the kitchen table. It said he'd dropped by but I'd been sleeping so sound he didn't try to wake me. Instead he'd taken Fancy for a walk (bless the man) and also left a few more containers of food to try from the resort restaurants courtesy of Jamie.

The food looked delicious but I had heartburn that felt like it was going to turn my esophagus into ash, so I settled for much more boring food for my afternoon snack.

The day was warm enough I took Fancy outside and sat on the back porch with her. I only needed a scarf and coat, not the big blanket from the couch. But after twenty minutes I started to shiver a bit and went back in. Fancy stayed out.

I wondered what else there was to do to find Spots. I really couldn't do much until he came back around. I was at a dead-end with the animal control and shelter.

I called Mason and asked him about the house they'd bought as part of the resort development. He was able to point me to his contracts guy who looked the information up for me and confirm that the house Spots had lived at before all of this was only about a quarter mile from where the cabin was located.

"It's still standing if you want to see it," he said. "That section is part of Phase II development. I think they're going to put some horse stables out there."

"We're going to let people bring their horses on vacation?" I asked, mildly appalled.

"I don't know. That's above my pay grade. Might just have horseback riding. But that's not going to happen until next summer according to the development plans."

"Can you tell me exactly where the house is located?"

He rattled off an address and how I could walk there as well as the roads that would get me there. According to his guesstimate, the house was probably only about two-tenths of a mile from where we were if you walked.

"Thank you," I told him and hung up.

Now, knowing me, you are probably thinking to yourself, *"Please tell me she did not try to walk there, end up in labor, and give birth to twins in an abandoned house where she didn't have cellphone service."*

And, granted, that is a valid concern to have, given certain of my past decisions. But I am happy to say that I was a mature, married, mother-to-be who actually took into account the fact that it was not just my personal safety on the line, but the lives of my two little girls as well.

I won't tell you I didn't think about it. Because that would be a lie. But in my defense I did not think about it for long.

Mostly because Matt came home.

And also, my feet were killing me and walking even two-tenths of a mile with ankles as swollen as mine seemed some fresh hell I just could not imagine inflicting upon myself.

So as I lay on the couch with my feet propped up as best I could while dealing with my very large, awkward, uncomfortable belly I instead filled Matt in on everything I'd found out and suggested that maybe we could take a little bit of a drive later?

"It's going to be dark soon, Maggie."

"I know. But…Spots. Another night out there alone without his owner. Struggling to survive in the snow and the cold. Not understanding why he's been abandoned…" I gave him my best hopeful look, but he shook his head.

"Tell ya what. We'll go in the morning. I don't have to be to work until ten and you are always up by six. That should give us plenty of time to drive over there, see if the dog is there, and drive back before I have to leave."

"Thank you. I'd kiss you if I wasn't actually too comfortable to move right this minute."

Of course, the babies being the babies, one of them chose that moment to make me decidedly uncomfortable. I still didn't kiss Matt, though. I was too busy trying to get to the bathroom in time.

Ah, the joys of pregnancy.

CHAPTER 22

Matt and I drove over to the address I'd been given the next morning. It was weird having to put on real clothes. I'd gotten away with hanging out in really soft baggy pajamas since we'd moved to the cabin because the only people who were going to see me were basically family.

Well, and Mason, but who cares about impressing Mason? I was pretty sure he already had his opinions of me and my wearing comfortable pajamas for a lunchtime meeting weren't going to change them.

Greta, too, I guess, but she has a way of not seeing what she doesn't want to see, so if she was offended I never noticed.

The house was down a dirt road that had clearly not been plowed or leveled recently. We were fortunate that Matt's police vehicle was built for pretty much any terrain.

And that it had good shocks. Even with good shocks it was a bumpy drive. After the third time I put my hand against my belly and said, "Oof", Matt suggested that maybe we should turn back.

But no way no how was I giving up on my one chance

to check out the house and find Spots.

We'd had a decent run of good weather for Colorado in winter, but we were due for snow that night and I did not want him out in it. (Sometimes in Colorado the forecast and the actual timing of the snow don't exactly match, but they're usually within a day or two and a foot or two of one another.)

Finally, when I was really starting to question the woman who'd lived there's sanity for living in the absolute Boondocks, we turned a corner and saw the place.

I understood in that moment why she'd lived there. It was so peaceful. And the house was so cute. It was one story with a fenced-in yard and trees all around. Not too close—fire danger and all—but close enough to make it feel cozy.

I loved it. I could see why Spots had come back to it, too. It was perfect.

(Okay, so maybe I was anthropomorphizing the dog a bit, his feelings were probably not complex human emotions, he just wanted to get back to his person and his home. But I did really love the place and could see why someone would want to live there even if it was in the butt end of nowhere.)

You know, I think it's a travesty for people who've grown up somewhere like New York City or downtown DC to not at least be given a chance to experience nature like that.

Get them away from the concrete and tall buildings, and the people everywhere and the non-stop noise, and the lights and stress, and let them see what else the world can be. Take them somewhere where they can only hear birds chirping in the distance or wind blowing through the trees.

Yes, I know, some people would shudder at the thought of so much loneliness and silence. But in my opinion there is almost no manmade beauty that can trump nature.

Although mankind does come close sometimes. I'm not particularly religious but I still think of a stone carving I saw of Jesus once in an old church in Avila, Spain. Took my breath away.

And if you've ever watched the Keira Knightley version of *Pride and Prejudice* there's a carving in there when she's walking through Darcy's house that gets me every time. Like how did they do that? That stone carving of a woman with a veil? Remarkable.

But nature. Nature is epic on a scale that a tall building can never touch. At least for me.

We pulled up in front of the house and I glanced at Matt. "What do you think of the house?"

We'd tried looking for homes in the valley, but there were barely any listings. And almost all of them had multiple stories which I was not going to do unless it was the house I already hated that was next door to my grandpa and was at least saved by virtue of its location. The other houses in our price range—which was not a high-priced range—were rundown sorts of places missing key features like running water and electricity.

So that house…Even with its dirt road…Looked like perfection.

"What do you mean?" Matt asked. "What about it?"

"Well, we haven't found a place to live yet. I mean, we can stay next to Grandpa, but that place has stairs and with two small kids and two dogs…"

"*Two* dogs?"

"Uh, sorry. One dog."

He narrowed his eyes at me. "You don't make that kind of mistake, Maggie."

I held up a hand. "Look, I don't know what'll happen here. But if we find the dog and we can't find the owners, maybe instead of sending it back to the pound…"

"Right." He gave me a look.

"Just think about it. And I'll see what the situation with this house is. If it's available, would you want to live here?"

"Just like that? You haven't even been inside. It could be falling down, rat-infested, stink like cat urine…"

"But it's perfect. Especially if we're both going to be working for the resort. It's close enough to be on call, but far enough to be private. And one story. You know how much I hate stairs. I mean, I assume it's one story. It could have a basement I guess. In which case, that's yours. Do you like doing laundry?"

He didn't dignify my question with an answer, but instead studied the house and the area around us. "I do like it. If the inside matches the outside, it has some potential. We'd need to get that road paved, though. Or at least planed and some potholes filled in."

"Ha. Yes! I knew it."

"But only if the inside looks doable. We're too close to your due date for massive renovations. Whatever it looks like inside, we're going to have to go with."

"But otherwise?" I stared at him hopefully. "Let me remind you how much I love you."

"Because I go along with everything you want?"

"Because you go along with *almost* everything I want but push back when I take it too far. So?"

"Let's find out more and then we can decide. But for now…A tentative yes."

I bounced in my seat. Which really made me want to pee, but that was just going to have to not happen. "Great. Let's find the dog."

We stepped out of the vehicle and I took a deep breath of the crisp winter air. It even smelled good.

"Spots," I called. "Come here boy. Come here, Spots."

"I'll go look around back," Matt said.

"Okay."

As he disappeared around the side of the house, I hustled up to the porch and peeked in the window by the front door. It was…not rat-infested.

I could see a cute little kitchen. It had those old brown wood cabinets from back in the day—that would need to be painted over at some point—but at least there were actual cabinets. *And* no granite countertops or stainless steel appliances. Yay.

(I know. People love those things. But did you know that you have to reseal granite countertops? And that you have to be careful not to get acidic things—like lemon juice—on them or they'll stain? And the last stainless steel fridge I'd had wouldn't take a fridge magnet either. Now, granted my putting twenty fridge magnets from all the places I've traveled on a fridge should probably be strongly discouraged, but to not even be able to put a memo pad up? And I was about to have kids. I needed somewhere for their artwork.)

The other window showed a living room with wood

paneling and some unfortunate carpet. I winced at that. I actually like carpet, but not shag orange carpet. And it did make me worry about potential smells.

But it could all be dealt with. The structure seemed sound at least. I didn't see dirt or pine needles on the floor. And, really, what other choice did we have at that point? We had tried, trust me. The location was perfect and that's what really counted. All the rest could be fixed.

Even if it did take us ten years to do it, because, you know, twins. I winced again. Orange shag carpet for a decade?

Not ideal. But it was what it was. I turned my attention back to calling for Spots, but he never appeared.

Matt did, about five minutes later. "I found an old dog house in the backyard. It was in pretty rough shape but I scavenged some loose boards and patched it up as best I could. I'm going to put that blanket we brought and the water bowl out, just in case.

"Good idea. We can come back in a few days and see if maybe it's being used."

He chuckled. "Probably find a fox or raccoon or something when we do."

"Well, if there is we'll still have done a good deed. All God's creatures and what not. As long as it's not a skunk family. Not that they don't also deserve shelter, just, you know, I'd rather you didn't come home smelling like skunk."

"Agreed."

As he went back to put the blanket and water bowl in place I shook a bag of treats and called for Spots one more time, but still nothing. Either he wasn't there or he was so scared he wouldn't come out.

I really hoped we'd find him before the next big snowstorm. Poor guy. But at that point we'd pretty much done what we could. If he wanted to be found he was going to have to come to us.

CHAPTER 23

When we returned to the cabin, Matt left for work and I took a couple-hour nap until my meeting with Jamie. She came in with Max in his carrier and a big smile on her face.

"Good morning," she almost sang.

"You seem happy."

"I am. Look what just arrived. Aren't they gorgeous?"

She held up one of those "We Believe" signs. You know the signs I'm talking about? They're all pretty and cute and start with "In this house we believe" and then list things like "love is love" and "kindness is everything" and all that?

"Uh. Nice. For your front yard?"

"No. For here. I thought we could put them in the windows of all the cabins."

I pressed my lips together.

Jamie stared at me in horror. I think it was the first time I'd ever seen her worry that something was fundamentally wrong with me.

(Which, given my history, says a lot.)

"You don't support these signs? You don't believe that

black lives matter and science is real and no human is illegal? Maggie, I…I don't know what to say."

I put my hands together and pressed them to my lips. I knew Jamie meant well, but…

I sighed and laced my fingers together.

"Okay. Sorry, but you're about to get a rant you probably didn't want to hear." I opened my mouth to continue but had to pause to figure out how to put into words what I wanted to say. "First, I think having a sign like that in your yard is good, right? Because it's a public statement of some very important beliefs that I think are good beliefs to have. And publicly stating these things matters. It lets others know they're not alone in believing these things and maybe makes people who don't believe these things pause for a moment and reconsider. Maybe."

"But?" She stared at me like a wide-eyed doe seeing a hunter about to shoot its mom.

"But…" I took a deep breath. "I think for the most part those signs are performative bullshit used by upper middle class white people to pretend they care."

As she stared at me like I'd just shot her, I continued my rant. Might as well. I'd gone too far at that point to stop. "I mean, really, Black Lives Matter is in bright pink and No Human Is Illegal is in a pretty shade of blue. I get that people want a lawn sign that's attractive, but come on. Not to mention, probably eighty percent of the people who put a sign like that in their window or their yard are then going to turn around and explain to you how their husband absolutely deserves to earn three hundred thousand a year for all his hard work while his company won't even hire a black person for a similar role because 'it wasn't a good cultural fit' which is just privilege-speak for doesn't sound and look like me."

I barely paused for breath as I added, "And ask one of those people to vote on something that might infringe their perfect life to help black people or immigrants or anyone else captured by that sign and they're going to vote it down in a second. Because as much as they're willing to put a pretty sign up and sound outraged about the world today they're not willing to actually give up something *they* have to make things better."

I shrugged and turned towards the kitchen. "Sorry. It's just a pet peeve of mine. Too much time on Twitter where people talk about their outrage instead of logging off and actually sitting down with frustrating people to try to create real, impactful change."

As I made a cup of tea, I added, "At least you didn't bring in a blue line flag. Nothing like desecrating the symbol of your own country to show your support for the police. Frickin' idiots."

There was absolute silence until I returned to the table. Jamie looked at the sign in front of her and then back at me, stricken. I wanted to apologize for what I'd said, but it was true. At least in my opinion.

(Of course, not saying I'm any better. I try to vote for the collective good which is why even before I had kids I voted for school funding and libraries and things like that. But I'm just as prone to sit on my butt as the next person and just as prone to complain without taking action. I just happen to also complain about the people who complain is all. Ah, irony, my good friend.)

I squeezed Jamie's hand. "Ignore me. Please. I'm pregnant and cranky and full of weird ideas. All I ask is if you are going to put those up around the property—and you may want to check with your husband first since, you know, he may vote differently than you think—is that you also remember all those pithy sayings du jour next time you go to vote and that you try to live them. And that if we as a corporate entity donate money, that we do so to politicians or causes that actually support what those signs say and not to the assholes who'll lower our corporate taxes while going against everything listed there."

I hated to upset my friend, especially when I knew she meant well and believed in what was on those signs. But there'd been a time in my life when I tried not to talk politics or religion with anyone ever and look where that got us.

"So," I said. "How's Max doing? He looks great, as always."

Her shoulders sagged in relief. Jamie is the most competent person I know, but conflict is not something she enjoys.

"He's been fidgety this week. I think it's probably just growing pains. But I'm keeping an eye on it. After I took him into the doctor four times in the first four weeks I try to let things work themselves out before I involve her. But it's hard."

I laughed. "I can imagine. Did I ever tell you about the time I took Fancy into the vet because I thought she'd cracked a tooth?"

"No. What happened?"

"She lost one of her back baby teeth but it looked so completely different from her front teeth that I assumed she'd cracked a tooth and rushed her to the vet. He was so embarrassed on my behalf he told me to sneak out the back door and pretend I'd never been there. At least he didn't bill me for it."

"What a nice vet."

"He was. One of my big regrets about moving was losing that vet and gaining Mr. Crankypants Your Dog Is Fat as a replacement."

"He said that about Lulu, too!"

We talked dogs and babies for the next half hour. I was glad we'd been able to find our way back to a middle ground where we could joke and laugh. I hadn't meant to single her out about the sign thing, it was just something that really irked me, this modern trend of trying to boil serious issues down to slogans and signage.

It made me worry for my girls, what our world was becoming.

(I know these stories I tell you are supposed to be light and fluffy and fun and an escape for both of us, but the world is right there, you know, and I can't help but being shaped by it, and sometimes that leaks through. Sorry. Not sorry. But sorry.)

Anyway. I digress.

Jamie and I had a good visit in the end. She promised to look into that house for me and see if we could live in it, which was good progress, but I still hadn't found Spots and my delivery date was coming closer every single day that passed.

CHAPTER 24

The next week was uneventful.

Given the number of times Fancy went racing outside barking her head off either Spots was lurking nearby or a mountain lion was. Or maybe both.

My stomach continued to get bigger—something I really hadn't thought was possible—and my back pretty much ached non-stop all day no matter what position I was in.

To cheer me up the doctor did one of those creepy 3D ultrasounds. Have you ever seen one of those things? The babies look like aliens because they're in this reddish-copper color that is not the color of human skin. At all. And they're not quite done developing just yet, so it's even more freaky.

It's just not right. Give me the blurry black and white images of the old days anytime, because the last thing I needed as I approached the end of my pregnancy was something that made me wonder exactly what was growing inside me.

I'd also taken to listening to music all the time to keep the babies entertained. I'd like to tell you I listened to calming, beautiful classical music that would elevate their tastes, but that would be a lie.

I figured if my girls were going to have to grow up on classical rock like Cream and Blood, Sweat, & Tears they might as well get used to it now. That and Taylor Swift, P!nk, Jim Croce, and Kenny Rogers.

What can I say? I'm eclectic. (Right, that's the word for it. Eclectic. Better than describing me as someone with as many personalities as there are sides on a thirty-sided die.)

Even though most of my research had indicated that bed rest was not the best idea in the world for most women, I did end up getting a lot of rest simply because I was tired.

The day I made it to 36 weeks I wanted to get up and dance around the room, but I settled for a "hell yeah" as I walked to the kitchen for another glass of tea.

That's when Spots made his next appearance. Fancy was in the living room sleeping when I saw him out in the yard. Quietly I blocked the doggie door, grabbed a bag of treats, put on my coat and warm slippers, and went outside.

The treats woke Fancy up, of course, but I was able to throw her a few and sneak out the door before she tried to follow.

"Hey, Spots," I said in my friendliest dog voice. "How are you, buddy?"

His little tail wagged.

"Do you want a treat?" I tossed one of the treats near him. He flinched when it hit the ground but then approached it cautiously, sniffed it for a few seconds, and gobbled it up.

I kept throwing him treats, each one closer to me than the last, until he was on the porch next to me. He was in rough shape. The scratch on his nose did not look good at all. He was also limping on one foot. And there were more than just pine needles tangled in his coat. On his hip he had a whole branch tangled up in his hair.

"Ah, you poor thing." I wanted to pet him, but he was still pretty skittish. Also, fleas and dirt and what-have-you.

"Hm. What to do with you now?"

The porch had a gate you could pull shut so that it was closed in. The railing was slatted and only hip-height, but with Fancy that would've been more than enough to keep her contained. I figured I could shut him in on the porch and then call Jamie or Matt or my grandpa to come help.

I slowly eased around behind him and pulled the gate shut as he ate another treat.

But that's when I learned that the little guy was quite the escape artist. The railing on the patio was about three feet high maybe? He jumped right over it.

From a standing position.

No running leap like I would've needed (and still failed). Nope, just a quick, pop! right over the railing.

He took off for the woods as I called after him to come back and never even hesitated for a moment as he reached the bigger fence and jumped right over that one, too. At least that let me know how he'd been getting into the yard since I never had found a loose board or hole.

He was gone in a moment.

I let Fancy out into the yard and she raced over every inch of it, her nose pressed to the ground, pausing to pee occasionally, presumably where he'd tried to mark his territory.

Great.

I'd missed him again and all I had to show for it was a very sulky, very big dog who ignored me for the rest of the afternoon. Joy.

CHAPTER 25

Jamie came over about twenty minutes later.

"Any word on that house?" I asked. "Do you think Matt and I could rent it? I wish we could buy it, but since it's part of the resort I know that's not an option…"

I was still nervous about renting a house from the resort. I mean, what if it failed? Matt and I would both lose our jobs, *and* we'd lose our home all in one big fell swoop.

But I put that aside because that kind of paranoid catastrophizing is just what I call a normal Tuesday.

Jamie wouldn't meet my eyes. "Um, you know, still looking into it."

I knew I should let it go, but I was worried. Time was running short. And if we couldn't have the house to rent then I needed to know. I wondered if my asking had been some sort of unspoken breach of etiquette. Sometimes I miss class differences and maybe Mason had been offended by the idea we'd rent from the resort and Jamie just didn't want to tell me.

See, this is why you don't involve family and friends in money or business. Because it gets awkward.

I rubbed at my back. I could not get comfortable anymore. "Jamie, please be honest with me. If we can't have the place, just say so." I winced as the muscles in my belly tightened.

"Are you okay?" she asked.

"Fine. Just the normal aches and pains of being a living, breathing incubator. I can't believe that one woman had eight babies at once. Like, how?"

"Well, they're really small when that happens. She probably had an easier birth than a woman who has one really big baby."

"Right. That makes sense. Miserable pregnancy, easier birth. If all you had to do was carry and give birth to the kids then multiples would be the best choice. But then you also have to raise them…Can you imagine? Eight kids at once? As a single mom."

"I know. Crazy, right?"

"Me, I'm just in the sad middle ground where I get both a miserable pregnancy and a hard birth." I winced again.

"Maggie?"

"It's fine. When you get this big, it hurts. And I'm just a little stressed is all. You sure you don't have news on the house? It would really help to know. One way or the other."

She shook her head. "Sorry. You know Mason and business and all that…"

I tried to hide my disappointment. Where were we going to live? I guess we could always go back to the place by my grandpa. It wasn't *bad*. And maybe we could move in a couple years? Although, moving with toddlers? Ugh.

I frowned. I knew we were going to be stuck in that place for the next decade. And…I didn't want to be. But nothing to do about it. If I'd crossed some horrible invisible line with Mason I'd just have to hope it didn't impact anything else. See, this is why you didn't work with friends and family.

Work-only relationships were so much cleaner.

Although, no, not really. I'd always been stepping in it when I had a corporate job. I mean, seriously, casually mention that your grandpa had spent fifteen years in prison and suddenly everyone is like, "Oh, you're not one of us."

Well, at least they are after they find out it was for armed robbery and not some white-collared version of stealing from people. A little Ponzi scheme is just a misstep between friends. But armed robbery? That's simply not done. If you're wealthy you don't use *guns* to take people's money. How crass and obvious.

I sighed deeply.

Jamie squeezed my arm. "It'll work out. Trust me."

"Heh. Yeah. Right. It'll work out. Of course it will."

Luckily for Jamie, because I think it was starting to get awkward at that point, the babies decided that was the perfect time to arrive.

What had been sort of consistent but widely-spaced pains in my stomach suddenly started to get a lot more regular and a lot more frequent.

I stared up at her. "Oh God. I think it's time. You need to take me to the hospital."

"It's time? For the babies?"

I nodded. "Yep."

"I'll call Matt."

"Do that. But tell him to meet us at the hospital. We need to go. Now."

"Now?"

I nodded my head vigorously as another contraction came. "Yep. Now. Right now. Let's go. Now."

"Maggie…"

"You know those pains I'd been feeling the last day or so? Pretty sure those were labor. So, yeah, now. Right now."

CHAPTER 26

One of the reasons Jamie is my best friend is because there is almost no occasion she can't handle. So when I told her "now", she took control. She had me and my go bag bundled into the back of her vehicle within five minutes and had called Matt and my grandpa by the time we pulled out of the cabin's driveway.

As we drove to the hospital at a slightly-above-speed-limit-but-not-dangerously-fast speed she called Mason and asked him to drop in and grab Fancy.

I wanted to object—I mean, Mason?—but she was right. Who else would she call? I wanted my husband and my grandpa at the hospital and at least Fancy knew Mason and would tolerate him well enough.

The folks at the hospital knew about me and fortunately didn't drag their feet when we showed up. Which, as it turns out, was a very good thing. Because despite my mom's stories of being in labor with me for like twenty-four-plus hours, I was in labor at the hospital for a grand total of thirty-five minutes.

The doctors were not happy with me for waiting so long and thought I'd done it deliberately, but I swear, I had not. I just couldn't tell the difference between "this is labor" and "this is the unending miserable, cramping existence that you have been condemned to until you give birth" that had been my last week or so of pregnancy.

They made me deliver in an operating room since there was a chance that even if I got baby one out just fine that baby two would need to come out via C-section. Doctors take a woman giving birth to twins seriously. Which, I should be glad for, but it's a little stressful, you know?

Like, *Here, we've got this whole surgical tray set up right there by your side so we can cut into you and grab that baby out if we need to at any moment. Ready to push?* Cue fake smile.

Oh, and just because it was a short labor does not mean it was a painless labor. No epidural for me. And things…yeah. Let's just not go there, huh?

At least the twins were on the smaller side, which made it easier. But not too small, thankfully. They squeaked in just under the line.

I was almost nine pounds when I was born (ouch), but my little girls weighed in at 5.5 lbs each. And by some miracle they were both fine to breathe on their own, too. And both had ten fingers and ten toes and everything else in the right place. No hair, though. They were as bald as I'd been when I was born.

Baby one had some seriously good lungs. Holy cow. She came into the world letting everybody know exactly what she thought of being removed from her very comfortable home.

Baby number two came out wide-eyed and calm and looking around like she already knew more than all of us combined.

(Which, well, that's pretty much how my girls have gone through the world since. Baby one leading with a screaming charge, baby two coming along behind and not missing a thing.)

And, yeah, in that moment I felt what everyone says you feel. That as covered in who-knows-what and as screaming as baby one was and as much as it had hurt and I'd ached and suffered to get to that moment, that it was worth it to hold those little girls in my arms and know that they were mine in a way that nothing in this world had ever been before.

I expected they weren't going to appreciate me as a mom when they were stubborn-minded independent teenagers, but even then they'd still be a part of me. And a part of Matt.

Hopefully they'd be the best of the both of us combined and two unique, amazing individuals at the same time.

It was amazing.

And also the beginning of one of the scariest, most rewarding journeys of my life. Heck, it was even scarier than jumping out of a plane.

Fortunately, I was so exhausted after weeks of not getting enough sleep that even the thought of what was ahead couldn't keep me awake for more than the time it took to have everyone tell me how happy they were for me.

CHAPTER 27

I woke up sometime that night to find Matt sitting in a chair by my bed, wide awake.

"Hey, did you get some sleep?" I asked, rubbing at my eyes.

He shook his head. "No. I've been sitting here watching over you and the girls. Your superstitiousness must've rubbed off. I had this crazy thought that if I closed my eyes, it would all go away. This was the most amazing day of my life and I didn't want it to end."

I reached out and he laced his fingers through mine.

"We did pretty good, you know," I said.

"We did. Now can we name them, though?"

I laughed softly as I rested my head against the pillow. "Right. They can't just be our bundles of joy anymore. They need real live names."

"We could name one Joy, so they still are in a sense." He raised an eyebrow, looking at me expectantly.

I nodded. "We could..."

I'd gone to school with a girl named Muffie whose parents had given her that name because they'd told her older brother there was a muffin in the oven for the entire pregnancy, and they figured that would help him understand that the little baby they brought home was the same as that muffin in the oven.

Poor girl. Stuck with an unfortunate name like that for her entire life just so her brother would be able to connect the two. (In some weird way the name actually fit even though she was not an east coast prep school student or bubbly cheerleader. I guess that's what happens when you have such a unique name. You can make it your own.)

Anyway. I was still in post-delivery, pregnancy delirium, so I added, "And, maybe, I mean, right now, things seem to finally be turning the corner in the world after a dark stretch, so maybe the other one could be Hope? Hope and Joy?"

(I know. How cheesy can you get? But I'd just given birth. There was blood loss involved. Do you think my mind was working in a rational way? I think there are some cultures that wait something like forty-five days to give newborns names. Those people are smart. Because, well…)

Matt smiled. "I like that. Hope and Joy."

(I don't know what Matt's excuse was. He was supposed to be the one that stopped me from making bad life decisions, not enabled them. But, maybe he was tired, too.)

I glanced over to where the babies were starting to stir. "They're going to hate us for it, you know that, right? And it pretty much guarantees that at least one of them is going to be a bitter and jaded goth princess when she's a teenager who sneaks out of the house, smokes, drinks, and tells us she hates us all the time."

He laughed. "If her entry into the world is any indication, I'm pretty sure baby number one is going to be that way no matter what name we give her."

"True. Less than twenty-four hours in and we're already in trouble. Hm. Maybe Joy isn't such a great choice for her." I chuckled.

"We could name them after your mom and your grandma."

I shook my head. "We could. But I want them to be their own people, you know? Not burdened by some legacy of an earlier generation. Also Olivia, Emma, Ava, Charlotte, and Sophia are out, too."

"Why?"

"Most common baby names last year. I always pitied the Sarahs and Jennifers in my class who had to be Sarah B or Jenny J so you could tell them apart from the other Sarahs and Jennifers. I was always the only Maggie, you know, which was nice."

"Hm."

I realized he'd probably been a Matt B himself. Maybe it wasn't so bad being on that end of things after all.

We sat there for a long moment, thinking about our choices.

"So Hope and Joy?" Matt finally asked.

"You realize we're bringing on the apocalypse if we name them that? The world is just going to go to shit if we do this. That means we also need a good solid middle name they might actually want to use, unlike May for me. My mom used to tell me I could use my middle name if I didn't like my first name, but May just never had any flavor to it, you know."

(No offense, of course, to anyone named May. But when you move from Maggie to May there's a shift there. People do react to names and the way they view a Maggie is not the way they view a May. Sorry to say it.)

"What are you thinking?" he asked.

"I don't know. I kind of want to give them both the same middle name, but we can't do that. Can we?"

"Why not?"

"What if they *both* hate their names? And then they both want to go by their middle name? Twins with the same name? How awful would that be."

He shrugged. "If they do, they do. I know you're going to dress them alike. You won't be able to resist."

"Only for birthdays and holidays, I swear. When we can really have fun with it and take lots of photos. The rest of the time they can do whatever they want. Maybe they'll each get a signature color, you know. For years when I was a kid it seemed like everything I was given was lilac."

"And did you like that?"

"No."

"Well, then maybe we skip the colors. At least until they're old enough to choose them themselves."

We lapsed back into silence.

Matt squeezed my hand. "So. What middle name can we choose that will work for both of them?"

"What about Rosenda? It's a family middle name on my side if you go back a few generations, but no one ever used it as their main name. And there's a lot of variations they could use so they could be the same but different."

He nodded. "I like it. So baby one is Joy Rosenda Barnes-Carver and baby two is Hope Rosenda Barnes-Carver."

I squeezed his hand. "Just Barnes, no need to hyphenate."

"Does that mean you changed your mind about taking my last name?"

"Nope. But I also don't think our babies need hyphenated last names either. Imagine learning how to write that. Ugh. Hey, that's another reason Hope and Joy are good choices. They're short. Ooh, and Barnes, too. Lucky kids."

He smiled. "Okay, then. Joy Rosenda Barnes and Hope Rosenda Barnes who will likely end up calling themselves Roz and Rosie by the time they're eighteen."

I laughed. "Perfect."

Our eyes met and I shivered. "I can't believe we're doing this. I'm glad I have you by my side. I don't think I could do it alone."

He kissed my forehead. "You could. And you would. But I'm glad I'm here, too. There is nowhere I'd rather be than with my girls."

(Yes, it was hokey. Optimism, exhaustion, and lack of sleep do that to you. And, yes, we probably did bring on ten years of bad luck with those names. But it was a really good moment. Of course, I still hadn't found Spots yet and we still didn't have anywhere to live permanently…but life is messy like that sometimes. And you gotta take the wins when they come.)

CHAPTER 28

Two days after I gave birth, we headed "home" with the twins.

Of course, home was still the cabin at the resort, because we still had no idea where we were going to live. At least I didn't. Matt had promised me that he had something in the works, but he wouldn't tell me what. I figured it was some sort of renovation on the house next to my grandpa's or maybe we were swapping out with Jack and Trish and we'd live in Matt's dad's old mobile home and they'd live next to my grandpa.

I didn't really mind the thought of living there. The views were gorgeous. And, sure, yeah, it was a mobile home not a home home, but really when you're in one it doesn't feel any different. It's more the tornado risks and freezing pipes and predatory landlords that are the issue with a mobile home. But if we owned the property and were well-insulated…

It wasn't a bad option. It wasn't the house on the resort property, but, you know, you don't always get what you want. Sometimes you just have to find a solution that at least gives you what you need. (Thanks,

Rolling Stones, for that life lesson.)

I was so exhausted learning how to nurse and then nursing two babies that I really didn't care at that point. Give me a roof over my head, food, and a safe place to sleep and that was good enough for me.

Poor Fancy was beside herself when we got there. (Matt had already been by earlier in the day to get her settled back into the cabin and to arrange the basics we were going to need, but last she'd seen me I'd rushed out in pain and then she'd had *Mason* show up. I don't know what she had to be thinking at that point.)

I figured she'd be pretty emotional about everything so when we pulled up I left Matt with the babies in the van and went in on my own first. I was actually able to sit on the floor with her for the first time in a couple of months. (Even though that wasn't the best of ideas post delivery, I knew she needed it.)

I let her crawl all over me as she gave me a long lecture and licked at my face frantically.

"It's okay, Fancy. I promise."

She finally settled enough for me to pet her some and give her a kiss on the forehead. I rubbed at her velvety soft ears. "You and me, kiddo. It's going to be a wild ride, but we'll make it work."

When I stood back up and reached for the door she looked at me in panic. "I'll be right back. I promise. I'm coming right back. It's okay." I gently closed the door in her face.

I could've probably let her come out to the van with me, I was pretty sure she wouldn't run away, but you never know, and I did not need to lose her when trying to care for two newborns.

She was right there at the door when Matt and I came back in with a carrier each. I had to nudge her to the side as she tried to sniff at Joy who was just starting to stir from what had been a nice, peaceful nap.

I set the carrier down on the couch. "What do you think, Fancy?"

She sniffed at Joy and then turned to sniff at Hope when Matt set her down, too. After she'd finished her inspection she turned to look at me.

"Do you like them?"

In answer she laid herself down along the length of the couch between the two carriers and closed her eyes with a contented sigh.

"I'd say that's a yes. I bet she's going to be their Nana dog like in the Peter Pan books."

Matt put his arm around my shoulders. "I couldn't think of a better protector for my girls."

As Matt went off to reheat one of the casseroles Lesley had left us and I settled in for (yet another) nursing session with the twins, Fancy stayed right where she was, keeping an eye on me as I nursed Joy and then Hope.

When I moved to the table to eat, she didn't budge, though. Not even when I set down a sharing plate for her. It seemed babies trumped food in Fancyworld. Interesting.

Matt laughed. "I wonder if Fancy will ever leave their sides again."

"She'll have to at some point."

We ate that whole meal without Fancy even looking in our direction once. She only moved when Joy woke up again and started crying for milk. And then all she did was jump to her feet and look at me like, "Alright, do something already. Help my baby out here, would ya?"

I'd been so worried that Fancy would feel left out when we brought the babies home, but honestly I was the one that felt like I'd been abandoned, because from that day forward those little girls were her world.

CHAPTER 29

That afternoon my grandpa and Lesley came by.

"Don't look," my grandpa told me as he had Matt go back out to the truck with him.

Lesley—with her pure white hair in an adorable bob and her tactful pearls—distracted me by showing me all of the meals she'd brought to fill up our freezer.

"Has anyone ever told you you're a lifesaver?" I asked her.

She smiled. "I know what it's like in those first few days. Which is why there are also boxes of snacks in the truck that we'll bring in in a minute just in case the effort of heating something up feels like too much."

Each container was labeled in her perfect-looking script. It was every type of casserole you could possibly want.

"Good thing I have Matt around to be my home helper. He can heat the food while I lounge on the couch being a milk-producing factory."

Lesley laughed and patted my hand. "You'll get used to it eventually."

(I wasn't sure I actually believed that, but I was willing to pretend in the hopes that she was right.)

My grandpa and Matt came back inside muttering to one another as they maneuvered something through the door.

The cradle!

I'd forgotten. In all the excitement and stress and insanity I'd forgotten that my grandpa was making the babies a cradle.

"Don't turn around yet, Maggie May," my grandpa called as he and Matt headed back outside.

"What on earth did he make?" I asked Lesley as they came in and went back outside a third time.

"You'll see. Some of it isn't what he made. We have goodies for you as well."

Finally, my grandpa said, "Okay, Maggie May. Turn around."

I turned. There were *two* wooden cradles sitting in the middle of the living room. They were exquisite. Gorgeous.

Honestly, I can't do them justice.

They smelled like cedar (which is such a good smell) but my grandpa had inlaid different types of wood at each end on the outside to make these gorgeous patterns so that they looked like works of art.

They *were* works of art.

And at the top above where the babies heads would go, each one had an arch with the baby's name carved in cursive in the center with roses around the perimeter.

"How did you find the time to make two of them? And when did you add the names?" I asked as I ran my fingers over the intricate carvings.

He flexed his hand and winced. "Spent the whole day yesterday finishing 'em up. Everything was set except for the names. And the roses. I added those when Matt told us what their middle names were going to be."

"These are so amazing, Grandpa." I started crying.

Matt chuckled and put his arm around my shoulder. "Ignore her. She's been doing that a lot since she got pregnant."

I wiped the tears away. "I hope it stops soon. This crying at everything is getting to be a bit much."

I stepped away from Matt to give my grandpa a big hug. "Thank you so much. These are so special to me." I wiped at my cheeks again. "Sorry."

"Don't worry. It's not a bad thing to cry." He pulled back and looked me in the eyes. "But if you find that you're crying for no reason, then you tell someone. I had a friend whose wife had that post-partum and it was bad. So no going it alone. I know we have to limit our visits to keep you and the babies safe, but I'm going to call you every day and check on you."

I smiled and hugged him again. "Thank you. I'm so glad I have you."

"Oh, and the name plaques at the top of the cradles there? Those can be removed when the babies are done with the cradles. Maybe you can put them on the wall above their beds or on their doors or something."

"That's amazing, Grandpa. You think of everything."

Lesley grabbed my hand and led me to the corner where there were two large plastic bins. "Now, I know you didn't want a baby shower, but people still wanted to buy you cute gifts. So I collected them on your behalf. With twins we didn't know what size they'd be or when they'd arrive, so I did most of the clothes shopping in a rush after you delivered. That'll all arrive tomorrow—

gotta love two-day shipping—but in these bins there are diapers and baby wipes and diaper cream and burp cloths and the rest of it to get you started."

I stared at her, wide-eyed. "To get me started? There's two bins of stuff there."

She laughed. "Oh, you just wait. You'll be amazed at how much stuff you have by the time you hit the six-month mark."

I glanced around the small living room area of the cabin and then at Matt, horror in my eyes.

He came and hugged me. "Deep breaths. We've got this."

"Right. Deep breaths. We've got this."

But did we? All my research online and I honestly did not know what I was doing. Other girls babysat or had younger siblings growing up, but I'd had none of that. And I'd studiously avoided being around babies my whole adult life because I didn't want to break one.

(And you think I'm exaggerating, but I actually had a friend's kid stand on my leg at one point when he was not that old. I was holding him, kind of bouncing him, and then that kid pushed off against my leg and twisted around like a salmon. I almost dropped him on his head on the floor. No way I was going to try to hold another baby after that...)

So my entire baby experience was limited to a few times when I was brave enough to try to hold Max. But Matt had been around when Jack was young, so maybe he had a clue what to do about all of it. Maybe.

Fortunately, Lesley spent the next hour walking me through all the things she'd brought and why I needed them and how to use them, or I would've been completely lost.

There were so many things. And so much to do. I had flashbacks to when Fancy was a puppy and how hard that had been, but Lesley patted my hand. "You'll be fine. Don't worry."

We had a good meal together and then they left.

And that's when it hit me, Matt and I were committed to this path for the next eighteen years. I didn't have time to freak out about it, though, because Joy woke up screaming for food.

"Time to feed 'em, yet again." I collapsed onto the couch as Matt picked her up from her cradle.

Fancy, who had established herself between the two cradles watched Matt carefully to make sure he didn't drop her and then put her head back down on her paws when he'd successfully handed her off to me.

Do you know how hard breastfeeding is? I knew all the reasons to do it, so I was determined to give a good try, but with two babies to feed? Holy…

Not easy. But I did it because that's what you do. And then…

When the babies were settled and changed and back asleep?

I took a nap. The nurses had said I needed lots of rest and that I should get it while the babies were sleeping, so that's exactly what I did, leaving poor Matt and Fancy to entertain themselves.

CHAPTER 30

I hadn't forgotten about Spots. If he was still out there all alone he couldn't be doing well. I mean, snow and wilderness. It had to be rough.

I'd actually once seen a picture of a Newfie who'd gone "wild". Poor thing had a matted coat six inches thick that had to be shaved off when it was finally brought in. I didn't want that to happen to Spots. But, giving birth had sort of derailed my plans to find the poor guy.

Day three of being home I was finally working myself up to having enough energy to drive over there and track him down, but I wasn't quite there yet.

I decided I'd do it after the babies, Matt, and I spent a little time outside. Fancy had been inside with me while I was pregnant and then with them, so I knew she had to be dying to get outside and just lie in some grass for a bit.

I figured after we had our outing maybe Matt could watch the girls for me while I drove over there.

(Yes, the logical option would've been to have Matt drive over, but I was a little stir-crazy, too, by that point.

I needed a reminder that I was more than just a milk-vending and diaper-changing machine.)

At least the weather had finally started to turn towards spring so it was warm enough to sit in the shade and not freeze. Matt and I bundled the girls up, though, just to be safe.

They were in adorable matching coats and pink hats with bear ears. (I hadn't wanted to go the matchy-matchy route, but it seems Lesley or whoever else ordered clothes for them had. I'd given in because how can you resist such adorable cuteness as matching ladybug outfits? I'd also had to give in on the pink and sparkly thing or else the kids wouldn't have had much to wear.)

As soon as Fancy was satisfied that we were settled in on the porch and her girls were safe she walked out into the yard and collapsed. She was asleep in a minute.

"Told you she'd go outside if we did," I said to Matt.

He nodded. He looked as exhausted as I was. He'd agreed to bring the babies to me for middle of the night feedings so he'd been as sleep-deprived as I was the last few days.

But he at least had the military training that let him drop immediately back asleep, so he was actually in much better shape than I was. Plus, he was not having his nutrients sucked out of his body to support his spawn.

(Don't get mad at me. I loved my girls with my whole heart. But that is what happens.)

We'd just settled into a happy stupor when I saw Spots on the edge of the woods. Fancy saw him, too. Her head lifted and she stared right at him.

"Fancy," I called. "Leave him be. He needs us. If he

jumps that fence, you stay right where you are and do not chase him off, you hear me?"

I know, that was a lot to tell her, but I figured it was worth a try.

When Fancy was a puppy she was too clever for her own good and would eat around whatever you hid a pill in. Cheese, peanut butter, pill pockets. Didn't matter. She'd eat whatever it was and spit out the pill.

Finally, after shoving a pill down her throat for the third time because I had no other option, I looked her in the eyes and told her that she could accept pills with peanut butter or spend the rest of her life having pills shoved down her throat. Her choice.

And from that day forward? She took pills in peanut butter without an issue.

Probably me hallucinating that she understood what I was telling her, but it worked, so I tried it again with Spots.

I handed my baby (Joy) off to Matt and went inside for treats and a doggie ice cream. Before Fancy could scramble to her feet, I put the ice cream in front of her. It was the only thing that might keep her occupied for more than thirty seconds.

While Fancy diligently licked away at her ice cream, I approached the gate in the fence, treats in hand.

"Come here, Spots," I coaxed. "That's a good boy. Look what I've got for you." I opened the side gate and motioned for him to come inside, holding a Pumpkin Puff in my hand.

I glanced back at Fancy. She was still licking away at the ice cream, but watching us. Once she's started in on an ice cream she won't abandon it until it's all gone.

"Come on, Spots. Come on. You've gotta be exhausted, buddy. Come on. Let us take care of you."

He hesitated for another moment and then came forward and took the treat from my hand. He was in rough shape. I could see his ribs and his coat was a mess and that cut on his nose looked even worse than before.

And the amount of dirt and pine needles he was carrying around…

I knelt down and held my hand out and let him sniff it. He did so, but was still tensed to run away.

I offered him another treat and gently scratched behind his ears as he ate it. "That's a good boy, Spots. Good boy."

"Come on." I motioned him through the gate and he stepped through, taking another treat from my hand.

Fancy finished her ice cream and got to her feet. I glared at her. "Fancy…Be nice."

She gave me a look and then ambled over to sniff at Spots. He tensed at first, but didn't move away as she sniffed him over. Slowly, his tail started to wag.

Before I could stop them they were running through the yard, playing.

I watched them intently, waiting for any sign things were going to turn ugly, but they didn't. They played for about two minutes and then both collapsed side by side in the yard.

I smiled and looked at Matt.

He sighed. "I take it we have a new dog."

"Maybe. If his new owner doesn't want him back. But what we definitely need to do is get that guy a good bath and vet visit ASAP. Which means we better tuck the girls away for now so you can take care of that."

"Me? I thought you wanted an outing."

"I did, but no idea how long it'll take to sort all that and well…" I gestured at myself and then the kids. "Unfortunately, not all parenting duties can be done by both parents."

CHAPTER 31

Fancy didn't know what to do with herself when Matt left with Spots. She wanted to watch the girls, but she also didn't want to lose her new best friend. She ended up stationing herself by their cradles but facing the front door of the cabin and didn't move from there until Matt returned with Spots three hours later.

Luckily, since the resort was almost ready to open he'd been able to take Spots to the groomers in the main resort building and call in the vet we'd hired to work the property. (A new vet, I was so excited.)

Spots gave the groomers quite the challenge, because he really was an absolute dirty mess. They had to almost shave him in a few places which meant he came back looking spotted in a whole new way. But the vet declared him surprisingly healthy. His nose had needed some cleaning and two stitches, but that was it.

He looked like a new pup when Matt brought him back home. He seemed to feel like one, too, because he was full of energy. He and Fancy raced out the back the minute Matt walked him through the door and they didn't come back for a full ten minutes, after which they sprawled in the middle of the living room, their paws covered in mud.

I sighed. "Well, I never was one for cleanliness."

"Me neither," Matt said, but we were both staring at those muddy, muddy paws. "Maybe we should think about hiring someone to come and clean once a week now that we have two babies and two dogs."

I wrinkled my nose. "I don't like people in my stuff. I'd have to clean before they came to clean." I turned to look at him. "Did you say two dogs?" I grinned.

He nodded. "If we can keep him. Have you called yet?"

I shook my head. "No. Not yet."

I really didn't want to. Somehow I'd fallen in love with the shaggy little mutt and I didn't want to lose him. I knew it was the right thing to do, so we'd do it. Eventually. Just…maybe in a few more days?

(I know, I know. Somewhere out there his current owner was probably frantic to find him. It wasn't nice to hold onto him for a few days. Which is why we didn't try to.)

"Give me the number. It'll be the last thing I do as a cop." Matt pulled out his phone.

"Okay." I read the number off to him and went to slump down on the couch as he called the shelter down in Denver.

The woman gave him the same runaround she'd given me so he got all official and told her to look him up online and call back through the police switchboard if she didn't trust him.

(I was surprised she didn't pull out the "just because you're a cop doesn't mean you aren't a stalker" card to shut him down, but she didn't.)

She did, however, call back through the main number for the police department. Fortunately, Marlene, the receptionist at the police station, put the call through to Matt's cell instead of saying he didn't work there anymore.

After a little more convincing, he finally had a phone number to call.

I bit my lip as he dialed the number. All I could hear from where I was sitting was his side of the conversation.

He explained that we'd found Spots and where and why we thought he'd run away. And then he nodded and uh-uh'ed in sympathy as the person on the other end of the line talked. "No, yeah, that is rough," he said once before going back to non-committal sounds of agreement.

My fingernails were digging grooves in my palms by then, but Matt has the patience of a saint.

Finally, when it seemed the person on the other end of the line had wound down with whatever they had to say, he said, "We're happy to bring Spots back to you if you want him back. Changing homes is hard on a dog and we want what's best for him."

I sighed. Well, adding Spots to our family had been a nice thought but looked like it wasn't going to happen.

He continued, "But it sounds like you've had a rough time of it lately and if you don't think you're up to taking him back I can promise you we'll give him a great home. He's already bonded with our existing dog and he'll be living in his old home and have a yard and everything. Your call."

I sat up, holding my breath. Was there a chance? Were we going to get to keep Spots?

Matt did some more of that uh-uh nonsense and then he hung up.

"So?" I asked. "You didn't write down an address. Is he…ours?"

He nodded.

"Yes." I pumped my fist in the air. "But, what happened? Why didn't they want him back?"

"It was a young couple who adopted him. But they lost him on a hike near Winter Park. Let him off leash and he kept going. They did try to find him, but no luck."

"They didn't call shelters or anything, though."

He shrugged. "He was microchipped so they assumed they'd get a call when he was found."

"Huh." Me and Fancy, I'd never stop driving around until I found her. I'd camp out in that park and hand out flyers and call everyone and anyone I could think of. But, okay, whatever. Different strokes and all.

"Maggie, don't judge."

I shrugged that off. I always judge. That's like telling water not to be wet. "So that's how they lost him, why don't they want him back?"

"They split up. The woman did want him back, but she's now living in an apartment and the pet deposit, pet rent, etc. would push her over the edge financially. Also, she said he's pretty high energy for an apartment. She made it sound like he might be pretty high energy for a yard."

I looked at the sleeping dog on the floor and raised my eyebrows.

"She said he escaped their yard more than once."

"Oh that I'm not surprised about. He can hop that fence out there no problem. But maybe he kept escaping because he wanted to come home."

"Maybe."

I narrowed my eyes at him. "It doesn't sound like you had to lie to her, though, so why did you?"

"About what?"

"About him living in his old home."

Matt's eyes got a little wide.

"Matt? What aren't you telling me?"

"It was supposed to be a surprise."

I leaned forward. "What was?" I was on the edge of my seat with excitement.

"Maggie…"

"No. No. You said it, you now have to tell me."

He shook his head. "Fine. It's almost ready anyway. We got the house. Not just to rent, to buy. Mason made us a good deal."

I stared at him wide-eyed. "We got the house?" I stood up and did a little jig. "Then why aren't we living there right now?"

He laughed. "Because even when both parties want to you can't just buy a house in a day."

"So we rent it or whatever until the closing."

"Also…"

"What? Just tell me. If we can move out of this cabin and into a real home, Matt, why haven't we?"

He shook his head. "Do you like orange shag carpet and brown wooden kitchen cabinets?"

"No. They're hideous. But, a home. Our home."

"And would you want to renovate those things while we're living there with two newborns?"

"Of course not. I just figured we'd live with it for the time being."

Which, granted, probably meant living with it for the next decade. Something that did not seem all that appealing when I stopped to think about it. But newborns and home reno? Not a good combination.

"Well, lucky for you, and me, for us, your friends and family like you very much. *Our* friends and family like us very much. Jamie is overseeing a whirlwind renovation of the house. Jack and your grandpa have chipped in with free labor. And Greta has used her questionable connections to make things happen I wouldn't have thought possible. Another five days or so and it'll be like a brand new home."

I stared at him. "Really? You mean we get the home and it will be all new and shiny?"

He nodded.

I smiled. But then a thought occurred to me. I opened and closed my mouth. My grandpa had always told me not to look a gift horse in the mouth, so all I said was, "That's great."

"Maggie…"

"It is. It's great. I'm so happy."

"How come you don't sound happy?"

I licked my lips. "I am happy. I am so, so grateful that they're doing this for us."

I pressed my lips together so I wouldn't say anything else.

"But…? Maggie I know you. Just spit it out, whatever it is."

I sighed. "Fine. It's incredibly generous and I am so, so grateful. But…What colors are they using? Because if they went with realtor gray it will make me sad…And are they using carpet? Because Fancy and those modern floors that everyone likes so much do not go well together. I know it's weird, but I like carpet, Matt. And have you seen Jamie and Mason's house? All that wood and stone. I can't live like that."

He laughed, loud and from the belly.

"What? I'm serious."

"I know." He came over and gave me a kiss on the forehead. "Don't you think your family know you well by now? That they know your tastes? And the colors you like? Look at the quilts that Elaine made. Look at the cradles that your grandpa made. Did you like those?"

I nodded. "They were perfect."

"So don't you think that if your best friend, who is the one who told Elaine what colors to use, and your grandpa, who made those cradles, are in charge of this project that they might come pretty close to what you want?"

I chewed on my thumbnail. "Yeah, I guess. You're right. It might not be exactly what I would've chosen, but they know me. I'm sure it'll be amazing." I beamed at him. "And we'll have the perfect home, Matt. That's all ours."

"We will. It's perfect. And, as it turns out, big enough for at least one more kid."

"No. Give me time for some amnesia about pregnancy and childbirth before you even try to go there. Because right now two sounds like a good number."

I settled back into the couch, smiling. We were going to have a house. A renovated house. And we were going to own it. But then something occurred to me and I frowned.

"What now?" Matt asked.

"I was just thinking about my grandpa and how he's going to feel about us moving away. We were next door before and now…"

"Oh, well, that's more news."

"What?"

"Your grandpa is selling his place so he can move in with Lesley."

"When did that happen? Why does no one ever tell me anything?"

Just then Joy started to cry and I went to pick her up and feed her.

Matt nodded towards the babies. "You were pretty busy the last few weeks. We figured you didn't need to know everything."

But I did. I did need to know everything.

I would've argued with him further about that, but between dealing with Joy and then Hope waking up, too, I had to let it drop.

Maybe I did have enough on my plate already. Still. I did not like being left out of the loop.

CHAPTER 32

It took another two weeks for the house to be ready. But the nice part of that was that by the time we finally were able to see the house and move in everyone we knew and loved was also fully vaccinated which meant we could have a real, honest-to-goodness house-warming party.

(Ah, the good old days when vaccines were much more effective…How I miss thee.)

The house was painted a nice deep blue with white trim and had a bright turquoise door for a pop of color. I loved it even more than the first time I'd seen it.

And inside…Jamie led me straight to the nursery.

It was already a little late for it to matter but she'd included a border along the top of the walls that was white with black geometric shapes. Below that the walls were a deep teal that was absolutely gorgeous.

The teal was accented with bright yellow and orange stuffed animals on the shelves and on the pillows on the nursing chairs (one for Matt, one for me). Elaine's quilts matched perfectly and the room looked like it was made to host the cradles my grandpa had made.

It was a peaceful haven built just to my tastes.

And the kitchen…The kitchen was heaven.

My friends and family really did know me. Through some miracle I probably didn't want to look too closely at they'd found me a blue Sub-Zero fridge.

When I saw it I turned to Jamie, wide-eyed. "Jamie…"

"You have been talking about how you want one of those fridges since you were twenty and saw it in a design magazine."

"But, you know why I never bought one. They're pricey."

"Greta said to consider it a baby gift."

Since Greta wasn't there to argue with, I continued my inspection.

The lower cabinets in the rest of the kitchen matched the fridge. The top cabinets were light gray. (Thankfully no white painted cabinets. Those things get *dirty*.) And the countertops were white quartz, not granite. Jamie really did know me well.

But quartz…Once more I looked at Jamie, but she just shook her head. "Mason said to tell you that the upgrade expenses were a great way to reduce the taxable amount of the sale and to stop complaining."

I frowned at her. "Tax write-off or no, the money was still spent. That's like people who don't want to earn too much because they'll have to pay a higher tax rate on the extra income. At the end of the day, it's still more money in their pocket even at the higher rate."

She shrugged and smiled serenely. "Take it up with him. I was just the designer."

"Liar."

"Then take it up with Matt. He's the one who negotiated the house price with Mason that included all of this."

I narrowed my eyes, but only nodded. I knew Matt. He'd accept some help from others, but not too much, so I expected the negotiation with Mason had involved Matt negotiating the price *up* enough to make him feel like it was a fair deal for the house we actually got.

"Well, thank you. For the design help." I gave her a hug.

"Wait until you see the rest of it…"

It was all amazing. There was a home office. With a built-in floor to ceiling bookcase along the longest wall that was already crammed full with all of my books. And all my little tchotchkes. The mementos I'd picked up on travels around the world.

Matt joined us there. "What are all these?" he asked, picking up a vase with a dolphin painted on the side.

"Memories. I bought that one in Greece. And this line drawing of a baby tiger I bought in Prague. And this little carved stone elephant I bought in Spain. Don't you collect things like that?"

He shook his head.

Glancing around the room I laughed. "That's probably a good thing. I don't know where we'd put it all if we were both quasi-hoarders."

He looked a little wide-eyed at the sheer number of books and things on the shelf, so I gave him a kiss on the cheek. "Don't worry. Now that we have the kiddos it'll probably stop."

Jamie laughed. "Maggie, as long as I've known you, you've always had a book in hand. Always. I don't think that's going to stop, even with kids."

"Okay, so maybe not the books. But the things, because, really, when are we ever going to travel again?"

"Mason and I are already talking about Max's first trip to Paris. You know you can travel with kids."

"Theoretically," I said. "But I have seen those parents at airports with their kids and their carriers and their exhausted, panicked expressions. I'll wait until my kids are like six for that kind of trip, thank you."

"So be it. Well?" She waved her hand through the air. "Are you happy?"

I nodded. "I am. This is amazing." I gave her a quick hug. "It's perfect, Jamie. Thank you."

Mason walked into the room and I turned to him arms spread wide. "Come here. You, too. Thank you."

He shook his head and held his hands out in front of his chest, fending me off. "A thank you is enough. No hugs needed."

"Mason. This may be the only time in our lives I like you this much. Just go with it." I opened my arms again.

"Fine. But make it fast."

(Just for that I hugged him for an extra five seconds and then winked at him when I pulled away.)

I smiled at the room once more. It was amazing. "Okay, I need to go find everyone else involved in this and thank them, too. You guys are the best."

🐾 🐾 🐾

Later that afternoon we all gathered in the backyard for barbecue and burgers. It felt good to be there with that taste of spring in the air and all our friends gathered round. Everyone was laughing and smiling and talking about how excited they were for the new resort.

I stood off to the side, Fancy at my feet, and took it all in.

Greta and Jean-Philippe were sitting at the picnic table whispering quietly together, their hands intertwined. Abe and Evan joined them, all smiles, and I saw Abe reach for the ultrasound picture in his pocket.

I think I'd already seen it myself three times that day. They had baby fever like I have never seen before. It was adorable.

My grandpa and Jack were standing next to the fence having a spirited conversation as they gestured at the boards and around the yard. They were up to something, that's for sure, but I didn't know what.

Sam, red-hair flopping into his eyes, was chasing after Spots, laughing and screaming his head off with glee as Spots barked happily.

Elaine and Dennis stood together in the doorway talking to Mason looking mildly nervous, but definitely comfortable with one another.

Lesley was bustling around with a pitcher of lemonade refilling everyone's glasses while Trish brought out the onion dip, chips, and veggie trays.

Matt was inside checking on the babies who'd gone down for their afternoon nap.

Jamie came over and handed me a bottle of Wooly Booger. "We did pretty good, didn't we? Who would've thought three years ago that we'd be here, now, with all of this."

(Don't worry. Before you freak out about my bad mothering because I was drinking a beer while breastfeeding, I'd done my research. Jamie and I had both banked enough extra milk to let us have one lousy beer at the housewarming without it impacting our kids. Mason and Matt were on baby-feeding duty for the rest of the day and happy to do it.)

I clinked my bottle against hers. "We did do pretty

good, didn't we? Cheers to us. Could you imagine if we hadn't moved here? With the last year?"

She shuddered. "I'd rather not."

We each took a sip of our beer and turned back to watch the small little community we'd built of family, and friends that were like family.

Finally, in that moment I understood why you'd want your family and friends working alongside you to build a business like we were.

Losing so many people so young I'd learned to do it all myself. Better that than to turn around and find that someone you relied on wasn't there anymore. The first time I tried to call my mom after she was gone and remembered she wasn't there…

It had been hard. And I'd had to handle that heartbreak all alone.

And then I'd gone out into the bigger world that pushes us all into these isolated little family units and then makes us so busy we're just struggling to keep our own heads above the water…

It had never occurred to me to look around and offer to help. Or to ask for help.

But there we were, stronger together. I could finally see that. It was hard to accept, and scary to think about relying on others that way.

There was still a small part of me that worried I'd lose one of these people and be all alone again. Or that they'd let me down somehow. But I couldn't let that fear keep them at arms' length anymore

I had to trust. I had to open up. So we could all succeed. Together. So we could *all* have a better life.

Jamie and Mason, Greta and (as weird as it was)

Jean-Philippe, Evan and Abe, me and Matt. Our kids. Our families. All of the other friends we'd made along the way.

It was going to be all of us, working together to pull one another up, to build something from the best of each of us.

(As long as I made sure that Mason and Greta shared out the results equally, but from what I'd seen that wasn't going to be an issue.)

I shook my head.

How had I not wanted everyone I knew and loved involved? How had I thought it would be better to keep it arms' length and distant and professional?

I wiped a tear from my eye as Matt came over and joined us.

"You okay?" he murmured, giving me a quick kiss on the cheek.

I leaned into him. "Couldn't be better."

I knew in the years ahead we'd add more people to our circle, bringing in those who were lost or looking for community, like Elaine. And that there would be new adventures (and mysteries) when the pet resort opened.

But right there in that moment I finally felt complete for the first time since I'd lost my parents. I had everything and everyone I needed.

Life was good. It was really, really good.

CLOSING NOTES

So there we have it. The end of the Maggie May and Miss Fancypants mystery series. As I was finalizing this series I realized that maybe it wasn't so much a cozy mystery series as a small-town family drama with equal amounts of mystery and romance as well as lots of dogs to love.

But, well, a book has to go somewhere on the shelves. And when I started writing this series I had no idea where it was going or how it was going to end and I figured Fancy was such a large part of why I was writing the first story that cozy pet mysteries was as good a fit as any.

Thank you, first and foremost to you, dear reader for sticking through to the end. I selfishly write these books for my own enjoyment but at the end of the day it's readers buying and talking about the books that makes it possible to keep writing.

And so every purchase and every positive review and every reader who comes back for more has a special place in my heart. Especially nine books deep on a wacky little series like this one.

I don't normally write one of these acknowledgement sections because when you self-publish there's not a lot to put into one of these things when it comes to the production side. At least for me.

I don't have an agent or an editor or a cover designer or a book formatter or an advertising team or a foreign rights team to thank. Everything you saw in the last nine books and the related short stories was all me. The good and the bad.

But at the same time, I didn't do this alone.

And while I am fiercely protective of my friends and family and try not to call them out into public because they didn't choose to have me be a writer and they just want to live their lives in peace, I figure here's the place to thank them since if you made it this far (and weren't hate-reading the series for some weird reason that likely requires therapy) then under other circumstances or settings you would be a friend, too.

So let me introduce you to some of the people whose support helped make this happen and maybe give you a little more insight into the series.

First, we have to start with Miss Priss, my real-world version of Fancy.

She's an old lady now. Just celebrated her ninth birthday and I hope will be one of those Newfies who makes it to fifteen. I know that's not likely, but at least she'll always live on in these books.

She's been by my side for every word written and is the reason you have all the little Fancy bits in this series. (Currently she is snoring away right behind me on one of the two dog beds that are in my office. Spoiled? Never.)

She's actually the reason the series exists at all. Because she does in fact like to pee on dead things. Writer-brain took that and thought, "What would happen if she ever peed on a dead body?" and a few years later, off we went.

She's also the one that drags me out for walks and makes sure I eat, mostly because she needs to eat. I hadn't planned on getting a dog at the time she came into my life (I'd been focused on moving to New Zealand), but I wouldn't give up these last nine years for anything.

Next, I should thank all the people and places in Grand County, Colorado in the early 80's. The Baker Valley in these books is made up, as are the characters, but there are definite inspirations in these books from when I lived in the Colorado mountains when I was young.

Grandpa Lou's house in the corner of Creek, for example, is very much inspired by the house we used to live in in Hot Sulphur Springs. And that flat rock on the side of a mountainside that let a little kid watch the train go by while eating sliced peaches covered in sugar absolutely exists.

Although last time I passed through there were too many aspens and too much grass that had grown up on the mountainside to let me reach it. (That's where my dad's ashes are scattered, so it made me sad, but the world changes like that.)

Someone reading these books who was there then will notice some familiar names. Those are my nod to a time and place that I loved. But the characters in these books with those names are not those people.

(I really did write the name MATT on the wall of that house. But that Matt was a cute little toe-headed boy. I have no idea what became of him or my big crush of those years who was a red-headed boy named Sam. Sadly, Sam dumped me in 3rd grade and left me crying to the Grease soundtrack. I'm not sure I ever recovered. Haha.)

After that are my family.

I lost my Grandpa Lee last year. He was part of the inspiration behind Grandpa Lou in the books. I hope I did justice to the core of who he was to me.

The real-life man was a kinder man than Grandpa Lou, and less prone to doling out life advice. But if I were ever in trouble, he would've been the man I wanted in my corner. Just by being himself he taught me some really powerful lessons about life. Although, it might've taken some years for those lessons to sink in…

I want to also thank his widow, Sybil, for reaching out and putting us back in touch after too many years apart. I didn't have the relationship with him that Maggie has with her grandpa, but I am glad that I was able to visit and reconnect before it was too late.

My mom is still very much alive. Every single release she buys five copies of the book in print even though I don't think she has five people to give them to. (Thank you, Mom.)

She's also the only person who gets most of the little "Easter eggs" I've sprinkled throughout the book. (Easter eggs are little inside jokes or references that authors include in stories for those "in the know". Since she was up there in the mountains with me she recognizes the names and places and descriptions. And since she raised me she recognizes the little stories borrowed from my life like the infamous pea incident where I wouldn't eat my peas but she insisted that I do so and we had a three-hour standoff.)

She's also the one who named me Muffie, for better or worse. (That's my real name. And now if you made it to the end of the series, you know why that's my name. Haha. Sigh.)

Thank you, Mom, for reading my books and supporting me with all of this. I appreciate it more than I can say.

I also want to thank my stepdad, Tom, for reading these books. He's far more a reader of Brad Thor-type books, but he's stuck in there until the end. So thank you. Tom, you're a good man and we're lucky to have you in our lives.

Even though he won't read these words, I have to also thank my dad who has been gone for 27 years at this point. No book I write is without his influence. Even all these years later he has a profound impact on who I am and who I became.

He was the best dad I could have hoped for. Not perfect, no one is, but a really, really good dad.

I don't think the rest of my family read these books (and as a writer you can't expect that anyone you know will), but if you're family and you're reading this and I didn't call you out specifically, know that I love you. And I appreciate you making it here to the end with me.

I think I do have some friends who've stuck with this series to this point, too. Thank you to them as well.

You didn't have to, so I hope you made it this far because you enjoyed spending time with a more neurotic version of me. And I appreciate that you're here and also that after reading these books you're still my friend in real life, too.

As a writer I am always both incredibly grateful and somewhat nervous when people I know read what I write. Because the books all come from me, but sometimes they are more than me or they highlight parts of me that I wouldn't highlight in real life.

For those who are readers but don't know me in real life, Maggie's voice is very much my real-life voice. But she's also a version of me that takes all my worst insecurities and instincts and dials them up to ten.

So Maggie is me without normal limits.

I figured if I was going to write a character I might as well give them my flaws because then if people hated the character I could write them off the same way I do in real life when someone doesn't like me. Somehow it's easier to write-off people in real life who don't like me as a person than it is to write-off people online who don't like what I write. It's weird how that works.

Now, I do want to call out one friend in particular, Lindsay.

She is one of my best friends and part of the inspiration behind Jamie in the books.

(Jamie is actually a compilation of my two best friends as well as some additional friends I've had over the years and then some random character traits that none of my close friends have ever had. None have been quite as boy happy as Jamie is.)

Lindsay is a great cook, competent as hell, always put together, and I don't think has ever said a mean word to me even though it's possible she should have at some point. (That's pretty much what it takes to make my close inner friend circle. It's why it's so small. Haha.)

Each time I release a new book she somehow makes

time to read it even though she's juggling two young kids, live-in in-laws, a high-pressure job, and a world that's generally on fire these days.

Sadly we live in different states and I haven't traveled since 2019 so I think at this point it's possible that she's spent more time with Maggie-me than me-me in the last few years, but life does that to you. (Just remember Lindsay, I'm crazy, but not quite as crazy as Maggie.)

Hopefully sometime in the next few years the world will settle down enough for me to visit and we'll get to go out for a dinner involving a tasting-menu and cheese board at some fancy restaurant. I don't care if they're both out of style by then. Cheese is the best. And a surprise meal delivered by a talented chef can't be beat. Especially when paired with good wine.

Okay, then.

I think that's everyone. I'm glad I got to write this series. I'm glad there were readers who read it. This may not be the last of Maggie, Matt, and crew, but it is the end of this series.

I am sorry for anchoring it to the events of the last few years. But I hope I did so with some humor. No matter how dark times get, there's always beauty and humor to be found. Remember that as we go forward.

Anyway. I'm glad you're here. I appreciate your support more than I can express. And may we meet again on the pages of another novel someday. Until then I wish you laughter, health, happiness, and good books to read.

ABOUT THE AUTHOR

When Aleksa Baxter decided to write what she loves it was a no-brainer to write a cozy mystery set in the mountains of Colorado where she grew up and starring a Newfie, Miss Fancypants, that is very much like her own Newfie, in both the good ways and the bad.

You can reach her at aleksabaxterwriter@gmail.com or on her website aleksabaxter.com.

* 9 7 8 1 9 5 0 9 0 2 8 6 6 *